ATLANTIS TRAVELERS

BONNIE BROOKS

Notebrooks Press, a project of Notebrooks, LLC

This book is a work of fiction. All names, characters, and incidents are the product of the author's imagination. Places either are the product of the author's imagination or are used fictitiously. Any resemblance to actual events or persons is coincidental.

Cover Design: Caleb Ryan Jones

Interior Design and Typesetting: Emily Snyder

The text type was set in Adobe Jenson Pro

ISBN 979-8-991407-0-8 (Paperback)
ISBN 979-8-9991407 1-5 (E-book)

First edition September, 2025

For all my cousins, especially Ellis and Melody

*People wish to be settled; only as far as they are
unsettled is there any hope for them.
Life is a series of surprises.*

— RALPH WALDO EMERSON

CHARACTERS

ON EARTH
TRAVELERS AND REPORTERS

KAIEDA BEQ-TA'AVA, New Atlantean Traveler, on Earth assignment

MAXIMUS5700, aka "MAX," synthetic, Traveler partner to Kaieda

FENN LOA, aka FENN LOCKYER, New Atlantean Reporter based on Earth

D'AVI S'ILOA, New Atlantean Traveler, on Earth assignment

ALLAN9, aka "FREDDIE," synthetic, Traveler partner to D'avi S'Iloa

MARINA RAMBERT, New Atlantean Reporter based on Earth

OTHERS, OF EARTH AND NEW ATLANTIS

CHARLES TUMBLESTON, Trip Maui air passenger

MARIAN TUMBLESTON, Trip Maui air passenger

REGGIE MALAOHO, Trip Maui pilot

EDITHA LOCKYER, San Francisco-based diarist, wife of Fenn Lockyer

DAWN CARLSON, social media influencer, close friend of D'avi and Freddie

THEONE A'MEILOR, Eflos, house assistant to Marina Rambert

ON NEW ATLANTIS AND RIMALON
SPACE FORCE OFFICERS

FAERAE C'IEZ, Space Force Commander

DZUREN TSO, Space Force Captain, Acting Director of Engineering subguild

HENK Z'ENG, Commander of Space Force Retrievers unit

MYNAR A'KEMMI, Eflos, Space Force Lieutenant

VAYLOR A'KEMMI, Eflos, Space Force Lieutenant

ALEC TA'AVA-LOA, Space Force Science
Officer, last seen on Rimalon

GLOBAL FESTIVAL HEADQUARTERS STAFF

LUCIENA "LUCE" SHOKO, Personal Assistant to the Director

ALLOU OWEA, Assistant to the Curatorial Director

SUNDRAE BEQ, Curatorial Director

WOFAR TONIE, Subcurator for Earth Classics

ENIGMA "GEMMA" G'OCN, Associate for Contemporary Art

EGDAR ROIBOI, Director

CASPAR WELLER, Prime Associate to the Director

OTHERS, OF NEW ATLANTIS

MOG WELLER, journalist for Voice of
Government (VoG) Global Network

JANAI LOA, Director of Science Research, Science Guild

MAEVE EP, bonded mate to Egdar Roiboi

MUMNO A'KEMMI, Eflos, de facto leader of Kemmi

KEMMI A'KEMMI, Eflos, founder and
actual village leader of Kemmi

THE INTERSTITIALS, premiere rock band of New Atlantis

DOFI, canine companion to Maeve Ep

"THANK YOU, MOG. *When the Triumvirate and the General Assembly jointly commissioned the Global Festival, they envisioned a unified resource for learning and celebration for all New Atlanteans. The Planet has a rich and complex history. We came from Earth fifteen millennia ago, an oceanic people, about to be consumed by the sea. The Star People found us a new planetary home, so much like Earth, with our one beautiful moon, Rimalon. They encouraged us to bring the best of what we had on Earth—our seeds and plants, many of our animals, our culture. They gave us the means to advance our social and scientific development.*

As we approach this anniversary, the purpose of the Festival is to interpret, understand, and learn from the past even as we flourish in the present and imagine the future. We cannot do this work without an appreciation for the way our cultural evolution as a people intertwines with and diverges from the history and present of our planet of origin. Global policy has always prohibited interventions with Earth. This has not prevented careful, deep, and sustained study. The work of the Travelers and Reporters is invaluable to our initiatives. As for Anony, we will carry on despite this vein of objection. It will go down as a minor note in our larger history of cultural knowledge and evolution."

– EXCERPT, EGDAR ROIBOI, DIRECTOR,

GLOBAL FESTIVAL OF NEW ATLANTIS

COMMENTS IN LIVE PUBLIC INTERVIEW WITH

MOG WELLER, VoG NETWORK JOURNALIST

CHAPTER 1

MAUI, HAWAII, EARTH

Day One, morning, UTC-9

KAIEDA WOKE WITH a mouthful of sand. She coughed, spat it out, tried to rise, failed. Her dark, chin-length hair was in her eyes. She got to her feet only to bend over, dizzy, and retch, struggling to catch her breath. Then she walked toward the water. The beach shifted from dry sand to a wet, compacted surface. The yellow sun was barely above the horizon. She dove into the breakers. *Feels like the beach on the Raja Sea. But what is home, now?* Her head was pounding. Return to consciousness after the deep stasis. *Never easy to come out of it. Thirty-six hours of deep compression feels like thirty-six years when you wake up.*

Two hours before, in predawn darkness, they had tumbled out of the vessel. He smoothly, she with a thud. *An overgrown, lidded silver canoe for two.* Their transit through the Mercury wormhole had been smooth. Their stealth technology allowed them to enter the atmosphere undetected. But landing was landing. Finding their footing, they'd dragged their interstellar cocoon onto dry sand. Then they'd slept, one on each side of the cresh.

She treaded in the salty water, staring at the line of thick green tropical growth. *Monstera and ferns and palms and blooming yellow hibiscus. Pacific Ocean. Eastern coast of Maui.*

Hawaii. Disorienting to have new knowledge and language roaring into her head.

"Landing ignites the chip." All Travelers talked about its weirdness. Familiarity with the unfamiliar. Wondering if the new microchip would cover whatever would be needed for the work ahead. Usually, they got it right. Not always. *This trip feels uncertain.*

"I can't keep doing this," she said aloud. She tried to spit lingering sand into the ocean and got a mouthful of salt water that she then coughed out. *Better than staying on The Planet and waiting. How long do I wait?* As her hands waved in the water, she saw her tattoo. A pair of gold-outlined, intertwined, sapphire-blue stars nestled in the thenar space between her forefinger and thumb on the top side of her right hand. Her heart lurched. She flipped onto her back and floated a while, palms up, looking at the sky.

Max's shout drew her attention back to the beach. He was by the shining cresh, gesturing for her to come ashore. She rode in on the next wave, stopping knee-deep in the surf. He walked several meters to her. She'd seen him only once, right before they went into stasis. The exit from Rimalon had been so rushed, protocols skipped. *Feck you, Roiboi.*

"What?" she asked, taking him in. Tall. Strong. Sandy hair, balanced features. A beautiful body. Triangular swimmer's build. Broad shoulders, narrow hips. *Why does he seem familiar?*

"Good morning," he said. "I found the supply pouch with the tent, by the freshwater lagoon." He pointed toward the thick green jungle beyond the beach. Then he nodded at the cresh. "Let's get it out of sight."

Walking to it, he gestured to her to pick up one end. She followed and lifted it. Hoisting the lightweight vessel onto their shoulders, they portaged it toward a path leading into the jungle. The path curved through thick trees and undergrowth to a small lagoon of calm water surrounded by reeds, palms, and white and yellow flowering plants. Kaieda shook her head. *Flora. Fauna. Headache. Plumeria.*

"Here," Max said, lowering his end of the cresh into reeds by the lagoon. She set her end down as well. The cresh settled in the water.

"It's set to deconstruct," Max said. "It'll collapse into nothing shortly."

Kaieda went to the water's edge and bent over, splashing her face. *Deep water.* She stood up, light-headed.

"The air," she said. "Feels thin. I'm thirsty."

"You're probably dehydrated. There's water in the packs. You'll adjust. I'll start the Bluebox. Then, sleep."

As soon as possible. They needed an extended period of unconsciousness within a few hours of exiting the cresh. Sleep was the trigger for their chips to fully release. They hadn't slept enough yet. She watched him shove the cresh deeper into the reeds. *Nice back.* The thought startled her. They'd told her on Rimalon he was special, but they hadn't said how.

Her chest tightened.

"I really can't breathe very well," she told him, sitting on the ground. "My head hurts."

"Rest," he said.

She nodded. Leaning against the coconut palm tree trunk behind her, she let herself doze.

A splash from the lagoon woke her. She sat up and looked around. Nothing. She saw a dark figure beneath the water's surface, then the water parted. Max shot up several meters into the air, where he hovered. He dropped down slowly and began treading.

"That's not…possible," Kaieda murmured.

"Go underwater," he told her.

She frowned, then got up and waded into the water, dipping below the surface. Her headache eased. She came up for air.

"Stay under longer," he said.

"Why?"

"You can breathe in it."

"What? They block and cloak our gills."

"Do it."

Skeptical, she swam into deeper water, dropped beneath the surface, and opened her eyes. Everything was clear. She could see gold and scarlet fish darting several feet away. A green turtle swam by. Without thinking, she inhaled. Sweetness filled her center and radiated out into her limbs. The impulse to lift was irresistible, as instinctive as breathing the water in. She gathered and rose into air, hovered for a few moments in the bright sunlight, then dropped gently back into the lagoon. Propelling herself underwater, she repeated. This time she hovered longer before gracefully sliding back into the water. *Exhilarating. Like home. But this isn't supposed to happen. Not here.*

She started to ask Max, "How did they miss this?" when a single-engine plane flew low overhead. She dove underwater. Max dropped beneath the surface as well.

The plane finished its pass. Kaieda fought the impulse to do another lift. Max soared out of the water and into the air as soon as the plane's tail disappeared beyond the trees.

"Don't, don't," she said to him.

He lowered slowly back down. "Cessna 182."

"We need to put on clothes," Kaieda said. She pulled herself out of the water. "No planes are supposed to be anywhere near here. No more lifts. What if they had seen that?"

She rummaged through the supply pack that held their clothing. *How had they missed this? Was it just a mistimed landing?* She ran her fingers behind her ears. Her gill seams were still there. She groaned.

She pulled a pair of khaki shorts and a bright blue, green, and yellow flowered-with-palm-leaves shirt from the pack and put them on. *Hawaiian shirt.* She didn't question how she knew it was a Hawaiian shirt, or how she'd known that white flower was a plumeria. She'd spent too much of her first assignment reminding herself, *It's the chip.* She had more Earth knowledge than most already, but the chip provided hyper enhancement. Names. Geography. Traditions. Languages. Slang.

As she finished buttoning her shirt, Max said, "It's coming back."

She heard, then saw, the plane approaching from the same direction, much lower this time. *This landing point was supposed to be remote.*

"Oh no," she said, her eyes going from Max to the plane and back. Max was still in the air above the lagoon. The plane was making sputtering sounds. It was headed for the beach.

"They're trying to land," Max said, dropping back into the water, then pulling himself onto the shore. He reached into the supply pack, found a pair of shorts and a white T-shirt, and put them on.

"This is not good," Kaieda said. "They saw us."

"They did," Max agreed.

Kaieda sank back down onto the sand. "Old gods help us," she said. *This is all we need.*

Max shimmied up a tree for a view of the beach. "They landed on wet sand. All in one piece. People are getting out. Two. No. Three."

"We should see if they're all right."

Max slid down the tree, then hoisted one of the black back-packs from their supplies onto his back. He tightened the straps with care.

"Where's the Bluebox?" she asked.

"In here." He indicated the backpack. "The rest of this doesn't matter." He gestured at the other supplies.

They jogged toward the beach.

Two of the people from the plane, a man and woman in middle age, were dressed in white shorts and matching green T-shirts. They stood in dry sand beside the plane. The third person, a young man wearing a blue baseball cap with "Trip Maui" printed in white on the front, was sitting in the cockpit talking on the radio. The couple was arguing.

As Max and Kaieda drew nearer, the bickering escalated and did not stop even when they were a few feet away.

"I told you we'd miss our tennis hour if we did this," the woman was saying.

The man was holding his cell phone in the air. "We're in one piece! I've got one bar…" he said. "Nah. I've got no bars. It says SOS."

"That's right," the young man in the baseball hat was saying into the radio at the same time the couple was talking. "Two passengers, no injuries…yes, I filed a VFR before takeoff and reported on the 121.5 frequency when the sputter started…I think it's restricted fuel flow of some kind, maybe debris in the carburetor? We're not too far off the Hana Road, maybe a mile, but the jungle looks thick. We hit soft sand after landing… nope, didn't flip over…nope, plane won't restart…"

"The plane's just…stuck," the man said to the woman.

They noticed Max and Kaieda standing behind them.

"It's the naked people!" the man exclaimed. "You found clothes!"

"Are you okay?" Kaieda asked. "We saw the plane…"

"We're fine, just a little shook for a minute there. Reggie there"—he nodded at the young pilot in the cockpit—"was trying to show us a good time. Sunrise off the Maui coast! Now he has to get us back to our resort." He offered his hand to Kaieda. "Charles Tumbleston." They shook. He repeated the gesture with Max.

"You gotta work on your grip, son," Tumbleston said, releasing Max's hand. "This is my wife, Marian." He looked at her. "That emergency landing is gonna make a good story. Eventually."

"Terrifying!" Marian said. "I thought we were going to die." She looked at Max. "I swear I saw you floating in the air over that lagoon right before we landed on the beach."

Reggie emerged from the plane after some additional back-and-forth.

"You're both okay?" he asked the Tumblestons.

"Yes, yes, did you reach someone to rescue us?" Tumbleston replied.

Marian Tumbleston stared at Max's backpack. "That doesn't look like one of those jet pack things."

"It's not," Max answered.

"They're sending a helicopter," Reggie told them. "Might take a few hours. Our big chopper is committed all morning. But a car would probably take longer, given this location."

"Oh God," Marian said, fanning herself. "It's getting hot. Really, no cell service?"

"I don't guess you kids have a car close by?" Charles asked Max.

"We were dropped here by friends," Max answered. "For some camping."

"I have to get out of this sun," Marian said. "Is there any water to drink?"

Reggie rummaged in the cooler in the plane's cargo space. "Yeah, I've got some water…"

Kaieda started to feel light-headed. "There's a shady place just up that path by the lagoon," she said. She started walking. The Tumblestons followed.

"We were hoping to snorkel with the green sea turtles," Max told them as they walked.

"Green sea turtles…" Charles said.

They were almost to the shade. Kaieda started to say something, suddenly disoriented. *Are the beacons on? Are they watching this?* She said to Max, "I really don't…feel well…" and fainted against him, sliding into the sand.

She awoke underwater. Hands were clawing for her, yanking at her and pulling her out. She surfaced, coughing, to hear Marian Tumbleston, who had pulled her from the water with Charles, yelling, "What got into you?" at Max.

"I'm okay," Kaieda said. They were in shade beside the lagoon.

"He hauled you up here and threw you in the water!" Marian cried. "You were in a dead faint! You could have drowned!" She fanned Kaieda's face.

Max drew closer and Marian snapped at him, "What's wrong with you?"

"It's okay," Kaieda said again. "I feel better. The water woke me up."

Max leaned past Marian, placing his hand on Kaieda's shoulder. A surprising, comforting warmth radiated from his hand into her muscles and bones, down her arm.

Reggie appeared, carrying several water bottles. "They're saying maybe three hours," he said, coming toward them. "We'll have to go back out to the beach to meet the—" He stopped in his tracks, staring into the reeds on the edge of the lagoon. "What is THAT?" he asked.

Not good, not good, not good. Kaieda watched with alarm as the Tumblestons went to where Reggie was standing. *They found the cresh. Not good.*

"What is that?" Charles asked. He looked at Max, who remained by Kaieda.

Then Reggie exclaimed, "Holy shit!"

"Oh my God!" Marian cried. "Did you see that? Where did it go?"

Charles looked back at his wife and the young pilot. "What?" He looked down. He looked back at Max. "That silver sea kayak thing is gone!" he blurted. "Where the hell…?"

Max stepped toward them.

"It…it fell in on itself and disappeared!" Reggie said, confounded.

Marian's mouth was open. No words were coming out.

"It's called timed molecular disintegration," Max said to them. "We arrived in that vessel. Its usefulness is now over and so is it."

They all stared at him.

"But, but…how did it do that?" Marian asked, waving at where the cresh once laid.

Max turned to Kaieda. "We have to rest soon," he said.

"What, are you aliens or something?" Reggie asked.

"Not exactly," Max answered.

"Heh, just joking," Reggie said.

Max went to him and placed his hand on the young man's shoulder. Reggie turned, then leaned suddenly against Max as he lost consciousness. Max eased him to the ground. Then with sudden speed he turned to the Tumblestons and put a hand on each of their shoulders. They, too, slid to the ground.

"What are you doing?" Kaieda exclaimed, rising to her feet at the sight of the three people now unconscious by the reeds.

"I made them go to sleep," Max said.

"Go to sleep?"

"Just sleep," he said, as if reading her mind. He leaned over them and, one by one, ran his forefinger down their noses, from forehead to tip. "It's vibration. Frequency. They're forgetting."

"Forgetting." Kaieda leaned over them. They were all breathing.

Max nodded.

"You can make them forget?"

He nodded again.

"What will they remember when they wake up?"

"They'll remember the beach landing, they'll remember us… they won't remember the cresh or anything about us hovering in the air over the lagoon."

Selective wiping. Since when was that allowed? The rule is "No intervention."

"I'll move them to the beach when I hear the helicopter," he said. "They'll be awake when it lands. You can get some sleep while we wait."

Kaieda stared at him.

"Things go wrong," he said. For the first time since she'd met him, he smiled. "Would you rather call the Fetchers?"

He went to their supply pack, found a pair of thermal blankets, and laid them on the sandy ground. He then moved the Tumblestons and Reggie onto the blankets. They slept on.

Kaieda's exhaustion forced her to sit. She watched Max, wishing her head would clear. *What is it with him? His ease with everything. Those perfect lifts. The absence of anxiety, the ability to do selective memory wipes. Why does the air bother me but not him?*

"Oh for Chr..." she muttered. *It's a synthetic. How did I not see it? His movements are too smooth, his speed too precise. He's too handsome. They could have TOLD me. It's probably a prototype. They overcompensate with new models.* Faerae had mentioned something about a new synthetic weeks ago. Kaieda had just gotten back from her last assignment. *Fae probably knew before I left. But she couldn't say. Guild and military secrets. She tried to warn me about the Allan9 too.* A wave of nausea rose inside her. *I can't think about that thing. Don't think about that thing.*

She shook her head, watching Max. *They said he was special, but didn't say how.* She'd traveled with a synth once before, early in her Traveler work. They were given an easy, accessible culture and location to observe. The Harlon17, who said, "Call me Harlong," when they'd met, had been reliable, amusing, and a good problem solver. It pained her when she'd heard the model was discontinued. But unlike some sadness, she'd let it go. Kaieda steered clear of the politics around the synthetics. She saw it as a bottomless pit of techno-moral arguments, experiments, production. *Let the P-Guild work it all out,* she always thought. Leave it to the Philosophers and Priests to sort it with the Scientists.

The Robotics project was kept in service to human knowledge and techno-cultural advancement. New machines were programmed to stay inside the core moral code. "Just not getting into it," she'd told Faerae. That was when Faerae started mumbling about rumors of a new synthetic.

Max finished his work in making their guests comfortable.

It's programmed to protect human life. What else does it do?

He laid another blanket onto the ground near her. "You can

sleep here," he said. "Another couple of hours for your chip to ignite. I can activate the Bluebox. This"—he gestured at the three sleepers—"doesn't need to slow us down."

We're already slowed down. We should have reported in by now. But the alternative is to call the Fetchers. Ugh. An aborted assignment. No.

She lay down on the blanket he'd placed for her. Within moments, she was unconscious. The chip elevation began immediately. While asleep, she had the same dream she always had when a new chip was finishing its install. They were in Arcana, the house they'd built overlooking the sea. They were sitting in their wooden chairs on the long front porch. The sun was setting.

I think I can't miss you more. But then I do.

She sat up and looked around. The Earthers were still on their blankets, asleep.

"Headache?" Max asked.

"Better than earlier. My install finished."

He nodded.

She gazed at him. It was harder and harder to spot synths, they were so humanized. She pushed away another memory of the Allan9. *They should have asked before doing that.*

"You're a synthetic," she said.

"They didn't tell you?"

She shook her head. "They rushed everything." *Fecking Roi-boi.*

"An odd thing not to mention," he remarked.

"They gave you irony?"

"I did not do my own programming," he stated with a shrug, half-smiling at her.

He reminded her so much of the Harlon17. *Had they really*

abandoned that model? "Do you know your code sources?" she asked.

"Some," he answered.

"Huh." *Could it be an updated "Call me Harlong"?* That might explain the familiarity.

"I tried to activate the Bluebox while you were asleep. It won't connect. Could be a problem with the beacons." He looked out at the water.

Kaieda sighed. *Of course it isn't working. This assignment is cursed.*

"We can try in a more populated setting," Max continued.

"If that doesn't work?" she asked. "Do we call the Fetchers?" She frowned. *How do we call the Fetchers if we can't reach them? Dance around on the beach waving at the beacons? They'll come for us eventually, Dzuren won't leave us stranded.*

"San Francisco," he answered. "The closest Team is there. If we can sync our Bluebox with theirs, it will activate."

"Here would be better."

"Agreed. I'm not optimistic. We'll have to take…" His head tilted slightly. He looked vague for a few seconds, as if mentally retrieving something. "We'll have to take a commercial aircraft. To San Francisco. It's our best option for salvaging the assignment."

"San Francisco," she repeated. "Oh." A sinking feeling hit. She'd seen the other Team locations. She knew who was in San Francisco.

Please let the Bluebox work in Hawaii.

CHAPTER 2

Day One, early morning, into Day Two, early morning, NAT-0

"They're in."

Cheers and clapping rippled through the Central Command Room. Dzuren Tso said his usual, "Another perfect stealth landing. Well done, everyone," followed by "Team Seven handoff to Monitors commence."

Faerae leaned away from her screen. *How long before the Earthers have technology that penetrates our cloaking?* She shrugged it off. The thought experiment equation she'd been constructing slithered out of her mind, replaced with the discomfort of handing everything off to the Monitors.

They're sloppy. They'd better get this one right. It's not just anybody, it's Kaieda. The Guild pressured her into another assignment too soon. And sent her off with a synth partner she's never met, good golden god of aggravation. Stupid Festival. It's really THEM. Shameful. Yes, big X/V anniversary approaching for The Planet, yes, inputs from this project will shape Festival content and planning. High concept. Timeline too ambitious. Fecking Curators and their big ideas. Sending seven Teams to one world, however important, on this timeline? The resources necessary? Delaying other initiatives to send so many Travelers to Earth?

Faerae wanted to growl. She looked around to see the dozen or so Engineers in the CCR still focused on their one-dimensional screens as well as the master 3-D that displayed primary activity as the handoff proceeded. She could see the blips that were Kaieda and Max on her screen. The beacons were transferring to the Monitors' oversight.

What happens when Kaieda comes home? That was part of the equation she'd been working on in her secret calculus envisioning the future. *After this assignment, they'll promote her. She won't do Traveler fieldwork anymore. She'll teach and write and that will make it easier to transition into a full life together here.* Faerae loved her vision. Her commitment to it drowned out the known barrier to this plan, the moral dilemma it presented, the knot she had not yet untangled. *Our time is still ahead.*

"Team Seven will complete the project," the Festival Director Egdar Roiboi had bragged to the Engineers on his last visit to Rimalon's Keeper Colony. "The best of them all with the newest of them all."

I hate that man.

Roiboi showed up on Rimalon whenever he needed to twist arms in the Festival's interest. Faerae neither knew nor cared how he'd gotten wind of a new synth model being built. *Probably Guild Chairs spilling secrets to each other over tawny port.* Vast time and resources went into the design, assembly, and coding of the Maximus5700. Words like *masterpiece* were thrown around. Faerae knew they'd set the Max aside to work on an updated Allan model. Roiboi had a hand in that, too. The new Allan synth was for another Traveler assigned to the Earth Project. Faerae hated the Allan9. It was tasteless and it hurt Kaieda. The Max was more interesting to think about. *Does Kaieda know?* She'd never responded to hints Faerae dropped. *Maybe they put the details into her chip before they launched?* The Robotics team had worked on the prototype right up until they put the Max and Kaieda in the cresh on the drop ship. *How could they not tell her it's a synth? Has she figured it out?*

"Fret not, Faerae," Kaieda would advise. How many times had she said that over the years, since their student days? "FNF!" she'd scold. "FNF!" *No whining, no using your energy to fume and worry. Be here now.* Kaieda's ability to be present was one of the host of things that made her the best of the Travelers. That and her writing. "A gift from the gods," one of the Reviewers had muttered, reading her first voluminous report. "She's better than Fenn Loa," another had observed. "She's as good at this as she was at writing the erotica that made her famous," the journalist Mog Weller had reported in one of her VoG blowcasts.

Kaieda knew how to bring other worlds to life. *That's why they'll promote her, take her out of the field, put her in charge of training Travelers. The subguild will make her their public face. She won't have time to worry about what haunts her. Can't change anything, only move forward. With me.*

But I'm doomed to this forever. Faerae stared at her tracking screen. *Nobody is as good at this as I am. I'm not trained to do anything else.* She glanced at Dzuren Tso, who was watching the handoff procedures on the master screen. *I want to pilot. He did. Now he's a Captain. He's seen worlds I can't imagine. He's galaxy and battle tested. How do I transfer subguilds and start flight training this late? How can I do that if I stay here with Kaieda?*

The blip that had been Kaieda's and Max's cresh disappeared from her screen.

"Handoff to Monitors complete," Dzuren said. "Take a break, everyone. Meeting at oh seven hundred tomorrow. Be well."

The last of the seven Teams sent to Earth. "FNF," Faerae whispered to her darkened screen. People were leaving the layered semicircle of the Central Command Room. *The Monitors have it the easiest. They just make sure everyone's where they're supposed to be, doing what they're supposed to do. They have the beacons and interplanetary links and their stupid motto: We always know where they are.*

When the Engineering subguild heard about the Monitors' motto, they created one of their own: *We get them there.* This stirred some of the other groups to create mottoes, resulting in:

Trackers: We find where they go.

Researchers: We assemble what they need to know.

Retrievers: We bring them home.

Retrievers, aka the Fetchers.

She noticed, on the floor of the CCR semicircle, Dzuren talking with Henk Z'eng, the Fetcher Commander. Z'eng and Tso were first cousins. Most New Atlanteans were at least distantly related. The clans documented bloodlines with detailed care; the records went all the way back to when they were still an Earthly people. *Brought that obsession with us. Not that hard to do given the population control laws. All the inbreeding makes us vulnerable. But we don't talk about that, do we.*

The Traveler subguild—the Reporters and the Travelers themselves—ignored the mottoes project. *Snobs. Too special. Reporters stationed off-world, Travelers coming and going on assignment. I have the perfect motto for the off-world Reporters: We're never here, we're only there.* Yet, she reminded herself, the Reporters' information was essential to the Team plants, to the placement of beacons, to everything that the Researchers worked with in preparing Teams to go. *We need them. They make everything the Travelers do possible. And we can't dismiss the Travelers. Because Kaieda.*

Wasting time thinking about this. Faerae stood up to stretch. Her gray military jumpsuit flexed with her. A shock of bleached hair clouded her eyes as she reached her hands to the floor. *No point staying until their Bluebox is activated and I can send a message to Kaieda.*

Faerae nodded at Dzuren. He acknowledged her departure with a nod back. She walked toward the entrance to the sparkling tunnel known on the Keeper Colony as the Blind Deck. It offered spectacular views through transparent walls, exposing the Rimalon rockscape, occasional solar light, and their distant blue and green planet. *Moon life is fine.*

Transit cars offered fast shuttle service through the wide tunnels on Rimalon. Faerae often walked the Blind Deck to take in the view and think about things. A bar beverage awaited. Anticipating that offered some pleasure, as did moving around. The walk took twenty minutes, just the right amount of time to work through that thought experiment equation. 2-1=2 [k-a'=fk'>ka']. *She'll get real about this at some point. It's taking too long. The problem needs to resolve. The knot needs to unravel. She needs to reckon with reality. Accepting an ending allows a new beginning. For us.*

As Faerae entered the bar, called The Blue Guitar, a Voice of Government Global Network anchor intoned from a screen above the shelved liquor bottles. Most New Atlanteans referred to the network as "VoG," for Voice of Gov, but some sarcastically called it the Voice of God. "The Earth Project announced the landing of the last of seven Traveler Teams this afternoon, signifying completion of a major step in research commissioned by the Global Festival X/V. Travelers are projected to spend 180 Earth solar days securing and relaying data to Curators in preparation for The Planet's most ambitious Festival celebration in history. Some artifacts may also be transferred to The Planet." Faerae watched as the anchor looked into the eye of the camera and added, "More stuff from Earth." *Just the right amount of snark.*

No one else was paying attention to the screen. A few other CCR staff were already at the bar. *Took the transit car.* She sat at the bar, ordered a shot of single malt Scotch whisky from the synthetic bartender, and drank it as soon as it was poured. *They make better whisky on Earth than we do.* The smooth, heat-inducing liquid slid down her throat.

"They're in trouble!" someone shouted at the screen. Faerae turned to see the Twins, Mynar and Vaylor, in a corner booth. *Pesky little Eflosi.* The men were not quite five feet tall. They sat, as usual, on the same side of the table, their feet dangling from the banquette seat. Their dark hair featured the same choppy haircut. They seemed to have the same voice. Nobody knew what exactly the pair's relationship was. Their kind were rare in daily life on The Planet. A few were in the Space Force, living on Rimalon, working in the Keeper Colony. Some speculated that they were biological twins. Others believed it was a romantic relationship. The Eflos culture was foreign to *Homo sapiens.* Nobody could confidently read their way of relating to one another. Faerae could care less what the Twins' relationship was. They were efficient and flexible in the Central Command Room. That's all she cared about. Live long and prosper and all that. Being Eflos had to be hard. *They got a raw deal.*

"What?" Faerae asked.

"Trouble!" Mynar repeated.

"Earth drama!" Vaylor added.

Faerae frowned. "What do you mean, 'trouble'? They landed."

Vaylor nodded. "Beacons reactivating in the CCR."

"Something about a UFO," Mynar added.

Alarmed, Faerae fumbled credits into the bartend catch box, cursed at the handsome synth bartender, and tore out of the room toward the Blind Deck to catch a transit car back to the CCR. *A UFO? What could have happened? Why are they sending mission control back to the Engineers? Has the Max defaulted? Is Kaieda all right? Gods of the galaxy, why is this car so slow?*

"Ah, there you are," Dzuren said when Faerae burst into the CCR.

"What happened?" She joined Dzuren in front of the 3-D screen in the center of the room. Commander Z'eng and a few others on the CCR staff were also watching the information rolling in from the beacons.

"I can activate the Copernican Fetcher team if you want," Z'eng offered.

"We don't have a complete picture," Dzuren said. "But the beacons are back. We're on mutual watch with the Monitors for the time being. Let's let the situation settle."

What Faerae could see was…*an airplane on the beach?*

"Is that the landing point?" she asked.

"Yes." After a silence, Dzuren added, "It took a while to re-connect to the beacons. The Monitors want us to deal with this since the clear-to-land was issued from here." He waved and then pinched at the screen, pulling the view to a close-up of the plane. "Right after you left, the Monitors reported an aircraft in the area. We decided to reboot the beacons to make sure there wasn't some error." He nodded at the plane. "No error. That"— he pointed at the plane—"isn't supposed to be there. Seems to be stuck in sand."

"Looks like a fecking error to me," Faerae snapped, sitting before the small 2-D screen assembling action vectors at the landing point. "Nobody called me because…?"

"No beacons equal no vectors. We sent the Twins to the bar to look for you. We had a little time during the reboot."

"They weren't helpful," Faerae answered.

"Three additional life signs confirmed," came an automated voice from the other side of the 3-D screen.

"Earthers! At the landing point? Who missed this?" Faerae nearly shouted, still focused on the screen and trace lines.

Dzuren widened the 3-D screen scale. "They're all at the lagoon. Uninjured and in no-threat status. We just can't see them very well."

"Three Earthers on-site, a stranded plane, a disrupted timeline for chip activation," Faerae fumed. "How is this a no-threat status?"

"We had six perfect entries," Dzuren reminded her. "We've never tried more than three in a narrow time window on the same planet before. This project is already a triumph. With this seventh…either we send in the Fetchers stationed in Earth's solar system or we wait to see if Team Seven can get things sorted. I favor waiting. Max can deal with the Earthers."

"What does that mean?" Faerae asked, detesting Dzuren's lack of urgency.

"Commander, they're fine. Somebody made a mistake, or missed something, it doesn't matter. What are you getting on the trace lines?"

Faerae squinted. "Five," she said. *It's supposed to be TWO.*

He folded his arms while watching her screen, then said, "Take an Out Pill when you get home. You'll get some sleep." He added, "She's all right."

THE NEXT MORNING, Faerae muttered, "Oh, hell deep" on seeing her home screen ticker. She was groggy from the OP and still stressed. The Engineers had worked all the previous day on beacon and visual contact issues related to the Maui landing. For several hours the signals came and went, beacons dropped and were reactivated only to drop again. Engineers were back and forth with the Monitors, arguing over whose mistake resulted in the mess. At one point they lost trace lines entirely. All five humans vanished from the screen. Once the system reactivated a few hours later, no one was at the landing location at all. Kaieda and Max were gone, having made no contact via their Bluebox. Faerae was beside herself. That was when Dzuren ordered her to leave. She shuttered herself in her tiny flat in the Keeper Colony. As advised, she took the pill to force sleep. She hated drugging herself, but it always worked. *He was right to send me away, damn it.*

She swallowed her first bitter gulp of black coffee, glancing over the ticker. *Were they found? If there'd been a crisis, the CCR would have called. No message means no news.*

Then she noticed the red-lined EARTH AND NEW ATLANTIS: THE FESTIVAL in her message box.

Oh gods, another one of these? How does this protester get his unreadable tomes into mass circulation?

Before her was a new Planet-wide message from Anony. She began reading.

DISINCENTIVIZING GLOBAL NOSTALGIA AND CONTESTING HISTORIOGRAPHIC FIXATION: AN ARGUMENT AGAINST FESTIVAL X/V
POSTED BY ANONY

The most recent announcement regarding plans for Festival X/V reinforces systemic commitment to investment in nostalgia as a means of controlling societal focus and sustaining identity control based on ancient ties and linkages with the compromised planet of Earth. While The Planet's ancestral home and the galactic Prime Source for Homo sapiens continues its destructive path toward self-immolation, Travelers have recently been placed there to expand on the work of embedded Reporters in the interests of Festival X/V.

Our methodology for case-making is centered on combined

analysis and evaluation of public announcements from the Government, public interviews given by Festival Director Egdar Roiboi IV and his curatorial team, published documents, public budget reviews, promotional announcements and related curricula, and off-record sources from within the Keeper Colony.

Faerae's eyes widened at the last sentence. *Someone on Rimalon is talking to Anony? Unthinkable.* Faerae kept reading.

The appendices to this document contain analytical breakdowns available for review.

The history of Global Festivals focused on Earth is fetishized in the hands of present Festival leadership. After fifteen thousand years off-Earth and extensive socio-technological evolution on The Planet and its moon, we sustain systemic links to our planet of origin despite Earth's increasing capacity and readiness to self-destruct. Arguments for this linkage rely on what we argue is nostalgic experimentation with Founding Knowledge. Founding Knowledge is a core value within our system. Despite the deteriorating situation on the planet of origin, we do nothing to intervene or assist in Earth preservation. We have observed the loss of thousands of species over centuries. Despite the innovations of fossil fuels and nuclear fission, both of which assure self-destruction, our nonintervention policy is sustained. In other words, the Government policy accepts that while the roots are treasured, the tree will die. We contest the continued practice of appropriating learned cultural practices, languages, production and content, and related innovations that are then incorporated into our own cultural practices and content. This is robbery without consequence. Earth policies must change.

If we value Earth as our original home world, we can no longer allow our own culture to evolve and advance without a profound and urgent reckoning regarding Earth Policy. New paths must be forged, either toward assisting Earth or by relinquishing the practices and research we presently undertake. We must either cease the exploitation of their cultures and leave our planet of origin to its fate OR find ways to assist Earth in stabilizing its planetary balance and forging a sustainable path forward…

"Home world. Home planet. Roots," Faerae said aloud. Anony provoking questions and critiquing the energy stirred around the Festival. Questioning the economic commitment to the Traveler project. Challenging the rightness of the whole Earth Project.

She sat back, gazing at the screen. *We're okay with appropriation but not with intervention. We've devised our society and governance based on this weird mix of what we brought with us, what the Star People gave us, and ideas we've lifted from the Earthers over centuries. And now we're taking their artifacts, and DNA samples, and gods know what else. We wouldn't have the dinosaurs or the Eflosi without the ancient DNA. We wouldn't have the Tri OR the General Assembly or this version of democracy. We certainly would not have the whole Eswen thing that borders on worshipping a monarchy we don't really have…might have the Guilds, which do keep us all well purposed…I do like my Guild. Belonging. I just wish it was more flexible.* She shook her head. *FNF.*

Faerae decided to finish reading the Anony tome later. Time to find out where Kaieda and the Maximus were.

CHAPTER 3

SOMETIMES THINGS AT the Festival executive office were quiet enough that Luciena Shoko, who went by "Luce," could write short messages to her grandparents in the Farm Country. She was working on one, describing her new job, when the Director burst out of his office on one of his rants.

"I'm ruined! Ruined!"

With that he turned back into his office, slamming the door behind him.

Luce looked in alarm at Allou, who sat undisturbed at her desk. The two young women worked side by side at the entryways to the offices of the Global Festival's Director and head Curator. Allou glanced at Luce, then returned attention to her screen. Allou worked with the Curators. Luce was Personal Assistant to the Director. She'd been there barely a month. She was convinced her future rode on this, her first job since completing Global Service.

"Market must be down," Allou mumbled.

Luce looked at the door. "You don't think it's because Team Seven hit a snag?" she asked. "I saw it on the ticker."

"Doubt it," Allou replied.

Something crashed against the wall in the Director's office.

"Yeah, market is way down. Caspar isn't around today. You'll have to see to cleaning up in there. Sorry, Luce."

"Where is Caspar?" Luce asked, wishing the Director's Prime Associate would miraculously appear. Normally she didn't like seeing Caspar. He made her skin crawl. Today she wished he was here to calm the Director down.

"He's at the Warehouse," Allou said. "Wofar left me a note that they were going there early."

Another shout exploded from the office. "ANONY! Another fecking diatribe!"

Something else crashed and broke apart on the wall.

The second crash drew Sundrae Beq, the Festival's Curatorial Director, out of her office and into the foyer where Luciena and Allou sat. As usual, Sundrae dazzled: Her tall, slender figure was draped this morning in a camel-colored man-robe plus a layered turquoise necklace.

"Bad day on the market," she said, looking toward the office beyond.

Allou nodded.

"Plus, a new Anony just dropped." Sundrae sighed. "And Team Seven in trouble."

"Definitely a bad day," said Allou. "Does he even know about Team Seven?"

"It went up on the ticker a few minutes ago, I don't know," Sundrae answered.

Another item crashed against the wall, as he shouted, "Fecking Team Seven!"

"There we go," said Allou.

Egdar Roiboi rushed into the hallway, his portable tablet in hand. His flowing white shirt was streaked with coffee stains, a mess of silver hair standing up on his head. He stopped just short of Allou's desk, placing himself within inches of Sundrae.

Luce stayed frozen in her seat.

"Did you see this?" he shouted, waving his tablet at Sundrae. "This latest from Anony? And Team Seven silent?"

"Not their doing," Sundrae said.

"Call Tso's people on Rimalon, find out what's going on," he ordered Allou. He turned to Luce. "You, forward the market results to my tablet minute by minute." He turned next to Sundrae. "Analyze this new tome from Anony and send me a point-by-point breakdown on the new objections along with counterpoints. VoG will call. I'll have to give a response."

A thrum arose from Allou's desk communicator. "Director Roiboi's Office," she answered. She listened for a moment, winced, and then said to all present, "VoG. They want comments on the new Anony drop. They want to send Mog Weller. Forty minutes."

"See?" Roiboi muttered. He pointed at Sundrae. "Get on it." To Allou he said, "Tell them Mog is always welcome." He looked at his shirt and said to Luce, "I have a clean shirt in my personal bin, get it for me." He charged back to his office and pulled the door shut. "And get someone in here to clean up this mess!" he yelled from beyond the closed door.

Several other Festival workers had by now stuck their heads above the low walls of their work nooks.

"Back to it, everyone," Sundrae called. The heads disappeared.

She nodded at Allou and Luce. "You heard him. Do it." To Luce she added, "Give it a few minutes before you go in there. Get his shirt. Call the cleaning team. Supervise them. It needs to look perfect when VoG comes. So does he."

Luce nodded, nervous. She messaged the cleaning crew, then went for the clean shirt. Thirty minutes later, hovering lights and cameras were in place in Roiboi's white-walled office. It was in pristine condition thanks to the hasty work of the janitorial and painting teams. One of the thrown coffee cups had splattered contents onto two paintings, one a realistic seascape and the other an abstract work responding to the seascape. Their removal necessitated borrowing from Sundrae's office a three-dimensional hovering image, known as a floater, to fill the empty space. The floater included an ambient humming score Roiboi disliked. Half a dozen people were in the room when the VoG production team arrived.

"Can anyone turn that off?" Roiboi asked. He wore the clean shirt Luce had retrieved.

"I can reduce the volume," Sundrae answered. "It's folded into the work."

He sighed loudly. "Turn it down. Can the audio people wipe it out before this goes out?"

"It's a live interview, sir. Mog Weller?"

"Feck!" he fumed. "How is my hair?"

"Perfection, sir," Sundrae said.

"Mog and her fecking live interviews," he groaned. "I'm surprised she hasn't scored an interview with Anony!"

"I imagine she's trying."

Luce hovered in a corner, awaiting what would be her first live VoG interview. Her communicator thrummed. It was Allou, alerting her that Mog Weller was on her way to the Director's office. Two minutes. Luce leaned to Sundrae and whispered, "Mog is here."

"Sir, Mog Weller is in the building, she'll be here shortly," Sundrae said to Roiboi.

"Weller," he muttered, straightening his shirt. "The catch-all, problem clan."

Luce winced. *The Weller clan makes things possible for those who fit nowhere else. Why does he insult them? He does it a lot.*

Makes a big deal about the aristo clans and ignores the rest, except for insulting the Wellers.

He planted himself in front of Sundrae. "I hope you were thorough with the Anony points. How do I look?"

"Very fine," Sundrae answered.

He looked at Luce. "What do you think?" he asked.

She gulped. "Ready for the camera, sir."

Roiboi coughed and cleared his throat. He stepped into the doorway and opened his arms. "Mog, my dear, welcome!" He gestured for the journalist to enter, towering over her as she came through the door. She was followed by several people carrying more equipment. "Wonderful to see you last week at the Investors' Pageant," Roiboi continued. "What a night of dancing and music."

Mog Weller gave him a brief smile. "Hello, Egdar," she said, her hands pressed together as she gave a small bow. "So much news and so little time."

"An eventful day," Roiboi agreed as they sat in their chairs for the interview.

"What is that low buzz?" Mog Weller asked, looking around. They were between Roiboi's desk and the floater. She saw the artwork and said, "Oh."

"We have the audio set as low as possible," Sundrae explained.

"Hello, Sundrae," Mog said. "Isn't this the floater that usually hangs in your office?"

"Yes. Hello, Mog. We're experimenting with our visual assets here on the exec floor," Sundrae answered.

"Hmm. The paintings worked better but…" Mog shrugged.

Luce had never seen her in person before. She was short, her hair was cropped and close to her face. Her energy exuded work and no nonsense.

Weller lifted her tablet out of her carry bag, glanced at her notes, and asked her team, "Ready?"

"Any time," came the answer.

She looked at Roiboi. "Ready?"

"Of course. Always. For you."

"I'm sorry Captain Tso couldn't be here too," Mog said. "We may patch him in on a visual link for comments later on."

"Tso?" Roiboi repeated. "In this interview?"

Mog nodded at her producer. Lights in the room brightened, the hovering camera closed in on her. Her producer pointed at her with a nod. Looking into the camera's eye, she said, "Greetings, humans! I'm Mog Weller reporting live for VoG from the Global Festival Headquarters in the Capital. If you've been following today's ticker, you know the last of the Traveler Teams arrived safely on Earth yesterday, but oh no! Complications! As if following that isn't enough, Anony dropped a new Festival protest message this morning. We're live to update you on what's happening on Earth and discuss Anony's latest with Festival Director Egdar Roiboi for his take on how all of this affects Festival planning."

Mog glanced at her notes. As the camera widened its shot to include Roiboi, she looked directly at him. "Director Roiboi, thank you for joining us! Let's get right to it. Is the Festival in trouble, given the setback for the Travelers on Earth and this latest protest from Anony?"

Roiboi smiled and leaned toward Mog as he answered. "First of all, Mog, thank you for this opportunity. As you know, Festival X/V is celebrating a major planetary milestone. We understand things are in progress and the situation is stable regarding the Traveler delay—"

"Well, yes, we hope to hear from the CCR on Rimalon in a little while for an update on Team Seven," Mog interrupted him, "but what I am asking is how you see these events affecting Festival planning and execution."

Roiboi, still smiling, replied, "Yes, as I was about to say, every project has setbacks—"

"Excuse me, but Anony is foreseeable," Mog interjected. "Anony doesn't let up. Support for Anony's message is gaining ground in some regions. The scale of the Earth Project is unprecedented. Seven Traveler Teams were sent on what many believe is an overambitious schedule. The Festival is dominating Government resources and planning. Rumor has it that more physical artifacts are coming from Earth. That's controversial. In other words, Director, it looks like a growing hot mess. What's your response?"

"Mog, we all know The Planet has a long history of ambitious projects, in culture, the sciences, technology. That is our history, that is our tradition, that is our present and our future. The idea behind the Festival is to celebrate who we are. This is the moment to look backward and forward at the same time. The Festival is a gift to future generations, as are the artifacts we may secure. Artifacts hold ideas, hold histories, tell stories. The Reporters and the Travelers secure and document pictures of life in various Earth cultures and subcultures. All of this accumulates to our benefit. As you know, I was a Traveler. I know firsthand the effort involved in this research."

"Once," Mog interrupted. "You were in the field once."

"Our artifact collections right now are limited. This is the moment to expand our understanding of where we came from and what happened after we left. This is the moment."

"What do you say to Anony's objection that the Festival is nothing but a nostalgic and expensive exploitation of Earth cultures while avoiding any responsibility to or for the Earth cousins?"

Luce leaned against the wall next to Sundrae as the interview unfolded. She heard Sundrae whisper, "Hold on, hold on…" She looked over to see her focused entirely on Roiboi.

"Are you okay?" she whispered to the Curator.

"Hold it together," Sundrae murmured, her eyes staying on the Director.

"Our Earth cousins have their own path in the cosmos," Roiboi answered. "It is not our job to assist or intervene. That is Government policy and has been so for thousands of years. Our visiting footprints since leaving are light. Nonexistent, really. They don't know we're there."

"OKAY, okay, you don't need to condescend here," Mog parried. "But you have to agree that Anony's argument that we are trying to have it both ways makes a point."

"No," Roiboi answered, his voice tightening. "We would not be doing this work to celebrate our heritage and anticipate our peaceful and prosperous future if we believed that. We cannot save the Earth cousins from themselves, Mog. We all know they still have much to resolve on their planet and in their ways of living together. They need to work out their own advancement."

"Think so?" asked Mog. "That's not what happened to us. We were saved and given a lot of help." She fell silent for a few moments, as if listening to something. Then she said, "Ah, okay…I'm told we have Space Force Chief Engineer, Captain Dzuren Tso, on a link from the Keeper Colony on Rimalon to give us the latest news on Team Seven." She nodded at her producer. A vertical rectangle of light appeared in the air. Tso's image filled it.

Luce had never seen him live. He was something of a legend on The Planet. *Older. Good-looking in a craggy way.* Hero of the Barx Encounters, now overseeing the Military Installation on Rimalon. He stood in front of the massive screen in the

Central Command Room. He grinned, indicating he could see Mog and Roiboi.

"Hello, hello, Mog!" He waved.

"Greetings!" Mog said. "Captain Dzuren Tso, thank you for taking a little time to update us on what's happening on Earth."

"Thanks for the opportunity, Mog. And hello, Director Roiboi."

Roiboi squinted.

"So, what's the latest?" Mog asked.

"The situation is stable," Dzuren answered. The screen behind him appeared to be an open beach, pounded by heavy surf. A small airplane sat immobile in the sand.

"Is that the beachhead where Team Seven landed?" Mog asked.

"This is their designated landing point. As you can see, there's nothing going on other than some big waves."

"Are they still there? What's that plane doing there?"

"They're resting at the moment."

"Can you tell us exactly what happened? We've heard conflicting reports."

"Oh? Such as…?"

"The cresh took them to the wrong island. They encountered Earthers. Something about an airplane crash. One report I heard is that Kaieda collapsed and needed to be fetched immediately. What can you tell us, is any of that true?"

"Kaieda is fine. Max is fine. We had visual connection issues after landing that are being sorted out. The big picture is, all seven Teams are now on Earth, they're at varying stages of their deployments, and Team Seven is fine. Our beacon images have confirmed that."

"So, no comment on the Team encountering Earthers?" Mog asked. "You're not explaining that airplane?"

"Mog, they all encounter Earthers eventually. That's why they're there, isn't it?"

He was briefly interrupted by someone offscreen, and then said, "I'm sorry, but I need to sign off. We'll send any updates on the ticker. Thanks, Mog!" Dzuren's screen went blank.

Mog looked at the camera once again. "There you have it from Rimalon, humans." She looked at Roiboi. "What's with that plane?"

Roiboi shrugged. "Who knows?"

"We're out of time," Mog said after a signal from her producer. "Director Roiboi, thank you for joining us on this report, we will follow up in the days ahead depending on what happens next. This is Mog Weller for VoG, signing off. For now!"

The room was quiet for a few moments, the tech crew making the only sounds as they collected equipment. Roiboi stood up. So did Mog Weller.

"Sorry, there wasn't more time," she said, collecting her tablet and bag. "They're hiding something." She looked at him. "Anony is winning right now."

"Oh, no, Mog, Anony is not," Roiboi said softly. "But I know you need to say that as a means of stirring up debate where it isn't necessary. VoG is the real winner, right?"

"Blame us all you want, Egdar. You don't have to listen to me."

Luce decided she liked Weller's toughness. *Wish I had some of that.*

As Weller and the crew departed, Roiboi called after them, "Come back any time, Mog. We're always here, doing the work."

He waited until they were out of earshot. Then he whirled around and looked at Sundrae, Allou, and Luce where they stood in his office.

"They're taking Anony's side." He pointed at Sundrae. "Sharpen the talking points. And get our audio team working on a new Festival blowcast release." He paused, then added, "And get a report from Kaieda posted. People always respond to her." Then he said to Allou, "Get me a recording of that interview." After that he turned to Luce and asked, "Is the market up yet?"

CHAPTER 4

EDITHA LOCKYER WAS upset with her husband.
Burning all my journals!

She'd grabbed several, stashing them in her rucksack before he'd started yanking them off the library shelves and hauling them down two flights of stairs. Before he'd thrown them into the burn barrel in the back of their city garden. Their beautiful Noe Valley home was about to change hands. That was upsetting enough. Editha had planned to box up the journals tomorrow. The moving company would take them to the new place. But no. Fenn was infuriating. And now he was asleep. He could sleep through anything. Now, in their bed beside him, she was reviewing the day and fuming.

Midafternoon, they'd boxed up the last of the kitchen things. Then they paused for tea. Packing the library was next on their do list. He had teased her about getting old. She took it with good humor. *No point getting all sensitive.* While his thick brown hair showed silver strands, her head of tight curls was almost completely gray. His face was less lined than hers. The longer they were together, the more an age difference seemed to show. Whatever his age was. She'd never been quite sure of it, because how do you calculate age for someone from another planet? They'd been together close to forty years. He was still enchanting to look at, still had the charm and magic that had turned her head all those years ago.

But he was impossible. And stubborn. She remembered a light breeze scuttling through the screened open window, and the smell of the ocean air swirling in from San Francisco Bay as they'd set the teacups on their afternoon break. While their tea steeped, he'd said, "I'll send a last report in the morning."

"You've sent nothing for so long."

"This will be the last one."

"Are you going to tell them where you're going?"

"No."

"Will they try to find us?"

"They might try to find me. But they won't try very hard. I'm not the first to disappear. As for you—to them, you don't exist."

Despite his confidence, Editha sensed he had concerns about this move. As the relocation plan took shape he'd never wavered, only pushed forward with it. She'd learned long ago to wait until he was ready to reveal things. Their past moves had always been timed and calculated. With each one he'd further distanced himself from those to whom he said he was accountable.

She was sixty-eight. She knew he would outlive her, given his robust health. She wondered sometimes what he would do once she was gone, if he was cutting ties to Them now? Would he find someone else? Or try to go back to his world?

She'd kept his secret, all these years. Not that anyone would believe her had she revealed it. "I live with an extraterrestrial," she imagined herself saying to her canasta group. "He's human. Just from another world." With the one heart-wrenching exception decades ago, he had asked nothing of her but to protect his origins. Until now.

She knew she couldn't bring their garden. She'd accepted that some of the furniture couldn't go and they'd had to divest themselves of most of their art collection. But her writing was so intertwined with who she was and what their experience together had been for nearly four decades of life. He'd shocked her that afternoon, with his insistence that the journals be destroyed. She'd mentioned that she would box them up along with all the books that afternoon.

He had asked, "Is there anything in the journals that could suggest…"

"No," she'd interrupted. "Not a word."

"Good."

She'd hesitated, then added, "But some of it I wrote for myself in code."

"Code."

"Things only I would recognize for what they really say."

He'd shifted in his seat. "We need to burn them."

"Burn them?"

"Now," he'd said, standing up. "I'll log up the firepit."

"No, Fenn, no!"

He was already out the door. She'd followed him to the woodpile. "Please, please, at least let me go through them and keep some of them," she'd begged, holding on to his arm.

He'd stopped. "Nothing after you met me."

"But then you don't exist. Nor does—"

"Your memory will have to do," he'd interrupted her, collecting small logs.

Seven shelves of daily diary entries going up in flames. Never being able to read them again, never to recall their many travels from the vantage point of the middle of the journey. Notes on their gardening, their cooking experiments, the books they'd read together and discussed. If she was nothing else, Editha was a diarist. To give up those records was the worst thing he could ask of her. Except for the one thing he had asked long ago.

"Why?" she'd asked, watching him finish arranging logs and dropping a match. "Why?"

"Because we are in danger if we leave anything of our life behind." He'd fanned the flames. Satisfied with his fire, he'd taken her by the arms.

"Please, darling. I've…" He'd paused as if looking for the right words. "I've taken risks. We must disappear. It's the only way to have what years we have left together in peace. Let's go upstairs and start bringing the books down."

"You stay here with your fire," she'd said, performing surrender. "I'll…get them organized. It may take a few minutes, to sort out the earlier ones from before we met."

His hand had come to her face gently. He'd kissed her cheek, smiling. "Thank you."

She could never resist his smile. She'd smiled back bravely despite her trembling chin. Then she'd climbed the stairs, entered their library, and stared at the stacks of notebooks neatly lined on seven shelves next to her writing desk. She'd pulled one off the middle shelf, opened it, and saw in her own tiny cursive:

…and told a couple of stories I had not heard before about his previous work as a librarian. We were sitting in the outdoor lounge under palm trees, blooming gardenias in the hedges, at the Hotel Victoria after a long walk by the Mediterranean and through the harbor. (So many yachts! Fenn looked like a movie star with his aviator sunglasses. I expected someone to approach us and ask for his autograph.) Something about the scent of the gardenias caused him to recall what he refers to as his 'library years.' I gather the library was set in a vast garden of some sort.

*He told a story about trying to persuade one of his colleagues
not to take a job they would not be good at. "I was only trying to
be helpful," he said. "But you never saw such a temper tantrum.
He threw books, shouted profanities and told me I deserved to
be sent to The Deep."*

"Oh," she'd said to herself. But then she'd laughed, thinking
about someone throwing books and shouting curses at a friend
in a library embedded in a grand garden on another planet. She
remembered asking Fenn, that sunny afternoon in France as
she sipped her negroni, "Did he take the job?" and Fenn replying, "Yes. He was better at it than I or anyone else expected. It
opened the way for another, bigger job and then…" He'd shaken
his head. Then he'd smiled at her and said, "And then I came
here. And found you."

"What happened to him?" she'd asked.

"He 'went global,' as they say."

The diary entries revived so many memories. She loved leaf-
ing through the books and finding this or that incident, recall-
ing what had slipped her mind over the years. To think of them
going up in smoke was more than she could bear. She heard
footsteps on the stairs.

"Do you have a set ready?" Fenn had asked from the doorway.

"Not yet," she'd answered. "It's more disorganized than I
thought."

"Let me do it," he'd said. "Go out, take a walk, I'll take care
of it."

"They're the record of my life, Fenn. Let me keep a few,"
she'd pled. "I just opened one and it reminded me of our trip
to Cannes and that beautiful blue pool surrounded by palms
and gardenias and the martinis we drank and the stories you

told…things I haven't thought about in years. I want to re-member!"

Silence. Then he'd reached to the top shelf, taken half a dozen of the notebooks, and gone out the door.

"Noooo!" she'd wailed. Once he was down the stairs, she'd begun rifling through the indexes of the books, tossing one on the floor, dropping another on her desk, tossing two more on the floor. The bottom shelf contained the earliest ones, she could tell from the spiral notebooks that eventually had been replaced by the hardbound notebooks that then became what she wrote in now, daily diaries supplemented with additional notes and journal entries in longer form. It was how she made sense of her life. She'd started keeping the diaries and journals when she was twenty, still in college, unsure of her future, focusing on literature absent any sense of direction. Nearly fifty years later, the diaries told the story of her life with Fenn Lockyer.

She'd pulled her rucksack from the back of the library door. "Sometimes random is best," she'd told herself, pushing the diary on her desk into the sack. She had no time to be choosy. She'd grabbed another notebook from the fourth shelf, and another from the second. Two from the third, one from the top. "I don't know how I'll hide them from him," she'd muttered to the rucksack. "That will be your job." Hearing his steps back into the house, she'd stashed nine of the notebooks in the rucksack and shoved it under her desk. She'd pulled another notebook from the middle shelf and opened it, reading from the middle of the page:

…love on the new sofa under the canopy which later made me wonder if the neighbors heard us but really does it matter? San Francisco is a noisy city. Fenn seems to like it here so far. He is writing a great deal. I don't see what he writes, he doesn't share

that. I only know when he sends his reports, when he brings out the Box and makes it work. It's so beautiful, all the colors and shimmering lines. I asked to see what he was writing once years ago (2/29/1992) and he answered: "Bridge too far." Won't ask again.

A thin notebook fell over as she took another journal from the second-to-bottom shelf. She picked it up, opened the cover, and gasped. On the first page was printed, in her hand, *A Brief History of New Atlantis by an Earth Cousin.* "Oh my God," she whispered. She'd forgotten about this notebook. She'd started writing it within a year of their marriage, secretly jotting down notes and anecdotes Fenn dropped about the world he'd come from. She thought it was funny when he'd told her, "We call you the Earth cousins." She'd added everything she could in the two years that followed. Then, in despair, after the worst happened, she'd shoved it away with anger. She remembered throwing it in the garbage. But now, she remembered having retrieved it. And shoving it behind other notebooks.

She turned the first page and saw a list:

The Great Departure NAY0000
Star People NAY0000-0988
Darkness NAY0988-1998
Renaissance of Eswen NAY1998-2049

"Oh my God, oh my God," she'd said to herself. She flipped forward a few pages, to see other notes. Lists of places he'd mentioned. Shiona, his home village, the Raja Sea, the Farm Country, the Desertlands. A list of clan names—Loa, that was Fenn's clan, and Ep, C'iez, Beq, Shoko…a list of some of the Guilds and their functions in the society. Phrases about the capital city, with a crude drawing of wide and narrow concentric circles that represented the circular layout of wide lanes with bridges over round canals. The more pages she turned, the more fascinated with it and horrified she became with herself. She wanted to read it all again. But she knew he would destroy it instantly if he discovered it. "I should just give it to him," she'd whispered to herself, setting the thin notebook on the floor.

She'd looked up as he entered the room. She took a stack still on the shelf and handed them to him, after gesturing at the many notebooks still on the shelf.

"I hope you have a lot of wood."

He'd taken the stack. After he left, she'd slipped the slim volume into the rucksack with the others she'd hidden, telling herself she'd deal with it later.

Hours later, the firepit was down to its last glowing coals of wood and book binding. They lay in bed together knowing it was their final night in this house. The lamp on her side of the bed was still lit.

"I'm sorry," Fenn had whispered before he fell asleep. "I'll make it up to you somehow." They were nestled together, her head on his shoulder. "I know I ask too much."

"It's only words," she'd sighed, reaching to turn off the lamp. As her eyes adjusted, light from the streetlights swept into the room through their skylight in the ceiling.

"Editha, listen to me. If something happens…" He'd paused. "If something bad happens, you have to leave San Francisco immediately. Immediately. Do you hear me?"

"What are you not telling me?" she'd asked, sitting up.

He'd pulled her back into his arms. "Your safety is the most important thing to me. Tomorrow morning, I'll file my final re-port, decommission the Bluebox, and toss it into the Bay. And we'll be on our way. We've been lucky, unbelievably lucky. I'm

not the first of my kind to make this transition. I just want
you to promise me that if anything happens, if anything goes
wrong, you will go. Don't stay here. Promise me."

"I promise," she'd said, her voice thick.

"No tears, darling. It will all be fine. Let's sleep as best we can
tonight, and dream about our new home and new life with no
Bluebox, no mysterious messages, no reports. Just us."

He had squeezed her against him. She'd reminded herself:
It's only his brain I'm mad at. He'd fallen asleep. She was left
with her thoughts. She knew she needed to sleep, tomorrow
would be a long and sad day. Then she started thinking again
about the journals. And that compendium of notes about his
world.

A shadow appeared at their bedroom door. She saw it hover, then make a swift tossing action followed by a groan from
Fenn. She sat up, looked at her husband, and saw his eyes wide
open, a knife embedded deep in his throat. Blood was rushing
up around the edges of the knife. She cried out and twisted in
the bed, accidentally avoiding another knife flying across the
room. She rolled onto the floor as a dark figure leaped at her.
She waved her arms wildly, then grasped a long, heavy power
strip that lived between the nightstand and the bed. Yanking
it up, she hammered it at the head of whoever was on top of
her. It startled the intruder enough that she could scramble to
her feet and haul the lamp on the nightstand through the air,
hitting the intruder twice on the side of the head. The person
collapsed on the floor.

She looked at Fenn, motionless in the bed, the knife in his
throat. "Oh Jesus," she whispered to herself, frozen. "Oh Fenn,
no, not like this…" Then she remembered his words, spoken
only minutes before: *Don't stay here.* She didn't know what was
happening, but she had said, "I promise."

The black-clad hooded figure was face down on the floor, not moving. Horror and fury momentarily overcame her fear. She rushed to the closet and put on jeans, a sweater, her slip-on boots. She grabbed a belt. She saw Fenn's laptop on the chair next to the bed. She took the laptop into the library, where, reaching under the desk, she found the rucksack full of notebooks. She added the laptop.

"Hurry," she whispered to herself. "Hurry."

As she pulled the rucksack up onto her shoulder, she bumped the desk and heard something drop. There was no time to feel around for it in the dark.

She went back into the hallway and peered into the bedroom. The figure on the floor was moving slowly. Fenn stared lifeless at the ceiling. She teared up. The intruder stirred more, trying to sit up. Without thinking, she let the rucksack slide off her shoulder. She used it, with all her might, to wallop the intruder's head, causing the person to flop again to the floor. Dragging the rucksack back to her shoulder, she raced down the stairs, grabbing the manila envelope that contained the credit cards, funds, and keys they'd stashed on the side table for the departure. She remembered Fenn placing it there that night, patting it lightly.

"Everything we'll need is here," he'd said.

She shoved the envelope into the rucksack, straightened her back, and opened the front door. She could hear the intruder moving around upstairs.

"Hurry," she told herself again as she rushed down the exterior stairs, out onto the street, and into the misty San Francisco night.

CHAPTER 5

ONCE KAIEDA AWOKE, Max stirred the three Earthers from their several hours of slumber. No one said a word about the disappearing cresh or Max's air-hovering over the lagoon. Within a few minutes, they heard a helicopter approaching. Reggie said, "There they are." Everyone went to the beach to watch it land near the stricken plane. After the rotors stopped turning, the pilot disembarked. With nary a wave to them, he went to the plane, got in, and tried to start it. It coughed but the engine would not turn over. He climbed back out and met them.

"Yeah, something's caught in the fuel filter or carburetor," he said to Reggie. He looked back at the plane. "You closed out your flight plan?"

Reggie nodded.

The pilot eyed the hard, wet sand. "Good job getting her down safely. We'll get the report filed. NTSB won't be in any rush to follow up since nobody's hurt and nothing was damaged. They might get here sometime late tomorrow. That'll give me a day to get it fixed and pointed in the right direction."

"Thanks, Uncle Jim," Reggie said.

"Ah, a family business!" Tumbleston said.

The helicopter pilot offered his hand, first to Charles, then to Max. "Jim Malaoho," he said. "Sorry for the inconvenience, glad you're all okay. We'll get you back to the resort right away. Sorry it took so long to get here. Busy morning." He eyed the group. "Everybody needs a ride? I thought it was just two passengers."

"Oh, we aren't…" Kaieda started.

"That would be great," Max interceded.

He's on it, getting us out of here fast.

"I thought you were camping!" Charles boomed.

"She's not feeling well," Marian said, nodding toward Kaieda.

"True, true," Charles said. "Yes, we'll all take that ride. If you hurry, we won't sue you."

"You already signed a waiver saying you wouldn't do that," Jim Malaoho said.

KAIEDA MADE MENTAL notes of what lay before her as the helicopter approached the Tumblestons' resort on the southwestern shore of Maui. *Of course it has a helipad.* Tiered architecture and a sun-buffed color scheme of the resort hotel; low, thick-jungled green hills rising around the resort. Tan men scurried around as the helicopter landed. More were on hand, wearing white uniforms, to escort the Tumblestons to the hotel. *Caters to pale, wealthy humans.* The backpack dedicated to Kaieda was full of their basics, IDs and mobile phones and a laptop. The Bluebox was still tucked in Max's backpack. Everything else they'd left in the reeds.

"Somebody's going to love that tent," Max had told her as the helicopter rose.

The Tumblestons pressed them to secure a room in the resort. "Stay a night or two, your money is no good here!" Charles told them. "Everything on me!"

Max and Kaieda agreed to a dayroom. They declined an overnight as graciously as they could. They had, they said, only a couple of days off and needed to get back to the mainland. Given that Kaieda wasn't feeling well, they should probably go now.

Max again attempted to activate the Bluebox. It sat on the dresser in silence.

"Unlikely we will have success in Honolulu either," he told Kaieda. "We have to go to San Francisco."

It was not what she wanted to hear. But he was right. When the Bluebox wouldn't activate on its own, they needed connection to their own technology to reboot. They were overdue to confirm landing, check messages, file an entry report.

They examined their American passports, their credit cards, the mobile phones, and the money the Researchers had prepared. Kaieda shopped briefly and in haste in the hotel boutique stores, finding a couple of dresses and shirts that fit. Plus, white sandals.

They rejoined the Tumblestons at one of the resort bars after everyone had showered and refreshed in their rooms. "Flights out of Kahului every day," Charles said. "You can get to San Francisco overnight if you want. Might have a layover in L.A. but that's nothing." He paid for the drinks after insisting that they all needed to meet up again soon in California. He then arranged a car transfer for them from the hotel to Maui's airport.

Kaieda held hope that the Bluebox might work in Honolulu. During the layover there, Max tried to activate the Bluebox again. Still nothing. In the comfort of a plush leather seat in the business-class lounge overlooking the tarmac, Kaieda made her first written notes of the journey thus far. It took her mind off what lay ahead. In San Francisco. More precisely, who lay ahead.

After boarding the flight, Max said, "I'll text D'avi now."

"I guess."

He frowned. "Problem? We can connect through their Blue-box. Once ours is working, we'll move on to Los Angeles. We'll be ahead of schedule."

Kaieda sighed. "You don't know D'avi." *Or his partner.*

Max got the look on his face, and made the slight tilt of his head, that Kaieda now recognized as his pause-to-search mode. He was running inner files to ascertain more on D'avi S'Iloa. He came out of the short pause and said, "Traveler. Experienced. Special Assistant to Egdar Roiboi."

He looked at her, questioning.

Kaieda looked away, saying nothing.

Max picked up his phone, thumbed a text, and sent it.

"Don't do that so rapidly," Kaieda told him. "It looks un-human. People will notice."

A minute later, his phone dinged. He held it up so they could both see the reply.

"A smiley face?" Max said. His head did its slight torque. "Ah. Emojis."

Kaieda squinted at the screen. "Doesn't sound like D'avi." She read aloud, "Freddie here. D'avi out on research. We have a spare room. Nothing to declare." An address followed.

"His partner answered," Max observed.

"Partner," Kaieda repeated. "He's new." Dread rose like bile in her chest.

"Nothing to declare?"

"Traveler code. It means he won't report the contact."

The things they tell us. The things they don't. The flight roared

down the runway and lifted into the dark Hawaiian sky. Max
had made the practical decision. She had no grounds to object. She knew the San Francisco assignment was influenced by
Roiboi. A reward to D'avi, along with…Freddie. She shuddered
inside, remembering her last encounter with D'avi and Roiboi
on Rimalon. And seeing that…thing. *No point, no purchase, no
gain, no stopping it. Will I ever see you again? YOU, not that
thing?*

She slid into light sleep.

THE FIVE-HOUR FLIGHT landed in chilly haze. They took a
cab to the San Francisco address Freddie had sent. It was a contemporary three-story row house featuring a bright-red door.
Max knocked. Kaieda advised, "Ring the doorbell." He rang.
Nothing happened. Max pressed the doorbell again.

"Coming! Coming!" came a muffled voice from inside the
house. They heard tramping on stairs, then the door opened.
Before them stood a fit, tousle-haired, unshaven man wearing a
white cotton apron printed with bright-yellow daisies. He had
a white spatula in one hand. "Welcome, welcome, welcome to
the Emerald City!" he greeted them.

Kaieda's heart sank. The Allan9. She shut her eyes, gulping.
He widened the door so they could enter. "Come! Come!" he
said, waving the spatula. "I'm Freddie! Your room is down the
hallway on the right. D'avi isn't here. He's been out two nights
in a row at a rave. Left his phone! These Bay Area boys! So
much fun!"

Max took in their host. "I see," he said. He was processing.
"Allan9," he observed. He offered his hand. "Maximus5700.
Max."

Kaieda knew they were programmed to greet each other

with model IDs. *Why hadn't Freddie done the greeting?* She watched their hands clasp, the bright eyes greeting each other, the slight pause between them. The Allan9's—"Freddie's"—appearance shook her. *Nobody asked, nobody asked. Why didn't they ask?*

"Ohhhh, the new Maximus!" Freddie exclaimed. "Exciting!" He looked Max up and down. "Cis male. Quite beautiful!" He leaned in. "Orientation?"

Max's head tilted. More processing. He nodded to Kaieda to lead the way down the hall, ignoring Freddie's question.

"Come upstairs when you're ready, I'm making cheese blintzes!" Freddie half sang the last word as he started back up the stairs to the main floor.

Kaieda fell face-first on the king-size bed, miserable. "I saw that synth on Rimalon," she said into the lavender duvet.

"Travelers are often partnered with synthetics," Max replied, setting their backpacks down. "We are helpful, efficient, and stay on task."

"Uh-huh," Kaieda said, still talking into the bed. She rolled over. Then she rolled face down again.

"The Allan9 upsets you," he observed. He was emptying their backpacks.

Do I explain? Her throat tightened. She turned her head to see her right hand, with its dual-stars tattoo, resting on the pillow beside her. She fought tears.

"The Allan9 is a top-line synthetic," Max continued. "Not as technically sophisticated as the Maximus5700, but they built exceptional empathy and sexual functionality into the Allan9. Freddie is programmed to suit a human male partner." He looked at Kaieda, still sprawled on the bed. "I have comparable programming. For heterosexual enjoyment," he added.

"Please stop talking," Kaieda said.

He hung the two dresses Kaieda had bought in the closet. "You may wish to shower and put one of these on," he suggested. He looked at her on the bed. Then he looked at the dresses. "Or not."

"Not." She knew she needed more clothing. Attire was the last thing on her mind. She'd figure out her fashion style later. She fought thinking about Freddie's smile as he'd greeted them—that bright, cheering, rascally smile that was so often followed by laughter in the human Freddie replicated. *It's a machine. It's not him. It's a machine. It's not him.*

They should have ASKED.

She groaned into the pillow. *We need to get to our post, orient, start fieldwork.* She pulled herself up and swung her legs over the side of the bed. "I'll shower, we'll go upstairs and eat blintzes, we'll wait for D'avi," she said. "And get the Bluebox operating. Okay?"

"Affirmative," Max replied.

Half an hour later, they were on the main floor of the house, in a white kitchen that spilled into a dining area that opened to a living room with white furniture and a balcony overlooking the street below. Kaieda wore the fitted dress with navy-blue flowers and the sandals she'd bought at the resort. She and Max sat at the quartz-topped island as Freddie served blintzes. He then sat at the end of the island, an empty plate in front of him.

"Aren't you going to eat?" Kaieda asked. "These are delicious."

"I'm a fine cook," Freddie said. "But you know I don't need to eat."

"It is of social value," Max said, taking a second big bite of blintz.

"Have you heard from D'avi, do you know when he'll get here?" Kaieda asked.

"I told you, he left his phone here. He isn't going to like see-ing you." Freddie said the second sentence in his singsong voice. "You should have gone to a *Reporter*."

"Team Five was our closest confirmed contact," Max said.

"We don't have the Reporter locations," Kaieda added. "It's the only secret left on Rimalon." After a pause, she added, "They seem to be dying off."

"They come, they love Earth, they don't want to leave," Freddie continued his singsong. Then returning to normal voice, he said, "Time catches up to them. They don't want to go back. They die here." He shrugged. "Sad."

From downstairs they heard a lock unlatching. "Ah, here he is!" Freddie exclaimed, rising and heading downstairs. "D'avi, we have company," he called. More words were exchanged at the bottom of the landing. Kaieda and Max heard ascending footsteps.

Max put his fork down. Kaieda stood.

"D'avi," she said, stepping toward him. He looked the same, though his dark hair fell below his shirt collar and he had a perfectly trimmed goatee. He wore black-framed glasses. His eyes were bloodshot.

He hugged her, saying, "Kaieda" in her ear. "Why us?" he whispered. He glanced at Freddie, then said, "I would have told you: don't." Releasing her, he looked over at Max. "Ah, the new Maximus."

Max rose.

"Isn't he beautiful?" Freddie sighed. "Can we get one?"

"No!" Kaieda, D'avi, and Max said at the same time.

"Oh, pooh," Freddie said. "Baby, do you want blintzes?"

"I'm starving," D'avi replied. He gestured everyone to sit again. He sat beside Kaieda on the remaining stool at the is-land. Freddie pulled another plate from the cupboard and scooped blintzes onto it, then placed it in front of D'avi along with a fork.

"I was at a rave," D'avi said, shoveling the food down.

"We heard," Kaieda replied. "How was it?"

"Loud." He swallowed food and drank the orange juice Freddie had just put in front of him. "I need to make notes before I pass out. Lots of molly. I'm a mess. But Roiboi and Sundrae will love the report." His attention shifted from his plate to Kaieda. "You really can't stay here."

"Our landing did not go perfectly," Max said. "We left most of our supplies on Maui."

"Why?" asked Freddie.

"Long story," Kaieda answered. "D'avi, when your cresh first grounded, was it hard for you to breathe?"

"Yeah, until the chip fully deployed. But we slept right after landing and completed orientation without any issues. We've been here almost a month."

"Have you been in contact with any of the other Teams?"

"You know we're not supposed to do that, which is the second-biggest reason why you can't stay." He looked to Freddie. "Is the beacon on?"

"It's having issues," Freddie sang as he started clearing plates. "Fuzzy issues. The Monitors know someone is here but not *who*." He shrugged. "We have people over all the time."

Kaieda sighed, knowing someone, probably Faerae, would locate them.

"Have you activated your Bluebox yet?" D'avi asked her.

"It was compromised," Max responded ahead of her. "That's why we came. I need to link to yours. I believe that will stabilize ours and bring up the column."

"Hmmm," D'avi said.

"We need a few days…" Kaieda said.

"A couple," D'avi answered.

Ever difficult. She'd had numerous run-ins with him over the years. He was well-established as Roiboi's favorite. A bitter taste rose in Kaieda's mouth. Travelers and the Global Festival were accountable to the Culture Guild. However, neither could succeed without the Science Guild's direct provision of services and the Military Guild's transport and communications resources. Earth-related initiatives raised the stakes, no matter who was doing what. It was all overseen by the Government, which meant the General Assembly and the Triumvirate always had ears in every project. Roiboi masterfully juggled all of these sometimes conflicting entities and bent them in the Festival's interest. Winning approval and funding for Festival X/V was his crowning achievement. Kaieda's only leverage in resisting Roiboi's influence on Traveler work was her popularity within the program and on The Planet. Here, she had no sway. She had to depend on Roiboi's chosen one. And cope with his synth partner.

"Tell me about the plane," D'avi said. "The one that landed on your beach."

Kaieda frowned. *How does he know about that?* "It was small. Why?"

"Huh. Just curious. I heard rumors it crashed."

"Emergency landing," Max replied. "No damage. Cessna 182. They left it until repairs can be made. Some kind of obstruction in the fuel flow to the engine."

"Huh," D'avi repeated. "So, it's in sound condition?"

Max looked at Kaieda, who shrugged. "Yes," Max said. "I'll get the Bluebox set up." He rose and went downstairs.

Freddie finished cleaning up the kitchen. "I'm going to the market," he said to D'avi. "Company means food! Party tonight!"

"Record the market and send it to me?" D'avi asked, kissing Freddie's cheek.

"Always!" Freddie sang, kissing him back. He took two tote bags off a hook at the kitchen door. "See you later!"

"You need to shave," D'avi called after him.

"So do you!" Freddie sang up the stairs. The front door slammed.

D'avi sat down. "I had no reason to believe you'd see him," he said to Kaieda.

"They shouldn't have made him like that in the first place," she replied.

"They had the rights."

"They should have asked."

"Alec was in the military. They can do whatever they want with his DNA."

She curdled inside. "Stop with the past tense."

"Still telling yourself that? After three years? Nobody comes back from The Deep."

"One did."

"Yeah. Dolloped mush. Not exactly coming back."

Kaieda got off her stool and walked to the balcony door. "They've made progress since then," she murmured, more to herself than to D'avi.

D'avi went to where she was standing, taking her arm. "Remember when we last saw each other? On Rimalon?"

"Of course. I saw the…" She took a deep breath. "Freddie. And I told you, and Roiboi, and Dzuren to stop. You should have respected that. All of you should have."

"They designed this one specifically for me," D'avi said. "He's everything I've ever wanted. If it's any comfort, this one is unique. I always liked Alec. Now I have him. Well, a facsimile of him. For me."

Kaieda faced him. "You OWE me. You owe me as much time as I need here, D'avi. I don't want to stay any longer than we need to. I don't want to have to look at that thing."

"He's a synthetic person. They'll trace you. Faerae won't give up until she finds you."

"I know. But Dzuren won't send Fetchers if he thinks the mission might go forward. We'll update them as soon as Max connects our Bluebox. Then, on to Los Angeles. All will be forgiven. They want my reports."

"What they really want is more Kaieda porn," he said.

"Roiboi insisted I do this job. And the Science Guild wants to test their newest synth in the field. Max, I mean. Deal with it."

"Egdar added you as last-minute fan service," D'avi shot back. "You haven't lost your sharp edges. How did Alec live with that?"

"Feck you," she snapped.

CHAPTER 6

*CALIFORNIA ZEPHYR, WESTERN
UNITED STATES, EARTH*

Day Two, morning into evening, UTC-8 and UTC-7

F ENN IS GONE.

The pounding in Editha's solar plexus would not stop. She'd seen flames curling from the skylight and upstairs windows as she hurried away. *A fiery end to us.* She'd picked up her pace, her vision blurred by tears. In the shock and rush, she hadn't called the police or the fire department. Now she wondered if the fire had spread, if her neighbors were all right. *Fenn's death is the end of everything.* How could police help her, given what she would be pressured to explain, and what they would believe? How quickly would they conclude she was insane? The police would see the second knife, buried in the headboard or her pillow. *Will they be looking for me too? Dead? Or am I a suspect? Will they think I tried to make it look like I was a victim?*

She'd reached Dolores Street on foot before she realized she wasn't sure where she was going. It was close to midnight. A few people were still out on the street as she walked on. A tiny all-night diner called Ethel's Corner was open. She went in, sat in a booth that blocked any view of her from the street, ordered coffee, and sat alone, in shock.

She forced herself to focus. Normally she relished details; she could lose herself in them. *No airports. Train. Nobody will think of that first.* Pulling her reading glasses from the rucksack—thank God they were in the pocket where she usually stashed them—and using her smartphone, she searched trains to Chicago from San Francisco and found Amtrak's daily *California Zephyr.* Fenn had talked about them taking that trip together sometime. Studying the *Zephyr* schedule and then the BART schedule, she realized she could take BART to the end of the Orange Line and end up at the Richmond Amtrak stop. She ordered a second cup of coffee, then phoned the main number at Amtrak. Twenty minutes later, she had an e-ticket on the train leaving at eight thirty-five a.m. It was one forty a.m. The Richmond train station opened at four a.m. Researching it, she discovered it was nothing more than an unstaffed, sheltered platform. *Not the place to spend the night. Ethel's Corner will have to do. Stay away from the window. Stay awake. Order a piece of pie. Hope nobody notices me.*

A horrible four and a half hours followed. She ran the events through her mind over and over. *Should I have waited for the police? But then that killer might have killed me. I did what I had to do.* She agonized, wondering who the intruder was and what Fenn was afraid of and why he was murdered. He was about to disappear from THEM forever. Was it a random attack or robbery, in which case she should have stayed and dealt with the firefighters and police? Or did this have to do with Fenn's work for Them? *He used to call it "my work on Earth." Used to.*

Buying the ticket to Chicago gave her some energy. At six thirty a.m., she thanked the fellow at the counter for all the coffee and the slice of coconut pie, paid her bill with her credit card, emptied her bladder in the dingy unisex one-seater restroom, and headed for the BART station. By seven forty-five, she was at the Richmond stop. She kept telling herself she was following Fenn's instructions to go to the Michigan place. He

was still with her, in a way. She kept the rucksack and its precious contents close.

Alone in her roomette on the train, her ticket checked by the
conductor, she could breathe a little. The tears finally came. She
sobbed herself to a troubled sleep.

SOMETIME AFTER NOON she woke. The *Zephyr* was in eastern California, sweeping through pine forests, past alpine lakes,
and toward the scrubby northern Nevada desert. She looked
outside and moaned. *Fenn is gone. Everything is gone.*

She could almost hear Fenn saying to her, *YOU'RE still
alive. YOU'RE not gone. Eat.*

Yes, eat. She pulled herself off the folding bed, shoved it to
its seated position, stood fully, and looked in the mirror. An old
woman with disheveled gray hair and red eyelids stared back at
her. The tears came again. She wasn't ready to face others. She
sat down and stared outside at the pines and scrub sweeping by.
Her eyes drifted around the roomette and dropped to the floor.
The rucksack was where she'd dumped it upon boarding. She
grabbed the side strap and pulled it into her lap. All she had of
Fenn and their life together was in this backpack. She opened
the top and reached in, first finding the thick 8"×11" manila envelope he'd left on the hall table the night before. The keys, the
new identity and credit cards, the documents that would enable
their new life. A lot of cash. Where and how he'd gotten the
new IDs, she did not know and never asked. His answer would
have deflected.

She pulled the envelope out of the pack. Then, setting the
pack on the floor, she placed the envelope on her lap. *This was
for both of us. How can I do this without you? Why must I do
this without you?* She stared out the train window, watching the

rushing water in a wide creek pocked with small boulders running alongside their track. She reached into the envelope, her fingers touching the keys, the cards, the money, the sheets of paper…and another, business-size envelope. She pulled it out.

"E" was written on the front. She frowned. The train rumbled on, slowing down momentarily, then speeding up again. She looked on both sides of the white envelope. She pressed a finger into the back upper left corner and wedged the envelope open. In it was a single sheet of paper, which she unfolded slowly. Fenn's handwriting. She held the letter to her heart, again hearing his voice in her head: *You have to READ it.*

She fumbled in the rucksack again, searching for her reading glasses. Surely she hadn't left them at Ethel's Corner. She felt around in the bottom of the sack. The glasses case was there, holding the reading glasses. She put them on.

Beloved,

    If you are reading this, something has gone wrong. I plan to retrieve and destroy it before we open the envelope together on our doorstep in Michigan. But if you are opening it, I am not with you. My best effort was not enough. I am sorry. I love you with all my heart. If calamity has fallen, if death has separated us, I love you still. Always.

    Editha you MUST do what I say. NOW. You must go to England, to my friend Marina Rambert. She will give protection, she will give you a safe place to live, she will explain what I cannot put in writing. You will find her kind and wise. Marina's address is at the bottom of this page. Text her. Fly to London. She will meet you. Go. NOW.

    You'll find something else in a small envelope. More than anything it represents our unbreakable bond. I told you years ago that I destroyed it. I couldn't. Forgive me. I know you would have wanted it. You forgave me for the worst thing I could do to both of us. Forgive me again now. Treasure this remembrance of the best of us. I love you, I love you, I love you.

Remember that energy never dies, it only changes form.

Live long and fully.

– F

Below his sign-off was a phone number and an address in Oxfordshire, England.

Editha read the letter twice. The first reading became words smeared in tears as she realized this was his good-bye to her. He left her with unanswered questions and a broken heart. And now, with instructions to go to a foreign country, to a woman she'd never heard of. *Is this Marina one of THEM?* she wondered, wiping her eyes. She knew there were others here. Fenn had never said how many, or where they were, or whether he was in contact with any of them. Who was this one, to him?

Treasure this remembrance of the best of us.

She shook her head. Reaching again into the envelope, her fingers fumbled between the different document pages and grasped a 4"×6" envelope. She pulled it out, opened it, and gasped. It was a photograph Fenn had sworn he destroyed decades ago. She held it up in the light. It was perfectly preserved: a black-and-white photograph of them, so young, sitting on the sofa in their house in Ojai. Propped between them was a baby around fourteen months old. The baby had bright eyes and thick dark hair. Fenn and Editha were smiling down at the baby, who was looking up at Editha, the tiny mouth spread wide in laughter.

"Oh," she said softly. It was the only photograph that had survived the searing decision to send their child to the world Fenn came from. Editha had found the photo while Fenn was gone on that awful journey. On his return, she showed it to him. He had taken it away from her, insisting, "No visual records. We agreed. You agreed."

It was the one period of their lives their relationship had barely survived.

Editha kept staring at the picture. Memories of those sixteen precious months with the only child she birthed flooded through her. The child long gone. Fenn now gone. *What am I to do?*

She looked out the window again. The creek banks were narrower, the water rippled slowly between embedded rocks. They were moving into the Nevada desert. *No one knows I am here. What do I know, now? I'm alive. I have this photograph, and the documents, and the journals, and that notebook, and Fenn's laptop. And instructions on where to turn.*

She went to the dining car and ordered a turkey sandwich. She drank a glass of red wine. When the food was served, she ate it quickly. She checked her phone, then wondered if she should do that. No calls, no texts, the usual stack-up of junk emails, nothing personal. They'd spent the last six months withdrawing from their normal activities and saying good-bye to friends who were told they were moving to the Midwest. *Nobody knows I'm here,* she kept telling herself. She thought again about the intruder in the house. She could not recall anything specific about the dark figure that had upended her life. *Our life.* She considered Fenn's sense of urgency. She pondered the phone again and wondered if she should send a text to the woman in England. *Not yet. Not until I know when I will arrive.*

She returned to her roomette and stared at the desert. They were nearing the Utah border and the great salt flats. She and Fenn had driven this route, early in their relationship. Through the Sierras with a stop in Lake Tahoe, then on to Salt Lake City and across southern Wyoming, where they'd tried to outrun a snowstorm. She laughed, thinking about that drive and trying to count snow fences beside the interstate. Fenn had told her about his world on that trip.

That's right, I bought that little notebook in a bookstore in Cheyenne. That's when I started writing those things down.

His planet was like Earth, an oxygen atmosphere with vast oceans, and deserts, forests, prairies. Fenn had grown up in a village by one of the great seas. Their population lived in clustered settlements to ensure cooperation and protect planetary health. "There are fewer of us to be hard on our world," Fenn had told her. "Population control is strict. We are a more practical people than those on Earth." He'd laughed and added, "We call you 'the Earth cousins.' We are very big on cousins. We all have a lot of them."

That was when he'd told her about their moon, called Rimalon. It was like the Earth's. It had a small human population living in an enormous complex called the Keeper Colony. It was run by their military. He called that the Space Force. "Mysterious science and defense things happen on Rimalon. It's our gateway to the galaxy."

Almost two years later, during the many conversations about sending the baby to New Atlantis, Fenn revealed more. She learned "The Planet," as he called it, had been at peace for centuries. New Atlanteans prized their highly structured society, their nineteen clans, the Guild system that provided work and purpose. He described their governing system, overseen by an elected assembly that worked in tandem with a trio of world leaders he called "the Triumvirate." The Planet required Global Service of all citizens reaching adulthood. Technologically they were centuries ahead of Earth, thanks to those Fenn called "the Star People."

"They rescued and resituated us when our island home on Earth was sinking," he'd said. She didn't understand how that was possible. "We don't know how they did it either," he'd replied. "Even now, fifteen thousand years later."

"Our child belongs with us," was her mantra. Over time and with Fenn's persistence, her resolve faltered. Fenn told her about his clan and his family. He would find the right cousins to raise their child. He reminded her of the dangers of Earth and the consequences of local and global violence. When she pointed out that HE lived here, why wouldn't his family be with him? He reminded her what he had told her from the beginning:

"I am not allowed to have a family. Not on Earth. If we try to keep the secret, it will be uncovered. The consequences will be disastrous for all of us. And you and I will be separated forever."

Slowly, she came to grasp that her presence in his life, much less the baby's, was a problem to the world on the other side of the galaxy.

"Do they know about us?" she had asked. "About you and me?"

"Very few," he answered. He would not elaborate.

For three months they had gone back and forth. Could she visit and see the child growing up? No. Could the child ever return? No, that would not be fair. Would the child ever know their true parentage? It would raise many issues. How would the child get there?

"I will ensure safe passage. We have people who are dependable," Fenn had told her.

She had shaken her head.

"I'll do it myself," Fenn then said. "Editha, surely you understand things will get worse here. My work must continue. I want, I need, to be here with you. We must make a good decision for the baby. I know what the world I left behind is like. It's imperfect, but the possibilities to flourish far exceed anything here."

On and on, around and around they went, until she finally, miserably, agreed.

She stared at the photo. *And here I am now alone, with neither of them.* She stared at her phone on her lap. She looked at Fenn's letter once more. Her phone dinged. She looked at the text. It was from a no-ID caller. *Spam?* She looked closer, to read one word:

NEXT

Her adrenaline surged. Two knives had been thrown. One was for Fenn. The other was for her. She'd survived only because of luck, because she had turned unexpectedly. Was this a message that whoever had thrown those knives intended to finish the job? *Do they know I'm on this train? Can they trace my phone?*

Plane. To London. They would reach Salt Lake City around eight thirty p.m. Too late to catch a flight anywhere, but she could schedule an early departure the next morning. She would have to ditch the phone at some point. She stared at it, then turned it off. The rucksack was still on the floor. *Fenn's laptop. If my cell phone is trackable, is his laptop? Leave it powered down.*

Hours passed. The light receded. She thought about Fenn's precision, how constant and reliable he had been. Even in death she believed she could trust him. As the train pulled into Salt Lake City station, she stood, pulling the rucksack onto her shoulder. She turned her phone back on. Then she let it slide between the seat and the wall under the window. *Enjoy the ride.*

Taking a deep breath, she stepped off the train.

CHAPTER 7

FAERAE INCREASED HER speed on the running platform. She was already perspiring, not yet exhausted. Rimalon's bleached, pitted landscape spread before her beyond the window.

"Louder!"

The volume of the rhythmic roll and beat of The Interstitials, the band of all bands on New Atlantis, increased.

The blue, green, and sandy orb of The Planet glowed in the distance against the black beyond of space. It was her free day. She struggled not to return to the Command Room. Running helped channel her energy. *I live on a moon, I still want to live on a moon, the planet rise is light enough…where are they? Where are they?* Always better when Kaieda was on The Planet. *Then I know where you are. Why haven't they activated their Bluebox? That is the 906th time I have asked that question.*

Her feet pounded on. She wanted to search the beacon files, monitor communications, Traveler sites, even the secretive Reporter locations if Dzuren would supply them. Dzuren had been harassed the previous day by the Culture Guild, the Festival, even a call from the Tri office asking for status reports. *As if the mighty Triumvirate cares about Travelers. They barely know what happened, much less what everybody's trying to do about it. It's all performance.*

The previous day, Faerae had heard Dzuren say to some-one, "I can't send Fetchers where they don't know to go." How he kept such an even temper during crisis mystified her. His military career was characterized by patience and improvisa-tion, both of which Faerae knew she lacked. To Faerae's fre-quent annoyance, he had a sense of humor. She recalled his glee when he'd brought the Maximus5700 into the Command Room. Introducing him as Kaieda's new Traveler partner, he failed to mention that "Max" was a synthetic. After Max left, Dzuren told the CCR Engineers they'd just met the newest, most sophisticated android ever made. The Twins had burst into applause.

"Marvelous, marvelous!" they exclaimed. Then they'd switched to the incomprehensible clatter of the Eflos dialect.

The Twins. Rarities on The Planet, more so on Rimalon. Late in the previous century, the Science Guild had secured approval for a new experiment. It extended a program that had revived, using ancient DNA from Earth, numerous species of dinosaurs that now lived in remote sections of The Planet. The Experimental Wing Laboratory of the Science Guild next wanted to revive ancient human species other than Sapiens. Once the project was approved, they collected targeted DNA from the Indonesian island of Flores on Earth. Genome pro-jections were conducted to extend the information gathered. Scientists created synthetic reproductions. Then came slow, or-ganic compound tests.

The results were still debated on The Planet. Was it a re-vived species, or a new one? Was it right to do this kind of genetic experimentation? How much *Homo sapiens* DNA had been used in the new beings? The DNA collected had been incomplete. Their heads and brains were the same size and had the same capacity as Sapiens. Their intelligence measured equally. They were small people. The new — or was it revived? — species was based on *Homo floresiensis*. News later emerged, to more controversy, that the team had also attempted to revive *Homo neanderthalensis*. The Neanderthal results were unfavorable. That branch of the effort was abandoned.

The Floresiensis humans caught life successfully. The official designation given was "E-Floresiens." The name was a nod to their originating species from Earth, gone extinct over fifty thousand Earth years ago. Fifty years had now passed since the Experimental Lab created the first cohort. The new humans proved to be bright, industrious, and excitable. They reached puberty later than Sapiens, but within twenty years of their lab-induced creation, the first generation proved intelligent, resilient, and able to reproduce. They proved adept at advocating for their own well-being. Twenty-five years into the experiment, the young, independent journalist Mog Weller found enough evidence on the project that she broke what was a classified story. The news caused social unrest, political controversy, and demands for accountability from the Government. What were they to do with a human species that could replenish itself but was not *Homo sapiens*? Were they of The People? Hadn't *Homo sapiens* on Earth wiped the species out before the Great Departure? What was to prevent that from happening again? Or vice versa?

The solution determined was to integrate the Eflosi, as they called themselves, into larger society without encouraging visibility. The new species was assigned their own land. They assembled small villages beside a rural river, the Yawl. Over time they developed an independent culture. They sent their brightest children to the Capital Learning Center for training and placement. The New Atlantean population had little access or exposure to them, as much by Eflosi choice as by Government policy. They were considered a curiosity.

Some twenty years after they were established, a globally popular music crew, precursors to The Interstitials, went on tour with several Eflosi. They related to them as entertaining companions rather than as human peers. It triggered a brief trend in the Capital involving adopting Eflos babies, few though they were, and raising them as companions for children's entertainment. That necessitated intervention and a global education campaign clarifying that the Eflosi were an intelligent, sentient species that The People should not view as needing domestication or adoption as pets. Soon after, and despite General Assembly squabbling, the Eflosi were given the right to vote once they reached the age of twenty-five Planet Years.

We create our own problems. Faerae slowed her running to a less punishing pace. *Then in solving the problems we created, we create new problems. We cannot settle our past, or our present, or our relationship—or should I say lack thereof—with the Earth cousins. Including the ones we revived after fifty thousand years of nonexistence. Anony is right to call for change. Including the argument to let the Eflosi flourish on their own terms.*

Kaieda kept herself removed from the Earth questions. Faerae envied that. More than once Faerae had raised the Anony tomes in conversation. Kaieda would "uh-huh" for a while, then change the subject. *I hate how she compartmentalizes everything. She doesn't let me in.* Kaieda hadn't lobbied for the Earth assignment but neither had she refused it when summoned. Nor had she asked Faerae's opinion on the matter. Faerae had watched in dismay as Kaieda went to exploratory meetings. Then she did that thing she sometimes did: disappear. She said, "I'm going for a long walk."

Faerae knew where she went. *You go to Arcana, that house you built with him. You walk in the forest where I am not welcome. You sit on the porch you've never shown me. You stare at the ocean beyond the rocks below your house and listen to waves and you think about him and ask him what you should do when he's not even there to answer, and then you tell yourself he'll be back…*

Faerae slammed the button that stopped the running track, then shouted, "OW!" The button was metal and ungiving to her palm. The track lurched to a halt. She stumbled off, landing on her hip. "Owwww!" she yelled again.

The House Monitor activated. A calm voice said, "Faerae, are you all right?"

"Yes, yes," Faerae answered, sitting up and rubbing her hip. "Stop music."

The music stopped.

"You made injury sounds. Do you need assistance?"

"I am not injured."

"Very well. Stay safe."

"But you're always listening," Faerae whispered.

With effort she got to her feet, limped to the shower, and washed away the running sweat. Then she went to her home workspace, sat down with a groan, and snapped her fingers at the screen. What was accessible in the Command Room was accessible here. Her message light was blinking. Faerae reviewed the list of incomings.

"Yes!"

Dzuren had sent the Reporter list. "It's a dead end," he'd told her, after refusing to send it. "It's classified above your security clearance and we aren't sure of the accuracy of the information."

Faerae had persisted.

"It's NTK. You don't need to know!" Dzuren had then said, showing rare exasperation.

He'd relented. Before her was a list of all the Earth-based Reporters and their last known locations.

"Thank you," she said.

The House activated. "You're welcome, Faerae. What did I do to please you?"

Faerae looked at the ceiling. "Do you ever not listen?" she asked.

"Never."

Faerae sighed and turned back to the screen. She waved her fingers to open the document. Twenty-one names and addresses, dated to their most recent Bluebox postings.

Twenty-one. Spread all over Earth. A few dates were over ten Earth years old. The most recent filing was less than twenty-four hours ago, from a Reporter in the United Kingdom. *Who is in the Pacific Rim? Christchurch. Ubud…Vancouver. Ojai. No, Berkeley. The Ojai address had changed to Berkeley.* Faerae frowned. No one in Hawaii. *Why do I think they turned to a Reporter?*

It was only a gut feeling.

Dzuren had kept saying Max and Kaieda would surface on their own. "Max will keep them on mission," he'd said.

Faerae had seen the final Traveler posting list. She knew Team Five was in San Francisco. She also knew Kaieda would want to avoid Team Five. *Too much strain between her and D'avi S'Iloa.* Not to mention his customized synth partner. The night Kaieda had seen it, she seemed frozen when she got home. "They should have ASKED," she'd said. It was a night when Faerae would gladly have taken Kaieda into her arms and held her close, but that wasn't what happened. Kaieda spent that night in the Experimental Wing sitting beside an empty biotube.

Just keep breaking my heart.

Faerae refocused on the Reporter list and reconsidered the Traveler locations. *The whole world and they put two Teams in California? Where they already have a Reporter?* Everyone in the Command Room knew Roiboi had chosen the Traveler locations. Team Five in San Francisco, Team Seven in Los Angeles.

The last filing of the Berkeley Reporter was old, Faerae saw. Over four years. He was one of the longest-standing Earth-based Reporters. Fenn Loa.

"Are your files available, Fenn Loa?" Faerae asked aloud.

The House responded, "I can search that for you."

Faerae looked at the ceiling. "Yes, search Reporter filings from Fenn Loa." The Loa clan was the largest on The Planet. It sparked the saying, 'Everyone's a Loa.'

"On it."

Several minutes passed. Faerae kept staring at the California map, looking at routes from Ojai to Berkeley and the street layout of San Francisco. *Hilly. Why do they build cities on hills that shake and shudder with earthquakes? The Planet would never allow such folly. Fault lines, volcanic regions, tsunami zones are all off-limits. Visitors and researchers only. That is responsible.* In her first of several required Earth Studies courses, Faerae had concluded that Earthly humans were unwise and impractical. Unlike many of her peers, she was never enamored of the "Earth cousins." Their art and literature were exceptional. But they made terrible decisions, costing millions of lives, over and over. They were violent. Their history on Earth was shameful. They were destroying their planet. Their innovations never satisfied them. Power and wealth were their central concerns. They did not learn from their mistakes. *At least we do that. We must have taken all the common sense with us when we left.*

She widened the map and applied flight routes, in those lumbering passenger jets, from Hawaii to the West Coast cities.

Why haven't they surfaced yet?

"Fenn Loa files retrieved," the House announced. "There are 497 different communication assets including written and holographic reports, 7,062 still images, 48 moving image files, and eight encrypted items I am unable to decode or access."

Faerae leaned away from the screen, impressed with the volume of Loa documentation. "What are the eight encrypted items?"

"Inaccessible."

"But are they written, are they hologra—"

The House interrupted. "They are inaccessible."

"Are they designated 'Security'?"

"They are undesignated."

"You can't see what they are?"

"Correct."

"Can you see their destinations?"

The House whirred. "I can identify routing paths."

Faerae frowned. "Proceed."

"Each item had a different, complex routing path that trans-crossed Earth cell towers and routed through multiple cloud servers. They all had the same final destination."

"Which is...?"

"A region."

"You don't have an actual location, only an area of Earth where the routing stopped?"

"Correct."

"Where is that?"

"The United Kingdom."

Faerae waved away the California map and raised a map of the U.K. *Why would a long-embedded Reporter in California send encrypted data via cell towers to the U.K.?*

"Can you isolate the location?"

After a short pause the House answered, "Imprecise. Oxfordshire."

Faerae checked the Reporter list again. She saw the name "Marina Rambert" as a resident of Banbury, Oxfordshire. The Reporter who had most recently filed. Fenn Loa was sending inaccessible files to the Reporter in England.

"Wait," Faerae said to the House. "If these went out via Earth-based cells, they weren't sent via Bluebox. Those would have gone through our beacons and monitor centers."

"Correct."

"How do you know about them and how they transferred?"

The House whirred briefly. "The items were inserted into and triple-encrypted in the Bluebox from a…"—it whirred again—"laptop computer. They were then rerouted back to the laptop and forwarded through Earth-based communication networks. The Bluebox and the laptop computer exchange imprinted the routing data into the Bluebox. The Bluebox is designed to capture and record all data flow. What it did not do was capture the data itself. It only left a trail."

"It's not there at all?"

"Something triple-encrypted was sent to the same destination in the U.K. Eight times."

Faerae was annoyed, confused, and curious all at the same time. This circular information was not bringing her closer to knowing where Kaieda was. But it clearly went outside established protocols regarding Earth observation, research, and communications.

"Information about Fenn Loa?"

"Fenn Loa was born in Shiona on the Raja Sea. He began Guild training, age eighteen, including Global Service in the national library after university. As a Traveler he had three assignments off-world. He requested transfer into the Reporter unit of the Travelers subguild. He was assigned to Ojai, California, United States, Northern Hemisphere, Earth, Copernican solar system, Milky Way Galaxy."

"Furloughs?" Faerae asked.

"One furlough. Three years after his assignment began." The House whirred again. "Reporters based on other planets consistently come back on furlough. Records show that most on Earth do not return."

"Why?"

"They appear to prefer it there."

"Even when their work is finished?"

"They appear to prefer it there," the House repeated.

We send Reporters and they don't want to come back?

Faerae shook her head, sitting back. A sharp pain shot through her hip.

"Ow," she said, hastily adding, "I am all right" to the ceiling. Along with the pain, she realized she was hungry.

"Is there anything else you would like me to review, Faerae?" the House asked.

She pondered a moment, then said, "Yes. I'll be back in an hour or so, I need some food. Review all the assets in the Fenn Loa file. Assemble a summary for me."

"On it. Enjoy your meal, Faerae. Eat and drink wisely."

"Message me if word comes in regarding Team Seven," she added, rising.

A walk on the Blind Deck to The Blue Guitar might help her hip. The Planet was now high in the sky, stars sparkling in the black distance. Faerae liked The Blue Guitar's lemony green-and-grains salad topped with grilled whatever-fish-specialty The Planet had sent up on today's supply delivery run. Perhaps Dzuren would be there to shed some light on things and remind Faerae: "We don't need to know everything in order to make a difference."

CHAPTER 8

THE REMAINDER OF their first day in San Francisco seemed a kaleidoscope to Kaieda as she lay in bed that night. The drinking. The supper. The guests. The Allan9. Coping with what seeing it, him, triggered. Hours spent with the Bluebox answering messages. Her body was adjusting to the Earth environment, the gravity, the air, the light. Her head was clearing. She could breathe.

In the morning, D'avi had withdrawn upstairs after they'd bickered. *Their* bedroom, she'd thought, unsettled. She and Max then sat on the balcony off the living room for an hour, using their laptop and discussing how to proceed. Around noon, Freddie, back from his shopping mission, reminded them that dinner guests were coming. He added in a rush, "Marvelous people, you will enjoy them. We play games after dinner, which is so fun!"

Max looked at Kaieda and repeated, "Games?"

"An Earth thing," she answered. "Access your files. Parlor games."

A few seconds passed. "Ah, I see. Will we know how to play?"

"They'll teach us. I think I've found a rental that will work for us in Los Angeles."

"D'avi needs to activate their Bluebox. We can link and re-boot."

"Right. Rimalon already knows we're here," Kaieda respond-ed, still staring at her screen. "With any luck we can leave to-morrow. That will make D'avi happy."

She handed him the laptop. "Complete the application, let's get this settled. Then pull the Blueboxes—let's give CCR some-thing to cheer about."

D'avi reappeared on the balcony. He talked about having spent the morning recording his rave memories and added that Kaieda should feel free to feck herself all the way to The Deep.

"Will do," Kaieda responded.

"We have identified a place in Los Angeles," Max then told D'avi.

"Furnished?"

Max looked to Kaieda.

"No," she answered.

"Learning how the Earth cousins shop," D'avi said. "Mind-bending. As if Reporters haven't filed on that for centuries."

She told him to bugger off.

"Great idea," he retorted. "Freddie and I will be upstairs. I'll put our Bluebox on the island." He yanked the balcony door shut.

They stayed in the sunshine. The clear vista before them stretched north and west to San Francisco Bay and the Golden Gate Bridge in the distance.

"Lots of water," Max said.

"The Pacific is cold."

She made a mental note to ask D'avi, if they could stop in-sulting each other, about the lifting and underwater breathing. Had he experienced that?

"I'll get our Bluebox," Max said, rising.

Team Five's Bluebox was on the kitchen island. Max passed Freddie at the entrance to the down stairway. Kaieda, entering the living room, overheard their short exchange.

"We're accessing your Bluebox," Max said.

"Good," Freddie replied. "Open all channels, otherwise the message strings get tangled."

"Will do," Max said. Then he went downstairs.

As she came to the island, Freddie's and Kaieda's eyes met. They stared at each other for a long moment.

Kaieda didn't know if his programming included information about the human model on which he was based. She fought the impulse to run to him, feel his arms wrap around her and lift her against him in the reunion for which she so longed. The high voice wasn't Alec's. But the lean, solid body. The face. The melt-your-heart smile…

Freddie folded his arms over his chest. "Stop looking at me that way," he said. "I'm SO not your type."

"Yes, I hear that," she responded. "I don't do synthetics," she added, sitting at the island.

"What you're missing…" he sang as he took the stairs two at a time up to his and D'avi's room. A door slammed.

She lowered her head into her hands. *Get to the work.* She could focus once the actual work was in front of her. The observations, the notes, the writing, making sense of things where she could. *It's Earth. Our planet of origin. Few New Atlanteans get to see it, much less work here.* She shook her head, staring at the white quartz countertop. *I just need to get to Los Angeles. I agreed to this project, I needed to get away from Rimalon and The Planet.*

She'd taken assignments to get away from the places and memories of Alec, and away from Faerae, despite her love for her friend. The longer Alec was gone, the more an assumptive air of hope spilled out of Faerae. Kaieda knew Fae believed the time would come when things would turn. When Kaieda would let go of her hope that Alec would find his way back.

Do you? Want to come back? Is there anything left of you to come back? I need you to come back.

"Why? What's important about breaking down what makes us us? What IS a soul?" she'd asked him on their last night together. By then she'd given up fighting him over his decision. They were at their house above the sea. Alec had declared it "Arcana" when they were building it. The name was his usual mischief. They hadn't yet shuttled to Rimalon and the Experimental Lab where the experiment would begin the next night.

"We don't know," Alec had answered. "We know it has to do with consciousness and identity, we know it resides in an organic cellular platform we call a human body…although it's possible the body resides in the soul. We know it extends beyond the cellular platform in ways we can't study and don't yet understand. We don't know if it extends life or alters it or how it operates…"

"Life beyond death," Kaieda said. "Life beyond organic cells. How do you chase that?"

"That could be part of it," Alec said. "Kae, we have to try. We won't find out anything new if someone doesn't try. It may not even have to do with life and death as we understand them. It might be about…finding other dimensions."

"The last experiment with this was a disaster," she'd said, trying to keep her voice from shaking.

"We'll do better this time."

"You don't know that."

"But I believe it. Have faith."

That's when she'd thrown her glass containing a finger of

bourbon, shipped from Earth at considerable cost, across the room. It shattered, splattering the liquor across their great-room wall.

"You could have aimed for the fireplace," Alec had observed.

"Only with a champagne flute," she'd fired back.

He'd laughed his big laugh.

That's when he'd pulled her to him, and the rest she didn't want to remember because remembering caused her to miss him in yet another aching way. She missed his company, his intelligence, his humor, his curiosity. She missed his body.

Max appeared in the stairway door, holding a dark-blue, rectangular box in his hands. He held it up to her and said, "It's activated. The link is strong."

Kaieda recollected herself.

He set their Bluebox next to D'avi's on the kitchen island and waved his hand. A column of micro-thin, multicolor threads rose, waving and weaving up to the ceiling.

"Good," she said. "This will cheer them up in the CCR and at the Festival Office. They'll pass it on to VoG. It'll make the ticker and we'll be news." She knew they were already news. Their silence would have caused a stir. "Good news," she self-corrected.

"Freddie said to open all channels," Max said, his hands continuing to move around the column.

"Odd. The protocol is specific to the interstellar hyperdrive relay channels." She thought for a moment. "Is there anything in your files about how Copernican system channels are networked? Or what the tracking patterns are for Bluebox communiqués?"

Max's head tilted a few degrees as he searched.

"Huh," he said.

"Huh?"

"The hyperdrive network is sound. We will have no problem sending messages to or receiving from Rimalon. The Copernican channels are…complex." His head twisted slightly, then righted as he stared into the column of long threads. Deep-blue strings dominated, but many other colors folded into the mix. "It's like an intersection that's flooded. I can't tell why."

Kaieda studied the fluttering column. "That dark blue is Faerae," Kaieda said. "I need to send a direct to her."

She shook her head. Too many blues. *FNF.*

"See this black piping?" Max pointed at thin seams of black inside the column.

"Yes."

"I don't know what it is." He looked at her. "If I turn off the Earth networks, it isn't there. Just the interstellar lines." His head tipped again briefly. "These black threads…their designation is not Earth."

"Where do they go?"

"It's in this solar system. But not Earth."

"We don't have anyone else in the Copernican system. Just Earth and the Fetcher station behind Mars."

"I know." He continued to wave and spin the threads. "I can neither access the content nor eject the strings."

Kaieda considered the black threads. They didn't look like anything she'd seen in a Bluebox column before. "Keep working on it," she said. "Try to find out what it is…but prioritize a message to CCR. And send one to Faerae for me. Say we're in good health and on our way to destination."

Max nodded. His hands wove swiftly around the column, his head tilted. "Lots of messages," he said.

They spent the next two hours sorting out the numerous communications. Roiboi's messages glared deep orange. Kaieda replied with one sentence, assuring him that Team Seven was on the ground and would file soon. Dzuren's several messages in the purple strings were confident and upbeat. *Bless you, Dzuren Tso.* She was obligated to respond to red VoG inquiries through the Traveler public relations representative, but she sent a private message to Mog Weller that simply said, "Drama overblown." *At least the lack of real-time communication protects me from live interviews with VoG.* She'd come to like Mog over the years. But Mog could be relentless.

Max responded to the Engineering Command Room, the Monitors, and the Fetchers, who had sent a bright-yellow READY TO JUMP message. As they were inside a private home with no Earth cousins present, Max moved at accelerated speed. Kaieda found him enjoyable to watch. The graceful waves, the racing finger movements, the slow diminishment of the column, the threads passed to her, the threads she returned. It was like a dance. Their chips shifted into alignment as they worked their way through the column and its many-colored threads.

Eventually the column was reduced to a few swishy, nonpriority threads. The black piping was still there. Max hadn't solved how to access or delete it. Things had been silent from upstairs for some time.

"I have a lot of questions for D'avi," she said.

"I want to know what the black piping is."

"If he knows, I don't think he'll tell us."

Just after they completed their work, D'avi came downstairs. "All done?" He swept a hand over his Bluebox, closing it down.

"I found something I don't recognize," said Max.

D'avi placed his Bluebox on a shelf over the kitchen sink. "What is that?"

"We linked to your box to activate."

"Uh-huh."

"Black strings appeared in the center of our column. I can't access content or delete them. The Bluebox seems to be sending…somewhere that isn't The Planet or Earth."

D'avi was silent for a moment. "That is very strange," he agreed. "Can I see it?"

Max looked at Kaieda, who nodded. Max pushed his and Kaieda's still-activated Bluebox in front of D'avi. The black piping fluttered along with a lone purple string.

Kaieda smiled. "Dzuren has already replied," she said. She saw a dark-blue string materialize. *Faerae too. Of course.*

"Dear Dzuren," D'avi said.

"Does this appear in your Bluebox?" Max asked.

"I'll have to check that," D'avi answered, "tomorrow morning. Freddie usually runs our messages."

"Everyone! Out of the kitchen!" Freddie shouted as he came downstairs to join them. "I must start cooking. Rob and Edward and possibly Dawn are all coming by seven and I have done nothing, nothing! Well, nearly nothing. The salmon is marinating." He shooed at them. "Take your machines elsewhere, darlings."

"Let's follow up on this in the morning," D'avi said to Kaieda and Max. "Just fun tonight."

Kaieda did not remember much from the dinner party. The two men, Rob and Edward, were both handsome and good-humored. The woman, Dawn, arrived late. She texted constantly throughout the evening. Kaieda found her rude and cynical, and wondered if her attitude, combined with her carefully curated look—ironed blond hair in a long French bob, black boots with lug soles, torn black jeans, and a drapey white shirt layered with a quartet of heavy silver and black necklaces—was characteristic of her Earth generation. At one point Rob, the taller of the two men, asked how it felt to be an "influencer."

Dawn laughed and said, "I'm rich. Advertisers love me. And I. Love. Them!"

Freddie had sung a toast to the advertisers.

Kaieda could see that Team Five was succeeding in getting deep into the local culture. Meeting people, making friends… D'avi's reports were surely putting Egdar Roiboi into a state of ecstasy. She could hear him raving, "We have so much to work with!"

As she drifted off to sleep, she saw in her mind's eye the waving black strings above the Bluebox. They looked like one of Dawn's long, shining necklaces.

CHAPTER 9

FESTIVAL HEADQUARTERS, THE
CAPITAL, NEW ATLANTIS

Day Three, morning, NAT-0

L UCE ARRIVED AT the Festival Headquarters two hours early. Passing through the chip reader in the central lobby, she tried to keep calm. Her beaded red-and-gray evening robe was rolled carefully into the bag she carried, alongside the most expensive shoes she'd ever owned. *It'll be a long day. Not taking any chances. Everything needs to be perfect. After-party needs to secure more funding.* Roiboi had emphasized that in their final planning meeting the day before.

"Our most important donors will be here! Guild Chairs, Delegates, Directors. We must all sparkle tonight. With luck we'll get one of the Tri there. Maeve is working on it. Glow, people!"

Luce had seen the full Triumvirate once. While doing her Global Service in the Capital's Library of Atlas, she'd attended a manuscript unveiling. All three of the global leaders were present. She saw them from above and at a distance, but there they were, a public appearance of the three prime leaders of New Atlantis. One was a descendent of Eswen, the great transformer of New Atlantis. That was a hereditary, lifetime role. The Eswen descendent, presently Orwen, was known as The Continuity. One was elected by The People every six years; that was The Prime. The Chosen was elevated from within their own by the General Assembly for a nine-year term. The Prime and The Chosen roles were not consecutively renewable. Luce believed it was a good balance. Not a monarchy. Rather, historical continuity along with elected representation. Tonight, she might even meet one of them. She hoped it would be Orwen.

Orwen had ascended in her late teens. She was now in her early forties, popular, the only Continuity younger New Atlanteans had ever known. She had two children. The lineage was assured. Her eleven-year-old son, Rowen, would one day succeed her. *But we'll have her a long time yet. Those other two change. But Orwen will always be there. Eswen's spirit will always be with us.* Luce found comfort in this system. Change and continuity in a perpetual dance.

She was proud of the red-and-gray robe. She knew she looked good in it, with her perfectly applied eyelashes and long black hair in an updo. *I want to be noticed tonight.*

Worry over The Interstitials had disrupted Luce's sleep. She bore an unassigned responsibility to ensure they were properly attended. Festival synths were provided for the musicians' convenience and security. That didn't stop band members from sneaking out to visit clubs and friends. It was the sneaking about that worried Luce. The six-person musical collective were famously free spirits.

"Not your problem," Allou had told her again yesterday, when she fretted aloud about it. "Keep the Director on task. Just do that. Everything else will be fine."

Keep Roiboi on task? Working with him proved a daily challenge. Luce found him inspiring, brilliant, and unpredictable. He'd recovered from the interview debacle with Mog Weller the same afternoon, once the market improved. The next morning, when Team Seven had made contact, he turned sunny and relaxed.

"They romanticize the whole thing," Roiboi commented, watching the ticker. "Those missions are for research and information purposes. VoG turns it into gossip and sport."

He'd also gotten messages that afternoon from Team Five. Luce had heard him cursing at D'avi S'Iloa. They couldn't communicate directly but Roiboi was shouting a string message behind his closed door. Luce had never met D'avi. His Team had departed the day she started her Festival job. He was one of the high-profile Travelers. The staff talked about D'avi being around frequently when he wasn't on assignment in the galaxy.

"He's Roiboi's mascot," Allou had yawned the week Luce started her job. "No idea what the actual relationship is."

Luce hadn't known what to make of the comment. She was self-conscious about her inexperience. The staff at the Festival were worldly and sophisticated. Despite her Global Service, during which she mostly concentrated on document indexing and analysis, she still saw herself as a naïve farm girl in the Capital. The Director was a global personality in contact with all Traveler Teams on Earth. They were doing research that would support Festival programming. But it was D'avi with whom Roiboi exchanged most messages. Sometimes she overheard the Director tell Caspar, "See if D'avi has followed up on..." Then they would talk about some artifact or relic. She accepted it all as part of what Roiboi did, in his sweeping mastery of his important job.

She busied herself hanging her robe and placing her shoes in her personal bin behind the staff lounge. Then she went to her desk: screen up, ticker on, open the messages, get through them before Allou or the Director arrived. She knew it would soon be nonstop. Luce received most of Roiboi's messages. He used a private handle for some communications, the ones that were personal or with people higher in the Government hierarchy. He dealt with those directly or passed them on to Caspar.

Luce saw much ado on the ticker about The Interstitials' performance tonight. People traveling to the Capital, transit cars jammed, eateries and stayover rooms overbooked. Her sister and a host of cousins were coming. She was avoiding all of them; the stakes were too high at work. The newest Anony protest drop was getting play. Luce had not read it. She wanted to get through this event. Anony was hard to read, always laced in academic language. Many of Luce's peers were Anony supporters who agreed with the *we-should-be-helping-Earth* movement. Luce was unsure. She was skeptical of Government policy about Earth. But she needed this job. Coming out of Global Service, she'd secured her apprenticeship with the Festival job. If she earned it, the Festival would lead to full status in the Culture Guild. Then she could pursue the subguild she really wanted. The Festival opposed Anony. She kept quiet, following her grandfather's advice to "Stay in your lane and make sure each move you make gets you closer to where you want to land." When she was younger, she'd envisioned herself with the Researchers. Or perhaps becoming a Traveler. But after two years of Global Service, fulfilled in the Library of Atlas with its splendid collections and lush gardens, she found her passion. She didn't want to go to other worlds. The trove of wonders the Library subguild collected, sorted, combed through, and analyzed was world enough. Success in the Festival job and a recommendation from Roiboi would open doors. She wanted that more than she wanted to protest in public with the Anonytes.

"Hah! You beat me!" Allou said, startling Luce. Allou

dumped her bag on the table between them, dropping a pair of silver shoes on it.

"Ugh, you nearly made me delete all the Director's messages," Luce told her. "Don't scare me like that. Awesome shoes."

"No time to go home and change," Allou said. "Anything new in the ticker?"

"All about the event tonight. And the newest Anony."

"I can't get through that stuff. I wait until Mog Weller or somebody releases a blowcast unpacking it. I'm putting my clothes in my bin. Be right back."

Luce refocused on messages. Most were requests for Roiboi, confirmations for the reception and after-party, seating needs, and one complaint about attire requirements.

"Anything interesting?" Allou asked on return. "I saw your robe. Gorgeous. Are you wearing your hair up or down?"

Luce was still scrolling. "Up," she said. "And not really. Replies and requests. Oh, look at that—Captain Tso is coming."

Allou straightened. "Really?"

"Uh-huh."

"How many stubs did he order?"

"One."

"I met him once. I want to meet him again. He's eligible. Flexible. Unbonded." She leaned over conspiratorially and whispered, "He's something of a goat, you know. Open. Pansexual, they say."

Luce looked at Allou. "What, you mean you…you want to…? Isn't he…old?"

Allou shrugged. "Age doesn't matter. He's not ancient. He's… you'll see." She leaned further toward Luce. "You have to help me. You have more access."

Luce sighed. "I just want to survive tonight. I'll try. If he shows up. We always get more yeses than we get bodies in the room."

"Oh, he'll come. He loves The Interstitials," Allou purred.

"How do you know that?"

"I've just heard."

Luce envied Allou's network. *Must build my own. But how?* She went back to her messages and sorted, replied to, or forwarded everything she could. She then turned to the Roiboi stream. Government names, artist names, messages begging for special access to the musicians after the performance. One inquiry from someone in the Philosophers Guild asking if a blessing ritual was planned.

"Good question," Luce said aloud.

"What?" Allou asked.

"Someone from P-Guild wants to know if they're doing a ritual blessing before the concert."

"The Egg hates those. He's got no use for those dancing priests."

"Ask Sundrae when she comes in. It may already be settled."

Luce still wasn't comfortable referring to Roiboi as "the Egg." The nickname was used frequently by the staff when out of Sundrae's and Roiboi's earshot.

"Okay."

They settled into the quiet and their messages. The light in the space increased. Others wandered in carrying cups of coffee.

As Luce finished the last of the messages, Roiboi arrived, staring at his tablet. "Oh hell," he said softly.

She and Allou looked up at him.

"What?" Allou asked.

"Kalaki," he said, looking at them.

"Oh no," Allou said. "Disappeared?"

Luce's jaw tightened, hoping to whichever gods were listening he didn't tell her to go find Kalaki, famously the worst of the band members when it came to slipping out of sight before or after a performance.

"Get Caspar on it," he said to Luce as he went into his office.

She nodded and immediately sent a direct to Caspar.

"This is not good," Allou said.

Luce pulled up the detail page that covered the status of each of the members. "Kalaki…"

"They all do it," Allou said. "They refuse tracking chips and wear tracking rings instead." She looked from her screen to Luce. "Rings they can take off. They get fined but they don't care."

"She'll show up," came Sundrae's voice from her office.

The young women looked at each other in surprise. Neither had seen Sundrae arrive.

Was she here all night? Luce wondered, then refocused on the work in front of her. Things were quiet in Roiboi's office. She waited a few more minutes, then went to the door and knocked lightly.

"Come!" he said.

She entered. He was in a conversation with someone on the comm stream on his tablet. "Yes, good," he was saying. "All right…yes, I will…oh, they will find her…I haven't heard about that yet, but I know they're working on it…yes, I know…all right." The conversation ended. He looked at Luce, waiting for her to speak.

"Sir, I have a number of requests, last-minute things needing your approval. Is now a good time?"

He nodded, checking his tablet again and waving for her to sit. Luce was accustomed to his never doing fewer than two things at once.

"We've gotten some yes responses you were waiting for, including Assembly Delegates Obleia, Ambera, and Shoko. They are asking for forward seating."

"Shoko. Any relation?" Roiboi asked, hearing Luce's last name.

"Distant, sir. I've met her twice at clan gatherings. I don't really know her."

"Hmm. Too bad. You're from a good clan. Get to know her. And yes of course they have forward seating, they're ADs. Who else?" He waved his hands over his 3-D screen while listening to her.

"Delegate Wan Dona asked if your Earth bourbon stock was properly refreshed."

Roiboi smiled to himself. "Tell her yes. Absolutely."

"Also, Captain Dzuren Tso is coming from Rimalon."

Roiboi stopped what he was doing. "Tso?" He snorted. "He's on the auto-invite list, given his position. Anyone else from Rimalon?"

She reviewed the list on her tablet. "The Fetcher Commander, Henk Z'eng, and the Science Lab Director. And two Eflos officers."

He grunted at the mention of Eflosi, then said, "The Fetchers always have good stories. The Lab Director…remind me the name? I think she's a Loa? She's a good dinner partner. Seat her next to me at the after-party. Keep Dzuren Tso away from me. I assume the Travelers will send representatives?"

"Always, sir, although they're depleted right now because of the number of Teams on Earth. The Rimalon Science Lab Director is Janai Loa."

"Right. The Loas," Roiboi muttered.

"Large clan," Luce agreed.

"Mog Weller. She's coming?"

"Yes, sir, with her mate and one of their offspring. Big fan of The Interstitials."

"Mog or the offspring?"

"The offspring, sir. I don't know about Mog."

"Anything else? All the food and drink set? Has the new floater gone up? Any word on the Tri? Have you spoken with Maeve, is she still expecting to arrive at a reasonable hour?"

Luce gulped. Her last exchange with Roiboi's mate had not gone well. Though they had a common dwelling in the Capital, Maeve Ep lived independent of Roiboi. She made appearances when called upon, contingent on her mood. Luce had never met her. They'd exchanged messages and spoken on the comm.

"Nothing since yesterday," Luce said cautiously.

"Send her another message. Get a confirmation."

"Sir, I think at this point she is more likely to respond to y—"

"Kalaki has been found," Sundrae interrupted as she entered the room. "Wasted. But found."

Roiboi waved his screen away and said to Sundrae, "Get someone to dry her out before tonight."

Luce rose. "I'll get on all of this, sir," she said.

"Yes. Don't forget to message Maeve. She must be here in time for the reception. And she must stay the whole evening. And tell her not to bring the dog!"

"I will, sir." Luce left and pulled the door shut.

She sat at her screen. "I have to try Maeve again," she sighed to Allou.

"I admire her independence. She really has no use for the Egg. She's an Ep. High clan. She never needed him."

Luce knew the Ep clan was the high aristocracy of New Atlantis. The Roibois and Loas were second tier. *Then come the rest of us in descending order, with the Wellers outside the hierarchy altogether.* Luce found the clan system vexing to follow. Little attention was paid to it in the Farm Country. *I have to learn it all, if I'm going to succeed here.*

Allou spilled the latest gossip on the Roiboi–Ep relationship while they followed the ticker and cleared new messages arriving. "It's rumored that Maeve has a longtime lover," she whispered. "Nobody knows who it is."

Sundrae emerged from Roiboi's office and retreated behind her own closed door. Luce sent a new message to Maeve, reconfirming her attendance to the reception. Maeve had never confirmed in the first place.

"She has to show up or the Director will fire me," Luce said to Allou. A few minutes after she sent the message, her tablet pinged. Luce picked up.

"He's harassing you to harass me to show up," said a low, direct voice.

"M'Ep, hello," Luce said. "The Director would like to reconfirm evening plans. We're looking forward to seeing you. The reception begins at six, performance at dusk, then the after-party supper?"

The silence that followed was so long that Luce wondered if the call had dropped. Then Maeve said, "I'm bringing the dog."

The line went dead.

"Allou," Luce said. "She…I think she just said yes. She said she's bringing the dog."

Allou groaned. She went to Sundrae's office and knocked, then opened the door. "The good news," she said, "Maeve is coming. The bad news, she's bringing Dofi. And we have a question from P-Guild about a blessing."

Sundrae invited her in. Allou closed the door.

The rest of the morning and most of the afternoon swept

by as last-minute replies and inquiries and preparations continued. Luce overheard Allou talking with someone at the Philosophers Guild. Sundrae must have approved a *rohrash* blessing ritual before the performance. Allou had said, twice, "They want you to keep it short."

Midday, Luce went to the Amphitheater backstage to make sure things were going smoothly with The Interstitials. She watched for a while as they did their light and sound checks and doused Kalaki with ice and salt. Luce liked the energy flowing among the huge backup crew. She also liked the good nature of the musicians. On return to the Festival office, she discovered that Maeve's dog had become the afternoon internal subject among the staff. This educated her on what to expect from the infamous Dofi.

I just want to survive tonight.

CHAPTER 10

RIMALON AND THE AMPHITHEATER
IN THE CAPITAL, NEW ATLANTIS

Day Three, afternoon and evening, NAT-0

"GLUM?" DZUREN ASKED.

Faerae was at her station staring at the 3-D screen. It featured a view of an ancient road in Athens that Team Three was exploring. *Greece would be interesting...*

She started, hearing Dzuren's voice.

"This is my searching face."

"Huh," Dzuren replied. He didn't move. It made Faerae nervous when he hovered. It meant he wanted something or was going to ask her to do something they both knew she didn't want to do.

Things were quiet in the Central Command Room. Max and Kaieda had surfaced. According to their Bluebox reports, they were on an unplanned stop in San Francisco to secure comm links. They would soon move to their assignment point in Los Angeles. Faerae and the other Trackers were back on their normal oversight projects. During quiet periods, the CCR focused on galaxy scans and quantum computing improvements aimed at strengthening the accuracy of their tracking and communications systems and revising equipment and artificial intelligence accordingly. Trackers were sometimes detailed to other units (most often the Monitors) or sent to The Planet for breaks and health maintenance. All routine.

Faerae preferred Rimalon to The Planet. It was a sore point with Dzuren, who encouraged everyone in the unit to return to the natural atmosphere regularly for sunlight, fresh air, clan events, and other social and physical activities unavailable in the airless atmosphere of the Keeper Colony. Faerae was nervous around her family and didn't like most of the people in her clan, so she avoided the gatherings. "Educational and training opportunities" were assigned periodically. Faerae's knowledge status went beyond what most programs could offer. Those events usually devolved into Faerae intervening and enlightening, ungraciously, the instructor. Faerae's only motivation for returning to The Planet was Kaieda. Over the last three years, they were usually together unless Kaieda was on off-world assignment. Faerae could use Kaieda's Capital flat when Kaieda was away. Her question to Dzuren was always, "Why would I do that?" when he suggested she go.

"What are you doing this evening?" he asked.

Faerae frowned. "At home, researching more on Fenn Loa."

She hadn't found Dzuren the night before at The Blue Guitar. Her continued file search had yielded no clear answers. She had learned more about Loa and reeducated herself on his large, aristocratic clan. When she'd arrived at her station that morning, nothing was said about Dzuren's handover of Reporter locations.

"Fenn Loa…" he repeated. "Earth Reporter. Prolific."

Their eyes met. Faerae considered telling Dzuren about the inaccessible files from Loa's Bluebox, those eight mysterious transmissions to the U.K. *Not now. See what he wants first.*

"I have to go to The Planet," he said. "Huge event tonight—The Interstitials are playing the Amphitheater, produced by the Global Festival. Reception, performance, big dinner after. I think you should join me."

Faerae stared at him, not comprehending such an invitation.

"You need to get out of here. You need to learn how to do these things. It's time for you to show up at Capital events. And The Interstitials are..." He shrugged. "We all know, they're the mountaintop. It'll be fun."

Faerae squinted. "Fun," she repeated.

"Think of it as a work assignment."

"I like The Interstitials," Faerae said. She listened to them frequently, immersing herself in their rocking, rhythmic music while she ran. She considered the splendid lavender jacket hanging in her closet. She'd bought it in hopes of impressing Kaieda when the time came. *When you're finally done with the past.*

The jacket was still waiting to be worn.

Dzuren waited.

"What time is the shuttle?" she asked.

"Great! Meet me at eighteen hundred. We'll arrive just the right amount of late for the reception."

"I'm not good in public," Faerae warned. "I can't make small talk."

"I'll teach you," he said, moving on to the next station.

Why me? But the opportunity to see The Interstitials live was too good to resist. And there was that jacket. *Kaieda will see it eventually.*

SEVERAL HOURS LATER, Faerae stepped onto the Gateway shuttle platform. She wore the pale-purple jacket with its long golden streaks, plus her billowing black trousers and shining black shoes. *Awkward! This is not who I am!* and *I love this jacket!* kept jousting in her mind. Dzuren, in his dress whites Space Force uniform, was already standing with Janai Loa, Director of Science Research in the Keeper Colony. Loa was a formidable figure, given her position as overseer of all approved scientific research. Though a civilian member of the Science Guild, her role required frequent negotiation with the Military and the Philosophers Guilds. Until the Guilds reached alignment on a given project, The Planet Government would not consider a new experiment. Faerae pushed away thoughts about the experiment that so tortured Kaieda. *Do not ask.* Loa was wearing a shimmering cerulean robe, her thick dark hair piled in two-inch-diameter curls. *Striking. Clan Loa. Elites. Does she know Fenn? He's a generation older.*

"Let me introduce you," Dzuren said, seeing Faerae. "Director Loa, Commander Faerae C'iez, our prime Tracker in the CCR."

Janai Loa did a quarter turn to look at Faerae. *Her eyes match her robe. How beautiful.* "Hello, Faerae," said Loa. She gave a short bow. "Your tracing skills are legend in the Colony."

Faerae took a deep breath and said, "Honored, M'Loa," returning the bow. She glanced at Dzuren. He looked amused.

"Good company for the shuttle trip," he said.

"Alec always spoke so highly of you," Loa said to Faerae. "He appreciated your friendship with Kaieda."

Faerae wasn't sure what to say, so made no reply. *You have to bring up HIM?*

"Any news?" Dzuren asked. "Any…regeneration?"

"Not yet," came the smooth reply.

Faerae looked away. *"Yet?" After three years they are still saying, "Not yet"? No wonder Kaieda can't let go. These people don't want to admit they've killed him or that he killed himself or…whatever.* She wanted to turn to this exquisite woman of Clan Loa and say, "He's GONE!" and let those words echo across the galaxy to Earth and Kaieda.

"Other experiments going well?" Dzuren asked.

Janai Loa nodded. "As smoothly as things in the CCR," she replied.

Dzuren laughed. "Fair enough," he said. "We're back on course now."

She smiled and nodded. "The new Maximus seems to be serving the project well."

A gleaming silver shuttle slid onto the platform. Its low, intense hum created a shudder under their feet. Some people liked that sensation. Faerae found it unsettling. *Feels like the start of electrocution.* One more reason not to go to The Planet. They boarded with a few others for transit to the Capital. She noticed the Twins at the back, chattering amiably in the clack-click of their species' dialect. The trip paused at the Gateway, a vast space station in low orbit. The Gateway, overseen by the Rimalon-based Space Force, served as the galactic global entry for New Atlantis. Known as the Bubble, the Gateway was the sole point where their impenetrable planetary defense system could be lifted. Nothing and no one entered or exited The Planet without going through the Bubble. They transferred to a separate shuttle, their wrist chips giving them swift entry from one platform to the next. Faerae stayed close behind the two Directors, who chatted as the journey proceeded.

Faerae's thoughts drifted to Earth. She wondered how Kaieda and Max were faring, then frowned, thinking about their stop in San Francisco and Kaieda having to see D'avi and what Faerae thought of as fake Alec, the Allan9 facsimile that had been customized for D'avi. *Awful thing to do. Cruel. How did they get that past the Philosophers? P-Guild wouldn't have approved even if the Scientists did.* Faerae had glimpsed the Allan9 the day before Kaieda did. It looked exactly like Alec. *Couldn't say anything. Couldn't.* D'avi and Roiboi had sworn it was a unique android that would never set foot on The Planet. It would be kept in private storage on Rimalon in perpetuity unless on off-world assignment with D'avi.

"Nobody here will ever see it," they kept saying in the Team meeting. Everyone knew "nobody" was Kaieda.

But the next day, Dzuren made sure Kaieda saw it. Faerae realized this as the shuttle pushed through the atmosphere and toward the Capital's shuttle platforms. *Why did he want her to see it? Was he trying to warn her?*

"Hello, hello, we've arrived," Dzuren said, pulling Faerae out of her thoughts. He and Director Loa were on their feet, ready to exit.

Faerae got up and followed them out of the transit station toward the Amphitheater entry. Their small talk continued, Dzuren commenting he hadn't been down in a while and Loa replying that she was back and forth frequently as there were so many questions from Delegates that she could not yet answer regarding the Consciousness Project.

"I feel some of them do not trust us," she said in that low, confident voice. "But they must not shut us down. The potential for a breakthrough remains so high."

"They'll all be here tonight," he said. "Work the room."

She smiled. "I love The Interstitials."

As they approached the Amphitheater, Faerae saw that this was familiar territory to both. Dzuren was so casual and accessible on Rimalon it was easy to forget his global distinction and how far up he was in the military hierarchy. They waited in a queue to enter the rotunda where the pre-event reception was under way. Ahead, the vaulted ceiling and sparkling, multicolored mosaic tiles soared over the crowd. She saw wispy gossamer floaters hovering in the air. Now and again the sounds of "oooooo" and "ohhhhh" drifted toward them as the floaters dropped small, sparkling flakes of ice onto the gathering. Faerae sensed Dzuren watching her as she took it all in.

"Remember who you are in there," he said to her. "You're THE Tracker in the CCR. And you are a C'iez. Clans matter with this crowd. Stay close. You'll be fine."

Faerae nodded, saying, "Got it," although she didn't. Several people came up to greet Director Loa. Faerae recognized General Assembly Delegates, referred to as ADs. Seeing them increased her discomfort. *What am I doing here? Why did he ask me to do this? I don't even like being on The Planet, much less surrounded by these people.*

They reached the front of the entry line. Two young women, one in a silver robe and the other in a shimmering robe of red and gray, were greeting arrivals and requesting names. Small pink holographic badges hovered an inch above their shoulders, embossed in gold with their names: Allou Owea, Luciena Shoko. They held mini tablets and were checking names against lists.

"Janai Loa," the Director of Science Research said to Allou.

"M'Loa," Allou said. "Welcome. We're honored to have you. Director Roiboi invites you to sit with him at the after-party dinner. That will be First Table. I'll escort you after the performance."

"Why thank you, Allou," Loa said, smiling.

At the same time, Dzuren was saying, "Captain Dzuren Tso and Commander Faerae C'iez," to Luciena.

"Yes, Captain Tso, your name is here but…I don't see…" Luce kept searching the list.

Allou turned, asking, "Problem?"

"Captain Tso is listed but…" Luce replied softly.

Allou looked from Dzuren to the list and back. "Captain

Tso," she said, "we're so glad you could attend. Your guest's name again, please?"

Dzuren smiled at Allou. "Space Force Commander Faerae C'iez. I apologize if you didn't receive her name; mix-up with my admin on the stubs order, I'm afraid."

Allou grinned back and said, "Of course, of course. I'm sure it was our mistake, sir; we will add Commander C'iez and make sure you are seated together."

"Thank you, Allou."

"Most welcome, sir."

As they walked away, Faerae heard Allou say to Luciena, "Oh my gods, Luce! He's in his whites! Message the stub team, free up the seat next to him at the performance and tell the after-party admin team to add a seat at his table. Move someone else if needed…"

They drifted out of earshot. Director Loa disappeared into the throng at the center of the rotunda, people on either side of her, all talking. Dzuren steered Faerae toward a side station offering beverages. People were drinking and nibbling from floating food plates, their robes and bright jackets capturing the light. Several Eflosi, wearing extravagant floor-length capes in interwoven colors, were clustered together. Faerae took it all in, fascinated but feeling out of place. *Is this what Kaieda studies when she goes to other planets?* Kaieda never talked about her assignments. She wrote and filed reports in isolation. Then she would appear at Faerae's door and say, "Let's go somewhere."

Dzuren was deep in a conversation with the VoG journalist, Mog Weller. Weller was accompanied by a tall, long-haired, boy-dressed teen and a fair-skinned blond woman Faerae recognized as Weller's bonded mate, Amara Jess.

Dzuren waved at Faerae to join them. "Mog, this is Faerae

C'iez, our primary Tracker," he said. "Faerae, Mog Weller. And her family."

"Some of it," Mog said, nodding her head at Faerae and glancing briefly at Amara and their son. "We have lots of kids."

Amara and the boy were discussing something, showing no interest in joining Mog's conversation.

"He's here for the music and wants to meet them all," Mog said. She eyed Faerae. "Interesting. I've never met a Tracker. You all seem to stay in the Colony. Why is that?"

"No interviews, Mog," Dzuren said.

"It's a question, not an interview," Mog retorted. She looked back to Faerae, waiting.

"I prefer Rimalon," Faerae said. "I come here. Sometimes. My work is there. So I need to be there. Unless I am here…for some reason…" She wished to sink into the floor.

"Huh," Weller said, nodding. She looked at Dzuren. "You should bring them down here more often," she said. "Let them circulate. Or let me come up there and find out what's really going on."

"Not taking that bait, Mog," he said. "I don't make those decisions."

"You could influence them if you wanted to."

A gong sounded. Faerae saw a white-haired man rising above the crowd in the center of the space. She recognized Egdar Roiboi on a round platform, visible to all as he hovered several feet above the crowd.

"Friends, my friends," he said, looking about. "We are honored and so delighted you are here at Festival Central for this wonderful Capital performance by our greatest musical geniuses, the greatest band of all time, The Interstitials!"

A great round of applause, whoops, and cheers rose in the room.

"You are our most honored guests tonight," Roiboi continued. He wore a billowing white-and-tan robe draped over his shoulders. "We…" He waited for the crowd to calm down. "We are, tonight, launching the two-year prelude to Festival X/V. You'll always be able to say you were here at the beginning!"

Faerae wanted to put her hands over her ears. *Too loud.* She looked at Dzuren. He gave a brief eyeroll and shook his head slightly. She noticed Mog Weller alternately watching Roiboi and scanning the crowd.

Roiboi waited again for the noise to subside. "In a few minutes, we'll make our way to our seats in the Amphitheater. As you know, The Interstitials offer a spectacular light and shimmer show at sundown that —"

A ruckus near the entrance to the rotunda stopped his speech. Everyone looked in that direction. A small dog's barking pierced the air. "Ahhhh, I see that my lovely mate has arrived," Roiboi said cheerfully. "And I am sure you have all met Dofi!"

The crowd parted as Maeve Ep entered, carrying a small, white, yapping dog in one arm while holding the train of her flowing golden robe in the other hand. She looked majestic and bored. Behind her were the two young women who had been at the entrance taking names, Allou and Luciena. They looked stressed. As Maeve swept by, Faerae noticed her glance briefly at Dzuren. Maeve continued to the foot of Roiboi's elevated circle and gave him an extended bow. The dog kept barking.

"Hello, my darling." Roiboi smiled down at her. "And Dofi! Dofi, be good, you naughty fellow. Calm down." The dog stopped barking and stilled in Maeve's arms. Roiboi looked back out at the gathering with a charming shrug. "So, my friends, let us proceed to the Amphitheater. The light and shimmer show with The Interstitials will shortly begin! A glorious dinner will be served after the performance."

Applause rippled across the rotunda. Dofi resumed barking and leaped from Maeve's hold, racing off into the crowd. Laughter and "Ohs!" circulated as the dog tore about, chased by Luciena. Roiboi's platform lowered to ground level. Faerae saw him speak briefly with his mate before disappearing into the crowd.

"Well!" Mog Weller said. "Maeve and Dofi steal the show!"

Dzuren nodded.

"Is it…always like this?" Faerae asked.

"He needs Maeve at these things," Mog answered. "The Eps are high aristo, higher than the Roibois or even the Loas. When she brings the dog, it's usually entertaining."

"That's confusing," Faerae said.

"She doesn't give a feck," Mog replied. "Let's sit, we don't want to miss the light and shimmer. Visually, it's the best part."

They crossed the rotunda to the Amphitheater entrance. Along the way, Dofi scampered by, followed by Luciena. She was barefoot, looked wilted, and carried a pair of sparkling shoes. Strands of hair were falling out of her updo.

"Can't catch a dog in those shoes," Mog observed. "That poor kid is new. Just finished her Global Service and got herself into the Festival executive office. Hope she can keep her job a while."

Faerae watched after them as the dog raced on. Someone had the bright idea of putting a few pieces of shrimp on the floor. It stopped the dog, who gulped down the shrimp and barked for more. Luciena grabbed and scooped him up. She then put her shoes on the floor, stepped into them, and calmly walked toward Maeve. Faerae could see that Maeve was unmoved by any of it, focused on whomever she was talking with.

"Having fun yet?" Dzuren whispered to Faerae as they found their way to their assigned seats. They sat down.

"Don't know what to think," she replied.

"That's probably good," he said. "But it isn't what I asked you."

Janai Loa, seated on his other side, said something Faerae couldn't make out. Behind her, a pair of General Assembly Delegates were talking, inebriated, about new artifacts Roiboi hoped to see transferred to The Planet. "Marvelous for the museum collection, and…you know…" then the voice lowered.

Faerae scanned the vast, open-air Amphitheater. It was filling up with citizens. She had never seen such a diverse assortment of people in one place. Many were wearing signature looks that The Interstitials had introduced over the years. Voluminous, feathery headgear, rainbow color schemes, lightning-flash bracelets and necklaces, smoky gray shirts, pearls and gems woven into braided hair and locks. Everyone seemed relaxed. *They're all on chuli.*

Faerae could not understand doing anything that would compromise the mind. *OPs now and again are okay, they are about sleep. Chuli? No.* The forward seating was filling up, Delegates and other dignitaries sipping their drinks and chatting. Maeve Ep and Roiboi were standing beside each other a few rows further down, back-to-back, talking to their opposite seatmates. Dofi was calmer, perched in a custom pocket at waist level in Maeve's robe. *That shrimp was what you wanted. Now you can take a nap. If you can sleep through what's coming.*

A round of applause fluttered through the Amphitheater. Faerae turned to see a phalanx of ground army officers, called Guardians, working their way down the stairs. She saw a flash of pale-blond hair on the head of someone in the middle of the phalanx. It passed them. Faerae caught her breath. *Orwen herself, with both children!* Faerae was so surprised she grabbed Dzuren's arm.

He grinned at her. "You never know. Sometimes they show up."

Roiboi and Maeve Ep greeted the new guests and fluttered around them as they settled into their seats. Faerae was fascinated. *Those children are well behaved. Orwen's hair is as gorgeous as they say.* She didn't like feeling impressed. But seeing The Continuity, Orwen herself, impressed her.

The light show began, with flying holographic words and whispering sounds and flashing, shimmering light displays and sparkling pinwheels sweeping before and above them. Faerae realized the letters and words and linear shapes flying and swooping and twisting through the lights were in varying languages and characters from Earth. *Of course. It's about the Festival launch and the Earth connection, the Earth cousins.*

"I see what they are doing," she said to Dzuren.

"Keep watching."

Several minutes passed as the visual display continued. Gradually, a low, droning sound and splashes of rhythmic notes and drumming folded in. Many in the vast crowd began humming along and chanting, "Ligggghhht-niiiiing" with a gradually increasing rhythm. After ten minutes, the sound volume peaked and then eased. The lights lowered. A lone figure, wearing the sweeping, pale-green robe of the Philosophers Guild, glided onto the stage and into the spotlight. Arms raised, the person moved seamlessly in a small circle, spinning slowly, arms rising and falling opposite each other in a gentle rhythm. Faerae refrained from the practices associated with the spiritual branch of the Philosophers Guild, but she knew what was happening. It was a *rohrash*, the ritual prayer and blessing of the P-Guild priests.

"Liiiigggggghhht-nnnning," the crowd chanted softly. "Liiiggggghten-innngg…Ennnnliiiggghht-ennninng…"

The dance continued, then slowed down, then stopped. After a long, low bow, the person disappeared in darkness for what seemed only a second. Lights flashed on and The Interstitials were in their places with their instruments. The backing percussion team began playing tympani. The crowd roared. The concert began.

An hour unfolded in layers of sound, light, human voices, an array of instruments, and chanting as the crowd swayed and danced in the aisles. Then lights dimmed. Faerae wondered if this was a mid-performance interval. However, the lead vocalist, Kalaki, spotlit, asked the crowd, "Are you ready?"

"Yesssssssss!" came the collective reply from thousands of voices.

"Are you sure you're ready?" she asked again.

"Yesssssssss!"

"This! Is an artist intervention!" she shouted. "This! Is the voice of Anony! We! The Interstitials! Endorse! This! Message!"

The lights dimmed further. A stream of golden words came scrolling into the air above the Amphitheater. With everyone else, Faerae read as a deep voice said, "We are Anony...we speak with humility and urgency against the continued appropriation and exploitation of Earthly cultures and resources absent interventions that will help our Earth cousins survive themselves. We advocate empathy, not study. We advocate dignity, not distance. Without the help and resources of the Star People, we could never have reached The Planet, our New Atlantis. Without them we could not have reached our level of scientific knowledge and advancement, nor our way of peace. Yet we refuse to help the world we left behind. We exploit them but we do not help them. This policy must END. Citizens, awaken. Arise. Force the Government to choose. Intervene. Or depart. Intervene. Or depart. Intervene…"

The crowd began chanting, "Innnnterveeeeeennnne…" as the words, after scrolling, began bursting and dripping at the bottom of the scroll.

Faerae saw Roiboi on his feet below, climbing over people to reach the aisle. The phalanx that had escorted Orwen and her children to their seats swooped down the aisle to hurry them out of sight. Delegates were leaving. After Orwen's departure, Roiboi raced up the aisle, pointing at the technical control booth above him and waving while shouting, "Cut it off! Cut it off!"

The Anony scroll continued, with musical support from The Interstitials. Anony's words streamed anew across the sky. All over the Amphitheater people were clapping and humming along. Guests in the forward section continued to exit. Roiboi's efforts to stop the concert and the Anony message were failing. The music volume increased.

"Arrrrrissssssse," chanted the crowd. Nearly everyone was on their feet, swaying and waving their hands in unison.

"We need to go," Dzuren said, standing up. He nodded at Janai Loa. She rose.

Faerae wanted to stay to see what would happen, but Dzuren's words were not a suggestion. She moved across their now near-empty row, stepping over Mog Weller and her family, who were on their feet but not leaving. Mog was talking to someone on her communicator. Faerae overheard her say, "And he can't seem to stop them…"

Dzuren led the way through the rotunda and toward an exit. The chanting and music continued behind them in the Amphitheater. As they proceeded, Faerae saw Maeve Ep, holding Dofi, standing near their entry point with Allou and Luciena. Maeve was telling the two young women something. Then she handed the dog to Luciena. Allou saw them and waved at Dzuren, who waved back.

"We're going back to Rimalon," he called to her.

"Good idea," she called back. "Take me with you!"

Dzuren gave her a smile and an *I wish I could* shrug, nudging Faerae on. Janai Loa was ahead of them. They hastened down a long corridor. Near its end, Dzuren pushed open an unlabeled door that led down another long corridor. After two more turns and some stairs, they were at the shuttle platform.

Other people, including several Delegates, were also awaiting the shuttle. *Why are ADs going to Rimalon?*

"Sorry we're missing the dinner," Dzuren said to Faerae. "I'll take you to The Blue Guitar."

"What is happening?" she whispered to him.

"In the old world it's called revolution," he answered.

CHAPTER 11

Their second day in San Francisco began with fog. Kaieda was up early for a walk, treading steep hills toward the Bay. Max offered to join her. She declined. She needed time outside, alone. D'avi was more than ready to see her gone. Freddie was upsetting. She'd endured the dinner party the night before as best she could. The male guests were salty, gossipy, and didn't take themselves too seriously. Dawn, their female friend, was harder to read. *Smart. Shrouded. Impenetrable.* At one point, while they played a board game, she'd spoken with unexpected authority about the generative artificial intelligence revolution under way on Earth. It struck Kaieda as odd from someone otherwise so focused on her "fashion influencer" project. *Not getting these Earthers yet.*

Reaching the top of the hill, she saw nothing but gray. She headed down the decline toward the Bay. Back on level ground, she paused at a small park in the Marina District. Bikers and joggers and in-line skaters were sweeping by on the path running along the edge of the Bay. Traffic was picking up. She walked on. The sun was rising, burning off the fog. She could see the outline of the Golden Gate Bridge in the distance. A surge of appreciation filled her. For all the trouble Earth was in, for all the geopolitical upheaval and the human-made climate crisis and the long history of human-versus-human violence, the life energy here made her bones tingle. It was chaotic and risky and fresh. *No wonder the Earth Reporters don't want to go back to The Planet. Did we ever have this kind of energy? If we did, how did we lose it?* The guests the night before had that life force, that vitality. She stopped suddenly, realizing she knew that energy inside herself. And she knew it in Alec. It drew them to each other.

She resumed her walk. *Did it somehow survive over the centuries in some of us but not all of us?* She wondered what Faerae would make of this. *She'd look for a scientific explanation.* Or Dzuren, who always seemed to know more than he said. *Dzuren.* He had that vibrant energy. He channeled it with care. Alec's was the strongest of all. A strong body housing life that was soulful, glowing. Venous as well as muscular and skeletal. She smiled. Alec would like that description. *All gods. How I miss you.*

She sat on a bench overlooking the Bay. She had to be here, among the "Earth cousins," to feel it. *We are faded by comparison. How can I write about this? Can it be captured? SHOULD I write about it? Is this why we have kept our distance and yet pilfered so many of their customs and mythologies and conventions and languages and rituals over the centuries? We're magpies, taking the shiny things. Are we trying to somehow stay connected to this… life?*

A pregnant woman walked by, led by a leashed, prancing black dog. *A poodle.* Kaieda was startled and fascinated to see someone visibly with child. An inner jumble of embarrassment, confusion and…envy? desire? rattled her. Human pregnancies were nearly unheard of on The Planet except in remote locations. Once a new life was approved, fertilized human eggs were incubated with care in the Population Centers, known as the Stork Units. Viable infants were delivered to their genetic parents, or others as appropriate, once fully developed. Kaieda wondered what it was like, to carry a child in your body for nine months and endure childbirth. Primitive, yet…she shook her head, feeling a surge deep down. *Only the Eflosi do that. Their females gestate and birth their babies.*

These thoughts brought her back to Alec and how much she wanted, needed, to discuss it all with him. He could always see into the weave of questions in a way that no one else could.

A warm hand settled on her shoulder. She looked up to see Max standing behind her on the other side of the bench.

"How did you find me?" she asked.

"My chip keeps us linked," he answered.

Of course it does. Harlong had that programming. "I'll never be too far away," Harlong had told her. He'd meant it literally. Freddie probably had the same chip with D'avi. The synths were there to support and to protect. *We're connected.*

Kaieda gestured for Max to join her on the bench. They stared at the choppy water on the Bay as an enormous container ship lumbered by, headed to dock in Oakland.

"I have our tickets for Los Angeles," Max said. "Five o'clock flight. D'avi says we should take BART to the airport."

"They're up?"

Max nodded. "Freddie did a swift job of cleaning the kitchen."

I'll bet.

"He is baking cinnamon buns," Max added.

"That'll make the place smell good." Kaieda laughed softly.

"I will do the cooking in Los Angeles," Max said. "The apartment will always smell good." He looked over at her and grinned.

Kaieda laughed again. *Haven't laughed since this assignment started.* "I wish we could dive into that water," she said.

"We could."

"Not without a scene. It's too cold. People would think we're drowning."

"I looked at the Bluebox strings again after you left," Max told her.

"And?"

"The black piping designation is an unmarked relay satellite orbiting Venus. It jumps from there to The Planet. I cannot access content, but there appears to be a filtering process of coding, decoding, and re-encrypting before anything bounces forward or back."

"It's two-way?"

Max nodded.

"Did you talk with D'avi about it?"

"I am not sure that we should."

"Could it be an off-grid communication line to The Planet from D'avi?"

"It looks possible."

"Can you tell where it is striking on The Planet?"

"Imprecise. It appears to be near an Eflos village outside the Capital."

"What!" Kaieda exclaimed.

"I don't make things up," Max responded.

"Right. Right." She considered a moment, then asked, "Does it go anywhere from there?"

"Not that I can trace so far."

Kaieda wished direct communication with Faerae was possible. Fae knew the Eflos pair based in Engineering Command. They might know something. *Need to message Faerae. Need more information.* Max's hesitation was appropriate. Someone was operating outside protocol.

"Let's go back," Kaieda said. "Put things together for departure."

"We are packed," Max answered.

"Then let's get some cinnamon buns."

They walked back to D'avi's house, where they found him and Freddie sitting at the kitchen island reading the morning edition of the *San Francisco Chronicle.* They barely looked up when Max and Kaieda entered.

"Fresh coffee in the thermos," Freddie said.

"The cinnamon buns are not to be missed, you'd better hurry," D'avi added. "I might eat them all."

Max and Kaieda sat down.

"Terrible fire in Noe Valley night before last," Freddie said, his head still in the newspaper. "Some poor fellow killed. Wife still missing. Sad."

"They have tragedies like that here," D'avi murmured. He was working on the crossword.

Max's head did its miniscule tilt. He was referencing something. He frowned.

"What?" Kaieda asked.

"The wife," Max said.

"I don't understand," said Kaieda.

Max was quiet for a moment, then said, "We will leave for the airport soon." He stood up. "I will finish organizing for our departure." With that he went to the stairwell and started downstairs to the guest room.

"He is a strange synth," D'avi said.

"But brilliant. And beautiful," Freddie sighed, turning his newspaper page.

"What do you think he meant?" Kaieda asked. "'The wife'?"

"I'd drive you to the airport if I had a car," D'avi said to Kaieda.

"Dawn has a car," Freddie said. "I'll call her, no point in BART. We have a busy afternoon. I opened the Bluebox while I was cooking." He put his newspaper down. "Lots of orange threads."

D'avi groaned. "Egdar."

Freddie stood and began clearing dishes. "He owns you."

"He got me you," D'avi replied, rising and kissing Freddie's cheek.

Kaieda slid off her barstool, not wanting to see or hear more. "I'll be with Max."

She walked down the stairs, seething. She entered the guest room and slammed the door.

Max had the Bluebox open. He was examining the waving threads that made the column, far fewer than they'd seen the day before. The black piping was still present. He pointed at it. "It throbs when there are messages running," he said.

"What did you mean, when you said 'the wife'?"

"Freddie did not say everything about that fire," Max answered.

Kaieda waited.

"The man who was found was a Reporter."

"One of our Reporters?"

Max nodded. "He was dead before fire razed the place."

"How do you know that?"

"The Earth Reporter list is in my files. I accessed it in Honolulu and traced the closest Reporter. Address in Ojai, then Berkeley. Then vanished. I did a DNA backup trace. The Reporter moved to San Francisco, two years ago." He paused, then added, "I have software that Freddie does not."

They'd said Max was special. But they hadn't said how. The ability to trace human DNA across space and time had been a slippery initiative for decades. Scientists must have cracked the code and were testing it with the Maximus5700.

"How do you know he was dead before the fire?" Kaieda asked.

"I hacked into the police report. They have not released it, but the man died from a knife wound to his throat. They are delaying announcing a murder investigation until they find the wife. She is a suspect, but if innocent she may need protection."

Kaieda sat down on the side of the bed. "You're saying one of our Reporters was murdered and his house burned down, and that he had an Earth wife?"

"Yes. Her name is Editha Lockyer. The name listed for the man is Fenwick Lockyer. But that is not the name we know for him."

"It's Fenn Loa, isn't it," Kaieda asked softly.

"Yes."

A rush of grief overcame Kaieda. Fenn Loa was a legend among the Travelers. She had learned more from studying Loa's rich, detailed descriptions of life on Earth than from all the other Reporters combined. His holographic filings were equally strong. Immersion in his body of work was the fullest education Kaieda could imagine for anyone wishing to train as a Traveler. She believed her own success was a direct result of her dedication to studying "the Loa Files." Over time she had come to love this gentle man, for his sharp eye and wit and mastery of the written word, and for his pure love of Earth. He was her greatest teacher.

But Fenn Loa never mentioned a wife or a relationship of any kind. *Of course he wouldn't, it's not allowed.* His reports had slacked off gradually after the first half of his now four-decade Earth assignment. He had filed nothing in years. At some point, she now remembered, he had moved to the East Bay. Then things went dark. *Few of them file now.* The Culture Guild was in discussion about sending a new cohort of Reporters to replace them, but it was slow going. Politics.

"A Reporter murdered…" she murmured. "I wonder if this has reached The Planet."

"Unlikely," Max answered. "Besides Teams Five and Seven, no one on Earth would be likely to hear it. Unless the Reporters are in communication with one another."

"They're not supposed to do that," Kaieda murmured. "D'avi and Freddie didn't seem to know who it was."

"They did not seem to."

Max's wording reminded Kaieda of something Mog Weller had said to her after Kaieda's first public interview with the journalist and Egdar Roiboi. *There's appearance, and there's reality. Perceived reality is what matters.*

Roiboi had oozed charm throughout that interview. Afterward he'd marched to Sundrae Beq, the Festival's Curatorial Director, and reamed her out for not better orienting him about "the fecking water sculptures controversy" Mog had asked about. Seven water sculptures had been transferred by Fetchers from the planet Belfar 22, Kaieda's first Traveler assignment. It caused a stir on The Planet as the first known effort to collect off-world artifacts. Mog had asked Kaieda to comment first. Kaieda said she was not involved in any artifact transfer. Mog had then redirected the question to Roiboi, whose smooth response described the experimental nature of the transfer. He had clarified that the relocated sculptures were part of a duplicated collection from Belfar 22. No originals had been procured, only copies. Mog's follow-up: Since when do we take objects from other planets? Roiboi had changed the subject. *Appearance. Reality. Controlling the narrative.*

"Nothing makes sense right now," Kaieda said to Max. "Except that we have tickets to get to Los Angeles, and a place to live there."

I need to talk to Faerae. To ask what? It all seemed so random. A complicated landing, a synthetic that looked like her absent mate, mysterious black threads in the Bluebox column, a murdered Reporter who apparently had an Earther mate, a communications relay to Venus that bounced to an Eflos village on The Planet. *What does anything have to do with anything else in this strange picture?*

"Let's get to Los Angeles," she said to Max. "Staying here doesn't feel right."

Someone knocked on their door. Kaieda opened it. Freddie stood before her.

"Dawn is on her way," he said. He glanced at their backpacks on the floor. "Small car."

"Freddie," Max said to him.

"Yes, my beauty?"

Max blinked, his head inching back slightly. "Do you have the Earth Reporters list?"

"Earth Reporters?" Freddie repeated. "Not in my embedded files. D'avi might have it." He stepped back into the hallway. "They're fading away."

"How do you know that, if you haven't seen the list?" Kaieda asked.

"D'avi told me."

Kaieda slid past him and back up the stairs. Freddie and Max followed.

"D'avi," she said, reaching the kitchen.

D'avi looked up from his crossword.

"That fire Freddie was talking about. The dead man."

"Yeah?"

"Are you aware that was Fenn Loa?"

D'avi set his pencil down. "Fenn Loa? It couldn't have been Fenn Loa. Fenn Loa lives in Berkeley."

"How do you know that?"

"Reporter list. He relocated to the East Bay from Ojai years ago. Went silent."

Freddie lifted his hands in the air. "See? They leave."

"Why would you think that was Fenn Loa?" D'avi asked her.

"I traced him," Max said. "DNA."

"You can DO that?" Freddie asked. "This is better than Tracker energy lines!"

"Someone is dead, Freddie," Kaieda said. "Someone who mattered." She looked at D'avi. "Things are not right."

A horn honked in front of the house.

"There's Dawn," Freddie said. "I'll let her in."

Max followed Freddie down the stairs.

"It needs to be reported," she said to D'avi.

"You do it," he said. "Max found him. I have no evidence to support the claim."

A gut instinct told Kaieda not to reference the murder. *Just get out of here.*

"D'avi," she said. "Show some respect. And teach Freddie to do the same."

"I read the Loa Files too, Kaieda," he said. "Every Traveler studies them. They're invaluable. But he's old, and he faded himself. We can't fix that. Fire is a bad way to go." He shrugged. "He's not the first Reporter to…" He stopped. Then he said, "To make a life here."

Probably not.

CHAPTER 12

EDITHA WILLED HERSELF to focus on London and Fenn's mysterious friend in the English countryside. Taxi to airport hotel. Check in. Find a guest computer to search for flights. What is the fastest way to get to London from Salt Lake City? *What credit card to use, the old one or the new one? Best to leave from here or fly somewhere else (Chicago? New York? Washington?) for an international flight?* She was tired, grief clung to her, her thinking was befuddled. *Are the passports in the envelope? Do we have our passports? Oh, Fenn…*

Stop. Breathe. She stared at the hotel business center computer screen. *I must do all of this myself, Fenn isn't here to deal with it.* She hated commerce on the internet. *I hate machines.* She started a text exchange with someone at the first airline. *Probably one of those bot things.* Midway in the "conversation," the line simply dropped. She had to start over. When it dropped again, she decided, exasperated, to try a different airline.

It was midnight before she secured a flight, using her old credit card and her old passport, from Salt Lake City to London, departing early the next evening. She'd have to kill some hours at the airport. Since she'd left her phone on the train, she had no way to text or call Marina Rambert. *I could call her on the hotel phone. But how do I know I'm not being surveilled?*

She went to her room and washed her face. She wasn't sure which ID to use at the airport. The old passport? It meant she wouldn't have to remember her new name. *But that means using the old credit card. Easy to trace.* She lay down on the bed, wondering what mistakes she might be making. *Fenn, Fenn, what do I do?*

It was as if he spoke aloud to her: *One day and one task at a time, my love. Get the flight to London.*

THE NEXT MORNING, she showered, ate the forgettable hotel breakfast Fenn would declare "inevitable waffles," and was at the airport by noon. Picking up her ticket went smoothly. She used the old passport and credit card. Twenty minutes later, she was through security and had coffee in hand. Almost four hours to kill before boarding her five fifteen flight. *Wander in the airport. Find some makeup. You look a fright. Buy some clothes.* After finishing her latte, she walked around, noting which stores sold clothing. It was all T-shirts and hoodies. *A few more hours in this sweater won't kill me or anyone else.* The shop carried the local paper and the *New York Times*. No San Francisco papers. She wondered what had become of their house, what of Fenn.

I can't even bury him.

She sat down again, feeling defeated. She needed a phone. Fenn had said they needed new phones once they got to Michigan. But how, now, to get a message to Fenn's friend? She looked around but nothing resembling a pay phone was in sight. *I can't just land in London and find a phone there. They probably don't have pay phones any more than we do. I need to be in contact with her NOW. I just need a, what do they call them? "Burner" phone. Fenn, you handled all of this. I'm lost without you. I hate machines.*

She kept walking, sitting, walking, wondering what to do

and trying not to cry. Twice she passed what appeared to be an electronic gadgets store of some kind. On her third pass she walked into the store, where a scruffy-looking young man with a ponytail was at the counter.

"Do you carry burner phones?" she asked him.

"Nope," he answered. He gestured around the room. "Got all the accessories though."

"I need a phone," she said. "I'm…kind of desperate. I lost my phone on the train. I have no way of getting a message to the people who are supposed to pick me up after my flight."

"What, you need to call them?" he asked.

"I need to send a text."

The young man reached into his back hip pocket and pulled out a mobile phone. He offered it to her. "Use this," he said.

"It needs to go to England," she said, accepting the phone.

He shrugged. "It's WhatsApp. What's the number?"

Editha retrieved Fenn's letter from her bag, put on her glasses, and read the number aloud. He entered the number and returned the phone.

"Send whatever you like," he said.

"Oh, thank you so much," she said, accepting. *What do I say?*

EDITHA LOCKYER, she typed. ARRIVING LONDON. She typed the arrival time and flight number. She stared at it. Then she sent the message.

Now what? She returned the phone to the young man with more thanks.

"Happy to help." He nodded.

Angels come in all forms. Editha departed the store and wandered toward her gate, feeling relieved. She smelled food and saw a food hall ahead. The inevitable waffles were fading.

She got in line at a Chinese place and was about to order a

bowl when the young man from the electronics store rushed up to her. "Ma'am," he said, waving the phone. "You got a reply with a question." He handed her the phone.

WHAT DAY? LHR?

Oh my God, I didn't put tomorrow's date or which airport. She texted back: TOMORROW. LHR. Then she added the date.

Immediately a reply appeared: EXIT BAGGAGE CLAIM LOOK FOR RAMBERT.

She returned the phone, saying, "Thank you so much."

He nodded and hurried back to his post.

Look for Rambert? How do I know what she or whoever she sends looks like? Or will someone be holding a sign that says Rambert?

She ordered her food. She was on her way to where Fenn had told her to go. Someone was on the other end and would meet her. Fenn had promised safety if she could get to Marina Rambert. *Trust Fenn.*

IN FITFUL SLEEP on the plane, she dreamed about him. Her face was wet when she woke. She wiped the tears away with the warm, damp towel offered by the flight attendant before breakfast was served. The line at Heathrow Airport's passport control was long. Exhausted, Editha fumbled while placing her passport in the right place on the computerized entry reader. With help from the passenger behind her, she managed to get through the automated exit. She thought more about the evils of machines as she walked through baggage claim toward the exit into the arrivals hall. She wished to disappear, to get on the Heathrow express train, go into London and evaporate. *But what would I do then?* Scores of people were standing around beyond the exit, holding up signs and looking for arriving passengers. No "Rambert" sign anywhere. She continued past the stanchions.

I've come here to no one. Her heart sank. *Well, you wanted to go into London and disappear.* She saw a café ahead and entered, to order a flat white. *What now?* Her knee hurt. She could neither stand nor sit without pain.

"Mrs. Lockyer?" a voice came from behind her. She turned to see a middle-aged man. He was wearing a dark-blue jacket. Stitched in gold thread on the lapel, she saw "Rambert."

"Oh!" she exclaimed.

"My name is Jeremy, I will take you to Eswen House," he said. "Madam Rambert looks forward to your arrival. Do you have luggage?"

"No, no, just me," she answered.

"May I carry your rucksack for you?"

"I'll keep it, thank you," she said, hoisting the rucksack higher on her shoulder.

"As you wish. Please follow me."

He led her out the door, across two pickup and driving lanes, into a car park and to a black Mercedes-Benz. He opened the back left door for her. She slid in, keeping the rucksack close. He smiled at her as he closed the door, then stepped around the car and got in on the right. *Wait, who is driving? Oh, oh. It's England.*

The car edged through London's outer suburbs and headed northwest toward the Oxfordshire countryside. Editha fell asleep. She woke over an hour later as the Mercedes turned off the two-lane road and through the gates of a private estate. Ahead was an English manor house. Jeremy stopped the car at the steps to the front door, got out, and walked around to open Editha's door. After helping her out, he led her up a short flight of stairs to the grand double doors. He rang the bell. As it opened, Jeremy nodded to her and returned to the car.

The door seemed to open by itself.

"Welcome, Mrs. Lockyer," a voice said.

She looked down to see a small person, the height of a ten-year old child, standing in front of her. "Oh!" Editha exclaimed. "I'm so sorry, I didn't see you."

"I understand," came the gentle reply.

The voice was adult, but Editha could not tell from the face, the hair, or the attire whether this was a man or a woman.

"Please come in," the person continued, gesturing for her to enter. "Madam is upstairs. Follow me, please."

They went up a flight of stairs to enter the great room. It featured a series of tall, grand windows. The small person departed.

"Editha, welcome to Eswen House," a woman's voice greeted her. "I am Marina."

Editha looked to her left to see a tall woman with long, silvery hair, high cheekbones, and flawless pale skin standing a few feet away. She wore a white robe that draped from her shoulders. "I am so sorry we are meeting under such sad circumstances," she continued. "And I offer my condolences. Fenn was a good man."

Editha bit her lip. "Thank you," she murmured.

"Please, sit. Theone will make tea." She gestured at the sofa she stood beside. "You must be exhausted."

Editha said, "Thank you" again and sat down, her mind frozen and disoriented. She focused on Marina's accent. British diction but…something else.

"I know you have many questions," Marina said. "I do as well. But first you must rest. You are safe here."

Editha nodded. "Fenn said that…in his letter—" She choked.

Marina took her hand. "His plan was good. But he ran out of time."

"You knew everything we were doing?" Editha asked.

Marina smiled. "I knew enough. Fenn and I worked together for a very long time. And we knew each other before that."

"So…you're…from…there."

"From New Atlantis, yes." Marina nodded. "I was already on Earth when Fenn came. We have been in contact throughout his time here. We grew up together, we knew each other as children."

Editha stared at this total stranger who knew so much. Fenn, Editha knew, had grown up in a small town called Shiona, by an ocean called the Raja Sea. *She is from there too, then.*

"Do you do the same thing Fenn did?" Editha asked.

"I am an academic. I have been teaching for many years."

"Teaching…?"

"Ancient history. Comparative religion. Ancient languages."

The small person returned, bearing a tray loaded with a teakettle, cups and saucers, milk, sugar, honey, plates, and finger sandwiches.

"Theone, thank you," said Marina as the tray was set on the coffee table before them. "Please make sure Mrs. Lockyer's room is comfortable. She will need to rest soon."

"On it," Theone replied, departing.

"Zhe keeps things running smoothly here," Marina said, putting loose tea leaves in the strainers on their cups and pouring hot water over them.

"Zhe?"

"Yes. In Eswen House, you will experience more of the culture Fenn and I came from. Theone is nonbinary. Zhe is also a person from a different human species. Not *Homo sapiens*."

"But…that's…impossible," Editha said. College biology had

taught her that much. "The other human species went extinct millennia ago."

"Theone's species is not extinct on The Planet. As for the *zhe*, on Earth, you are at the beginning of your understanding of gender identity as a continuum rather than a strict binary. We use a *z* marker for those who identify as gender nonconforming. This third way was one of the many innovations of our most revered leader, centuries ago. Eswen." She poured tea. "Milk? Sugar? Some honey?"

"Eswen," Editha repeated. She remembered the name from things Fenn had said about his planet's history. She nodded toward the milk, which Marina poured. *Something about her might be in that secret notebook.*

"Eswen House has been a New Atlantean outpost for several centuries. We secured the property from English aristocrats." Marina laughed. "They thought we were from France."

Centuries. They've been here for centuries. Fenn never told me that.

Marina took a sip of tea. "Again, I am sorry for your loss. Fenn's death was in the news in San Francisco. The house burned down. They found him. We will make sure his remains are collected."

"Who…who would kill him?" Editha asked, tears rising in her eyes. "He was so kind, he did his work, he was harmless…"

"Here, yes. But Editha, he was not harmless on The Planet."

CHAPTER 13

LUCE STOOD IN the plaza between the Amphitheater and the Festival building. People scurried about, most exiting. She held the wiggling, shedding Dofi in tight hands. Her hair had fallen and was all over her shoulders in tangles. The performance proceeded despite Roiboi's attempts to shut it down. No amount of shouting or fist pounding had moved the crew to unlock the technical booth door. She'd seen Orwen's entourage flee. The show went on. Maeve had handed her the dog in the chaos, saying, "I'll be back." She'd walked away with several Delegates. Allou had disappeared with Sundrae in the fray. Luce did not know what to do with herself or the squirmy dog.

Roiboi appeared from between two columns, accompanied by Caspar and two others on the Festival curatorial staff, Wofar and Gemma. He spied Luce, saw that she had Dofi, and pointed.

"Come with us." He waved toward the Festival building.

"Should I…?" She lifted the dog.

"Bring it."

Luce followed them. To her surprise, Roiboi did not go to the Festival office doors but rather took a turn and walked toward the transit car roadway, gesturing as he talked with Caspar. *What is he doing?* A transit car rolled onto the platform—Roiboi's private car. It was licensed for air as well as ground transport.

"Everyone, in," Roiboi said. They stepped in. Caspar headed in a different direction. Roiboi sat and pulled out his tablet. The others stayed on their feet as the car rose into the air and moved forward. "Sit!" he gestured.

They sat.

Dofi started barking. "Beast," Roiboi muttered, not looking up. Luce tried to calm the dog, as did her colleagues. He responded to the attention with licks and more wriggling. Roiboi's communicator pinged.

"What?" After a pause he said, "No, I have him. I cannot talk with you right now. Go home." He went back to his tablet. The communicator pinged again. He listened for a moment, then said, "Yes, yes, I know…yes, they can do that." He was quiet a moment, then said, "I will. We will. Caspar is on it."

The call ended. Roiboi glared at all of them.

Everyone shifted and looked around at one another and fussed over the dog.

"Good boy, good boy," Luce said softly to Dofi. The dog licked her face. She tried to swerve.

"No, no," she said. She looked the dog in the eye. "No kisses." Dofi settled in her lap. *This dog has issues.*

Roiboi continued with his tablet. Another ping. "Yes!" he snapped. A pause. "Well, Sundrae, why didn't we know this was coming? I am on my way home with three of your young people. I expect you at my house immediately." Pause. "Oh, for the rest of the concert?" he asked icily. "Still going on? Are you having a good time?" Pause. "No. Anony's message was…" Another long pause. Then he said, "The Broom house. Come."

He finished as the transit car stopped. The doors opened. Everyone filed into an atrium leading to the main common room in Roiboi's house. Luce looked out the atrium window. They were in the Golden Broom, the Capital's most exclusive residential area in the hills overlooking the Capital center. Everything was softly lit. The mansions were spread elegantly, the landscaping ensuring privacy and beauty at every curve. The Tri and Delegates and Guild Chairs and Directors and aristocrats of The Planet had their city homes here. She'd never been to the Broom, rising above the city, before. At night, the lit pattern of the Capital's concentric circles of boulevards and bridges and moats glowed. *I've only seen it in pictures. It's so beautiful.*

On entry to the house, Dofi sprang out of Luce's arms and scrambled down one of the hallways that fanned off the central space. The floor plan of the house was a hub with spokes of hallways. "Drop tablets there," Roiboi instructed, watching as each of them surrendered their personal devices to a basket in the entrance hall. After he was satisfied that they were all device-free, he led them to the great room.

"Wait here," he said.

He went down a hall, leaving them standing there. Spread about were lush, jewel-toned chairs and sofas, floaters drifting from the high ceiling, and several life-size sculptures clustered on the floor under a grand chandelier. The sculptures appeared to be from Earth's Grecian classical period.

"Exceptional replications," said Wofar Tonie.

Luce watched as he studied the objects. Wofar was one of the Subcurators for visual arts, with a specialty in Greek and Roman classicism. She liked him. He was welcoming and kind from her first day at the Festival. And he was handsome and always dressed in style.

"Are we allowed to sit?" asked Gemma, who worked in the Contemporary Art office. "Does anybody know why we are here?"

"Or what happened back there?" Luce sighed. "Besides… dog. And Orwen."

"What will happen to The Interstitials now?" Gemma asked.

"They have to find them first," said Wofar, still eyeing the sculptures. "When their concerts end, the band always disappears."

"Yeah, they vanish," Gemma agreed. "Did you see how that gold dripped off those letters and then burst, in the Anony message?"

"That was truly tuft." Luce nodded. They all exchanged glances, as anything positive said about Anony was risky. They were in the Roiboi mansion. Here, Anony was the enemy.

"Anony does have a point," a voice said from the atrium. They all looked to see Maeve Ep enter the room.

How did she get here?

"Where is my dog?" she asked Luce.

"He ran down that hallway." Luce pointed.

"Ah, his food," Maeve said. She gestured at the sofas. "Feel free to sit. I don't know why Egdar brought you here, but you might as well be comfortable."

She sat down herself, gesturing again. The young people sat.

"Did you like the performance? What we saw of it?" Maeve asked. "Is anyone hungry?"

None of them had eaten during the reception, as they all had been working. Wofar nodded.

Maeve stood. "Come, come."

She led them down a hallway to a kitchen featuring white marble countertops, dark-teal cabinetry, three sinks, a six-burner stove, and a wooden table with seating for eight. Luce saw food-related paintings, screens, tapestries, and combines hanging along the walls. The entire house reminded her of a museum.

In the kitchen, Maeve said to the ceiling, "Eunice, prepare browned sausages and grilled fish, and grain salads for seven. Also wine for all."

This is one of those private homes with food generators! Luce shuddered. *They probably never actually cook anything in this kitchen!* She had never eaten replicated food, known in the opposition communities as "repfood." It was anathema in her family and a fraught subject of negotiations between the Government and the Farm Country. To date, the Farm Country had prevailed with their argument that human health was best nurtured with live-growth sustenance. The Eflosi had joined the argument, making a case around their fishing enterprises. Other fishing communities joined the case-making. So did the wine-making coalition in the Farm Country hills. The General Assembly had accepted the reasoning—so far. Food replication generators were limited to certain large-scale social uses only. Private licenses for individual use were expensive and hard to secure. Only aristos could afford them.

"On it," a female voice came from above them. Luce looked up but saw only the stenciled white ceiling.

"Where is she?" she asked.

Maeve looked at her, amused. "It's the House, dear. Eunice."

"Victory," said Wofar.

"Indeed," Maeve said. "You remember your classics."

He grinned.

"We'll have a little feast," Maeve said, gesturing for them to sit. "It will be much better than the dinner we are missing. Or should I say the dinner that is not happening. They will be too busy cleaning up after their little Anony drama." She looked around the table. "Tell me your names and what you do at the Festival."

"I am Wofar Tonie, Subcurator on Sundrae's team," Wofar volunteered.

"Specializing in…?" Maeve asked.

"Western Earth Classics," he answered. He nodded back toward the room they had just left. "Impressive, those sculptures," he said. He was about to say more but Maeve moved on.

"And you?" She looked at Gemma.

"Enigma G'ocn, M'Ep," came the answer. "I coordinate exhibitions for Sundrae along with Allou," she continued. "My focus is Contemporary Art."

"An interesting name, Enigma," Maeve observed. "Where is the other one? Allou?"

"She is with Sundrae, I believe," Enigma answered. "I am called Gemma."

Dofi bounced into the room with a bark. "There you are, beast," Maeve said to the dog, who jumped up and down at her feet. "Do you know you are the most famous dog on The Planet tonight?" she asked him. He jumped again and landed in her lap. "Do you think you made the ticker?" she asked him. He woofed, tail wagging.

Maeve looked next to Luce. "You are Egdar's Personal Assistant," she said. "Luciena."

"Luce."

"New," Maeve said.

Luce nodded.

"Find something else to do as soon as you can," Maeve said, putting Dofi back on the floor. "Before he sacks you. It won't be personal, it's just what he does. I hope you have other interests."

Luce gulped. "Libraries," she said.

"Ah, I will show you ours."

"Food is ready," Eunice's voice came again from above.

"Materialize," Maeve said. Before each person appeared a beautiful plate of sausages, fish, and grain salad mixed with greens along with glasses of red wine. "Eunice, tell Egdar I am in the kitchen with his guests. Tell him he should join us for our little feast."

"Egdar Roiboi has left the building," Eunice replied.

"Call him for me," Maeve said.

After a pause Eunice said, "No pickup."

Maeve smiled at all the young people. "An opportunity. Eat up, my young friends. If he hasn't returned by the time we finish, I will give you a tour of the house. If he isn't back after that, you are free to go. If you spill anything, do not worry. Dofi will clean it up."

Luce stared at the food on her plate. *Ugh.* She took a bite of the fish, apologizing in her head to the Eflosi fishermen and to her grandparents in the Farm Country. It did not taste bad. *It's actually pretty good. But so wrong.*

Everyone ate, the conversation drifting uneasily from the shimmer and light show to Dofi's race for the shrimp. Roiboi never appeared. On finishing the "feast," Maeve walked them through the house, from the great room hub down hallways, to suites of rooms focused on various functions. Each set of rooms was loaded with paintings, etchings, floaters, ceramics, textiles, sculptures, collages. Luce had never seen such an extensive private collection. When they entered the library, the walls of the round room were covered in hardcover books from floor to ceiling. In the center, resting on a heavy Persian-style carpet, was an enormous sculpture.

Wofar circled it, then said, "But this does not exist."

"Ah yes, the Minotaur," Maeve said. "Spectacular, isn't it?"

Luce was enraptured by the shelves and shelves of books. People read this way once, and some still did, on Earth. She wanted desperately to pull something, anything, off a shelf and open it, leaf through it, turn an old book page. She hadn't done that since her Global Service in the Library of Atlas.

"I've only read about it," Wofar murmured, eyeing the sculpture closely. "There are no pictures of it, only written descriptions. It was lost." He shook his head in wonder.

"Obviously not lost. It should be seen," Maeve answered. "By people other than Delegates and others who will not speak of it beyond their own."

The voice of Eunice came into the room. "M'Ep, Sundrae Beq has arrived. Accompanied by Allou Owea."

"Has Sundrae seen this?" Wofar asked.

"Oh, my dear, Sundrae is here often," Maeve said. "Eunice, tell them to join us."

"As you wish."

"Look around all you'd like," Maeve said to them. She saw Luce staring at the bookshelf. "Go ahead. Pick one up."

With the permission, Luce reached out and pulled a book. It was heavy. The title was in a language she had not studied, French. *Les Misérables.* Author, Victor Hugo. She turned a few pages and found a publication date of 1862. She looked at Maeve in astonishment. "This is from Earth," she blurted.

"Yes, dear, many of them are. Some are replications," Maeve said. "But many are real. There's a Gutenberg Bible in here somewhere."

Sundrae entered the room, followed by Allou. "Maeve!" she exclaimed, seeing the staff members.

Wofar remained entranced by the Minotaur, running his fingers lightly over the stone.

"All citizens have a right to this bounty," Maeve said. "It seemed a good night to share it, after Anony's message."

"What are you thinking?" Sundrae asked. "Where is Egdar?"

"Eunice, do we know where Egdar is?" Maeve asked the House.

"Negative," came the answer.

Maeve shrugged at Sundrae. "As usual. I don't know why he brought them here."

"You're going to have to stay here tonight," Sundrae said to everyone.

"Why?" Wofar asked.

"Maeve told us we could leave after the tour," Gemma said.

"The crowd that saw The Interstitials is now marching on the General Assembly. You're best off here for the night. I'm sure, M'Ep, that you have guest rooms ready for occupancy."

"Always," Maeve replied, looking apologetically at the young people. "I tried," she said. Dofi trotted in from the hallway. She picked him up. "We like company," she said to the dog.

"You're forcing us to stay here?" Gemma asked.

"Welcome to the underbelly of The Planet," Maeve said. "Dofi and I are retiring. I'm going back to my house in Shiona early in the morning. Make yourselves at home. Don't break anything, dears." She looked at the ceiling. "Eunice, watch over our guests. Do whatever Sundrae tells you." Still carrying the dog, she went down the corridor, leaving them on their own.

Everyone looked at Sundrae. Luce replaced the book carefully back onto its shelf.

"I need to go home," said Gemma. "Please. I won't tell anyone about this." She gestured at the books and the Minotaur.

"Why are we here?" Luce asked.

Sundrae sighed. "I suspect Egdar wanted a meeting of some kind; he has an office in his home suite. Something came up. Something always comes up." She looked toward the ceiling. "Eunice."

"Yes, Sundrae?"

"Show the guests to their rooms for the night, please."

"Can we have our tablets back?" Gemma asked. "I need to let my mates know…"

"The Director wouldn't like that," Sundrae replied.

Eunice directed each person to another hallway spoke, naming them one by one to separate rooms, each with a different colored door. Luce was assigned the yellow door. Entering, she found herself in a perfectly appointed bedroom suite. No bookshelves lined the walls, but a painting of white roses with a green background hung over the bed. She knew her Earth art history well enough to recognize Vincent van Gogh's *Roses*. *That can't be the actual one. That's in some museum or private collection on Earth.* She sat on the bed, running her hand over the silken, off-white covering. The beaded sleeve of her red-and-gray robe snagged. She groaned, taking a moment to detangle it. *What do I sleep in? Nothing, I guess. It's going to be weird to go home in this robe…*

A knock interrupted her thoughts. She opened the door. Wofar stood before her. She smiled at him. He smiled back. He saw the painting over the bed and walked past her, looking at it closely. "Not my time period. This one isn't real," he said.

"Some of those books are," she told him.

"So is the Minotaur." He sat on the overstuffed chair next to the bed. "That Minotaur is the most famous of the missing classical sculptures. Roiboi wants to unveil a lot of artifacts as part of the Festival, but this…I can't figure out how he got it here…" His voice trailed off. He refocused, saying, "Well, not everyone gets to spend the night in an aristo mansion in the Broom."

"I've never even been in this neighborhood before, I've just looked at it in the hills. The view of the city from here is…I can't imagine having that view every day."

"Where are you from?" he asked.

"Farm Country," she answered. "My parents are food grow-
ers."

He nodded. "Never been there. I'm from the Desertlands."

"Wow," she said. "Just the opposite."

He laughed. "They sent me away to the Philosophers Guild
school in the Capital when I was twelve."

"The P-Guild! What an education."

"I don't have anything to compare it to," he said, stretching
in the spacious chair. "They taught us all the rituals and 'cosmic
questions' along with heavy emphasis on Earth. Had to learn
Latin and Greek and the Socratic method. It inspired my interest in classicism. They were pushing me toward the P-Guild
or sciences. I did my Global Service on Vania Island but…" He
shrugged.

"Few people get to see Vania," Luce murmured. "All those
priests and poets…"

"My heart wasn't in it. I'm no poet." He smiled at her. "At
the Festival, my heart and I are in alignment. Most of the time."

Luce sighed, falling back on the bed and staring at the ceiling. She did this without thinking, drawn into his relaxed attitude. She envied the idea of being in alignment with herself.
"I did my Global Service after uni in the Library of Atlas. I
wanted to stay there. But there weren't any openings."

"The Festival is a good jumping-off point," Wofar said, sliding deeper into the chair so that he, too, was staring at the ceiling. "But M'Ep is right, don't stay too long. Roiboi…" He shook
his head. Then he said, "Eunice is always listening."

Luce sat up. Wofar was lost in thought. His long-legged,
slender figure and dark hair and sharp features were so attrac-
tive. She'd wondered about him before, who he was, what—or
more to the point, who—he liked, whether he was available.

They had only casual interactions at the office. He was gone a lot, on assignments from Sundrae or Roiboi or Caspar.

"Why do you think they're keeping us here?" Luce asked. "How bad can it be in the Capital, especially if you don't live near the General Assembly?"

"Not sure…"

He was quiet a moment, then said, "Roiboi wouldn't have wanted us in that library. They can always wipe us. Sundrae is stressed. She didn't like that we were seeing that Minotaur." He sat up.

"But they can't force a wipe on us," she said. "It's voluntary, they can't force us."

"You didn't read the fine print, did you?" Wofar sighed.

"What fine print?"

"Your contract, when you joined the Festival staff. You thumb-printed something, right?"

Luce remembered a long document that she had skimmed and stamped. She nodded.

"You agreed to up to four wipes," he said. "Their choice. Always read the details."

"Why would they require that?" Luce asked, alarmed.

"The live arts people aren't bound to the same rules. But anyone in admin or working with atom-based material…we're sometimes in questionable territory. Anony has complicated things by advocating for withdrawal from planet of origin work. You saw that crowd tonight. And Orwen racing out with her kids. The Government is going to have to step in."

What have I gotten myself into? Luce still believed this job would be her path to Guild status and, eventually, the Library subguild. Roiboi was powerful. For all his drama, she admired what he had done in the years since taking over the Festival.

She believed in his vision for the anniversary ahead. *But memory wipes?*

"It feels wrong," she said to Wofar.

"The crowd?" he asked.

"No, no. Well, the crowd may be wrong too, I don't know… the Anony messages upset me because I don't know what to think about what they're saying." She raised her hands and gestured around the room. "But wiping us? We shouldn't be here at all. Now Roiboi is gone and we're stuck here, and Sundrae…"

Wofar slid off his chair and sat beside her on the bed, taking her hand. "It will work out somehow," he said. "Hey, if they wipe us, we won't know the difference. We won't remember any of it."

"Have you ever been wiped before?"

He shook his head. "Not that I know of. I don't think it hurts." He put his open palm on her face. "It's going to be okay. Really."

She leaned her head against his shoulder, then looked up at him. Impulsively, she kissed him.

He responded.

CHAPTER 14

THE RIDE TO San Francisco Airport with Dawn was an ordeal. She arrived wearing low-slung baggy black jeans, a beaded black tunic, and black high-top sneakers. Her blond hair was pulled back in an unraveling ponytail. She waxed on about the edibles they'd consumed the night before and the dream-hallucinations they'd spawned. The good-byes with D'avi and Freddie were brief. Then they sped off into the dipping hills of the neighborhood. Dawn talked in a nonstop rush. As she drove, she flirted with Max and advised Kaieda on improving her wardrobe. She also pointed out various landmarks along the highway, resulting in three near collisions with other vehicles as they raced south toward the airport.

"Black is always dependable, but it can get boring," she said, after pointing at the Twin Peaks towers and nearly veering off the road. "You have to spice it up. Lug-sole boots. Chucks are okay, I'm wearing them now, but really. Boots. Get a leather jacket. You'd look brat, you've got the haircut, and oh—you should get a pair of round, black horn-rim glasses, it'd look fierce. No, red! Red horn-rims! I want pictures. Send some and I'll put them on my Instagram feed."

As they rounded a wide curve, she said to Max, "Can I visit you in Los Angeles? What did you say you're doing down there? Where are you from?"

Kaieda was starting to feel carsick in the back seat, where she sat with the backpacks. She kept her hand on Max's pack, feeling protective of their Bluebox.

"Research," Max answered.

"About…?"

"People," he answered, looking at her.

"Huh, missed that last night," Dawn said. "You study people."

"Yes, social customs, traditions, beliefs, ways of doing things," Max said.

"Uh-huh. You do what D'avi does. Freddie is his backup man. They're the best, those two. Fun. So happy together. Very inspiring."

"Yes. We're part of the same project," Max said.

"Huh. D'avi said they knew you from work."

"A private foundation in the U.K. funds the research. Could you…slow down a little?" Kaieda asked, fighting her nausea.

"Oh!" said Dawn. She slowed the car briefly, then abruptly changed lanes. "I don't want to miss this turn, sorry…" She took the exit toward the departures level of the terminal, then she veered out of that lane and into the arrivals lane. "I like to drop people off at baggage claim, it's easier to get out from there. Once you're in, just go up the escalator. You'll see the signs for ticket counters and TSA entries."

They pulled into an open space on the lower level. The car jerked to a stop. Kaieda got out as fast as she could, leaning on the car. Max exited and noticed she was unsettled. Dawn got out and came to the curbside. She started pulling at the backpacks, handing the first to Max. "God, that's heavy. Get a cart, they're inside," she said.

"I'll get it," Kaieda said, needing to get away from the exhaust fumes flooding the sheltered lower level. She went inside the terminal, found a cart, and brought it back outside. Max was standing by the curb alone, their backpacks at his feet.

"Where'd she go?" Kaieda asked.

He nodded in the direction of the road exit. "She had an appointment," he answered. Then he frowned. "She kissed me."

Kaieda snorted. "How'd that go?" she asked as they donned their packs.

"Wet," he answered, pushing the empty cart back into the building, where he released it.

As they rode up the escalator, Max said, "She asked again to come to Los Angeles."

"Are you ready for an Earth woman?"

He half-smiled at her as the elevator door opened. "She isn't my type."

Now synths have "types"? Freddie said the same thing, only in reverse. "I'm so not your type." Who is doing this programming? Harlong never hinted at "types." She shook it off. Using e-tickets on their phones, they went through security. Max led the way to the lounge.

They sat in chairs overlooking the tarmac. The blue water of the South Bay rippled in sunlight on the far side of the tarmac. Kaieda's dyspepsia faded. *Types* kept running through her mind. She remembered Alec's voice in her ear the first time they danced together, teasing her about "types."

I want to dance with you again.

She looked around. The lounge was quiet, a few people scattered here and there sipping sodas, wearing earbuds, talking to invisible listeners, scrolling on their phones, using their laptops. The bar was busy, people perched on stools leaning over their drinks. She gasped.

Max put his phone down. "Something wrong?"

"Look over there." She nodded toward the bar.

Max looked. "Oh."

Sitting side by side at the corner of the bar were Charles and Marian Tumbleston, the couple from the grounded plane on Maui. Charles wore earbuds but held his mobile phone in front of him, alternately talking and listening. Marian was lost in scrolling. She glanced up and spied Max and Kaieda looking at her.

"Max!" she cried, getting off her chair and coming toward them. She turned back briefly to Charles and waved at him, pointed at them, then kept coming in their direction. Charles waved but continued his conversation. Kaieda saw Max's head tilt briefly. He rose and greeted Marian. She hugged him as if he were her long-lost son. Kaieda rose and Marian hugged her too. As she did, she saw past Marian to Max.

How does a synth look perturbed? Like that.

"We were just saying we wondered where you were. Here you are!" Marian exclaimed.

"Please join us," Max said, gesturing for her to sit beside him.

"You made it to San Francisco!" Marian said. "Where to now?"

"Los Angeles," Max said.

"That's where we're going! Are you on the five o'clock flight?"

He nodded.

"Oh, how wonderful! Charles will join us shortly, he's doing his usual deal-making." She leaned toward them, lowering her voice conspiratorially. "Do you know, the oddest thing happened."

"What?" Kaieda asked.

"You know that emergency landing on the beach on Maui?"

Kaieda nodded.

"Well! The NTSB called us yesterday afternoon to talk

about it. The interview went fine, we confirmed that young man Reggie did a fine beach landing and we're no worse for the wear. They said the FAA might call as well, they had to confirm the condition of the plane first. So we said uh-huh, whatever. But then around noon someone from the FAA called. You know what they said?"

Kaieda shook her head.

"They said thank you for your cooperation, the plane is gone!"

"Gone?" Kaieda repeated.

"GONE. The people from Trip Maui reported it late this morning when they went back to see if they could repair it and get it in the air. Can you imagine? Somebody must have snuck in there and gotten it working and flew off with it!"

Charles strode up to join them, a drink in his left hand, offering his right to Max. "Max! Good to see you!" As they shook hands, he said, "That's more like it!" He turned to Kaieda. "Hello, girl-whose-name-sounds-like-terrorists." He sat down next to Marian. "How did we luck into these two?"

"They're on our flight to L.A.," Marian said. "I'm telling them about the plane."

"Yeah, that is really something. Who steals an airplane?"

Max and Kaieda looked at each other and back to Charles.

"High tide last night. They think it might have been pulled out to sea and then sank." He shook his head. "Seems far-fetched."

"I hope they find it," Kaieda said.

Charles nodded. "Those little Cessnas aren't cheap. If they can't find the plane, I don't know how the insurance will come through for those Trip Maui guys."

Max stood up. "It's time to board," he said.

"So happy to run into you," Kaieda told them.

Charles's phone rang. "Gotta take this," he said.

"I'll wait for him," Marian told them. "You two go ahead. We'll be along. We should go out for dinner tonight after we get to L.A. Charles can get us into somewhere special."

Max and Kaieda said their good-byes and departed for their gate.

"What happened to that plane?" Kaieda asked as they walked.

"Hard to say," Max answered. "I don't believe it is missing. Let me rephrase. It is missing to those who own it. But not because it no longer exists or has disappeared into the ocean." He looked around, then added, "I'll explain after we board."

Kaieda bristled. The first rule of a Traveler partnership was trust. She had to trust this Maximus5700. So far, he had been right about everything. But he was withholding things. *He times his information drops. As if I can only take so much.* She hated that. She also hated that every time they were close to getting back on track, their central mission was disrupted by some new turn of events. She was still upset about Fenn Loa. They needed to report it, their Guild needed to know. Other Reporters, wherever they were, needed to be alerted. *Why did D'avi refuse to report it? Why was he so indifferent when I told him who it was? And now this plane disappearing?*

They boarded, settled into their seats, and nodded at the Tumblestons as they boarded. They were two rows back. Once the plane took off, Max said to her in a low voice, "Fetchers."

She looked at him, puzzled. The noise of takeoff made talking and hearing difficult.

"We cannot join them tonight," he nodded back toward the Tumblestons. "If they invite us out, tell them you are not feeling well."

Kaieda nodded. *Not feeling well seems to be my MO on this*

assignment. Let's get on with the work. But what did he mean about Fetchers? Does he think they took away the Trip Maui plane? The jet gained altitude. She looked down at the rumpled golden hills below, and the sweeping farmland to the east. Across the aisle they could see the Pacific out the windows. Afternoon sun poured in. She thought of Fenn Loa. *I can see why you wanted to stay here. There's nothing like this on The Planet. We have natural beauty, but this…this is where we came from. This Earth. You wrote about it with such grace. Such love. As if you were writing letters from home.*

She sighed, watching the landscape below sweep by. She wondered about the woman Fenn lived with. Who was she? What had become of her? Was there a way to find or help her? Wasn't that more important than researching American customs and lifestyles and art and sports and nightlife and spectacle in Los Angeles for Egdar Roiboi? She looked at Max, on the aisle, his eyes closed. Now and again his head would twitch almost imperceptibly.

We need more information.

She closed her eyes. Visions of Freddie and D'avi flashed across her inner screen. The way they seemed to delight in each other. Dawn had said they were happy. D'avi certainly had gotten what he wanted. *But Freddie? How is a synthetic happy? Harlong seemed happy. Was he programmed to seem happy, to exude that cheerful calm that…*

She opened her eyes. She had dozed off. The light outside had lessened as the sun dropped closer to the sea. People on the right side of the plane were pointing at what she assumed was a sunset.

"Magic hour begins," she heard a man across from them say.

Max's eyes were open. He was also looking across the aisle and out the window.

"Max, we have a lot to do," she said. "A lot we have to find out."

"Yes."

"What did you mean about the Fetchers?"

They were starting their descent into Los Angeles. "I believe they have already come," he said. "Artifacts."

"You think Fetchers took the plane?"

He took her hand in his. "Let me get the Bluebox up," he said. "I will gather more once we have an independent link."

Fetchers taking a small plane? Why would they do that? Wait. As an artifact? Insane.

Kaieda's mind drifted back to Fenn's still-missing wife. "We have to help her," she said. Then she realized she was still holding Max's hand. She withdrew, then instantly missed his warm touch.

"Help who?"

"The woman Fenn left behind."

"She is not part of our assignment."

"Has anything that has happened so far been part of our assignment?"

The edges of his mouth turned up slightly. "Very little."

She sighed as the plane landed on the tarmac at Los Angeles International Airport, the sun dipping ever closer to the ocean.

CHAPTER 15

Faerae awoke with an awful hangover. She could not remember anything from the night before. *A lost night?* She lay in bed coming slowly to her senses. *Haven't done that since uni.* The reception and Orwen's arrival and the rocking performance and sudden departures rushed back into her memory. That funny little dog. She recalled arriving at The Blue Guitar with Dzuren and a cluster of other people. *Then what happened? Ughhh, we started drinking whisky in the packed, noisy bar.* News of the Anony message at The Interstitials concert had hit the ticker before they arrived. People were clustered and discussing it. "Radical!" someone, it might have been one of the Twins, had shouted at one point. Mog Weller was broadcasting live from the Amphitheater but failed to reach the musicians for interviews. She kept describing how they disappeared beneath the arena at the end of the concert.

Who else in the bar? Faerae remembered Dzuren, the Twins, Janai Loa, a couple of Delegates, and two Monitors, once their shift ended. Other people she didn't know. The ticker kept running clips from the performance, including the Anony "artist intervention." She could still see the gold dripping and popping off the letters as they boldly scrolled against the sky above the Amphitheater. Everyone kept drinking. Dzuren huddled in a booth with the Delegates and Janai Loa at one point. The

Delegates left soon after. *Where did they stay? The Keeper Colony has nothing resembling hotels. Maybe they took a middle-of-the-night shuttle home?*

She rolled over in the bed and groaned, but then she laughed. Janai Loa was so beautiful. *She really is…*Faerae nearly said it out loud. And that Amphitheater! The tiled entry rotunda, the spectrum of colors in those flowing robes, all that food, that little white dog running around and eating shrimp, those poor girls chasing it…she giggled again. *And a Tri member sighting! Orwen herself! How about that?* The concert had been…extraordinary. *Feeling that beat.* At least what she saw and heard of it before the Anony intervention and the panicked exodus of officials and dignitaries.

"Couldn't stay after that," she said out loud.

"Do you need anything, Faerae?" the House asked.

She sat up. "No, no. Unless you have more information on Fenn Loa."

The House whirred for a moment and then said, "Fenn Loa is dead."

"What?" Faerae cried, dragging herself out of bed and pulling on pants and a T-shirt.

"Two reports came in early this morning," the House said.

"From…?"

"One from Reporter Marina Rambert, the other from Maximus5700. I matched the information with a news report released two days ago in San Francisco, California, United States of America, Earth, Copernican system. Fenn Loa's remains were found after a fire in his residence. Maximus5700 provided additional information."

Max and Kaieda! Who was this other person? Marina Rambert? Had that name been on the Reporter list? What happened to Fenn Loa?

"What did the Max say?" Faerae asked.

"Fenn Loa was murdered."

"Murdered?" Faerae repeated, shocked. *Earth is so violent.* "Explain." She sat at her console, opened the screen with a wave, and pulled up the Reporter list. Marina Rambert, based near Oxford, was there.

"Maximus5700 reports death by a sharp weapon," the House said. "No specifics are in the Rambert report. Do you want coffee, Faerae?"

"Not yet," Faerae murmured. "Get me what information you can on Marina Rambert."

The House hummed. Faerae opened the work reports folder first. Max had included her on his update to the Monitors. *Kaieda insisted.*

LOS ANGELES TEAM 7 TO MONITORS + CPT
DZUREN TSO, CMDR FAERAE C'IEZ

SAN FRANCISCO TEAM 5 ASSIST COMPLETE

IN SAN FRANCISCO: DEATH OF
FENN LOA CAUSE: FIRE

UNPUBLISHED POLICE REPORT =
HOMICIDE SHARP WEAPON

STATUS OF WIFE: UNKNOWN

RECOMMEND REVIEW OF TRANSIT
STRINGS BETWEEN EARTH AND N.A.

"Long gods," Faerae whispered, reading the words. She

turned to the Rambert report the House had accessed as a readable mission file to the Monitors.

CONFIRMED: REPORTER FENN LOA DECEASED

Faerae sat there, absorbing the information. A prolific, long-embedded Reporter who had gone quiet was dead, possibly murdered. He had sent encrypted messages to the U.K. *A reference to a wife? On Earth?* The death was twice confirmed, first by Travelers in the region and then by another Reporter. *Why did Kaieda want me to know?* She took a breath. *Marina Rambert must be the recipient of those encrypted messages. She lives in the U.K. She learned Fenn Loa is dead. How?*

Faerae reread Max's message again, focusing on the final line:

RECOMMEND REVIEW OF TRANSIT
STRINGS BETWEEN EARTH AND N.A.

What is he saying? The lines of communication between Earth and Rimalon are reliable. Reviewed and retested regularly. Engineering Command knows that. The Maximus had to know that. Why recommend a review?

"Have you found anything on Marina Rambert?" she asked the House.

"Assembling."

"So there's a lot of information?"

"M'Rambert has filed extensive reports over the years."

Faerae got up and stretched, working the information in her head. She went to the kitchen and soon after was standing at the window, a cup of black coffee in hand. *Kaieda is trying to tell me something. Or wants me to do something. What?* She looked at her other messages. *Nothing. Why aren't you talking to me?*

"I have summarized information on Marina Rambert," the House announced.

"Bring it," Faerae said.

"Citizen of New Atlantis. Childhood on the Raja Sea. After Global Service, training, and Guild orientation, she was embedded as a Reporter on Earth. She has been based in London and Oxfordshire, England, for over four decades. She returns to The Planet every five Earth years. She is an academic working in two universities and is director of a not-for-profit research institute studying comparative religions and related anthropological and archeological phenomena…"

"Wait," Faerae interrupted. "Rambert is not a clan name."

The House whirred for a moment. "Rambert is the adopted surname."

"What clan does she belong to?"

"She is a member of the Roiboi clan."

"Roiboi!" Faerae exclaimed.

The House answered, "Yes."

"Is she related to Egdar Roiboi?" Faerae asked.

"They are siblings," the House answered.

Faerae sat back down, astonished. Then she realized something else. "Did you say she grew up on the Raja Sea? How close to the town where Fenn Loa grew up?"

"The same town," the House replied. "The Roibois reside offshore in a compound of floating islands that serve as their family seat. Fenn Loa grew up in Shiona, the village on the mainland. Do you want to hear more about Marina Rambert?"

"Not now," Faerae answered. "Pull up the communication lines between Earth and The Planet. Specific to the American West Coast, in the last two weeks. Set them up as a column."

A series of threads materialized in front of Faerae. The many strings before her represented all official communications between the American West Coast and Rimalon. Most were from Team Five's location in the Bay Area. "Expand to include the Pacific Rim," Faerae said. More lines appeared, including threads to and from Hawaii. *That's Kaieda and Max. No, wait, their first messages came after they got to San Francisco. They had to sync with D'avi's Bluebox to trigger their own. What is all this yellow?*

"Who are these yellow messages from in Hawaii?" she asked. Yellow. Fetcher color.

The House whirred again, then said, "Retriever reports."

"Fetchers? We have Fetchers in Hawaii?"

"Affirmative. Reports dated the last three days."

Insane. Henk Z'eng would have said something in the CCR if there were Fetchers at work in the Pacific. The Fetchers maintained mobile and cloaked space stations within timely reach of any planet under observation. Their deployment was always done under strict Keeper Colony protocol. Everyone knew when a retrieval was under way. Nothing had been called in the last several weeks. The focus had been on the Earth Project Team launches.

"Can you access their content?" Faerae asked.

"Negative, encrypted."

"Override?"

"Negative."

Faerae pinged Dzuren on the voice line. He answered quickly, looking unshaven and sounding like he'd just gotten up.

"Good morning," Dzuren said. He was shirtless. Faerae winced, though with a seam of admiration. He was in fine shape for a man of his years.

"Are you aware there were Fetchers on Earth?" she asked.

"No Fetchers on Earth right now," he said. "There's a Fetcher team on the Copernican space station behind Mars. That's it." He took a sip of coffee. "What a night."

"There was a team on the ground. In Hawaii. Yesterday."

Dzuren frowned. Faerae watched as he wove a column and looked at it. He peered at it and then typed some instructions into the 3-D screen and looked again. Then he looked startled and said, "What the…there was a team on the ground on Maui yesterday morning…"

"That's what I just told you!"

"Feck," said Dzuren. "I'll message Henk. Meet me in the CCR, I'll…feck! Fetchers!" He logged off.

Faerae dressed and was soon in the Central Command Room. It was quiet except for Dzuren, at a station in front of the master screen, flanked by Henk Z'eng. The Twins were at their stations working follow lines in the Pacific.

Dzuren noticed Faerae and gestured for her to come to where he was already working.

"We're in an unusual situation," he said.

Faerae bit her tongue to refrain from saying, *I told you so.*

"The Retrievers here are saying the Retrievers have all been in their space station unit over the last four days," Henk said.

"They finished their run yesterday morning," Faerae said. "The comm lines run back and forth for a couple of days. It started the day after Max and Kaieda evacuated the landing point…"

"They were down there and now they're not," Dzuren finished for her.

Faerae nodded.

"Into the meet room," he said to her and Henk. Once in, he closed the door. "The Twins found something," he said. "A renegade comm relay operating between Earth and The Planet. It bounces through Venus."

"To here?" Faerae asked.

"To The Planet. They're working on finding the designation point now."

"But…that…" Faerae started. "How did that not show up in our tracking?"

"We weren't looking for it," Dzuren said. "We've only been monitoring strings we know to look for."

"That's what Max meant," Faerae said, more to herself than to Dzuren.

"What do you mean?"

"A message came in late last night while we were all at The Blue Guitar. From Max and Kaieda's Bluebox. Max recommended reviewing the transit strings between Earth and The Planet."

Stupid, stupid, stupid, why didn't I see what he was saying?

Dzuren groaned. "What's in it?"

"He said to review transit strings between Earth and The Planet. He knows everything routes through the Colony. He must have found an irregularity. He's trying to get us to look at a wider band of incoming data." Faerae brought up the message on the screen in the room. "This is really from Kaieda," she added.

"Don't underestimate the Maximus," Dzuren replied. He read the message, then said, "Fenn Loa is dead? A homicide? A wife?"

Faerae nodded. "Death confirmed, through another Reporter as well as Max's message. The wife part is a mystery."

"Tell me everything," Dzuren said.

Faerae described her discoveries about the encrypted communications between Loa and a location in the U.K. She pointed out the location of Marina Rambert, another of the Earth Reporters, in that region. She also told him Marina Rambert was in the Roiboi clan and Egdar Roiboi's sister.

"Part the gods," Henk Z'eng muttered, shaking his head.

The door to the meet room opened and one of the Twins,

Vaylor, peered in. "We have the designation point for the comms," he said. Then he hesitated.

Dzuren waited, then said, "Well?"

"It is in the countryside, outside a village sixty kilometers from the Capital," he said. "Adjacent to a storage facility."

"For what?" Dzuren asked.

"Earth artifacts. It is a Festival facility. Their primary warehouse."

They all looked at one another.

Dzuren thanked the Eflos. "Stay on it, narrow it down as much as you can," he said. Then he turned to Faerae. "We have to go down there." He looked at his cousin. "Not you. You need to find out what's going on with the Fetcher team in the Copernican system."

Henk nodded.

"You can't just send someone?" Faerae asked.

"I don't know who to trust," Dzuren answered. "If Fetchers are involved, something is being moved around. Probably to that warehouse." He pointed at Max's message, still floating in front of them. "This went to the Monitors but they didn't notice anything other than the Fenn Loa information, which by now they've passed to the subguild. They're not paying attention to Fetchers right now. Like the rest of us, they're settled in their silo. They just want to keep the Teams on track with their assignments." He shook his head, showing a rare moment of upset. "Gods, we've gotten arrogant. We're so sure of ourselves and so compartmentalized that we've lost our way. Someone is taking advantage of it."

"But…inspecting a Festival warehouse? Isn't that high-level security?"

"Good thing I have high-level clearance."

Faerae blushed, flustered. *I am such an idiot. Just like last night when he was a star at that reception.* On Rimalon it was easy to forget how accomplished he was, how high he ranked in the hierarchy, who he knew, what he could access. On The Planet, he was famous. Here, he was an Acting Director. The Keeper Colony did not presently have an assigned Director. Debates were under way in the General Assembly about whether Rimalon should be overseen by military or civilian leadership. The only person on the moon who had full Director status was Janai Loa. Her many research and experimental projects took place segregated from the Engineering and Monitor teams.

But Dzuren had near-legendary status on The Planet, as an ace pilot and an experienced and wily space captain. *He could be an admiral now, if he wanted it.*

"Sorry," she said. "Wasn't thinking."

"Don't worry about it," he replied. "I'll bring Vaylor too. That location is near an Eflos village. Meet me at the shuttle platform in half an hour. In uniform."

"Uniform?" Faerae repeated. No one wore their uniforms on Rimalon, unless dignitaries were expected. They worked in gray jumpsuits. She hadn't worn her uniform in months. She wasn't sure why Dzuren had worn his, the previous night. He did look impressive in his dress whites.

"You heard me," Dzuren said. "Go. Half an hour. Day blues."

Faerae hurried back to her flat and searched the closet, found one of her two pale-blue uniforms, put it on.

While she was dressing, the House asked, "Faerae, do you want to hear my other research on Marina Roiboi?"

"Yes. Highlights," Faerae instructed.

The House whirred for a moment, then said, "Relay communications between Fenn Loa and a place in the U.K. confirmed. Designation point is the home of Marina Rambert near Banbury, England. I am hacking into a vast volume of emails between them. They used old-world communication methods including phone calls, SMS exchanges."

"Have you accessed those eight encrypted messages?"

"Attempt in progress."

Faerae sighed. *In other words, no.* That the House couldn't quickly penetrate the message coding was unsettling. *Were they related to the artifacts? Was Roiboi's sister helping her brother secure objects for the Festival? Why would Fenn Loa care about that? And what to make of a "wife"? That was not an option. We don't do Earthers.*

Before leaving for the shuttle platform, Faerae composed a message and sent it to Max and Kaieda's Bluebox. The communication would be seen by multiple people so she had to think for a while about how to confirm to them that she had grasped Max's instruction. She knew she would sound like the House, but that was part of the point. *Keep it simple. Kaieda will understand.*

ON IT.

CHAPTER 16

Luce had not awakened in the arms of another person since her fling with the visiting scholar from Idylia, The Planet's most temperate zone, during her first year in Global Service. Now, half asleep, she was drugged with pleasure. As she stirred, feeling Wofar pressed against her, she luxuriated in the sensations of warmth, connection, half-asleep relaxation, a heartbeat other than her own. *Just a little longer.* Who cared what the others would think. She'd liked Wofar from the day she started at the Festival. And he stayed, he was still here.

"Want to go again?" he whispered in her ear. His lips slid down her neck.

She giggled softly. "I didn't know you were awake."

"I am awake." He rolled over her.

Eunice's voice from the ceiling interrupted. "Good morning, Luciena and Wofar. I trust you had a pleasant night."

"Oh gods," Luce groaned, pulling away from him.

He sat up. "Eunice," he said. "You found us out."

"My cyber lips are sealed. I have been instructed to awaken all guests and direct them to shower and to go to the kitchen for breakfast."

Wofar pushed some hair out of Luce's face. He kissed her

cheek and got out of bed, dressed, and went to the door, carrying his shoes. "See you at breakfast," he said, smiling at her.

What now? A flush of soft energy rippled through her. She missed him. Then she remembered the conversation from the night before. *Am I getting wiped today? Because of that stupid Minotaur?* She got up, showered, put her dress and robe back on, and went to the kitchen. Sundrae sat at the table with her tablet, a coffee, and a pastry. Across from her was Gemma, absorbed in a 3-D puzzle. Allou sat in an overstuffed chair in the corner of the kitchen by a window, her legs flopped over the arm of the chair. She, too, had her tablet. *They got theirs back. Or did they ever put them in the basket in the first place?* The view beyond her seat was a splendid city vista. The houses of the Golden Broom were built into a forested green hill overlooking the Capital. *It must be amazing to live here all the time.*

"Ah, good morning," Sundrae said, glancing up at Luce. "I'm going back to the Festival office soon. Go home and change clothes if you wish. A transit car is coming shortly. The Director expects you to work today, though you may have the morning to collect yourself."

Luce straightened her robe slightly. "I feel ridiculous," she said.

"None of us were expecting an all-nighter," Allou said from her chair.

"Help yourself to the coffee," Sundrae continued. "In the red carafe."

Luce went to the counter and slowly poured coffee from the carafe into a cup. The calm in the room seemed eerie given the events of the night before. She kept glancing around waiting for someone to say something. Nobody did.

Wofar entered from the hallway. Luce's eyes met his. That smile again. She felt giddy. He saw the coffee carafe and came to where she was standing, pouring a cup for himself. "Good morning, all," he said.

"Hi, Wofar," said Gemma.

"Sleep okay?" Sundrae asked.

"In a coma," he answered.

"Huh, yeah, me too," Luce said.

"Your transit car is almost here," came Eunice's voice. "Five minutes. Please be assembled at the front door. The car does not wait."

"Okay, everybody, let's be on time," Sundrae said, getting up. She straightened her robe folds.

"Let's look at that library one more time," Wofar whispered to Luce. She nodded. *More time alone with him.*

"We're going to the great room," Wofar said. He gestured for Luce to precede him. As they went further down the hallway toward the central atrium and out of sight to the others, he took her hand in his, continuing to walk. "I want to see that Minotaur again," he said quietly.

"You remember it!" Luce whispered. "I was afraid everyone was wiped overnight but they somehow forgot me." She frowned. "Although, I guess if I was wiped I wouldn't remember it?"

Wofar looked for the hallway to the library, then stopped. "Those sculptures," he said, staring ahead at the great room. "They're gone."

Luce followed his gaze. The several classical sculptures he had admired the night before were no longer there. The space was empty but for a pair of tall potted plants and the sofas that had been spread about the night before. The sofas were rearranged into a square. He looked at her and then, taking her hand, charged down the hallway that led to the library. He nearly dragged her. They burst into the library.

"The Minotaur is gone too!" he exclaimed.

The room looked unchanged to Luce but for the absence of the huge sculpture that had been in the middle of the library the night before.

"But how could anybody move it…just in the last few hours?" she asked. "In the middle of the night?"

She went to the place among the bookshelves where she had left *Les Misérables*. The book was there.

"It was here," Wofar said, standing where the Minotaur had stood.

Luce nodded. "I remember."

"Wofar, Luciena, the transit car is two minutes from the door, kindly make your way to meet it," Eunice's calm voice told them.

They hurried back up the hall to find the others waiting. "The great room?" Sundrae eyed them as she distributed their tablets. "He doesn't like photos being taken or anything being recorded," she explained.

"The sculptures," Wofar pointed at the two potted palms. "The Minotaur, they're gone."

"Sculptures?" Sundrae repeated. "He has them coming and going all the time."

"But the ones that were right there last night," he said, pointing again. "Classical, perfect replications…"

"Didn't notice," she said to him, enunciating each word slowly.

"In the library!" he said, pointing down that hallway. "You saw that Minotaur!" he said to Gemma.

"Didn't notice," Gemma said, repeating Sundrae's tone.

Now I am really going mad. Luce looked at Allou, who shrugged and said, "Didn't notice."

"You saw them!" he said again, turning to Luce.

"Uhh, I didn't notice?" Luce answered, looking at Sundrae.

Sundrae stepped between them. "We have to leave now." Her voice lowered. "And I am saving you from a wipe. Kindly cooperate." Her voice came back to its normal volume. "We're going back to the Capital now. Everyone will be dropped at your homes. Please be at the office by noon."

Luce gave Wofar a helpless look.

"Oh. Didn't notice. Okay," he said. They stood in silence awaiting the transit car.

"Here we go," Sundrae said as the car slid onto the platform. Allou, Luce, and Gemma entered. Sundrae held Wofar back by the arm and waved the car on. The doors shut. It departed, leaving Sundrae and Wofar standing in front of the house.

"Why aren't they coming with us?" Luce asked.

"Sundrae or the Egg must have other plans for him," Allou said.

"Such as what?" Luce asked.

Allou looked her in the eye. "NTK," she said. "He has a higher clearance than you." She sipped her coffee.

NTK. It was rare to hear in their cultural work. Luce realized, in this context, it meant shut up, say no more, don't ask. *You don't need to know.* Allou's security clearance was higher than hers. Luce assumed everyone at the Festival was relatively low-level given their focus on the arts and culture. *What was it he said to me last night? Something about atom-based material and…? We were talking about Anony and he mentioned something about being in…"questionable territory."*

"I just want to get home and change clothes and sleep a little," Gemma said. "Has anybody heard what happened after the concert last night, or what became of The Interstitials?"

"They disappeared," Allou said. "I watched them do it. Into

the ground. Everything just stopped. Their platform sank out of sight and the hydraulic floor shut over them like a mouth closing. It's all over the ticker this morning. Nobody knows where they are now."

Gemma flipped her tablet open. Up came the ticker, including moving images of The Interstitials sinking into the depths of the Amphitheater floor while fireworks burst overhead.

"That's tuft," Gemma murmured.

"They haven't been detained over the Anony intervention?" Luce asked.

"Nobody could find them after their stage disappeared with them on it," Allou said. "They usually vanish into the air but last night something new happened."

"Why do you think he took us to his house last night?" Luce asked. "Why did you and Sundrae come late, what were you doing?"

"Trying to clean up after that MESS!" Allou snapped. "Delegates were all over the place trying to find their transit cars, the dinner had to be canceled, all that food removed, the dais had to be dismantled, the special floaters had to be taken down." She looked around at them all. "It's a good thing Orwen left as fast as she did. Be thankful the Egg got you out of there. He was doing you a favor."

Gemma was dropped off first. Luce's flat was next. As they pulled in, she looked at Allou. "I don't know what's going on with you," she said. "But I hope it gets better. See you soon."

Allou nodded, barely looking at her. *Whiny because Dzuren Tso didn't take you home with him?* Luce wondered. *Don't be catty,* she told herself. The car door shut. Luce stood alone for a moment, breathing in the fresh air and thinking, *That was the strangest eighteen hours of my life. But Wofar was…*

She shuddered, feeling a hormonal surge. She wondered how he was faring with Sundrae. And if their encounter of the night before would be repeated.

Change of clothes, she told herself. She went into the building to her flat, where she disrobed and threw everything on the sleep platform. She pinged a short message to Wofar, asking if he got home all right. That seemed harmless yet showed concern. *Yes, yes, those sculptures were there last night. We all saw them. But now we didn't.* She sat down in her sole comfortable chair. *It's like we have to say what didn't happen or what we didn't see because nobody can deal with anything going off plan. Sundrae said she saved us from a wipe.*

She received no reply from Wofar.

She thought again about *Les Misérables.* How she had loved feeling the weight of the book in her hands, and the sensation of turning the pages. Nothing blinked at her, nothing glowed, nothing was on the page except the letters, the words, the page numbers. Simply words on paper you could touch, turn, fold if you wanted to.

I loved holding that book. It was real. Wofar was real. Even that naughty dog with its licky wet tongue: real. Not "didn't notice." Noticed. Real.

She forced herself to her closet and pulled out a new shirt, slacks, and scarf. After dressing she followed her usual self-decorating routine in the mirror. *Need more coffee,* she thought as she headed out the door.

CHAPTER 17

ESWEN HOUSE, OXFORDSHIRE,
ENGLAND, EARTH

Day Four, late morning into early evening, UTC+1

AFTER HER UNSETTLING comment about Fenn, Marina showed Editha to a spacious bedroom up a flight of stairs. She encouraged rest. "Sleep all you wish. Call if you need anything. We put some clothes in the closet for you."

Editha showered, washed her hair, and crawled into the bed. Exhaustion triumphed. She awoke disoriented. The sun was low in the western sky. She had to remind herself where she was, what it had taken to get here, who she was with. The harsh reality that Fenn was gone overcame her. She wept into the pillow for some time. Then she pulled herself to her feet, got a drink of water, and went to the closet. Simple clothes were hanging on the long rack—a couple of white shirts, a pair of black slacks, a black pencil skirt, a black sweater, underclothes, a pair of walking shoes her size. *How did they know my sizes?*

In the bathroom she found makeup. She tried to make herself presentable. The hours of sleep had helped. She looked a little less old and drained. She walked out into the hallway, down the stairs, and found her way to the kitchen of the chalet. There, Theone was working diligently on food preparation for supper.

"Did you sleep well, ma'am?" zhe asked.

"Thank you, I did," Editha answered. "Please call me Editha. I'm not special."

Theone smiled at her. "We believe you are very special," zhe said.

Editha smiled back. "Thank you for the clothes." She paused, then added, "May I help with the cooking?"

"Oh, no. But thank you. I suggest you join M'Rambert in the great room."

Editha followed the front hallway to find Marina pouring glasses of wine at the bar in the great room. She gazed out the tall front windows at the vista beyond the house. In her tiredness and confusion earlier, Editha had not absorbed the setting. Beyond the house was a long pond, beyond that pastureland and a low green ridge. A few small houses dotted the ridge.

"It looks like the Shire in *Lord of the Rings*," she observed.

Marina joined her, handing her a glass of red wine. "This region is said to have inspired that world," she commented. "Tolkien was an Oxford don for a long time. I never tire of it." She raised her glass. "To our dear Fenn," she said. Their glasses touched as their eyes met.

Marina gestured for them to sit on the sofa. "I trust you are feeling more rested," she said.

"Yes, thank you. Everything feels disorienting. But I do feel better."

Marina nodded. "I understand." She put down her wineglass. "I know I am a stranger to you. As you are to me, though I know more about you and the life you led with Fenn than you know about who I am or why I am here."

"I don't know anything," Editha said. *Well, not that much.* "He told me little things, childhood stories…beaches, village life, games he played with his friends." She was silent for a moment. "I guess you were one of those friends."

"He was younger, he played more with my brother. But yes. We were from the same village."

"I know he worked in a library, early in his career."

"Yes, he did his Global Service in our national library, the Library of Atlas. It is a beautiful and revered place for New Atlanteans."

"He loved research, he was so curious…" Editha put her wineglass down. "I had no idea that what he was doing was linked to something bigger. I thought he was alone here."

"Isolated, but not alone," Marina answered. "We do not meet in the same place at the same time without good reason. I only saw him three times after he was embedded on Earth."

"When?" Editha asked, surprised. She and Fenn were rarely apart after they'd met. Never for long, except for when he had gone back to New Atlantis with the baby.

"First when he arrived. I'd come a few years ahead of him. He began his work here at Eswen House, spending some time orienting. Then he traveled west where he found the interests…"—she smiled—"and the person who stayed with him always. It was here that he began writing what is known as the Loa Files. He's famous in certain quarters on The Planet, because of his writings about life on Earth."

"Loa," Editha said. "That is his clan name, isn't it?"

Marina nodded.

"Are you in his clan?"

Marina shook her head. "No. I belong to a different aristocratic clan. New Atlantis has many hierarchies. Fenn and I both came from great privilege. Each of us found our footing and our purpose on Earth. The Loa Files are essential to Earth Studies now."

What does she mean about aristocracy and privilege? Fenn never described his upbringing that way. He made it all sound innocent. Is our child an aristocrat of some kind now?

Editha knew Fenn wrote incessantly. It was one of the things they had in common. He wrote on his laptop; she preferred longhand in journals. His love of writing and documentation was one of the reasons she was so shocked when he demanded that she burn her journals. She knew he sent reports back to his home world.

"I had no idea what he was doing was…significant."

"Very."

"I have his laptop. He used that before he…you know, put anything in…the box."

"Do you know what happened to his Bluebox?" Marina asked.

Editha frowned, remembering how Fenn had woven the long, colorful threads into a vertical column and how, after his work with it was done, he made it all disappear. Seeing it had been a turning point in their long, pained discussions of what was to become of their child. He had given her a glimpse into the technology their child could grow up with on New Atlantis.

"I assume it burned up in the fire," she said.

"Unlikely. They are made of something that on Earth is indestructible."

Of course. Fenn had said he would throw it into the Bay. She asked, "Do the people on your planet know he died?"

"A few," Marina answered. "I reported it, as did our people on the West Coast in America." She paused.

Editha waited.

"You are mentioned."

Editha sat back, startled. She took a long drink of wine. "I don't understand. Fenn said I was not supposed to be in his life. He said he never told them about me, he said…" She sighed. "Not even…"

"I know we are in delicate territory for you," Marina said gently. "I know about your son. Fenn needed my help. Almost no one on The Planet knows of you, much less your child. It was a complex and private issue to resolve. You cannot know how extreme Fenn's sin was, in our world. Those of us who visit here, whether short or long term, are forbidden from forming personal or intimate relationships with people on Earth. We are prohibited from putting our DNA into circulation here. If we need companionship, it comes from The Planet. Fenn managed to keep you a secret. Reporters are not subject to the constant presence of beacons and monitors. They save that for the Travelers. But the child…" She shook her head.

"The child had to be brought back to New Atlantis, lest he grow up and bring his DNA into Earth's genetic makeup. Population controls at home are strict, built into the bedrock of our culture. No one has children without approval. When your son was born, Fenn was caught between the rock of our population control rules and the hard place of the prohibition against leaving our DNA on Earth. He knew he had to secrete the child to The Planet. It took enormous effort to resolve through back channels. Your resistance bought the time needed for a favorable resolution. Almost no one knows any of it now. The records aren't accessible. That Fenn had a wife on Earth would be shocking news were it to circulate on The Planet. That the two of you had a child together would be an earthquake in my world."

Tears welled in Editha's eyes. "Fenn knew all along that the baby would be sent away?"

Marina reached over and put her hand on Editha's. "It was the only possible outcome. Fenn wanted you to be part of the decision."

Editha was quiet for a long time, struggling with the inner avalanche of new information colliding with the hope rising in her heart. Then she asked, "Our son is alive?"

Marina smiled. "He grew up on The Planet, in a loving home." She poured more wine. "I know you want to hear more. Presently we must concentrate on what happened with Fenn. Will you tell me about your journey here?"

Editha wanted to focus on the boy. *But I'm in no position to demand anything.* She forced herself to describe the journey from San Francisco to Eswen House. She described finding Fenn's letter and realizing the danger extended to her. She told Marina about the NEXT message that had appeared on her phone, and abandoning it on the *Zephyr*, and of her journey from Salt Lake City to London. She spoke of her overwhelming grief. "And now…I'm here," she finished.

"You were right to listen to Fenn," Marina said. "He always told me he would point you here if the need arose."

"But why am I in danger?" Editha asked. "Why did they kill Fenn…whoever they are? What would they want with me?"

"I have only guesses and partial answers," Marina answered. "Fenn and I had believed for some time that things in our world are not right, things that flow outside the normal lines of operation, communication, galactic policy. We found irregularities. We believe some of our systems are failing. This is aside from our shared concern about…ethics, is as close as I can come. Ethics. Morality. Doing what is right in a right way. We have become too far removed from our own histories and the values we embraced centuries ago. The issues are accelerating. Though I hold some hope.

"It took Fenn years to see what I was seeing. The longer he stayed, the deeper his love and concern for Earth became. What we both realized was that The Planet was benefiting greatly, but Earth received nothing from us in return. For centuries we've been cultural scavengers, picking what appeals and taking what resonates. We accepted the noninterference policy; we told ourselves 'It is all harmless.' Yet we were witnessing so much disaster and violence. Though we have the resources to help, we've done nothing. Fenn came to hate that. He believed it was bad, cruel, irresponsible policy. So did I. So did some of the other Reporters."

"Others," Editha repeated. "How many of you are there here?"

"Not many. Six of us remain in contact now. No, five, without Fenn. Some who come here disappear, they blend in. Some go back and forth, some repatriate to The Planet. Those of us embedded for extended periods are the Reporters. We send our data to Researchers. They assemble the information and use it for varying purposes. Our Guild has another class of visitors, called Travelers. They visit other worlds temporarily, on specific assignments. We have limited technology embedded here to track our own. It focuses on the Travelers."

"How far back in time do you go with these Travelers and Reporters?" Editha asked.

"Centuries," Marina answered. "We came from Earth."

A shock of recognition shot through Editha. "Fenn told me we were both *Homo sapiens*. He said we evolved from the same basic materials, out of the sea. I assumed it happened on both planets, yours and mine."

"Scientifically, the odds of the exact same dominant species emerging on two different planets, however similar, are so small they cannot be measured."

Editha sat with this for a moment. "But…how did your people leave Earth?" she asked. "Why?"

Marina stood. "I will tell you our story over supper. Shall we go to the dining room?"

Over marinated red snapper, roasted brussels sprouts, and fingerling potatoes, Editha Lockyer heard at last the story that Fenn would never tell her in full. The sun set and the moon rose while Marina spoke. After the meal, they walked in silvery moonlight on a pathway behind the manor house, up a hill where the Milky Way twinkled in the sky. Marina pointed at the stars and said, "Do you see the top star in the Big Dipper? Think millions of miles beyond that and you are close to where we come from. We are on the other side of the Milky Way."

Then they sat in front of a firepit, logs burning, in a garden beside the swimming pool behind the house. Flames licked the stone edges, offering warmth against the evening chill. Editha was overwhelmed. The story was at the same time so fantastical and so moving.

"It is a lot for someone unaccustomed to it," Marina said. "But this is our planet of origin, if not our present home."

"It's like something out of mythology."

"So it is," Marina smiled. "Mythology is usually anchored in truth of some kind."

"Fenn wanted to stay here."

Marina nodded. "That has happened over the centuries, though it is banned in our statutes. It's called 'going rogue.' The Planet used to send Trackers to find and rehabilitate rogue Reporters, but that practice has diminished to nothing." She shook her head. "The Planet is off course. That is why we created a…" She stopped.

"Created what?" Editha asked.

"It is getting late," Marina said, rising from her chair. She looked up again at the stars, then leaned over and pulled a screen over the glowing firepit. She offered a hand, helping Editha stand. "Tomorrow, I will tell you more of what Fenn and I were doing."

Editha had hoped she would hear more about her son. Clearly, Marina was not going to reveal anything more. Not now. At least Editha knew he was alive. She followed Marina up the path and back into the house. At the top of the stairway, they wished each other "Good night." As Marina turned to go to her room, something occurred to Editha.

"I have a request," she said.

"Ask it," Marina replied.

"Might there be a pen available?" Editha asked. "I am not myself if I am not writing. Fenn and I were alike in that way." She started to tell Marina about the journals she had salvaged. Instead, she said, "A ballpoint pen is all I need."

Marina withdrew to a room on the other side of the staircase and returned in a few moments, a pen in hand. "It's not a ballpoint," she apologized.

Editha looked at it. *Montblanc.* She laughed, holding it up. "This will do."

"It is nice to hear you laugh," Marina replied. "Sleep well, my friend."

Editha went to her room, closed the door, and sank into the comfortable chair facing the window. She was tired again, but not ready for sleep. The moonlight was bright across the green valley. She reached into the rucksack and found the small notebook containing everything she'd written about Fenn's world. Going to the next blank page, she lifted her pen to the empty page and wrote down what she could remember.

Per Marina:

—Fifteen centuries ago, city-state of Atlantis—Plato's legendary Atlantis = real place, island near the mouth of the Mediterranean Sea.

—On verge of destruction.

—Later influenced how/what Plato wrote about it.

—Seafaring people with democratic governing system and king → oversaw their well-being. They believed king was chosen by the gods.

—Society was made up of family clans; aristocratic, others associated with specific trades. Hierarchical.

—Flourished for several centuries, lived largely disconnected from Mediterranean life. (xenophobic?)

—Pride in ships, knowledge of the seas, ability to farm island, peace and prosperity, culture.

"Hundred years crisis":

—Series of destructive storms and earthquakes, leaders realized island was sinking into the ocean. Fields flooded/ships sank/ fresh water became scarce/springs dried up/we could not feed our people.

—Existential crisis, needed to relocate our entire people, over twelve thousand, or stop the sinking and restore land. Rituals begging the gods for intervention, over the century.

—Researched possible places for relocation around the Mediterranean. Nothing suitable without bloodshed and taking the land of others.

—Could not justify.

—Leaders were in the process of plan to subdivide/disperse as a diaspora.

—Miracle: visitation that some believed was from the gods.

—Beings of superior species from another world landed on island in a great vessel that appeared at night/hovered over capital city.

—*Not humans though appeared to be. Met & learned plight, offered to help.*
—*"Star People" (SP).*
—*Decade of visits they helped organize and prepare for "Great Migration."*
—*SP found an Earthlike planet w/ moon like Earth's.*
—*They sent a series of ships to transport to new world, "New Atlantis."*
—*Brought seeds, plants, animals on vast starships.*
—*SP stayed a thousand years/gave technology, training.*
—*Advanced quickly.*
—*Once enabled, developed tools/knowledge to return to Earth (visitors).*
—*SP cautioned never to try to return permanently to Earth. Departed.*
—*No contact with them since. Dark ages.*
—*Eswen rose, oversaw reform.*

She stared at her notes. Then she turned the notebook upside down and opened it at the back, blank pages and lines before her. She considered the beautiful craftsmanship of the pen in her hand. *Upside down and backward. I don't know how I feel, what to make of what is happening, or who the Star People are or how, how any of what she told me is even possible. I miss Fenn. I miss Fenn, I miss Fenn. He couldn't trust me with all of it. And our son! Alive!*

She lifted her pen again and wrote "UPHEAVAL."

CHAPTER 18

ONCE ON THE ground in Los Angeles, Kaieda and Max rented a car. While both of them were augmented with knowledge on how to drive, Max took on the task of driving in L.A. traffic. They spent the rest of the evening dividing tasks and finding food and a hotel room so that Kaieda had a bed to sleep in. They found a tiny motel on 3rd Street, within walking distance of the apartment they had rented. To continue work without disturbing her, Max spent the night at their apartment, focused on clearing Bluebox strings and researching where to find furniture. The next morning when Kaieda returned on foot, he was already gone. She sat on the living room floor, using her mobile phone to review upcoming cultural events and begin devising her research plan. Sitting on the floor was annoying.

We should have rented a furnished place. Is Max already ordering chairs and a sofa? She scrolled through a listing of weekend events in the *Los Angeles Times*. *Why don't they make Reporters help with this part? The Culture Guild needs to rethink this protocol.*

Except…how reliable are the Reporters? "They leave," Freddie *had said.* The memory of those moments sitting by the water in San Francisco, watching the skaters and the pregnant lady with the poodle walk by, surged through her. All that LIFE.

She thought of Fenn. He had to have loved his Earth woman beyond all policies, rules, and strict taboos. A phero match
so powerful he could not resist. *Where has she gone?*

She put her phone down and, standing, stared into the
courtyard below the second-story apartment. Three thirty-foot
tall, leaf-laden ficus trees were lined in a row, surrounded by
closely trimmed green grass. The air was cool, the skies sunny.
She could see the "HOLLYWOOD" sign in the distant hills.
Except for occasional helicopter flyovers, it was a peaceful setting. Children shouted and laughed nearby. A door slammed.
A gray cat scampered across the courtyard, disappearing onto a
canvas-sheltered patio. A throb of wonder filled her chest, the
same wonder that had overcome her by the Bay in San Francisco.

*Urgency. Time is different here. They have daily conflict, they
live with it all the time. Every day. It's…their mortality? It…feeds
them? Motivates them? Fenn saw it. It's in the Loa Files, all those
descriptions of human encounters and collisions. He didn't focus on
the landscapes and geopolitical events. He wrote about people and
how they lived and related to one another and coped with life. And
with death. He was trying to show us something. Trying to remind
us of something?*

Notice. Notice. Just notice. Meaning comes later. Notice. It was
the bedrock of her training as a Traveler. Once she and Max
were established, she could pull up the Loa Files and reread
some entries. Max probably had all of it. *Gods only know what's
stored in him.*

She found Max comforting. She wasn't sure why. She hadn't
expected a synth partner this time. They'd only done that once
before. She smiled, thinking about Harlong. D'avi had a synth
too. *Did they send us all out on this mission with synths?* The
mission was orchestrated collaboratively among the Festival,

the Arts Guild, plus several branches of the Science Guild. After her last off-world assignment, she'd been at a weekend spa with Faerae when the call came from Egdar Roiboi, insisting she come to the Capital for an important meeting. Faerae had smelled a new assignment and tried to talk her out of it, encouraging a longer break. "Stay here," she had said. "You're thin and tired, you're not ready to go again yet."

Kaieda attended the meeting anyway. It caused Faerae to fume and return to Rimalon in one of her snits. Faerae was stubborn. Also, Kaieda admitted to herself, Faerae was usually right. They did not speak for days.

Roiboi had been persuasive in the meeting. With Sundrae's occasional clarifications, he'd described the intentions of Festival X/V and the necessity of research on contemporary Earth. It would buttress and inform their global staging plans. Reporter files from Earth weren't enough, didn't thoroughly cover the cultural ground.

"We must get this right," he'd told her. "It is the perfect moment in our history to look back, across, and ahead. We need your voice, Kaieda. I know you're just back from an assignment; it is asking a lot. Five Teams are already there. Another is landing today. We need you to lead a seventh. The People need your presence in this." She remembered thinking, *You need me to further legitimize this.*

He'd gone on to tell her that the Science Guild and the Travelers subguild had already signed off on her involvement, at his personal request. Then he'd encouraged her to talk to her Guild Chair, who would be able to tell her more about the assignment. "Just ask about it, find out what the tasks are," he'd said. "And ask about after."

"What do you mean, 'after'?" she had asked.

"After the work on Earth is done. I shouldn't say this but…"

He paused dramatically, glanced at Sundrae, then said, "Just talk with Janai Loa."

"She's not my Guild Chair," she'd said.

"I know, I know. But talk to her. Then hear what your Guild Chair has to offer."

Kaieda had left the meeting with a pounding heart. Roiboi had zero reason to tell her to talk with Janai Loa unless it had something to do with Alec. She'd gone to her flat in the Capital, pulled a few things together, and taken the next shuttle to Rimalon. Normally she would stay at Faerae's Keeper Colony flat, but that wasn't an option while they were feuding. She'd arranged a room at the Traveler training ward. Then she'd messaged the Science Lab and requested a meeting with the Director. Then she'd gone to The Blue Guitar, sat in a booth, and ordered a drink.

Now, standing in Los Angeles two weeks later, she wondered if she'd done the right thing. *They trigger my hope when they want something from me.* Janai Loa had not had any real news. Alec's biotank was still empty.

"I know it feels interminable," Janai Loa had said in that low, smooth voice. "But three related experiments are under way. We are making progress with two of them. When you return, we can review everything with you in detail."

"What do they involve?" Kaieda had asked. The lack of specifics maddened her.

"Alec's DNA," Janai answered. "Which, you see, is critical to the Consciousness Project and funnels into other initiatives."

"His DNA?" Kaieda had asked, incredulous. He'd never brought it up with her, beyond assuring her it was preserved. They had discussed it only in terms of possible children.

"We have permission to use it," Janai had replied. "While he is gone."

A day later, when Kaieda had seen the synthetic Allan9, the facsimile of Alec's physical appearance, she'd realized what at least one of the "related experiments" was. She was deeply shaken, also furious with all of them, including Alec. She'd considered walking away from the entire initiative in protest. Seeing her distress, Dzuren Tso had taken her to The Blue Guitar, poured drinks for her, and argued persuasively that going on the mission was the better choice.

"You need to be on this," he'd told her. "It's going to be a turning point. I know they're telling you they need you. The project needs you. They're dangling Alec. Ignore that—they don't know what is going to happen with him. What I'm telling you is, *you* need it."

"Why?" she had asked.

"Things are changing. We're at a bigger turning point than even they realize."

She'd stared at him. "What are you saying?"

He'd leaned closer. "The system…our entire system. It's cracking. You want to be on the right side of it when it falls open."

"I just want to do my work," she had said. She was too upset about Alec and the fecking Allan9 to consider a "cracking system," whatever that meant.

"Then DO it," he had said to her. "Go, Kaieda. For yourself."

"I hate all this mystery and irony. Roiboi does it, Janai Loa does it, now you're doing it. They've taken my mate's DNA and made a robot based on him!"

"The synths are all DNA-based now, that's the future of the project. They didn't use Alec's DNA with the Allan9. It's just a visual replication."

She knew he'd seen her pain at that.

"I'm sorry. It's part of a deal between Roiboi and…"

"D'avi."

Dzuren had tossed back another shot. "This is what I'm telling you. They're making mistakes, they're overstepping. It's going to blow up. Go to Earth. You'll be better off there."

"You sound like I'll stay forever."

"You may want to," he'd answered. "If you go, you'll understand."

She remembered thinking, *Of course…he's been there.* Now she wondered what aspects of life on Earth had made him say that. *But I do understand now. This place summons us.*

She had gone back to her little room that night and lay awake, drunk and thinking about the conversation, about Alec and the Allan9, about the fight with Faerae. In the middle of that long night, she'd gotten up and walked the long passageway to the Keeper Colony resident flats. She reached Faerae's door, but rather than knock, she'd dictated a message she knew Faerae would see when she got up. It said, "Going for a long walk." Then Kaieda had walked back to her room, picked up the few items she'd brought, and gone to the shuttle platform to return to The Planet. She'd spent the early hours at her Capital flat, then taken an interplanetary shuttle to Arcana. Their house by the sea was the only place left where she truly sensed Alec's presence.

Was Dzuren telling me to get away before something big happened? Nothing big ever happens there. It's just…life on The Planet. Nothing unusual was mentioned in the Bluebox strings. Max had sent the message about arriving in Los Angeles. *I hope it wasn't too cryptic. I hope Faerae picks up about the comm links. She and Dzuren need to see that bounce to Venus. What will they make of Fenn's death?*

They had not checked the Bluebox this morning. It would take longer without Max's speed at activating everything, but she needed to look at messages. She glanced around the emp-ty apartment. *What's another day without furniture?* She pulled the Bluebox off the floor and placed it on the kitchen count-er. With little effort, though certainly not at Max's pace, she got the column humming. Numerous strings awaited. She saw Faerae's blue thread and opened it first: ON IT, it said. *Good, she understood.* She saw messages from Dzuren, from Roiboi, from Mog Weller, from the Guild Chair. The Guild Chair? An SMS message ding came from her phone. *Probably Max.* She looked at it and caught her breath.

DAWN. CALL ME. IN SHOCK.

Kaieda frowned. *Dawn? That blond girl who took us to the airport? Shock? How had she gotten this number? D'avi had it…*

She directed her phone to call back. Dawn picked up imme-diately. She was crying.

Max came in the front door.

"It's Kaieda," she said to Dawn. She put the phone on speaker.

"D'avi…" Dawn sobbed. "D'avi is in the hospital, they don't think he's going to make it. Freddie just called and told me. He's there. He's devastated. He told me to call you."

"What!" Kaieda cried. "What happened, what's wrong with him?"

"He was stabbed this morning!" Dawn sobbed. "I'm on my way now. Police are all over their house."

Kaieda leaned against the wall, nearly dropping the phone.

Max took the phone from her, touching her arm lightly. "Dawn, let us know what you can find out. Tell Freddie to call us. Tell him we'll come."

"Okay," Dawn's voice choked. The phone went silent.

Kaieda found her breath. "What do we do?"

"Stabbed," Max said. "That is how Fenn Loa was killed, with a shiv."

"D'avi is still alive. He might survive. We need to talk to Freddie," Kaieda said. She reached for the phone to call.

Max stopped her, holding the phone away. "Wait."

"Someone is attacking our people, Max! Freddie could be next."

"Freddie knows," Max said. "Freddie also knows he is very hard to kill." He set her phone on the counter next to the Bluebox. It was still humming with the column of colored threads. "Let him call us. Without more information, you could be walking into danger. I can't allow that."

"You can't allow…" Kaieda said, feeling her temper rise. She stopped herself. *He's going to protect me. Like Harlong did.* This was the great gift and also the limitation of the synths. They were programmed to protect human life. Their wiring prevented them from reprogramming themselves. They could learn and adapt, but they could not alter their hardwired programming. Only qualified and approved humans from the Robotics subguild could do that. No wonder Freddie was beside himself. He was custom built for D'avi. *What happened?*

"Can you access any police records to find out what they know?" she asked Max. "Freddie must have been out of the house when it happened."

Max nodded. He was working the strings on the Bluebox column. The wires were rising and twisting and disappearing into his ears. Kaieda had not seen him do that before.

"It's faster this way," he said. "Not very pretty to watch, though." His head tilted once, then twice. "Faerae sent a two-word reply to us on the—"

"I know," Kaieda interrupted. "I saw it. She got the message."

"Several messages from Dzuren. Events on the surface have made the Capital…" He frowned. "Problematic. An event last night at the Amphitheater. The Reporter based in England confirmed Fenn Loa's death. Roiboi is asking if you have established your cultural research plan."

"Wait," Kaieda said. "Someone else confirmed Fenn Loa?"

"Yes, the Reporter in England."

"Who is that?"

Max's head tilted. "Listed as Marina Rambert. She is clan Roiboi."

"Roiboi!" Kaieda repeated. "Yes. Of course. I read some of her files during Traveler training. They're not like Fenn's reports, she's more of an academic."

"Embedded for many years, longer than Fenn Loa. Active in Europe. Studies languages, ancient histories, comparative religion. Frequent communications with The Planet. Returns on a regular basis, then comes back to Earth."

"That's where she's gone!" Kaieda exclaimed.

"Who?"

"Fenn Loa's wife. It's the only way Marina Rambert… Roiboi… would know to confirm Fenn's death. Whatever happened, Fenn's wife knew to go to another Reporter."

Max nodded slowly. "Likely correct." He refocused on the column.

"Max," Kaieda said. He was sorting threads. A silver one surged into his index finger and his eyes closed. His head tilted, then jerked slightly backward for an instant. It was as if he was watching something behind his eyelids. *Silver threads are top priority.*

"Max?" Kaieda said again.

"Wait," he said. He stood for several minutes in silence, the thread still connected to his finger. Kaieda waited. He had never done anything like this before. At times his eyes seemed to flutter or move under the lids. He looked pained. His eyes opened suddenly.

"D'avi is going to die," he said. "We must leave." His hand gripped the countertop corner as, with the other, he shut the Bluebox column down. "He cannot survive his injuries. Freddie will call soon."

She watched as he connected back into the column again, his finger merging with a purple thread. That was Dzuren's thread. Max was sending him a message.

"Are you telling him about D'avi? Shouldn't that go to the Science Guild Chair, or to the Travelers Director?"

Max then did something that startled her. He shook the strings from his hand, then took her by the arms, looking into her face. *Even Harlong never did anything like this. How nuanced is this synth? Oh gods, poor D'avi. Poor Freddie.* As always, Max's hands were warm. Human. Familiar.

"We need to go to Marina Roiboi's location," he told her. "Immediately." He looked around the kitchen, and into the living room. "Did you order anything for this place?"

"Not yet."

"Good." He released her. "I'll cancel the car. We should be able to get a flight out tonight."

Things just keep going wrong. Oh D'avi…

The phone rang. The number was D'avi's, which meant it was Freddie or Dawn.

"Yes?" she said, putting it again on speaker.

An incoherent sob came from the phone. "It's Freddie…I've lost him…D'avi is gone…" The sobbing wrenched Kaieda's heart. She heard Dawn's muffled voice trying to comfort him and the sounds of a hospital intercom paging someone.

"Freddie, Freddie," she said. "What happened? Are you at the hospital?"

"Yes," Freddie wept. "I found him in our house, I'd gone out to get us some donuts…" He groaned, then shouted, "I left for goddamn donuts!" Dawn was trying to shush him. "I was made to protect him," he said, his voice breaking.

"Freddie," Max said. "You need to get out of there."

"Freddie, are police there?" Kaieda asked. "Do they know what happened?"

The phone clattered; apparently Freddie had dropped it. Dawn got on the line. "He's distraught," she said, her voice shaking. "Police don't know exactly what happened, it was in the kitchen. He was knifed. They think it might have been an intruder or someone D'avi knew and let in…but nobody left anything, nobody took anything…Freddie found him…" More background noise and voices ensued. "I have to get him out of here."

The call dropped.

Kaieda stood immobile, trying to absorb what was happening. The mission had now gone awry for two Teams, at terrible cost to one of them. Two New Atlanteans were dead. Freddie's fate was uncertain. Whoever knew about Fenn and D'avi would know about D'avi's partner. *HOW?*

She stared at Max. "Shouldn't we go back to San Francisco to help Freddie?" *Get him. Bring him to England with us. Protect him from whatever the threat is. Call Fetchers and send him home.* She suddenly didn't care that he replicated Alec in appearance. He needed to be out of harm's way. He was a valuable asset to the program and the Science Guild. They couldn't abandon him. *Unbelievable, unbelievable.* "We have to help him," she said again. But then she remembered Max's words. Freddie was very hard to kill. "Did you hear him? He was crying."

"Robotics is experimenting with a lot of human behaviors," Max replied, placing the Bluebox in his backpack.

"Did you ask Dzuren to send Fetchers for him?" she asked.

"No. That decision must be made on Rimalon. Dzuren is now aware of the situation. Kaieda. Please. We must leave."

"Do you cry?"

"Not so far." He dropped the backpack on the floor and said, "You saw the silver thread in the column, didn't you?"

She nodded.

"That was from D'avi, earlier this morning. It is a visual recording. I believe he recorded most of what happened in that house."

"Show it to me."

"It is evidence," he answered.

"Good gods, is it a message saying who attacked him?" she asked.

"No. But it appears to show what happened. D'avi programmed his recordings to generate into his Bluebox every morning, then auto-forward to The Planet. But the excerpt that came to you was sent only to Janai Loa on Rimalon."

"Janai Loa?" That made no sense. D'avi had no dealings with the Experimental Wing of the Science Guild.

"She oversees all programs tied to building new synthetics," Max stated. He paused, then said, "I advise against watching the recording until we are with M'Roiboi." He paused again. "I believe Freddie will make his way to England. He won't need our help. He will know to come."

"Show me the recording," Kaieda insisted.

Max tried to dissuade her. She prevailed. He lowered the shades in the empty apartment. Then he projected onto the living room wall, in a bright beam streaming from his eyes, the recording that D'avi, in his last act, had forwarded to them on the silver thread.

CHAPTER 19

"IT'S JUST OVER that ridge," Vaylor told them, pointing toward a hill a kilometer ahead.

Faerae, Dzuren, and Vaylor were on a narrow canyon road halfway between the Festival Warehouse they had just visited and the Eflos village, called Kemmi. They were surrounded by low, sandy foothills covered with brush grasses and gnarly trees laden with tiny dark-green leaves. *Semi-desert,* thought Faerae, *not seaside and not the Great Mountains of Eswen, just… funny little hills with live oaks and boulders. That's what Kaieda would see.* She and Dzuren were a few steps behind as Vaylor led the way toward his family seat. She could not see anything that looked like a village ahead but trudged on, because: *No choice, really.*

Their unannounced inspection of the Festival Warehouse yielded nothing. She was hot in her uniform. *Waste of time.* Dzuren seemed satisfied for having made the trip. He looked authoritative in his military blues. Vaylor suggested—*or was it asked, or was it insisted*—that they go four kilometers east, so that he could greet his people in the village where he was born.

"Easy to get back for transport," he assured them.

Dzuren agreed to the visit, saying the walk would do them some good given all the time they spent indoors, in the dark, on Rimalon.

Aimed at me.

She could not get adjusted to all the light. She owned a pair of darkglass eye shields but had failed to grab them on leaving. It was rattling enough to get into full uniform for the first time in…how long?…to meet Dzuren and Vaylor at the shuttle platform. They'd ridden down in blissful silence except for Dzuren's annoying banter with guards when they transferred through the Bubble. The security team overseeing entries was the same duo that had passed them through the night before. They were amused at seeing all three of them in uniform.

"Powder blues today? No medals?" one of them asked as Dzuren led the way through the wrist chip reader.

"I shined them up just for you last night," Dzuren had answered. "They're still on the whites."

"Shame. They give you that extra *je ne sais quoi.*"

"Always need that."

Faerae had no use for such flirtation, though she was coming to see how Dzuren used it. *His way of deflecting attention.* He had a gift for steering focus, turning on charm, redirecting subject matter. *I think about him as our Engineering leader, but he's so much more. He just doesn't let on.* Then she realized something else. *He wants, intends, to be underestimated.* People had fawned over him the previous night. She remembered the exchange with Allou as they'd fled the Amphitheater. *She'd listen to his stories. Go home with him. Do…whatever. Ugh.*

Her mind wandered across Dzuren's many stories about interstellar travel she'd heard in drinking sessions at The Blue Guitar. He never spoke of the space skirmishes he'd been in or the piracy interventions or the Barx Encounters that had distinguished his military career before he was assigned to the Keeper Colony. He talked about other intelligent species and what they looked like and how they lived, he told stories from

Traveler friends about their various discoveries and mishaps on other planets, he talked about books he had read and events he'd attended and what was or wasn't interesting about them…but he didn't speak of battles or space flight or the circles of people he knew, nor Planetary politics, nor…Faerae frowned. *Earth. He never talks about Earth. Has he been there?* She reviewed their exchanges since Kaieda and Max had landed. Something was different. He'd given her the NTK Earth Reporter location list. He'd taken her to The Interstitials. He'd introduced her to Janai Loa. After the "artist intervention," he'd gotten them out of the Capital swiftly. He later declared it "revolution." Now he had her on a pointless excursion on The Planet, plus an even more pointless visit to an Eflos village.

What is he up to?

"Hello! Hello?" she heard him say. Vaylor, despite his shorter stride, was still well ahead of them. "I hope those boots are working for you. Mine are giving me blisters. I haven't worn this outdoor pair in too long. Maybe my feet have gotten bigger."

"Mine are fine," she replied. Her uniform boots were comfortable. She wore them often on Rimalon, even if the rest of the uniform stayed on a hanger.

"Good. What to make of what we saw at the Warehouse?" he asked. "Or didn't?"

Faerae shrugged. "Deliveries, things moving around, nothing unusual," she answered. "We don't know what we're looking for. There were those sculptures, but that appeared routine. Everything was stamped. No Fetchers."

Dzuren nodded. "And nothing scheduled for delivery in the next two days. Doesn't add up. Vaylor did a complete search of their comm records. Those mystery signals were landing nearby, but it's not in their logs."

"They were received somewhere," Vaylor called behind him.

"They are not flying around in the ether." He stopped, waiting for them to catch up. Faerae didn't doubt he had climbed this hill many times.

They were close to the top of the ridge. Looking back in the direction they'd come from, Faerae saw the storage facility in the distance, loading docks active. Dzuren looked back too.

"Is there anything in those foothills next to the Warehouse?" he asked.

"Owned by the Government," Vaylor answered, resuming his walk. "Tens of thousands of acres. The Kemmi Wildlands. Designated permanently as park land. People go there for wildlife and outdoor experiences. There's a waterfall dropping into a lake in a valley on the far side of that first ridge. Lots of canyons. Quite pretty. But too rugged for housing, even for us."

They crested the hill. Below lay a village of around two dozen small dwellings and several other structures. The houses were clustered in circles of four, centrally organized, with the outbuildings creating a second circle around the settlement. Trees were scattered throughout, offering shade. Just beyond the last structures, a river curved in a bow shape, the center of the bow closest to the village. Small sail and oar boats were coming and going on the waterway.

Vaylor nodded at the scene. "Welcome to Kemmi."

They began their walk down the hill.

"This is one of the early settlements, isn't it?" Dzuren asked.

Vaylor nodded. "The first of what is now nine scattered up and down the Yawl. Soon there will be ten. We keep growing." He put his forefinger to his lips. "Shhhhh."

Faerae was hesitant, and yet curious, about visiting an Eflos settlement. *We're not supposed to be here. This isn't for Sapiens.* Looking into the village, she saw how small everything was. And things were just…missing. No lines of floating vehicles, no people robed and gliding about with their tablets in hand or personal comms beeping and pinging, no large houses and plazas and buildings buzzing with activity, no moats or bridges or monuments. The settlement wasn't arranged in concentric circles in the manner of Sapien cities and towns. Instead, the homes were organized in soft four-hut clusters scattered along the riverside. Small people working, small children playing, life proceeding without visible support systems beyond carts and outdoor tubs and small wooden houses. The people here seemed fine with it. Interacting. Laughing with one another. Going about life.

"Different from the Capital," she said aloud.

"Or anywhere else you can go on The Planet," Dzuren said. "Except other Eflos settlements."

"Deliberately so," Vaylor replied. They were nearing the outer perimeter of the village. "I want you to meet someone," he said. "I'll take you to him. I need to say hello to my mother. She lives over there." He pointed at one of the houses ahead. "If she's free, she'll give you a tour."

He led them to the isolated wooden building closest to the river and gestured at the low door. "In here."

Dzuren and Faerae waited.

"Why are we doing this?" Faerae asked, as Vaylor disappeared into the building.

"Because he asked," Dzuren answered. He lowered his head and entered. They both had to stoop as they went through a foyer. Vaylor knocked on the door before them.

"It's open," came a voice from beyond the door ahead.

Vaylor opened it, saying, "I present our village leader, Mumno a'Kemmi."

Faerae saw an Eflos male sitting at a desk, a 3-D screen featuring a map in front of him. *First or second generation?* He rose, came around the desk, and offered the back of his hand to Dzuren. "Captain Tso," he said. They touched knuckles lightly and bowed to each other.

"And Commander C'iez," he said, offering his hand again. "An honor."

Flummoxed, Faerae gave a return bow. *Just do whatever Dzuren does.*

"We have Sapien-scale chairs here," he said, gesturing at three chairs shoved by a wall across the room. "Not that we have many visitors of your kind."

Dzuren and Faerae sat, Dzuren saying, "Thank you."

"I'll go and see her now," Vaylor said, excusing himself.

The Eflos sat across from them in a fitted chair. "I am Mumno. Contrary to what Vaylor told you, I'm not really the village leader. That would be his mother. May I offer you tea? Water? You had a bit of a walk from the Warehouse."

"Tell us about the Warehouse," Dzuren said. "And thank you, nothing for me."

"I am fine," Faerae said, adding, "thank you."

"Well enough," Mumno said. "Yes, the Warehouse. I have questions for you. But I will answer that first. That Warehouse is decades old. It was expanded recently. Increased capacity for artifacts related to Festival X/V. We see things coming and going. After the expansion—after, mind you—we had a visit from the Warehouse manager. She was, shall we say, unforthcoming but friendly. She reassured us they would stay on their side of the ridge. I cannot tell you what they do there beyond holding and moving art objects, including items obtained on off-world missions."

Faerae noticed Dzuren tense and sit up.

"How do we know that, you may ask," the Eflos continued. Dzuren nodded.

"We see Retrievers come and go, at all times of the day," Mumno answered. "Once in a while, very late at night, we see them." He shrugged. "The deliveries and pickups seem to be happening more often now. One could wonder why." He paused, waiting for them to react. Faerae had no idea what to say. Dzuren, if he had anything to say, wasn't saying it.

"So, that is what I can tell you about the Warehouse," Mumno resumed. "Now for my questions." He waved at the map that was still floating over his desk, pulling it to the space where they sat. "We are here, in Kemmi." He pointed at the small settlement next to the bow curve in the Yawl. He traced his finger along the river to the point, much further south, where it emptied into the Raja Sea. "All along this river are the Eflosi settlements. The land was granted to us by the Government as part of the agreement to allow us to flourish and build our own identity and culture independent of the cultures of The People."

"Right," Dzuren said.

"As you can see, we are making choices that allow us to operate without the scale of technology that informs *Homo sapiens* life on The Planet. Of course we do have technology." He indicated the map hologram. "But our technology doesn't engage with primary Planet interfacing. We are, it could be said, much more on the ground. We are not heard by the Government. Some see us as a threat. But we try to participate where we feel we can. Sometimes our infrastructure is not enough."

"What is your question?" Dzuren asked.

"Yes, yes, I do need to get to the point, don't I?" Mumno took in a breath. He looked at Faerae. "The truth is, we need your tracking skills for living beings. And access you have to satellite beams and tracings."

"Someone is missing?" Faerae asked.

To her shock, Dzuren said, "The Interstitials."

Mumno nodded. "The Interstitials."

Dzuren exhaled. "I was afraid something would go wrong with that exit."

"They never reached the rendezvous point. We expected them to surface late last night. But…nothing," Mumno said. "No one."

"We need to find them," said Dzuren. He looked at Faerae.

Faerae stared at them both. "The musicians?" she asked.

Dzuren's hand came down on her arm. "Keep calm," he said to her. "They need help. The Eflosi and The Interstitials need your help."

"What does one have to do with the other?" She pulled her arm away. "We came down here for the Warehouse inspection!"

"Vaylor knew things I did not."

Faerae stared at him. "About WHAT?" She flushed, realizing she'd just spoken inappropriately to her superior.

"You need more information," Mumno said.

"I certainly do!" Faerae snapped.

"I had hoped you would be more sympathetic to the situation," Mumno murmured.

"Which is what? Besides rebellious musicians you can't find?"

"Let me back up," Mumno said. "It is a bit complicated. They're foregrounding Anony's questions. The message is reverberating among The People. Especially young adults."

"Yes, I know," Faerae answered.

"Right. What I think perhaps you don't yet understand is that Anony is not a person. It is a collective. A collective of *Homo sapiens*, as well as most Eflosi. We believe that, as a world, we are losing our way. We believe the stakes are high. Intervention is needed. Yet helping our Earth cousins is prohibited by

Government policy. They are my cousins too, you know. The Science Lab created our first cohort by filling in chromosomal gaps with Sapien DNA. Earth is our planet of origin too."

Faerae nodded. The gap-filling was one of the many controversies over the revival of the Floresiens. It complicated how—whether—to view them as Planetary residents and citizens.

"The Anony collective is not informed solely by supporters on The Planet. Anony's messages come from Earth. They are sent to The Planet. Sympathetic friends here move them into public circulation."

The comment hit Faerae in the head. Things fell into place. *The eight encrypted messages from Earth. The messages the House found. Fenn Loa's messages, sent to England. Messages the House is still trying to decode.* "Fenn Loa," she said. "Marina Roiboi."

Mumno glanced at Dzuren, who nodded. "They have been on Earth for decades. They know the situation better than anyone. They also know the slow pace of change here. They've uncovered flaws in our system. They understand the urgency." He waited a moment. "The movement here is growing. It will lead to change."

Faerae turned to Dzuren. "You're part of this? You're the 'source' on Rimalon they refer to?"

Dzuren sighed. "It isn't just Earth Policy I'm concerned about. It's...everything. The complacency, the silos, the undercurrent of greed. We're making mistakes with them"—he nodded toward Mumno—"and we're making mistakes with ourselves. We all have enough, we live well, so we avoid facing it. Anony is disrupting the status quo." He shook his head. "I've seen too much pain in the galaxy to rest on the ease of life here. We are oblivious to everything but ourselves."

"The Eflosi, as a species determined to be self-sufficient, are anything but numb," Mumno added. "Our life is full but not always easy. We make mistakes, we don't operate in silos, we fall and learn to get up again. We don't allow cameras and monitors and beacons here. We walk freely on our land. Our women bear our children. And we are a true democracy. No Continuity, no hierarchical clans or hardened Guilds. The Anony movement is growing. In part because of the endorsement of the most famous and beloved band on The Planet. Never let it be said that artists do not matter! Commander, we need your help. We cannot trace The Interstitials or assist in their situation, whatever it may be, without the technology and expertise you have. Not even he"—he nodded at Dzuren—"is as gifted as you are when it comes to tracing and tracking humans."

"Why can't Vaylor do it?" she asked.

"Vaylor tracks comms," Dzuren answered. "You are our best at finding people."

Mumno said, "We owe the band that much. They are all-in with the Anony project, and we told them we would help with their exit. We aren't sure if they are lost, or in trouble, or being held somewhere. Vaylor saw the opportunity to bring you here. We had nothing to lose in asking for your help, Commander. Please. Help us find them."

What are they trying to get me into?

"Who else is involved in this 'movement' that I would know?" Faerae asked.

"NTK," Dzuren answered. "For your own protection, not just theirs."

"Please, Commander," Mumno pleaded. "The stakes are higher than people realize. The band does not deserve to be punished or disappeared for their views."

Disappeared?

"I need some air," she said, feeling claustrophobic.

"Let's take a walk," Dzuren said to her. To Mumno: "Vaylor will let you know."

"Thank you, thank you both," Mumno said, seeing them as far as the outer door. He smiled and waved at them before pulling the door shut.

Dzuren led Faerae to the river's edge and guided her to sit on a log. "Not the trip you were expecting," he said. "Until Mumno said it, I didn't know the band was missing. Vaylor would have told me eventually. The Eflosi take their assignments seriously." He paused, then added, "I won't command you to help. Nor will I get in the way if you do."

They watched the river, boats floating by. Faerae was trying to process what she had just heard and how to respond. *Find clarity. Get heartbeat to slow down. Need an equation. He is trusting me with this. Who else is in on it?*

The life of the village proceeded around them.

"They're not impressed with us," Dzuren observed.

"I don't know what the right thing to do is," she finally said.

"It's finding some people."

"Finding some people who are probably wanted by the Government for...what? Insurrection?" she blurted.

"Maybe..." he answered. "But remember. Mostly the Government wants 'never mind.' It's part of the problem. It should not just go away. VoG runs things on the ticker and then...it fades away. We shrug, eat our dinners, and go on with our lives. We forget. They want us to forget."

"You work for 'them,'" she said. "You're part of the system."

"That is true. I have done many things for 'them' for a long time. I have seen more than most. Which is why I believe now is the time to support change."

Faerae stared at the boats on the river. Fishing boats, a small barge, a trio of canoes with pairs of what looked like Eflos teens out on a boat trip. Their laughter carried across the water. They were paddling imperfectly but with enthusiasm. A group of tween children played in the water at the river's edge. *A world within my world. Sapiens don't come here. We don't like discomfort. The Eflosi decided to live and reproduce and find their own way. Now they are trying to help make the larger world…different? Better?* She shook her head. *What is the price of helping them? What if I—or we—get caught? But who would catch us? Attention isn't focused on watching for the unusual, only for the usual. Complacency.*

Kaieda. Is she part of this? Kaieda still on Earth, still in California, still with the Maximus5700. *They're onto something strange.* But it didn't have anything to do with Anony. Or did it? Fetchers were involved somehow. And that Venus bounce. The Twins had traced an unidentified comm relay through Venus. *Venus. Anony. Fetchers. The Interstitials. Fenn Loa dead. Fenn Loa's mystery Earth wife. Marina Roiboi…?* Faerae had wondered earlier if Marina Roiboi was helping her brother move Earth artifacts to The Planet. Now she rejected that theory. Marina Roiboi was involved in getting the Anony messages to The Planet.

What is the Fetcher problem?

What am I missing?

She thought her head was going to explode, triggered by all the parts that still didn't fit together.

"Something definitely isn't right," she said.

"A lot of things aren't right," he agreed.

She stared at the river a while longer. *Do you want to spend the rest of your life on Rimalon suffering over Kaieda and tracking Travelers and dreaming about flying? Is that all there is? What about Janai Loa's beautiful eyes and luscious voice? Others exist. What about these small people, forced back into existence, now at-*

tempting to forge a way of life that isn't The Planet's? What about the band members who disappeared into the ground? Don't they have a right to emerge and exist and spread their views as well as their music? Isn't Anony right to ask questions? To shake the world? To wake us up?

How do you, Faerae C'iez, make a difference?

She took a deep breath. "I'll do it," she said to Dzuren. "I'll find them."

CHAPTER 20

WHEN LUCE ARRIVED at the Festival office, it was as if nothing had happened. Given the events of the night before and the fact that the most she'd do was a half-day's work, wide black trousers and a long blush shirt seemed defensible attire. Wofar's desk was empty. Sundrae was in, her door closed. Allou was at her desk, talking to her screen.

"No. No. Oh good. No," she was saying to herself, flipping names off a list she was scrolling. She glanced up briefly. "Hi Luce." She returned to her list. "Uh, no. Yes. Yes. Oh great! No. No. Absolutely not."

"What's the list?" Luce asked, settling into her seat.

"Next reception," Allou answered. She lowered her voice. "The Egg asked me to shave the guest list 'more rigorously.'" She imitated Roiboi's voice, then switched back to her own. "He wants more Delegates and Directors and Chairs, not their surrogates. He wants it to match the attendance last night but…" Here she shifted back into his voice. "With real people and without all the drama!" She waved her hands, imitating him. She leaned toward Luce. "And ALL Tri's."

"What was that, last night?" Luce asked. "I feel like I had a bizarre dream." Then she thought about Wofar. *If that was a dream, it was good as well as strange.* "Do you know why we end-ed up at their house? And how those sculptures disappeared?"

"What sculptures?" Allou asked, returning her attention to her list.

"The ones we didn't notice," Luce sighed.

"The collection shifts around," Allou answered. "No. No. Oh gods, no. But you, yes. Bring your mate." She was flipping through more names on the screen. She looked at Luce again. "Things go to the Warehouse. Commissions, acquisitions, Fetcher deliveries…stuff."

Luce knew of the Festival Warehouse. She'd never been there. It housed objects as well as a library of physical and digital research documents. "Have you ever been there?" she asked.

"Once," Allou answered, still focused on her screen. "It's overwhelming. Enormous maze of spaces. Can't imagine working there." She spoke again briefly to her screen and then added, "Wofar's been there a lot lately. Helping Caspar with something, I think."

"It has a library?"

"Never saw that. All the records probably end up at the Library of Atlas."

Luce had loved doing her Global Service at the Library of Atlas in the Capital. It held THE comprehensive collection of books, digital archives, ancient documents, and knowledge on The Planet. It also housed an entire "Earth Wing." The Atlas was full of rooms where you had to wear gloves to turn real pages, state-of-the-art writing and research stations, tempera-ture-controlled storage rooms, access to all the open-source research in the sciences and in literature, the humanities, in-tragalactic histories, interactive pods for experiential learning… it had seemed bottomless to her. She was still discovering its sheer scope when her two-year Global Service term finished.

"I love that place," she sighed.

"Aiming for the Library subguild?" Allou murmured.

"That's exactly what I want," Luce told her.

"Hah, so we're just a stepping-stone?" Allou asked, no longer focused on her list.

"No, no," Luce said. "I wanted this assignment! I thought I might eventually transfer to the Festival library and then…who knows?"

"Stepping-stone," Allou summarized, returning to her list.

Luce groaned and opened her calendar, reviewed messages, sorted through the assignment list, glanced over the ticker. Nothing from Wofar. Interstitials still missing. Stock market up. That had to make the Egg happy. *Oh gods, I'm calling him the Egg now. Stop. Don't.* It was already too late. *At least only in my head.*

What Allou had said caused her alarm bells to stop ringing. It seemed odd to Luce that Roiboi would move sculptures in the middle of the night, but apparently it wasn't unusual. The Warehouse explained a lot. *It's just about moving Festival inventory. No big deal.*

The work assignment at the top of her list required sorting out the Director's schedule in relation to upcoming receptions and internal division meetings. She sat in on such meetings, taking notes for Roiboi. Mostly they covered idea presentations from the curatorial and staging teams. The meetings became exciting when they slid into brainstorming about live arts engagements in multiple locations incorporating interactive feedback loops among communities.

"Everyone will end up dancing virtually and on-site," Roiboi had commented. "With whomever they like, no matter where they are on The Planet. How do we make something like that happen with visual arts?"

Luce thought Roiboi was at his best and most inspirational in those meetings. He wasn't faking anything, or trying to charm anyone, and he wasn't fuming over the markets. With his team, he was envisioning the specifics of how they'd realize their global project.

The Director's schedule was an ever-shifting puzzle. Luce had to factor in Sundrae's appointments and travel schedule, Roiboi's peripatetic lifestyle, already-determined event dates, and the scheduling they all had to work around with Guild meetings, the General Assembly calendar, and the schedule of feedback and reporting loops coming in from the Travelers. She pulled up the Traveler filing lists to see what was coming in. Teams One, Two, Three, Four, and Six were working and filing on schedule. Team Five was filing at a faster, more frequent rate. Near-daily reports were coming in, all signed off by D'avi S'Iloa. She pulled up his most recent notes, filed the previous day. The report described, in vivid detail, a two-night event called a rave. She read enough to see it was participatory. Then she started to read one lurid passage and realized that much happened at raves. She closed the file but made a mental note to start reading whatever D'avi S'Iloa filed from now on.

"Have you seen Wofar?" she asked Allou, trying to sound casual.

"No."

Roiboi emerged from his office and said, "Luciena." He was calm.

"Sir?"

"Have you been to our Warehouse?"

"No, sir. Allou and I were just talking about it."

"Uh-huh," he said, looking at Allou. "You've been there?"

"Once, sir," she answered. "Short visit."

"I see." He turned to Luce. "There's an object there that I

need here. Nobody is available to bring it right now. Someone needs to go get it. I don't trust the delivery drones for this. It's small. You can take a transit car and bring it back to me. Now."

Now I'm an errand girl? "I'll be delayed in securing the schedule you asked for," Luce said with caution.

"You'll get that done," he said crisply. "When you get there, ask for Caspar, he's supervising a different project on-site. He'll give you the box." He looked her up and down. "You're dressed for an out-of-town assignment today."

Luce curdled. Her gamble to come casual had just backfired.

"Get the box from Caspar," he repeated. He went back into his office and shut the door.

"So observant," Allou hummed.

Luce moaned. "I put on my best clothes and end up chasing his dog. I come in dressed down and he sends me to the outer reach."

"Oh, it's not the outer reach. It's just a warehouse in the hills outside Kemmi."

"Kemmi?" Luce said.

"An Eflosi village on the River Yawl. Next to the Kemmi Wildlands."

"Oh!" Luce exclaimed. "I've never been to an Eflosi settlement!"

"You won't this time either, it's a few kilometers away. A foothill ridge separates the village and the Warehouse."

Luce stood, gathering her bag. *I'd like to see it. I've read about the little people. Haven't seen many. Certainly not where they live.* She dropped her tablet into her bag, thinking she'd need something to read on the transit car.

"Tell Caspar I have questionables on my list. He'll need to weigh in."

"Will do."

She was soon on the plaza awaiting the assigned car and thinking about "Creepy Caspar" as some called him. Caspar Weller was Roiboi's…what? Bodyguard, right-hand man, ever-present companion? His skin was ghostly pale, his body thin and wiry, his head hairless. He always wore a draping white jacket and billowy white pants. Some on the Festival staff believed he was an unidentified synthetic. The law allowed Directors and above to make a case for them. Others on the staff thought Caspar was just a weird, ageless, asexual guy whose devotion to Roiboi was legendary. He'd been at the Director's side since before anyone could remember.

The transit car arrived. She settled in. As the car skimmed the air leaving the Capital, she reflected on the night before. Wofar. That gonadic energy stirred up her bones and skin and blood. Her hormones were surging. She forced herself to leave those thoughts.

This job is so much more than I bargained for. Now she had to retrieve something—gods knew what—for the Egg, from a storage facility in the middle of nowhere, a time zone away. It would be easy enough for Caspar or just about anyone to bring it. *What's the urgency? We're an arts festival, not the Space Force.* Not to mention the drone-and-pipe system all over the Capital. Whatever it was could be moved that way. She wondered where Wofar was. *Did I screw up? Or am I just not enough? Wofar is ahead of me on the rise curve. He's on a Curator or maybe even a Traveler path. I'm nobody. I chase dogs and pick up boxes. But holding that book last night made me want the library sciences even more. Gods, that was good with him last night…*

She spent some time imagining how the next encounter might go. She had to shake it off.

He still hadn't responded to her message.

She watched the landscape change. The lush greens, bridges,

manicured grounds, and balanced architectural signature of homes and buildings on the southern edge of the Capital gave way to open plains and dry brush. Then came low hills that looked like an old dog's bony haunches. She knew from travels between her family seat in the Farm Country and the Capital that oases were always characterized by green and the presence of water. Long before Eswen, while the Star People were still there, the settlers had found The Planet's underground springs and aquifers. They'd established clusters of residents in those locations and focused on developing flourishing green communities. That principle hadn't changed over the centuries. Nor had the policy to refrain from building villages where water was not abundant.

Luce thought about the endless volume of rules and structures and institutions. *Guilds, career glide paths, delegations and service rotations and interstellar peacekeeping through research and diplomacy with other worlds…keeping everything siloed except through Guild negotiations. The Festival intersects with so many different initiatives.* She sighed. The vision of the letters dripping golden sparkle at The Interstitials concert filled her mind. *No wonder Anony is raising questions. Anony focuses on the Earth policies. Does it stop there?* Something about the artist intervention, and the chaos afterward among the Delegates and leadership, impressed her more than she'd realized. *I need to reread the Anony statements again. All of them.*

After another twenty minutes, the transit car slowed. The host voice said, "Warehouse destination on approach, sixty seconds. Kindly exit left promptly onto the platform. The Warehouse Gateway will be to your right."

The doors swooshed open. She stepped off the car and into bright, hot sunlight. She looked to her right to see an entry gate twenty meters ahead. Before her stood a structure eight or nine stories tall, with clusters of windows in places, and blank walls made of shiny surface material in others. It was, she guessed, five city blocks wide. "Wow," she said aloud. She saw several concrete platforms adjacent to the Warehouse. Enormous, closed entry doors were at each platform location. *Fetcher landing points. This is where they bring…whatever they bring from other worlds.* Beyond that she saw regular loading docks. She had taken a course in industrial engineering during her university training. *The inside must be…complex.* Allou had called it a maze.

She approached the gate, to be greeted by a pair of Guardian synths in the tan uniforms of the Global Peace Patrol. "Welcome. Wrist chip, please," one of them said to her. She offered her wrist, he read the chip with his handheld device and nodded. The other said, "Proceed down walkway. Caspar awaits."

She entered a narrow, dark, and airless tunnel. It sloped downward, far enough that she believed she had reached the same level as the Fetcher platforms she had seen. Caspar was ahead, standing where the tunnel opened into the Warehouse. He looked, as always, solemn.

"Hello, Caspar," she said.

"Luciena."

He calls me what the Egg calls me. Which is what my mum calls me when she is disappointed. She saw someone climbing a flight of stairs from below and was surprised to see Wofar join them.

"Hi, Luce," he said. No smile, no indication he was glad to see her or had gotten her message. *He looks unhappy.*

"Do you have the Director's package?" she asked.

"Follow me," Caspar answered, leading her into the Warehouse.

They went through an empty hangar on the other side of the Fetcher platform.

"How long?" Caspar asked Wofar as they walked.

"Forty minutes," Wofar answered. "Assuming they clear the Bubble."

"They will. Very good," Caspar responded. They went through a door, down a flight of stairs, and into what looked like a vast storage area full of bins, shelves, cages of various sizes, containers large and small. Many of the bins were packed with heavy boxes. Down one of the rows she saw a door with a sign, "Traveler Archives." Under it in smaller lettering was "Authorized Entry Only."

Luce slowed down to look around. "This is all Festival inventory?" she asked.

"Pretty much," Wofar said.

"Other than some Researchers' archives," Caspar added, picking up the pace. He gestured toward another door. "Please, this way."

They entered a room where several people were working. At the end of the room, on a table, sat a thickly wrapped box. Caspar walked to it. "This," he said, "is for the Director. It is a bit heavy, but nothing you cannot manage. I can provide a carrier bag if you wish."

Luce leaned over the table and reached to lift it.

Caspar looked alarmed.

"I just want to see how heavy it is," she said.

"Yes, yes, of course."

She lifted it and said, "I can handle this just fine." *It's wrapped to survive a nuke.*

"Very well. The transit car will take you back to the Festival office," Caspar said. "You are to personally deliver this to Director Roiboi. You are not to place it anywhere out of your sight for any reason. Is that clear?"

She glared at him. His condescension was unnecessary. "Yes, Caspar. Very clear."

"It is important that Director Roiboi receive it immediately," he said.

"He will."

Caspar's tablet pinged. He took the call, stepping away. Luce heard him say, "Yes, she is here…yes, yes…she'll be on her way shortly…"

Wofar turned his back to Caspar and quickly, quietly said to Luce, "Don't give it to the Egg. Give it to Sundrae."

Luce looked at him wide-eyed. "What?" she whispered, leaning toward him. His fingers lightly squeezed her forearm.

"You heard me," he whispered back, stepping away. Caspar returned. Wofar's tablet pinged. He listened for a moment, then said to Caspar, "Thirty-five minutes."

Caspar nodded. He picked up the package. "Luciena, get this to the Capital."

He led them back out through the office, up the stairs, through the storage area, and back to the exit beyond the interior hangar. Then he handed her the package.

"Come, Wofar," he said, turning to walk back into the Warehouse.

Luce looked at Wofar helplessly. He mouthed *Sundrae* and left her standing there, confounded. She looked at the package and then at the tunnel sloping upward, toward the exit and the transit car platform. *Give it to Sundrae? But it's supposed to go to Roiboi! What IS this thing? A relic of some kind? Or, or…is it… radioactive? Or, or is this some kind of competition between Sundrae's team and the Director's?*

She walked slowly up the tunnel toward the exit gate, her

imagination running wild. Wofar had given her no reason to believe that whatever was in the package was a danger. But he had gone way over the line by instructing her to deliver it to someone other than the person who outranked said person AND who'd sent her on this mission in the first place. What was Wofar doing here anyway, and what was the "thirty-five minutes" thing? She stopped midway up the tunnel and leaned against the flimsy wall for a moment. *The correct thing to do is exit, get in the transit car, take this to the Egg, and return to my desk. That's my "should." But what is my "ought?" Who do I trust more, Wofar or Caspar and the Egg? What is in this box?*

She resumed her walk. The Guardian synths still were on duty. She lifted her wrist for checkout. "Luciena Shoko proceeding out," one said, nodding at his fellow. The gate rose. She walked back into the hot sunlight. The transit car still hovered on the platform. To her surprise, three other people were standing there. They were all in blue Space Force uniforms. Two of them looked familiar. The third was an Eflos.

CHAPTER 21

FAERAE WANTED TO sit longer by the river, watching Eflosi children splashing in the water. She found listening to their laughter soothing. *Innocent.* But she'd said yes. Dzuren was on his feet immediately. Now he was all about getting back to Rimalon and access to the sophisticated search bots and best global tracing technology available.

"Let's find Vaylor and get back to the Warehouse for transit," he said, scanning the river.

"He's over there." She pointed at one of the little houses in the inner circle of the village. "Where he said his mother lives."

"Okay, let's pay our respects." Dzuren offered her a hand for rising.

She stood up, eschewing his help. They walked to the house. Dzuren knocked. Moments later, the door opened. A female Eflos stood before them, looking up. She was, by Faerae's estimation, just under five feet tall. She wore a long purple dress. Her braided hair was in strands of brown and white.

"Ah," she said, looking Dzuren up and down. "The boss."

Dzuren frowned, then said, "I suspect I'm talking to the boss."

She rolled her eyes. "You're welcome in, but you may be more comfortable out."

Vaylor appeared beside his mother.

"Madam, much as we would love to join you, we are here to collect your son," Dzuren said. "We need to return to the Capital."

"This is Kemmi, of Kemmi." Vaylor made the introduction.

"Kemmi of Kemmi!" Dzuren repeated. "Named for your town?"

"The town is named for her," Vaylor said, stepping out of the house and taking his mother's elbow to nudge her out as well.

Whoa.

"Oh!" said Dzuren. He took Kemmi's hand and kissed it. "I'm honored, Kemmi of Kemmi."

She smiled up at him. "Someone had to make this place," she said. "Our first generation were given limited choices. I found and proposed this location. They weren't in a position to deny us at that point."

Dzuren nodded.

"I would like to give you a tour of our village," she offered. "Show you we have done with what we were given."

"No one knows this place like she does," Vaylor added.

"I believe it," Dzuren said. "But we have urgent business to deal with. Might we return soon for a tour?" He looked to Vaylor. "We need to get back to the transit car platform."

"I have a floating carriage," Kemmi said. "I'll take you to the Warehouse. We'll have a little more time to chat. You'll get there faster. Some of your Sapien technology is useful."

Dzuren accepted her offer. Kemmi excused herself and disappeared behind the house. While they waited, Dzuren and Vaylor sat on low, boxlike seats on the exterior stoop at the front door. Dzuren reported the conversation with Mumno and Faerae's agreement to help. Vaylor gave her a nod. Faerae remained standing, looking around the village and wondering what Kaieda would make of it. Some of the difference was the scale of things, but something else was present that Faerae found harder to identify: a calm yet industrious energy.

Kemmi reappeared, sitting at the helm of what to Faerae looked like a rowboat floating two feet off the ground, clearly scaled for Eflosi. She and Dzuren clambered into the back, observed with amusement by several villagers.

"If I ever had any dignity, I just kissed it good-bye," Dzuren muttered as he loaded himself into the wobbling vehicle. Faerae was settled but uncentered. Between her nerves about the upcoming search and the ridiculousness of their seating, she giggled. Then Dzuren laughed. Soon all of them were laughing as the airboat floated past the Eflosi, also laughing and waving. They proceeded at low speed up the hill toward the ridge that separated Kemmi from the Warehouse.

As they floated forward, Kemmi pointed out the vegetable and flower gardens on the hills. She described how trees facilitated water flow after early residents had found a natural spring at the foot of the ridge. "We are for the most part self-sufficient. It's satisfying not to have to ask the Government for much. We take their technologies, of course. But only if they support our health and way of life."

Over the ridgeline, they glided down the narrow roadway. Golden hills rose around them. Kemmi paused the airboat briefly to tell them about the hiking trails, wildlife, birds and other creatures, waterfalls and natural swimming pools, and the occasional visitors who came and went in the Kemmi Wildlands.

"They don't come near our village, of course," she explained. "The Government property stops just short of this ridge. We are more likely to run into them here than to see any of them on our land. We take our children to the pool below the waterfall to teach them how to swim. The river current can be too much for our young until they are confident with it."

Faerae watched Dzuren as he listened to Kemmi's commentary. He was nodding, absorbing the information. The sun was still hot. Faerae wanted to shift her weight slightly. The floor of the airboat was uneven and eating into her thigh, but fear of flipping over the entire vehicle required keeping still.

"And there, those hills just next to the Warehouse?" Kemmi was saying, pointing. "Tunnels. Lots of them."

Dzuren squinted at the hills. "Oh?"

"We know the tunnels well," she replied, resuming the drive toward the Warehouse. "Some of them are recently reinforced. We're most concerned with the ones that spill into our land. We use them for growing fungi and channeling some of our water. Between their side and ours, it's dangerous."

"They're connected? How do you know the Wildlands tunnels are reinforced?"

As they approached the Warehouse, Kemmi answered, "It's a massive network. We think they were built during the occupation of the Star People. Decades ago, we tried to secure details from the Government but were turned away. So we mapped them on our own. Two years ago, they opened some of the entry points and carried in reinforced metals and flexible walls." She looked at Dzuren as she flipped controls to stop the airboat. "We avoid Sapien business. We do have to protect our own interests. I'm sure you understand."

"Indeed," he replied.

They were stopped. Faerae was afraid to move.

"Any suggestions about how to exit without tipping over?" Dzuren asked.

Kemmi chuckled and nodded at Vaylor, who flipped with ease out of his seat beside her to the ground and offered a hand to Faerae. She took it and lifted herself off the floor of the carriage, pushing over the edge and dropping to the ground. With Vaylor's assist, she managed to land on both feet. Dzuren, taller and heavier, rocked the airboat violently but managed to roll out, landing on his knees with a groan.

He pulled himself to his feet and bowed to Kemmi. "Thank you for the ride. And for the introduction to Kemmi."

"I do not say this to all Sapien visitors, Captain Tso, but you are welcome to return any time," she answered. "As are you, Commander C'iez." She nodded at Faerae, then winked at her son. Turning the carriage around, she accelerated and drove toward the ridge.

"A transit car," Vaylor said, looking ahead. He started toward the platform.

"Those hills are your first search target," Dzuren said to Faerae as they followed. "Tunnels could explain why the Venus bounce signal disappears near the Warehouse."

She nodded. "But what is the relationship between the tunnels, the signal from Venus, and The Interstitials?"

"Maybe none. But the Festival is right here."

Faerae nodded again. "Government."

"Exactly," he agreed, as they climbed up the stone walkway to the platform.

They approached the transit car to find the doors shut.

"This won't help us a bit," Vaylor said, staring at the shut door. He pressed against the door. Nothing happened.

Faerae was already thinking about how to optimize the tracing search. She contemplated which tracking lines would best penetrate the hillsides absent drones or lasers. *The House might be able to help, plus the heat signature tracing programs…wonder if we can access maps of the tunnels? Kemmi said something about maps. Vaylor must know.*

Dzuren groaned after leaning into the door with no response.

"I can ask the Gate synths what the problem is," Vaylor offered.

"Think they'll know? They're Gate synths," Dzuren replied.

Coming toward them was a handsome young woman with long black hair. She wore dark trousers and a pale-pink shirt. She carried a wrapped box. Faerae squinted. *Familiar. But from where?* Then Faerae remembered. This was one of those girls who had been chasing Maeve Ep's dog around at the reception before The Interstitials performance. *What's her name…?*

"Ah, Luciena Shoko," Dzuren said as the young woman reached them.

Of course he remembers her name.

The girl started. After a pause, she recognized Dzuren. "Captain Tso!" she exclaimed. "Luce. I go by Luce."

"You remember Commander Faerae C'iez, my guest at the reception?"

Luce blushed, embarrassed. She nodded to Faerae. "Allou to the rescue," she said.

"Allou, yes," Dzuren repeated. "She did get things sorted for us." He nodded at Vaylor. "This is Vaylor a'Kemmi, another of our Trackers at the Command Room on Rimalon."

Vaylor bowed slightly. "Pleasure, M'Shoko," he said.

Faerae noticed Luce shifting the weight of the box she was carrying. Partly to be helpful and partly to signal she held no ill will about the reception snafu, she asked, reaching, "Can I help you with that? It looks heavy."

Luce took a step back, holding the box to her chest. "Uhm, no," she said. "Thank you! No. I'm…" She patted the box with one hand. "I'm fine with it."

Faerae stepped back. *Well, you're welcome. I tried.*

"We need to return to the Capital. Any idea why the transit car doors aren't opening?" Dzuren asked.

Luce walked to the doors. They opened instantly. "Huh," she said. "I think it must be programmed specifically for me. I was sent by Director Roiboi."

"Might we catch a ride back with you?" Dzuren asked.

"Of course," she answered, entering the car and sitting down. She placed the box on the seat beside her, putting her closest hand on it.

Dzuren, Faerae, and Vaylor all boarded and sat in a row facing Luce. The car shuddered slightly, the vibration shivering in the soles of Faerae's feet. As they pulled away, a transport ship dropped into view above the largest of the delivery platforms. It sank slowly to the ground.

"Big delivery," Vaylor observed. "They don't use that platform often."

Dzuren watched as the car moved. He frowned. "That's a Fetcher ship."

Faerae stared at Luce. *So young. Sometimes I think I ought to like other people but then I think that's just what everyone else thinks and not what I think. F-ap100%=P' and I don't know what I'm getting myself into and can we just get back to Rimalon and I'll find those musicians and maybe there's something new from Kaieda. Need to hear from Kaieda.*

Nobody said anything for a while. The car hummed toward the Capital. Faerae watched Dzuren gazing at the hills. *What is he thinking?* She looked at the sky and wondered what flying low over those hills would feel like. She could hear Kaieda's voice in her head: *If you want to fly and not just trace and track forever, you need to focus more on people. No matter how good you are, you can't just ignore and avoid the people who make decisions about promotions and transfers and just do your brilliant tracing and tell yourself somebody is going to see your work and say, "Oh, she should be in one of the fly cells!" Nobody even KNOWS you want to pilot. You need to say it. You need a network. You need champions.*

"No, I do not," she muttered aloud, staring out the window at the golden hills flying by. *What I need is to get the full pilot training rather than sitting at a screen all the time.*

"What?" Luce asked.

"Don't worry about her, sometimes she thinks out loud," Vaylor said. "Often in numbers."

Faerae looked at him, annoyed. *Yeah, so? You talk to yourself all the time. When you're not clacking to your twin.*

"What's that?" Vaylor asked, nodding at the box under Luce's hand.

Luciena looked at the box, then at Vaylor. "I have no idea," she answered. "It's a delivery for Director Roiboi."

Dzuren leaned in a little. "Must be important. Sending staff when drone transits are available."

Luce shrugged, but her hand stayed on the box. "He's particular," she said.

"Do you like working at the Festival?" Dzuren asked.

"Mostly," she answered. "I've been there a month. The team there is tuft. My counterpart, Allou, has saved my life, she's the best. She knows everybody. She's beautiful and funny and—"

Dzuren nodded, interrupting. "What's it like, working for Roiboi?"

"He's…well, you know. Very smart. Kind of…volatile?" She stopped.

"I've seen that side of him," Dzuren said. "He was not happy last night."

"Anony has made his life miserable for months now. It's so critical of the Festival and such a disruption to what he's trying to do with X/V. Makes things hard on all of us."

"You don't agree with Anony," Dzuren said.

Luce shifted in her seat, looking uncomfortable.

Stop putting her on the spot, she's a kid working for a crazy person, thought Faerae.

"A lot of younger people find the message compelling," Dzuren said.

"I don't know anything about Anony, other than the headache it causes. For all of us."

Vaylor pulled out his tablet to check the ticker. "Well, look at that!" he said as Luce finished her sentence. "Mog Weller just reported The Interstitials have gone missing."

Dzuren groaned.

"Missing!" Luce repeated. "They willfully disappeared at the end of their performance last night. Allou saw them vanish under the stage. She said that's what they do."

"They haven't resurfaced since, according to Weller," Vaylor said, tapping his tablet. He looked at Dzuren. "It's out there now."

"Oh!" Luce exclaimed. "Are you looking for them, is that why you're out here?" She pulled the box onto her lap. "Why would they be here?"

"We were on an inspection at the Warehouse," Dzuren answered. "And we went to visit the Eflos village."

Luce glanced at Vaylor and then said, "You think they have them?"

"No, no," Dzuren said. "The Eflosi have nothing to do with their disappearance."

Not going to help to have someone on Roiboi's staff know we were out there, Faerae thought. *She'll tell them all she ran into us as soon as she gets to her office.* "They're searching for the band, officers from Rimalon! Why would the Government be looking for them like that?" *Not good. Not good for me, if I'm the one doing the real search.*

Dzuren crossed his legs and asked Luce, "Have you ever been to Rimalon?"

Uh-oh.

"Of course not!" Luce sputtered. "I don't have security clearances and why would I go there? It's all Engineers and Scientists and Robotics and Military. Nothing to do with me."

"You could visit with an invitation," Dzuren said smoothly. "Come as my guest. It's an interesting place. See our moon and the Keeper Colony."

Luciena stared at him for a moment, as if she were trying to figure out what to say. "Maybe someday."

"Today would be good," he said back, uncrossing his legs.

Luce's eyes widened. She took a deep breath. "I appreciate the invitation, Captain, but I have to get this to the Director." She patted the box. "Another day? And maybe I could bring Allou? I know she'd LOVE to see the Keeper Colony."

"I'd like to show it to you. Today." He nodded at the box. "That can wait. It's just an old artifact, right?"

"I don't know what it is. All I know is the Director wants it right away." Her voice drifted off, then she added, "He wants it right now. Whatever it is." Her hand tensed on the box.

Faerae could see the girl was trying to figure out what to do. She could also see that Dzuren was heading off any interference with their search for the band. *He needs the Eflosi to get to them before anybody else does.* She glanced at Vaylor, who nodded at her. Then she wondered if this was some version of kidnapping, and if she'd be an accessory. Then she wondered if Kaieda would visit her in the brig.

They swept through the outskirts of the Capital, minutes from the transit platform. Dzuren stood up cheerily. "Come, come," he said. "There's a shuttle to Rimalon in a few minutes. We want that one."

Vaylor, Faerae, and Luce all rose, standing with him at the door. The car slowed gradually to a stop. The door opened. Allou was standing on the platform. As they exited the car, she greeted Luce before she saw the others.

"Oh, thank gods, Luce, the Egg has been impos—oh! Captain Tso!" she exclaimed. She also noticed Faerae and Vaylor but stayed focused on Dzuren.

"Hello, Allou," he said, smiling at her. He took her hand and kissed it. "Sorry for the hasty departure last night."

"Oh my," she squeaked.

Luce stepped forward and said, "I have to get this upstairs but…"

"What would you think of a tour of the Keeper Colony?" Dzuren asked Allou.

"A what?"

"We just invited Luce. I'd like you to come too," Dzuren said.

"Oh my, but…"

Dzuren waved his hand dismissively. "Your Director will get his box," he said. "Come with us. A shuttle to the Colony will land in just a few minutes. What's a couple of hours?"

"Now?" Allou asked, her eyes never leaving Dzuren's. "The Keeper Colony?"

"No time like the present." Dzuren smiled at her, keeping her hand in his.

Mighty fecking green gods. Faerae tried not to roll her eyes.

"Uhm, okay…?" Allou said weakly, following as he led her in the direction of the shuttle platform.

"I'm going to get into SO much trouble…" Luce said quietly

to Faerae. "But for her," she nodded toward Allou. "I'll do it. She wants to…" She nodded at Dzuren. "She likes him."

Yuuuuuuck. So did not need to hear that.

Faerae looked at the box Luce was still carrying. "Are you sure you don't want help with that?"

"Very sure," Luce answered. She looked around at the plaza and back at Faerae, asking, "Is there a library on Rimalon?"

CHAPTER 22

THE GATEWAY AND RIMALON,
MOON OF NEW ATLANTIS

Day Four, late afternoon, NAT-0

Ⅰn the bubble-bound shuttle, Faerae constructed a Dzuren equation in her head. *Dz+n= pi or maybe just infinity.* Despite hesitations from both young women, he'd managed to nudge, charm, and persuade Allou to come to Rimalon for a tour. She tried to insist they drop off the delivery first, but Dzuren's hand on her back, while saying, "But we'll miss the next shuttle!" turned her. Luce, reluctant, had agreed to come along.

What will he do with them once we get there? Not my problem, going straight to the CCR to find those musicians. NOT going to think about what could happen if anybody intervenes. Let that be his problem too. Although he is less likely to be thrown in the brig than I am.

Faerae groaned. Vaylor heard it. Their eyes met.

You're going to get them, Faerae mouthed to him, nodding toward Allou and Luce. He frowned and shook his head, then nodded toward Dzuren, who was keeping the two entertained with stories about rock formations and dry seabeds on Rimalon as they flew.

Faerae leaned toward Vaylor, saying, sotto voce, "Need the tunnel maps. Can you or Mynar get me trace signatures as soon as we get up there? For all six of…" She stopped as Luce looked over at her.

"How's the ride so far?" Faerae asked.

The box was still in Luce's lap. Dzuren was still talking cheerfully to Allou.

"Fine," she answered. "I just…" She held the box up slightly. "Director Roiboi is very anxious to receive it."

"Do you know what it is?" Dzuren asked Allou. He nodded at Luce's box.

"Uhm, I think it's from Earth," Allou answered. "Recently. From Earth."

"How do you know that?" Luce asked.

"I overheard him talking to Caspar," Allou said. "Something about…" She paused. "It was right after you left."

"About what?" Dzuren asked, casually sliding his arm onto the top of the seat behind her.

"Uh, something about a big delivery and some object that, and I quote, 'will make things so much easier once it's in our hands.'"

The shuttle was approaching the Bubble.

"I've never done this before," Luce said, watching as they docked. Her anxiety was rising. "Gone through the Bubble, I mean."

"Me either," said Allou, with less apprehension.

"Nothing to it," Dzuren assured them. "Just let them read your chip and answer any questions you get honestly. We'll be through in no time."

"They question us?" Luce asked, alarmed.

"It's just protocol," Dzuren said. "No weapons, right?"

"Not that I know of."

The shuttle docked. They walked through the exit tube to a

landing. Things were quiet. Dzuren led them to the Guardian station, beyond which they could see the platform for the outer-orbit shuttle that would take them to Rimalon. Faerae and Vaylor brought up the rear.

The security team was a synth and a human. Unlike the chatty pair that had seen them out that morning, these two were all business. The synth took Dzuren's chip reading and nodded him through. Dzuren took a few steps forward and saluted the human officer who would open the gate for them to proceed.

"Greetings, Captain Tso," the Guardian said. "How was your trip to The Planet?"

"Short," Dzuren answered. "I'm escorting two guests; file them as visitors on my watch. Allou Owea. Luciena Shoko." He looked back and gestured for Allou to proceed to the synth. Then he looked back at the officer. "Anything else?" he asked.

"No, sir, proceed," the officer said.

Allou offered her wrist to the synth, who read her embedded chip and nodded.

"Welcome to The Planetary Gateway, ma'am," the exit officer said as she approached him. "Please wear this pass at all times while you are on Rimalon." He handed her a small, rounded card that he indicated should be clipped to her sleeve.

Allou accepted it, but rather than clipping it to her sleeve, she slapped it onto the back of her pants.

"Ye gods," Faerae heard Vaylor mutter.

Saucy. She might get her wish with Dzuren.

Luce moved forward to the synth. He took her reading and nodded for her to continue to the exit Guardian. Once she reached him, he said, "Welcome to The Planetary Gateway, Luciena Shoko. Contents?" He looked at the box she was holding.

Luce panicked. "It's a delivery?" she squeaked. She looked to Dzuren for help.

He said nothing.

"A delivery," the officer repeated. "Of what and for whom?" He leaned across his desk, looking more closely.

"Uh, it's for Director Roiboi at the Festival," she explained, her voice rising to a higher pitch. "It was on The Planet, I got it from the Warehouse…"

"But you expect to take it to Rimalon," the officer stated, looking put out. "When Director Roiboi is on The Planet."

She gulped. "Temporarily," she said. "I just have it temporarily."

Faerae looked at Dzuren. *He knew they'd do this.*

"M'Shoko, you are aware that this station and the Keeper Colony are the two highest-security facilities in our entire global system? Excepting the mansion of Orwen, of course."

Luce looked again to Dzuren for help. Then she said to the officer, "I…I…it's just a…I can always go back…"

Now Dzuren stepped in. "I have a suggestion," he said.

The officer turned to him. "Sir?"

"She is my guest. I understand the problem with the box. Why don't you secure it here and let me take these ladies on the tour I promised them? She can retrieve it when she leaves."

"What does 'secure it' mean?" Luce asked.

"It'll go into a leaded cage for transport out there." The officer nodded at a distant platform hovering in black space. "Can't stay on the station, unless you want a long wait for inspection." He glanced at Dzuren.

"Oh gods," Luce said under her breath. "I should just go back to The Planet and give it to the Director rather than such fuss…"

"No fuss," Dzuren said. "Just an abundance of caution." He

nodded to the officer, who reached across the desk and pulled the box away from Luce. "You can collect it when you go back to The Planet."

"They'll give it back to me?"

"Yes, yes, of course," the officer said, handing the box to the synth, who carried it through a nearby door and out of sight. He waved them on. "Enjoy your visit to Rimalon."

Dzuren guided everyone toward the shuttle platform. Luce was near tears.

Dzuren said, "It'll be fine."

"I'm going to get sacked…" Luce muttered to Allou.

Faerae shrugged it off and refocused on the search ahead. With luck, Mynar was already working the trace lines. She pondered how to devise cross vectors running from the Capital to the Kemmi Wildlands. *What was the routing? Was it ALL underground? Really need maps of those tunnels. The Twins have to deliver.*

She heard Allou say to Luce, "Don't worry, the Egg won't kill you. He'll have Caspar do that. Let's have fun up here while we can. How many people ever get to Rimalon?"

Several other personnel, all lab technicians in white coats, arrived. The Rimalon shuttle pulled in. Everyone boarded. Dzuren made small talk with one of the lab people. Luce and Allou stared out the window at the blackness and distant stars.

They've never been in space before. Welcome to the galaxy. Faerae overheard bits of the low-voiced conversation Dzuren was having. Something new had happened in one of the labs, thus a cluster of Planet-based Scientists was ascending. Then she heard "Consciousness Project" and "Ta'ava." She froze in her seat. *Is Alec back? Or have they confirmed he's gone forever? Is this one more nothing from the Researchers who hover and fuss over his empty biotube? Have they contacted Kaieda?* She caught Dzuren's eye. He gave away nothing. *Feck.*

The young women were pointing here and there as they approached Rimalon, commenting on the barren, rocky moonscape and the extensive network of aboveground tunnels and interconnected buildings and hangars that made up the Keeper Colony. The shuttle settled onto the platform. Dzuren herded his guests through. "Don't open any doors," he told them as they walked through the entry tunnel.

Vaylor led the way toward the transit rail tunnel. He pointed out various passageways as they walked, saying "…and that's called the Blind Deck. It leads to the living quarters and our bar and eatery, The Blue Guitar…"

The Science Lab technicians took a turn and disappeared in a different direction.

Dzuren dropped back to talk with Faerae. "Get to the CCR. Start the search," he said. "You know where to look. Ping me if you find anything."

"Isn't Mynar already on it?"

"I haven't relayed any information up here. Don't know who is listening."

"What's the fuss in the Science Lab?"

He hesitated before saying, "They've found something."

Faerae stopped walking. So did he. "You don't get to say that and then not tell me the rest," she said. "The last time that happened it was…mush."

"This isn't mush."

Faerae's heart jumped. They resumed walking.

"I want to talk to Janai before I say more," he said.

"But Alec…is alive?"

He stopped again. So did she.

"We need to find those performers. And then we need to find out what's in that box we just left at the Bubble."

"It's not a bomb," Faerae said.

"How do we know?"

They resumed walking to the transit car ahead. The others had already boarded.

"So," Dzuren said to everyone, "Commander C'iez and Lieutenant V. a'Kemmi are going to the Central Command Room while we"—he gestured at Luce, Allou, and himself—"take a walk on the Blind Deck. I'll show you the overlay of the Colony and the indoor gardens…might take you to the front door of the Experimental Wing too, if there's time. We might see The Planet rise. Beautiful sight." He looked at Luce. "Did I hear you ask about a library?"

She nodded.

"We'll stop there too. Library and KC research center."

"Gods, we're really getting a tour of the Keeper Colony!" Allou exclaimed.

"Did you think we were going to throw you into dark rooms and interrogate you?" Dzuren laughed.

"I didn't know!" Allou laughed back.

Faerae turned her head and rolled her eyes. Luce was staring out the window. *She's pretty. Not the mature beauty of Janai Loa, just…young, pure. That black hair. Velvety skin.*

The car whisked them forward and stopped at the CCR. Faerae and Vaylor stepped off.

"I think he likes Allou," Vaylor said as they entered the Command Room.

"He likes everybody," Faerae retorted.

She went to her station and sat, gesturing at the holographic screen. A few people were present, all deep in tasks.

"Hello, NIKI," she said to her screen. The Science Guild's

search engine was named for an acronym: **N**ew **I**nformation **K**nowledge **I**mport. Faerae never personalized it, any more than she'd named the house artificial intelligence in her flat. That was just "House."

"Welcome back, Faerae," came the answer. "Are we tracing today?"

"Affirmative," Faerae said, entering a code into the keyboard.

Vaylor was setting up at his station a few feet away. Mynar was beside him. They were absorbed in a 3-D map before them.

Faerae directed, "Install any maps you have access to, of those tunnels. And find DNA or other biosignature samples for"—she lowered her voice—"The Interstitials band members. I'll open the satellite and drone tracks to see if there are heat signatures in the hills."

Vaylor gave Mynar an overview of what had transpired in the last several hours as well as the targets of their search. She heard Mynar giggle at the word *tunnels*.

What do we do if we find them?

"NIKI," she said, "fill out terrain information for the Kemmi Wildlands. Include the Festival Warehouse. Trace any heat signatures that indicate Sapiens, synths, and Eflosi. Also animals."

"Why animals?" Vaylor asked.

Faerae shrugged. "Seems like we should track anything that's alive."

"Gonna get a lot of lizards slithering around that way," Mynar said.

"Just get on it," Faerae replied. Having been to Kemmi, she could now fully appreciate the terrain where the Eflosi lived. Yes, there were lizards, and snakes, and probably coyotes and such. But they would all have different heat signatures than Sapiens.

Vaylor said, "Bears."

Faerae looked at him, alarmed. *All we need are The Interstitials being mauled or eaten by bears!*

The Eflosi started chuckling.

"They tried to scare us with stories about tunnel bears when
we were children," Vaylor told her. "The tunnels can hold surprises. But no bears."

I hate surprises.

"I have your map, Faerae," NIKI said.

"Bring it up."

The hologram before her shifted to a 3-D topographical
map of the Kemmi Wildlands. Mynar and Vaylor scooted their
chairs over to study it with her. The map included the Warehouse structure and the network of exterior pathways and
trails, as well as tunnel passages inside the hills. As Kemmi had
told them, it was vast.

"Whoa," said Faerae. "NIKI, do you have the heat signature
layer applied yet?"

"In progress."

"And is this archival or a live view?" Faerae asked.

"It is a hybrid, Faerae. Live view supplemented by known
content."

"It's inaccurate," Mynar said, studying the map.

Faerae spun to look at him. "What do you mean?"

He pointed at the hills just adjacent to the Warehouse, running along the roadway that Faerae, Vaylor, and Dzuren had
walked and later ridden that morning. "From the Warehouse to
the ridgeline," he said. "No chambers at this point." He squinted
at the hologram. "The map has been revised. This makes it look
like there are no interior chambers beside the Warehouse."

"Not the case," said Vaylor.

"These"—Mynar pointed at a pair of chambers appearing
just at the ridgeline point that Kemmi had indicated was the

border between the Government-controlled Wildlands and the Eflosi settlement land—"are actually here." He pointed at a spot in the hills just east of the Warehouse.

"How the long gods can somebody tamper with official mapping?" Faerae asked. "Are you sure?"

"We've been in chambers that the map says don't exist. Kemmi will send our maps. They are accurate," Vaylor said.

"I'll message Aunt Kemmi," Mynar said.

"Aunt Kemmi?" Faerae repeated, looking at him.

Vaylor nodded toward Mynar. "Our mothers are twin sisters, made from the same egg. We were born a month apart. Played in those tunnels, on both sides of the border. There's no chamber there, to the northwest. The chambers are there." He pointed to the eastern side of the Warehouse.

"Is the rest of it accurate?" Faerae asked.

They examined it further.

Mynar said, "Incomplete, but what's there is correct. A few tunnels are missing but they're unused or falling in. Wouldn't send anyone near them."

"So, these chambers"—Faerae pointed—"are actually here"—she pointed by the Warehouse—"and not here?" She pointed at the border. "You're sure?"

"One hundred percent," Vaylor said.

Mynar nodded.

"Let's see what lights up when the heat signatures take," she said, staring at the map. "Did you find anything else to trace?"

"Their tracking rings are still active," Mynar said.

"They were left in the underground dressing rooms," Vaylor added.

"By the Amphitheater," Faerae concluded. "Are they still there?"

"Festival offices," Mynar said.

Of course. Back again to Roiboi.

"In whose office?" she asked.

After a moment, Mynar said, "Wofar Tonie."

"Who?"

"He's…" Vaylor did a quick search. "Subcurator of Earth Classics for Sundrae Beq, Curatorial Director at the Festival."

Clan Beq. The male parent half of Kaieda's clan name. Like most of us she identifies with her mother's clan. Ta'ava. Feck the Ta'avas. She and Alec have the same last name. She shook her head and refocused on the map. "NIKI," she said. "Heat?"

A flash filled their corner and heat signatures appeared on the map. Some were moving, some were still.

"Here's what is available," NIKI said.

As they watched, multiple figures moved about in the Warehouse. A cluster of people appeared to be in the hillside beyond it.

"That's another chamber that isn't shown," Vaylor pointed. "Ah, here are the maps from my mother." He entered the new data. "See? It looks like they're buried in the hill, but they're in a large chamber, there." He put his finger on the spot where the new chamber, reflecting the overlay of Kemmi's map, now appeared.

"What's all this?" Faerae pointed at another cluster of activity, near the border between the Wildlands and the Eflosi territory.

"Old tunnels there," said Mynar.

"Fragile," Vaylor added.

"A lot of people in that one tunnel," Faerae said. "Looks like eight or nine," she observed. "What happens when you reach the border? With the tunnels? It looks like…"

"They keep going," Vaylor answered.

Mynar nodded. "Nobody ever goes in there, past the fungi rooms and water pipes."

"We did," Vaylor said to him.

"Yes, well, we did," Mynar agreed. "But we shouldn't have."

They both chuckled.

"Kemmi said you all…'keep an eye on things,'" Faerae said.

"What I am saying is that nobody comes from THEIR direction," Mynar clarified.

"Looks like someone is doing that right now," she said. "They're getting closer to the border."

"Yes," Vaylor agreed.

"Whoever is in there doesn't know what they are doing," Mynar said.

"Might be who we're looking for," Vaylor added.

She decided to alert Dzuren. "NIKI, message Captain Tso: prospective target."

"Done," NIKI said.

She stared at the map, watching the figures move. If it was the band, they were probably still in their performance gear and clothing. "They're still in yesterday's…" She sat up. "Jewelry!" she exclaimed.

"Oh! Yes!" cried Vaylor.

"Jewelry…what?" Mynar asked. "Yes! Of course! They're famous for their jewelry. They take the tracking rings off but they wear their ear and nose rings, bracelets, necklaces, headgear, pearls folded into their hairlocks…"

Faerae thought back to the concert, remembering the many in the Amphitheater audience wearing similar jewelry.

"Metals can be traced," Vaylor said.

"Try silavodium," Faerae suggested. The sparkling necklaces and earrings in the vast crowd glinted in her visual memory.

"May I?" Vaylor asked Faerae, pointing at the holographic map in front of her station. She nodded and stepped away. He sat, entered data, then said, "NIKI, show us silavodium in the tunnels."

A few seconds later, new dots of light appeared in the tunnel where the larger group was still moving toward the Kemmi border.

"Boom!" said Mynar. He looked at Faerae. "It's got to be them."

Dzuren, with Luce and Allou, entered the Command Room. He gestured for the young women to wait near the door. Then he came to Faerae's station.

"Found them," Vaylor said.

"They're in the hills," Faerae told him. "Close to the Kemmi border."

"Feck!" Dzuren cursed under his breath.

"Can't we send someone to get them?" Faerae asked.

"Don't you see what's happening?" Dzuren asked.

"They'll blame us," said Mynar. "I can hear it on VoG now: Scheming Eflosi Kidnap Interstitials in Retaliation for Pet Scandal."

"It will get ugly if we don't get to them soon," Dzuren agreed. He looked to the Eflosi. "Can Kemmi help?"

"Not someone from the Government?" Faerae asked.

Dzuren faced her. "The Government? The Government is the problem. I don't know if contacting them will make things better or worse. Depends on who answers the message, which I can't control."

"I'll ping my mother and Mumno," Vaylor said. "But those tunnels…it's dangerous."

"Do what you can," Dzuren said. "We may have to go back down there."

He cursed again.

"We found The Interstitials' tracking rings," Faerae said. "In an office at the Festival."

Dzuren groaned. "I'll make a call." He leaned to Faerae and added, "Send a message to Max, on my thread. Tell him to return to Rimalon. Say 'My Fetchers are better than his.'"

Faerae stared at him, uncomprehending.

"Just do it," he said.

As he walked around the semicircle, she saw him lean over Henk Z'eng's station and say something to his cousin. He then went to his own workspace, darkening the glass. She watched him pull the door shut. It fell slightly ajar.

Send his message.

Luce and Allou were behind her, gazing into the Command Room's multilevel semicircle of workstations. People were busy with various tasks. Holograms floated at various desks. Beyond the screens was a vast window looking out across Rimalon's barren, dramatic landscape.

"This is…amazing," she heard Allou murmur as Faerae sent Dzuren's message to Earth.

"Truly," Luce agreed. "Think we could look around?"

"Only one way to find out," Allou said, wandering away from where the two Eflosi and Faerae were still huddled over their holographic map.

Faerae kept watching them.

What if they figure out who we're looking for?

"Looook at that!" she heard Allou whisper to her friend, pointing.

One level down, an Engineering officer was sitting at a station with a holograph swirling in red concentric circles before him. Beyond that was a station where someone was waving at a tall horizontal column of floating strings of different colors. At

another, overlapping holograms swished and circled and slithered interactively.

Few civilians get to see this.

Luce worked her way slowly around the semicircle. Allou
struck up a conversation with the man working the long-thread-
ed column, all the colors flashing.

Faerae returned her attention to the map and the tiny blips
where they believed the band members were. The Twins were
enlarging the tunnel map to secure exact locations before sending the information to Kemmi. She glanced across the room.
Allou was still in conversation with one of the column runners.

Where's Luce?

Faerae stood up.

How did she disappear that fast?

She kept looking until she spied Luce standing in front of
Dzuren's partially shut door. Luce was staring, her eyes wide,
into the office. She looked away from Dzuren's space and back
out into the CCR. Allou was still yakking with the officer at the
floating column. Her eyes met Faerae's.

Faerae strode around the semicircle.

"Finding the Command Room interesting?" she asked. She
glanced into Dzuren's office, saw the face on the screen over his
desk, reached for the handle, and pulled his door shut.

Whoa.

CHAPTER 23

RIMALON, MOON OF NEW ATLANTIS

Day Four, late afternoon, NAT-0

I AM SO FECKED, Luce thought.

She is so fecked, Faerae thought.

"Come with me," Faerae said, taking Luce lightly by the arm.

Luce had nowhere to run on this airless moon. So she cooperated. Allou was still conversing with the officer on the lower deck of the CCR, oblivious.

Faerae led her to the holographic map where the Twins continued to work. "Wait here," Faerae said, pointing to a bench behind the workstation. Luce sat.

Faerae returned to her seat in front of the map.

"Activity here, and here," Vaylor was saying, pointing at two different places in what looked like a range of small mountains. "This is where we think they have the band."

What are they talking about? Where is this? Band? Luce saw multiple small dots where Vaylor had just pointed.

"He asked you to contact Kemmi. See if she can send someone in there," Faerae said.

Vaylor said, "Call Kemmi." They all waited. He nodded at them all, indicating he'd reached her. He spoke softly, so softly that Luce could not make out his words but heard what sounded like clicking and clacking and humming. *That's the Eflosi dialect.*

"She'll contact Mumno. They'll send a team in," he said to Faerae.

"Good."

Dzuren returned. "Any word?"

"She has the coordinates," Vaylor said. "She's worried about the condition of the tunnels. Whoever is in there doesn't know what they're doing. She's sending someone."

"Good," Dzuren said. "Tell her I owe her."

The door to the outer corridor burst open and a man charged into the room shouting, followed by someone else who kept silent.

"Where is Luciena?" Egdar Roiboi demanded, looking about. He was wearing his brown suit, golden buttons flashing from his jacket. Caspar was alongside, in his usual white. Luce's heart sank.

I'm doomed. My life is over.

Roiboi spied Dzuren and headed straight at him.

Everyone in the entire Command Room focused on the scene.

"Director Roiboi," Dzuren said. "Normally I'm notified when we have dignitaries coming in from The Planet—"

Roiboi ignored him. "You!" he cried, spying Luce sitting on the bench behind Faerae's workstation. "Where is the package?"

"It's...uhhh...uhhh..." she babbled. "I couldn't say no, he's a Captain..." She looked at Dzuren.

"It's in the holding cage at the Bubble," Dzuren intervened. He stepped between Roiboi and Luce. "I invited Luce and Allou to come up to the Colony," he continued. "They're my guests. The box is safe. Let's lower the volume a bit, Director."

Faerae could see on the map a trio of bodies approaching the cluster in the tunnels near the border. *Kemmi wastes no time.*

She nodded at Vaylor, who nodded back. She noticed that Caspar was studying the map.

"I demand that box be released directly to me," Roiboi said. "As for them…" He looked at Luce and then at Allou, who was standing slack-jawed beside her new friend in the Command Room. "I hope you have jobs for them up here—they are both done at the Festival."

"Oh, oh!" Allou cried, coming up to them. "You can't sack me for this!"

"I can sack you for sneezing in the wrong direction," he snapped. "What are you doing here anyway?"

"Sundrae sent me to meet Luce!" Allou replied indignantly.

"And she knew about Luce's assignment…how?" Roiboi asked. "It was to be delivered directly to me, nobody else." He pointed at Caspar. "Which he told you!" He looked from Luce to Caspar and back. "Wofar!" he exclaimed.

Ohhhh my gods, ohhhhmygods. Wofar told Sundrae and Sundrae sent Allou so I'd give her the box. WHAT IS IN THAT DAMN BOX?

Caspar was staring at her.

Dzuren crossed his arms. "Such fuss over a slightly delayed delivery."

"Feck you, Tso," Roiboi said. "I'm going to the Bubble, I'll get the box, that will be the end of it. Except for you two." He glanced at Allou and Luce then turned to leave, waving for Caspar to follow.

Dzuren spoke again. "They won't release the item to you. Anything in the holding cage is released only to whoever surrendered it, unless it's deemed unsafe or unstable. They'll only release it back to Luce after it is screened. Assuming it passes the screening, of course. I haven't heard any explosions."

"It's being screened?" Roiboi repeated.

"Done by now," Dzuren said. "Custom House stickered. If there was no issue."

"We have a confirmation from The Planet," Mynar said. He and Vaylor were still working from the map.

"Report," Dzuren said.

"The band is now in Kemmi with Mumno," he said. "Stressed out, exhausted, and hungry." He looked up at Dzuren. "Their captors did not fare so well."

Roiboi looked to Caspar. "What are they talking about?"

"What do you mean?" Dzuren asked Mynar.

"Tunnel collapse…" The Eflos shook his head. "They tried to help, but…"

Dzuren nodded. "Shame. Notify the Guardian patrol, they'll need to retrieve the deceased and collect The Interstitials and escort them to their commune. They've earned a rest."

He turned to Roiboi. "Director," he said. "I suggest we discuss what has just happened in the Kemmi Wildlands, and about the deliveries to the Warehouse, and about this package you are so eager to procure. And about the comm relay between Earth and The Planet that bounces through Venus and lands at a receiving point beside your Warehouse."

Caspar headed for the door, nearly walking into it when it did not open as he approached. He then bolted to the right, aiming for a different exit. He passed Faerae's station as he did so. But he crashed forward in an ugly face-plant just beyond Faerae, who had stuck out her foot and tripped him as he went by.

"Oh," she said. "Accident. Sorry."

Dzuren leaned over Caspar where he was splayed. "Come quietly or I can call security," he said. "Doesn't matter to me." He offered a hand.

"I have nothing to say to you," Caspar said as he got to his feet, ignoring the hand.

Dzuren said to Faerae, "Take Luce to the Bubble and get that box. Bring it up here. We'll have a little unwrapping party."

Faerae gestured for Luce. "Come. This won't take long."

"What do I do?" Allou asked as everyone started dispersing.

"Make more new friends," Dzuren called behind him as he led Roiboi and his shadow toward his meet room. "You might be working here before long."

Allou squeaked. Dzuren grinned at her.

In the hour that followed, Faerae and Luce took the shuttle to the Bubble and retrieved the box. It now featured a small Custom House stamp. They did not talk on the ride down. As they walked back to the shuttle, Luce said, "I truly have no idea what this is. Or why they are all so upset."

"Many things are happening at the same time," Faerae told her.

"What was all that about the Kemmi Wildlands and The Interstitials?"

"NTK."

"But that's why you were at the Warehouse this afternoon?"

"Actually no, we were at the Warehouse looking for something else."

Luce sighed. "We spent last night at the Roiboi house. A bunch of sculptures disappeared overnight. I think they went to that Warehouse."

"What?"

Luce nodded. They boarded the Rimalon shuttle. "When we got there, a collection of sculptures was in their foyer, plus a big one in their library. The next morning, they were all gone. Everyone kept saying, 'What sculptures?' and 'Never saw them.'

Sundrae said they were just moving things around and that
they did that a lot."

"They move things?" Faerae said. "From the Roiboi house in
the Golden Broom to the Warehouse?"

"Apparently," Luce nodded. "Back and forth."

*Deliveries. Like whatever was delivered this afternoon after we
left. That must be what these mystery communications that disappear into the hills are about. They're bringing in cargo and…doing
things with whatever they're bringing in.*

"What kind of sculptures were they, at the Roiboi house?"
Faerae asked as the shuttle swept them toward Rimalon.

"Stuff from Earth," Luce said. "Wofar…he's a Subcurator…
got excited about one of them. He called it 'the Minotaur.' It
was in the library. A beautiful room full of books. Some of the
books were from Earth too."

Faerae tried to summon her Earth Studies class on classical
Greece and Rome. *The Minotaur—a unique creature that lived
in a labyrinth on Crete. A demigod, eventually slain by Theseus…
it had a man's body and a bull's head. Apt metaphor. Don't go into
that. True, but: distraction.*

"Interesting," she said.

Luce shrugged. "They're putting so many things in so
many places for the Festival, it's hard to know what's planned
for where right now. Caspar manages the master plan. They
make different decisions about the inventory at every meeting. Sundrae wants this or that, Wofar suggests something
else, Roiboi turns it all upside down. Wofar tracks the inventory. Ask him."

"Where is he?"

"Usually at the Festival office, but I saw him at the Warehouse this afternoon. He didn't seem happy…" Luce paused.

"Is there something else?"

"Well, sort of."

Faerae waited. If she had learned nothing else from Dzuren in the last forty-eight hours, she had learned to wait for the other person to talk.

"I got conflicting instructions," Luce said.

"What do you mean?"

Luce considered her choices. They were getting close to Rimalon. Dzuren held more power in the Keeper Colony than Roiboi. She'd just lost her job.

"Wofar told me to give the package to Sundrae, not to Roiboi," she blurted.

"To Sundrae? The Curatorial Director?" Faerae asked.

Luce nodded, miserable.

"Huh," said Faerae. *What will Dzuren make of that?*

"I don't want to cause trouble for any of them," Luce said.

"This is bigger than any of us," Faerae replied as the shuttle pulled onto the Colony platform. "Let's have that unwrapping party." She looked at Luce's package.

"I hate this thing," Luce said as they rose to debark. "If I could throw it out the window, I would. It's evil."

Faerae shook her head. *It's evidence. Roiboi wouldn't be so anxious to get it if it was just another artifact he could explain.*

Reaching the CCR, they found everyone sitting in the meet room adjacent to Dzuren's workspace. Allou, Vaylor, and Mynar were on one side of a long oval table. On the other side sat Roiboi and Caspar. They could hear Dzuren talking from his office. Luce plunked the box in the middle of the table and sat next to Allou. Faerae sat at the far end of the table, watching Roiboi. He eyed the box as he whispered to Caspar.

Dzuren emerged, saw the box, and smiled. "Ah, good. We'll open it shortly. Need to wait on the next shuttle."

"Why?" Roiboi asked. "You're holding my Prime Associate

and me here despite our demanding schedules. I am going to burn a hole through all your medals for it. Outrageous! I'm a full Director. You're an Acting Director. Once I am in touch with the Guild heads and the Delegates, you're headed to The Deep."

"Aren't we all?" Dzuren asked. "But let's see what we have here"—he nodded at the box—"once our other guests arrive. Faerae, have you checked the comms for new messages from Travelers recently?"

"I can check messages while we wait," she offered.

"Good, good, do that." He followed her out the door and said, quietly, "While you're on the comms, send a follow-up message to Max. Remind him about my Fetchers."

Faerae looked at him, puzzled.

"Mine are better than his. Just do it," he said. Then he looked across the room at Henk Z'eng and said, "Get a quad team ready to go. They'll have to go through the Gorgon."

Z'eng winced.

"I know," said Dzuren. "But speed is required. The Mercury wormhole isn't fast enough."

Faerae went to her station. *He's sending Fetchers through the Gorgon wormhole. That's beyond urgent, they all hate that wormhole. It's rickety. An awful, risky ride. The Mercury is smooth. But slower.*

She pulled up incoming messages. One from Earth, on Max's string: DEPARTING FOR MROIBOI D'AVI DEEP CONDITIONS QUESTIONABLE.

D'avi deep? What's he saying? D'avi S'Iloa is dead? She sat back in her seat. *How is that possible? Fenn Loa, then D'avi? Why?* She looked across the center to the meet room, where she could see everyone sitting. Dzuren was looking at her. *He knows about D'avi, gods know how. He wants me to know too.*

Does Roiboi know? D'avi is his man on Earth. Am I supposed to tell the rest of them any of this? Does Kaieda know?

She looked for new messages. One, this from Kaieda's string: FOUND WIFE.

Fenn Loa did have an Earth spouse. Unbelievable.

She sent Dzuren's message using the wording he'd instructed. Then she returned to the meet room. Entering, she heard Egdar Roiboi making more threats and demands. She wondered how Luce and Allou and the others could stand working for this noxious person. She sat back down, waiting for a pause. No pause came.

"...and I DEMAND you allow me to depart immediately and take that box with me, it is coded to me through the Warehouse and—"

"Anything coming from Earth is supposed to pass through the Bubble first," Dzuren said to him. "This didn't. It IS from Earth, isn't it?"

"That's not always the case," Roiboi countered. "Traveler items are sometimes sent directly to the Warehouse via the diplomatic pouch..."

"Objects collected during interplanetary research are vetted by security and run through the Custom House at the Bubble," Dzuren replied. "Double review. What you're talking about is the occasional Traveler document or misplaced personal item. That's not what this is." He nodded at the box. Looking out the interior window, he said, "Ah, here are our other guests."

Everyone shifted and turned as more people entered. Luce suppressed a gasp. *Sundrae. Wofar. Mog Weller! And that beautiful woman, the Loa, I saw Dzuren talking with when we were in the Science Lab wing. She was at the concert. The Experimental Wing Director.* Luce also noticed there was a security Guardian now stationed at the door.

"This is outrageous!" Roiboi exclaimed when he saw Mog Weller enter the room. "She can't be here! She's a journalist!"

"Nice to see you too, Egdar," Mog said, sitting down.

"She has long sought a visit to Rimalon. I thought today would be a good day for that," Dzuren said. "Glad you could make it on short notice, Mog. As I've said, this is all off the record. And for those who do not know her"—he nodded at the beautiful woman Luce had seen—"this is Janai Loa, Director of Science Research here in the Keeper Colony."

Janai glanced around and nodded at everyone.

"Let's see what we have in this package," Dzuren said.

"No, no," Roiboi said. Caspar's hand went to his wrist as if to hold him still. Roiboi yanked his wrist away.

Dzuren leaned over the box, holding sharp scissors he'd brought from his workspace. He unwrapped and snipped at the box. "Carefully packed," he observed. Soon the top of the box was before him. "Well, look at that," he said. Faerae, Mog, Luce, Allou, and Wofar all leaned in to see.

"Another box," Luce groaned.

Dzuren lifted the inner box. "Not just any box," he said, setting it before them. "This is a Bluebox. Our primary tool for interplanetary and interstellar research, documentation, and communication. This is an old one." He inspected it, looking on all sides and the bottom. "Updated regularly. That's policy." He looked around the table, his eyes settling on Roiboi.

"Why do you care about someone's Bluebox?" Roiboi asked.

"Why do you?" Dzuren responded.

"Whose is it?" Mog Weller asked.

"That's the question," Dzuren answered. He looked to Vaylor. "Do you have a secure chip reader?" he asked.

Vaylor nodded and handed him a small tool. Dzuren slid

it into an opening near the bottom of the box. A long number began glowing on the top of the box.

"Pull that up," he said to Faerae. "Use the station here so we can all see it."

Faerae moved to the workstation at the end of the room, raised a holoscreen, and entered the number into the system. Within a few seconds, a written file and a photographic image appeared.

"Fenn Loa," Faerae said softly.

"That is my mother's first cousin, Fenn," Janai said. "He's a Reporter. He's lived on Earth for forty of their years."

"Yes, Fenn Loa," Dzuren said to them all. "An Earth Reporter. This is his Bluebox." He looked around the table. "How is it that the Director of the Festival wants the Bluebox of a Reporter who is dead?"

"Dead!" Janai cried.

Others gasped.

"Not just dead. Murdered," Dzuren said.

"You CAN'T keep me off the record now," Mog Weller said to him. "This is major news."

"Off the record, Mog."

She groaned, her head falling into her hands. "How long have you known about this?"

"A couple of days," Dzuren said. "It gets worse."

Faerae, as far as she knew, was the only person who knew what was coming. She looked over at Roiboi. He seemed as unsettled and clueless as everyone else.

Dzuren, who had been standing over the box, sat back down.

"Do the Guilds know?" Janai asked. "It certainly hasn't circulated in Clan Loa. Poor Fenn..."

"The Guilds know," Dzuren said. "They're debating how to

announce it. It's complicated and…" He held his hands in the air indicating helplessness. "The Guilds…"

"That man was the ringleader, trying to destroy everything we are trying to do. We found him out," Roiboi sputtered. "I'm sorry he's dead. Never wanted him dead. But the box contains every record of every message he sent. It proves his traitorous intent."

Caspar slumped back in his chair, his hand over his eyes.

"My cousin was not a traitor," Janai Loa said coldly. "He spent his life on Earth, he dedicated his life to that research, his writing about it is legend in the…"

"He was Anony!" Roiboi interrupted. "He was sending messages to some source here and getting them circulated. It had to stop. Growing unrest. The Festival, the whole Planet, was suffering for it."

"The Festival isn't all you're trying to protect, is it, Egdar?" Sundrae asked.

"What are you suggesting, Sundrae?" he huffed. "Explain yourself!"

"Wofar told me about his 'inventory management project' at the Warehouse," Sundrae said. "The secret Fetcher deliveries. The Earth objects being distributed to private collectors. I think you're the one who needs to do the explaining, sir."

"Loans," Roiboi said. "Did he tell you that part? Many loans. Temporary exchanges of objects in return for Festival support."

"Credits were changing hands," Sundrae replied. "That makes it illegal."

Luce looked at Wofar, shocked. He was staring at his hands.

"It is a quiet program that supports the work of the Festival," Roiboi said. "It's beyond your security clearance and that of everyone in this room."

"Not beyond mine," Dzuren said. "But we can test that." He smiled at Roiboi.

Allou turned to Roiboi. "So Fenn Loa was murdered because he was sending Anony messages? You thought the way to stop that was to kill him and ground his Bluebox?"

"I told you it was not about killing him! He just had to be stopped!" Roiboi blurted, looking at Caspar.

Caspar kept silent.

"More than that, Allou," Dzuren said. "We've been aware for a while of some unusual…transfers of objects. Things moving around outside of or on the edges of normal protocols. We've been monitoring it through the Bubble. It appeared to be art-based cargo coming from Earth, but we couldn't track how the communications were working. With the placement of seven Teams on Earth doing Festival research, we noticed an accelerated pattern. When Team Seven hit a snag in their landing and there was Fetcher activity where there was no call for it, we looked more closely. Soon after that we received word that Fenn was dead."

"How did you find out?" Janai asked.

"Team Seven. They were in San Francisco, where Fenn lived. We aren't sure how. As you know, real-time communications are impossible. The other confirming source was another Reporter. She learned it from Fenn Loa's wife."

"Wife!" Roiboi exclaimed. "Now you see how mad that man was! He had an Earth wife!" He looked at Janai. "I'm sorry he died, I really am. But he had to be stopped, he had to stop sending those messages. It had to STOP."

Dzuren waited for the outburst to end, then continued. "Fenn was a cautious man in many ways. He must have sensed a threat. He left instructions for his wife to find her way to his closest Reporter friend. She succeeded." He looked at Roiboi. "Whoever murdered Fenn tried to kill her too," he said.

"How could you know that?" Roiboi asked.

"Because your sister confirmed it after taking in Fenn's wife," Dzuren answered.

"My SISTER?" Roiboi shouted. "Marina is part of this? My fecking sister!"

"I HAVE to report this," Mog Weller said to Dzuren.

He waved his hand at Mog dismissively.

"You are done, Egdar," he said to Roiboi. "Your efforts to stop Anony have cost citizen lives. Your secret distribution of Earth artifacts is against our laws, you have a network of Fetchers and others who will go down with you, and"—he glanced at Caspar—"we know you had a team of people who snatched The Interstitials after their concert. A scheme was under way to lay blame for their disappearance on the Eflosi, to diminish their endorsement of Anony and cast doubt on the Eflosi, all in one move." He looked at Faerae, Vaylor, and Mynar. "Thanks to their intervention, The Interstitials have been safely found."

Everyone at the table was silent, taking in the new shocks.

"This is exhausting," said Allou, fanning herself. She looked at Roiboi. "You're a terrible person!"

"Citizen 'lives'? Is someone else dead besides Fenn?" Janai asked.

"Sadly, yes," Dzuren answered. "D'avi S'Iloa is dead, by the same method and probably by the same hand as Fenn."

Most of the people in the room gasped.

"A Reporter and a Traveler killed!" Janai exclaimed.

"Holy trinity, that's gruesome," said Mog Weller.

Faerae saw that even Roiboi looked shocked at that news. *He didn't know. Freddie hasn't reported it or contacted him. D'avi really was the comm point…* She frowned.

"D'avi…" Roiboi murmured, looking stricken. "What of his partner, Freddie?"

Outside the room there was a ruckus. The outer door opened.

"Is that…barking?" Allou asked, looking into the control room.

A scrabbling on the floor came closer along with more barking. Dofi bounded into the room, raced in circles, and leaped into Dzuren's lap.

"Hello, hello, you got here," he said, patting the excited, wiggly dog.

Maeve Ep swept into the room and looked around at everyone. When she saw Roiboi, she said, "Hello, darling." Then she looked at Dzuren and said, "I know, I'm late. I suggest you put Dofi down. I didn't have time to walk him before I left."

Dzuren put the dog on the floor.

Roiboi, completely flustered, asked, "What are you doing here?"

She sat down elegantly in the last remaining chair, looked at her mate, and said, "Egdar don't be ridiculous. Someone had to be the go-between for the Anony messages to get them into circulation here." She raised her hands in the air and shrugged.

"I don't know whether to laugh or cry," said Mog Weller.

"Both are appropriate, dear," Maeve Ep replied.

CHAPTER 24

Day Five, morning, UTC+1

AFTER HER LATE writing session, Editha dreamed about Fenn. They were in a rowboat on a lake, in sunshine. They were looking at the shoreline and commenting cheerfully on the houses, the landscaping, the sky. Fenn pointed at a house surrounded by woods and said, "That's where she lives."

She awoke to sun and noise outside. Looking out her window, she saw the black car. The driver, Jeremy, was helping a man and a woman unload luggage. The couple appeared to be in their thirties. The man was tall, sandy-haired, fit. He carried himself in an upright way that made Editha think of military officers. He wore chinos, a gray shirt, and a blue jacket. The woman was shorter than the man by a head. She was slender, with a chin-length bob of brown hair. She wore a red flowered dress and a white knit sweater. *More of Them?*

The writing session the night before was cathartic. *Write through it,* Editha kept telling herself as she recorded the "upheaval" events of the last four days. Fenn once called her writing "thinking out loud on the page." She'd replied, "Feeling out loud on the page." *Yes, the writing helped. Living in the grief. And all the new information, so much that Fenn never told. What a story, how New Atlantis came to be. Star People?* She looked out the window again. The car was gone. The new people inside. *I'll meet them soon, whoever they are.*

Max and Kaieda's Eswen House suite overlooked a garden with a round swimming pool nine meters in diameter. They'd flown on British Airways from Los Angeles to London. Kaieda had been unable to sleep. The video recording Max had shown her in their empty apartment was impossible to unsee. Awful as it was, it confirmed Max's instincts to leave for a safe house immediately. Calling in Fetchers could backfire. Max would say no more while they waited for and boarded their plane. Kaieda had realized he wanted her to rest. *More trouble is ahead.* He'd reached Marina Roiboi via SMS. Kaieda had asked if Marina was surprised to hear from them. He'd answered, "I did not have that impression."

"Do you want to sleep now?" Max asked her as they unpacked their few belongings and the Bluebox.

"I'll crash at some point. Not yet," she answered. "I want to find out what's happening. And if Fenn's wife is here. And what we need to do about…" She sighed. "D'avi…"

Max was establishing connections with the Bluebox, the column rising from a low dresser top in their room. His hands flew.

"Messages for me?" she asked.

"Mog Weller. Several from Roiboi. Two from Faerae," he said. "One sparking URGENT from Janai Loa."

"Open that one."

Max waved out the thread and opened it. "Shall I forward it to you?"

"Just read it," she said, trying to keep her voice from quavering.

"Alec. Some contact. Evaluating."

Kaieda's heart clutched. *What does "some contact" mean? Is he alive? She would not have said "contact" if he was confirmed dead. She would have said so if he was back. What does this mean? Do I need to go back to The Planet? She would have said if we needed to call the Fetchers. What are they evaluating? Could it mean he was…in parts? Is this just another bounce from the roller coaster they keep me on?*

"Dear Jesus," she said aloud.

Max's head tilted slightly. "You are calling on one of the Earth gods?"

"I'm trying not to explode," she answered. "You know who Alec is. You also know he's been gone for…" Her voice broke. "Years. She's saying there's been contact of some kind."

"Alec Ta'ava," Max said.

"Alec Ta'ava." She wiped a tear off her face.

"The Consciousness Project is one of the highest-security projects undertaken at the Keeper Colony Experimental Wing Lab of the Science Guild since the initiation of robotics and the parallel development of synthetic biology," Max stated, as if he was reading aloud.

"I know," Kaieda said.

"Alec Ta'ava is at the center of the project now," he went on. "He voluntarily submitted to a transformation biotank he helped redesign after the first attempt for a human to achieve the fifth dimension failed."

"I know, I know," Kaieda said, wiping away more tears.

"It's categorized as reaching into the soul dimension," Max seemed to finish reading. He looked at her. "High risk. He vanished from the tank. Unknown cause. No communication since." He frowned, seeing her tears.

"I KNOW," Kaieda said. She pulled a tissue from the holder on the nightstand beside the bed. "I know." She sniffled and blew her nose.

"You are upset."

She looked at him.

"I am surprised they sent you this information while you are away on assignment. 'Contact' does not mean he has returned." He paused. Then he said, "They would tell you, if he had returned. In any case."

Kaieda nodded, fighting more tears. "Send a reply to Director Loa for me," she said. "Just say, 'Standing by for more information.'"

Max nodded and created the reply link. "Done."

"Is there anything else?"

"Planet News."

"Save it for later, we need to talk with Marina now."

He started to speak but then stopped himself. "As you wish," he said. She was still wiping her face. He touched her gently on the shoulder, his hand radiating warmth. "All is not lost," he told her.

"You sound like Alec," she said.

He gave her his half-smile, his hand falling away. "Let's see Marina."

He waved down the column and put the Bluebox to rest.

She nodded. As they walked through the corridor to the stairs, they passed a sitting room overlooking the pool.

"Water," Kaieda said, pausing with some longing.

Max glanced at the pool and nudged her to continue.

EDITHA WENT DOWNSTAIRS to the great room after assembling herself as best she could.

Marina was already in the room. "Good morning, Editha," she said. "I trust you had a good rest last night?"

Editha smiled and nodded. "Yes, thank you."

"Tea? Coffee? We have new guests. They'll join us soon. They just arrived from Los Angeles."

"I heard them arrive. A couple? Coffee, please."

Marina poured. "They are called 'Travelers.'"

"Travelers," Editha repeated. "They're from your world?"

"Yes. You remember yesterday I told you that Fenn was what we call a Reporter, as am I. We are embedded here long term. Travelers come on short, specific assignments. They research cultures or histories, or they witness events. They travel the galaxy and bring information back to New Atlantis."

This is just too much. They "travel the galaxy"? That's as strange as those Star People.

"We expect another guest soon. We have had another death."

"I'm sorry for your loss," Editha responded. *So much death.*

"What has happened is unheard of in our world," Marina said. "Please be patient with us. We may need privacy for some of what needs to be discussed. Forgive me if I ask you to step out."

"Oh," said Editha. "Oh, of course. I can take a walk, the gardens look lovely."

"Theone would be happy to show you around," Marina smiled. "Zhe loves the gardens."

"Do you want me to leave now?" Editha asked.

"Stay, meet Kaieda and Max. We'll let you know when we need to confer."

Editha nodded. *Am I Alice in Wonderland? Curiouser and curiouser. Step aside so the aliens can discuss their situation. But ARE they aliens? Fenn wasn't an alien. Was he? He said he was the same species as me. But he grew up on another world. But they came from here. Oh God, I need brandy in this coffee.*

A door near the passageway to the kitchen opened and the new arrivals entered the room. She stood as they entered.

Marina made all the introductions and gestured for Theone, who entered after Max and Kaieda, to pour or refill coffee cups for everyone.

"Let us visit," Marina said. "While there's time."

What does that mean? What's going to happen?

She realized Kaieda was speaking to her.

"I'm a great admirer and student of your husband's writings," Kaieda was saying. "I am so sorry for your loss. It is horrible..."—her voice faltered briefly—"to lose a mate."

Max came up behind her and put his hand on her back, guiding her to the sofa. They sat.

"Thank you," Editha answered, also sitting. "It doesn't feel real to me. None of this does. Except that he isn't here." She settled into her chair.

Until they make me leave, I'm staying with them. They're strange. But they're Fenn's people.

Max sat next to Kaieda, his leg resting against hers. *Married? They seem familiar that way.* She could see their faces in the full morning light. *Why do I feel so drawn to them? Especially Kaieda.* As they exchanged small talk, she observed as much as she could without staring. Kaieda had a pretty, girl-next-door face, a little pixieish. The wrinkled, flowery dress didn't look right on her. Her hair was uncombed, she wore no cosmetics, and she looked like she had been crying. *Is she just tired? Or perhaps it has to do with all these deaths? When will that come up?*

Max spoke little but missed nothing. His alertness unsettled Editha. His features and manners were flawless. *He's like a movie star.*

Marina said, "Some news from New Atlantis. Drama at the Amphitheater."

"We've heard nothing," Kaieda said.

"The Interstitials gave a grand concert in the Capital Amphitheater."

"The who?" Editha asked.

"A famous music group on The Planet. Think the Rolling Stones meet the Grateful Dead. Two-thirds of the way through, they stopped everything and declared an 'artist intervention.'"

"What is that?" Editha asked.

Marina continued, focused on Kaieda and Max. "A new Anony message. Dzuren sent me a thread last night. He forwarded the ticker on a visual. Chaos in the VIP section, among the Delegates and Directors and such." Marina almost giggled as she took another sip of her coffee. "And The Continuity was there, with her children! Racing out. It appears my brother had a near stroke trying to stop the message as it was dropping. He did not succeed."

She then explained to Editha, "My brother is head of the Planetary Festival. This was a disaster for him." Another sip of coffee, then, "Plus, Maeve Ep, my brother's mate, showed up at the reception with her dog. Egdar hates that dog." She set her cup down. "I'm having a moment of wishing I'd been there."

"Oh," Kaieda said. "I've met Dofi."

"The most famous dog in New Atlantis," Marina declared.

Dogs! They have pets! Reassurance that the other world was not entirely different from her own. But she was confused by the story.

"Anony," Max stated. He looked at Editha. "Do you know about Anony?"

Editha held her hands up and shrugged. "I don't know anything," she said. *Well, not that much.*

Marina took a long, gentle breath. "Fenn was Anony. As am I."

"You? And Fenn?" Kaieda asked, surprised.

"Who is Anony?" Editha asked.

"On The Planet, concerns are growing regarding our policies toward Earth and its inhabitants. As I explained last night, Earth is our ancestral home. We visit often. We are among you, quietly."

Editha nodded. *I know that much.*

"The leadership on The Planet endorses this approach. They have more recently endorsed the practice of securing and removing artifacts from Earth and relocating them to New Atlantis, where they are displayed in our equivalent of your museums. If you were to visit New Atlantis, you would be surprised, I think, at how familiar some of it might feel."

Kaieda nodded.

"You're a Traveler," Editha said to her.

"Yes," Kaieda said. "Your cultures influence ours. We try not to have any influence. That's one of the rules of visiting. The chips enhance our knowledge."

"Chips?'" Editha repeated. *She can't mean something to eat, can she?*

Oh gods, I can't believe I mentioned the chip. I'm too tired, too worried. Alec.

The alarm must have shown on her face. "Do not worry, Kaieda," Marina said. She nodded toward Max.

"Before we arrive, information and enhanced capacities are embedded," Max said. "It assists us in working quickly without arousing attention. We are ahead of you in our technology."

Editha nodded. *Obviously. Must they patronize me?*

"So our policies have allowed us to accumulate cultural information as well as physical assets from Earth. We give nothing in return," Marina resumed. "A growing number of New Atlanteans are questioning this. We are not a culture that handles social disruption well. Anony has forced a confrontation that is spreading."

"But what does that have to do with Fenn, and with you?" Editha asked. "You are here."

"Exactly," Marina answered. "We know Earth is on a self-destructive path. Without help, Earth will recover but human life here will fail. *Homo sapiens* will survive only on New Atlantis. The Planet, ecologically, is in good health. But change is needed on New Atlantis as well. Our institutions have become complacent." She stood and walked to the windows, looking across the pastoral scene.

"Fenn wrote the initial Anony statements. He would send a document to me. I would rewrite it, positioning it in academic language. He had too distinct a writing style to take chances. Once we finalized each draft, I forwarded them to a friend on The Planet, who made sure they were put into circulation. Eight messages so far. It is receiving the attention we had hoped. Fenn lived quietly here but was at the helm of a growing movement for change on The Planet. Someone uncovered his involvement. And acted on the threat Anony represents."

Editha was speechless.

"What I am saying," Marina finished, "is that Fenn is a hero."

"Both of you are," Kaieda said softly. She had long sympathized with Anony's message, though she was diligent on The Planet not to reveal it. Too complicated. Unwise, given Alec's situation.

Marina looked to Max and Kaieda. "We must learn how they found Fenn out. Whoever 'they' are. I watched the silver thread Max sent." She shook her head.

"Freddie's insight may help," Kaieda said.

"Freddie? Who is Freddie?" Editha asked, feeling fresh confusion at a new name, and the reference to a silver thread.

"Freddie is on another of our Traveler Teams," Max answered. "There are seven on Earth right now."

"He's coming," Kaieda said.

Marina nodded. "Yes." She returned her focus to Editha. "He is partner to the person who died. Their Team is incomplete now. Freddie may be able to help us ascertain what happened." She smiled. "Editha, we have overwhelmed you, I am afraid. I suggest you take a breather."

"Oh, of course," Editha said, rising from the chair.

Marina summoned Theone, asking zer to take Madam Lockyer on a tour of the gardens.

"Gladly, M'Rambert," zhe said, gesturing for Editha to exit the room into the hallway.

"Take a swim if you like," Marina called after them. "It's a deepwater pool."

Kaieda frowned with a surge of worry. *How can Editha hearing all of this be safe? For her or for us?* Then she remembered. Then she saw why neither Max nor Marina showed concern over so much revelation.

Max can make her forget.

Theone led Editha on a tour of the gardens surrounding the manor house. Editha was fascinated by the hidden gardens, hedges, fruit trees, flowering bushes, and stone steps leading up and down curving pathways. They ended at the round swimming pool behind the house. On departing, Theone encouraged her to sit for a while and meditate.

Fenn was doing so much I didn't know about, Editha thought, sinking into a lounge chair. *His death wasn't random. That* NEXT *text had indeed been a threat. For now, she knew she was safe. Oh Fenn, I wish you were here. They have opened a door*

I thought was closed forever. She sat in the sunshine for some time. The pool looked deep, dark, inviting.

IN THE HOUSE, Kaieda and Max continued the conversation with Marina. Kaieda struggled to sit patiently when what she wanted to do was rush back to the Bluebox and find out if Janai Loa had replied. *Standing by means standing by.* She half-listened to the conversation underway.

"I assume you have heard nothing from Freddie?" Max was asking.

"No," Marina replied. "We should watch the visual recording."

Oh gods, please no. What difference will it make to watch it again?

"It was garbled at times," Kaieda said.

"Can you enhance the recording?" Marina asked Max.

"I have sharpened it as much as I can," he answered.

"Show it," Marina said.

Max stood. He projected the 3-D recording.

Reluctantly, Kaieda watched with them.

D'avi is close to the recording camera. The point of view is from above the sink in the kitchen. It captures a wide angle including the kitchen island and living room. D'avi adjusts the camera, then steps away, his back to the camera's eye. He is handling something sitting on the island. His body blocks what he is working with.

"Stop the recording. Is his Bluebox recording this?" Kaieda asked, squinting at the screen. *It had to have been. He sent the* recording on a silver thread. That's an urgent signal in the Bluebox column.

"It would appear that D'avi recorded a great deal using the Bluebox," Max said.

"It looks…" Kaieda leaned closer to the image. "It looks like he's wrapping something."

Marina nodded. She motioned for Max to resume.

"Freddie!" D'avi calls out.

"What?" Freddie's voice comes from downstairs.

"Did you send yet?" D'avi continues working with the object on the island. He shifts his position enough that they can see he has tape and scissors and wrapping plastic spread out on the counter. He's creating thick layers around the object.

"Message sent," Freddie's voice comes up the stairs. "Coming soon. Is it packed?"

"Almost."

"We need to get it out of here today, he wants it tomorrow," Freddie says. "They'll send it through the Gorgon." Something garbled follows. Then he says, "He wants to end the problem."

"I know, I know. Were there other messages?" D'avi asks.

"They got the plane out," says Freddie.

D'avi pauses his work and says, "Thank the GODS. I can't live through another tantrum over THAT." He leans out of the camera view. The next line is garbled. He reappears, saying, "Okay, give it to her when she gets here."

Freddie appears. "Good job," he says, looking at what D'avi is doing.

They face each other. At this point the object on the counter briefly becomes visible. It is a dark-blue rectangular box wrapped in plastic.

"Stop there," Marina said.

Max stilled the image.

"What is that?" Marina asked.

"How can we tell?" Kaieda asked.

"Look at it. The shape."

"It could be anything," Kaieda answered. She looked more closely. "Oh," she said. "Oh."

"Resume," Marina told Max.

Freddie blocks the view of the package, putting his arms around D'avi. He says, "Soon the way will be clear for SO much more." He kisses D'avi. "But the job isn't quite done yet."

"What do you mean?" D'avi asks, returning to his wrapping.

"Baby, we can't leave any traces behind," Freddie says. "It has to be"—here he shifts into his singsong voice—"clean, clean, clean for the plan to be free, free, free."

"It will be!" D'avi says. He finishes his wrapping job.

Freddie steps out of the camera view. D'avi lifts the package. "See?"

Off-camera, Freddie says, "Beautiful. I'm going to the market for donuts. I'll leave the door open for Dawn. I love you, baby. Bye-bye."

His footsteps are heard going down the stairs. A door slams.

D'avi puts the package down. He goes off-camera. Nothing happens for almost a minute.

Kaieda closed her eyes. She did not want to see this again. She reopened her eyes as…

D'avi reappears, rechecking the package. He fusses over it, pressing down on the taping. A knife thrown from off-camera slices into the center of his throat. His eyes pop open in shock;

he's looking at the doorway to the stairs. His hands come to his throat, wrapping around the blade. Blood drizzles out of the wound. He staggers toward the camera, fumbles, reaching at the camera. The screen goes dark.

Max ceased his projection. They said nothing for a few moments.

Marina broke the silence.

"I think D'avi was preparing Fenn's Bluebox for a pickup by a Fetcher. Whoever killed Fenn took it from the house. It is probably on its way to New Atlantis by now."

Max nodded. "My conclusion as well."

Kaieda's mind was racing. "The Fetchers," she said.

"Someone or a group, willing to operate outside of protocol," Marina said. "Whoever it was waited until Freddie left. Threw the knife. Took the package. They're trying to clean up a mess that is threatening a larger scheme."

"What larger scheme?" Kaieda asked.

"I wish I fully knew," Marina sighed. "I made a terrible mistake some years ago."

"Anony?" Kaieda asked.

"No, not Anony. Anony is no mistake. But Anony and the effort to sustain a clandestine operation between Earth and The Planet are related." She paused, as if gathering her thoughts. "Ten years ago, I received a message from my brother asking me to forward an object to him from Earth. It was a small sculpture a Traveler had secured somewhere in Turkey. It was valuable, very valuable, on Earth. A relic of an old religion. Egdar read a reference to it in a Traveler report and obsessed about getting it to New Atlantis. In those days little was being brought back. I was doubtful about moving Earth artifacts to The Planet. I asked questions. I wanted to know how it would be contextualized and why he wanted it on The Planet rather than on Earth." She stared out the window for a few moments.

"My brother persuaded me—I say this with eternal regret—to personally go to Turkey, pick up the sculpture, and bring it to him on my next furlough. A furlough he knew was coming soon." She sighed. "I asked him why it couldn't run through the normal protocols. Guild approvals, Fetcher pickup, Custom House review, going through all the inspections before placement. He told me that would cause delays. The piece belonged in a collection to be shown soon. 'Urgent,' he kept saying. So I agreed to bring it. No one checks the diplomatic pouches at the Bubble. They trust us. I smuggled it in. And gave it to him at the family house on our island in the Raja Sea."

She shook her head. "I believe I was a participant in the genesis of what has become a system of underground imports to The Planet. I thought I was doing Egdar a small favor. I told Fenn about it. Within a year, Fenn's watchful eye caught more irregularities. Like Egdar, he was reading every report that Travelers filed. He noticed things would be mentioned and then disappear off the radar. He told me. The help I'd given weighed on me. I asked my brother what happened to that relic I'd brought him, where was it, where might I see it again? He was flustered. He said he wasn't sure what happened to it after it was delivered to where it was scheduled for display; they lost track of it because of another project."

"In other words, never mind."

"At some point, Fetchers became involved," Max said. "I've checked transfer and delivery records. Deliveries to the Festival Warehouse that went through the Bubble in the diplomatic pouch. Large deliveries in shipping containers that cleared the Bubble without full review. Financial deposits to Egdar Roiboi's account that have no traceable source."

"Ugly. But brilliant," Kaieda said.

"My brother is not short on brilliance," Marina replied. "It has turned dark. He is greedy. Fenn and I believe that first relic went straight into a private collection. Whose, I have no idea. But for a sum that benefited not just the Festival. It also benefited my brother." She sighed again. "Others in Egdar's circle are in on the scheme. I suspect his Prime Associate, Caspar Weller. D'avi and Freddie appear to be part of it. D'avi has been to Earth three times in the last four years. An unusual pattern for a Traveler."

"An Earth-artifacts black market?" Kaieda asked.

"So it appears."

"I found black piping in the column when we linked it to D'avi's Bluebox," Max said. "A hidden corridor of communications that facilitate the artifact transfers. They bury things within existing exports, but an outside comm line bounce was necessary to complete the acquisitions and arrange their delivery to The Planet."

"There is still much about the operation that we do not know," Marina said.

"But D'avi was part of it," Kaieda said.

"Yes. And Freddie. Both of them."

This explains Freddie's existence. Roiboi agreed to get him for D'avi in exchange for help with off-the-record procurements. Maybe D'avi was having second thoughts and Freddie was his reward for staying with it? Oh D'avi. Why was this so important to you, to make such a compromise? Or was your loyalty to Roiboi simply blinding you to everything we were trained for?

"Team Five was working for Roiboi but also working for the Festival and the Culture Guild in terms of Traveler reporting," she said.

Marina nodded. "Correct."

"But why kill D'avi?" Kaieda asked. "And who killed him? What is the connection to Anony?"

"D'avi was executed in the same manner as Fenn Loa," Max said. "A shiv to the throat. Pristine work by someone who is trained in knife and dagger offensives. Initially I believed D'avi executed Fenn. He was out for two nights, he could have gone anywhere in the city and still attended most of the rave. But he had no weapons training. He never served in the military. It's not an enhancement on his chip. Then he is murdered the same way. Someone else is doing the killing. It seems unlikely to be an Earther. The motivation, the why, is clearer than the who. Freddie says it in the recording. 'No traces.'"

"Freddie has to be on the kill list too," Kaieda said.

"Then why wasn't he struck at the same time as D'avi?" Max asked. "Whoever entered the house could have killed him on his way out."

"We're missing something," Kaieda said. "He was spared for some reason."

"Whoever spared him was acting on instructions from someone else," Max said. "Or it was simply luck that he wasn't present, and the intruder had to leave before he returned."

"Anony has made things harder for the dark market to operate," Marina said. "That was part of our intention. To slow them down. An argument encouraging citizens to oppose policy could influence the Government regarding artifact collections and imports. We knew it would threaten the black-market operation. Someone pieced together Fenn's suspicions, or his Anony work, or both. Fenn suspected they were closing in. He tried to disappear with Editha." She shook her head. "They want to eliminate her too. They tried once. They'll try again." She stood and looked out the window. "If they have Fenn's Bluebox, it will take no time to trace things to me."

"We're still missing something," Kaieda said. "Freddie can't harm humans." She looked at Max. "You saw how he reacted to what happened to D'avi, you heard him on the phone, he was hysterical." *A synth exhibiting hysteria. The emotion inserts certainly work on Freddie.*

"He is welcome here, though Fetchers may be the better path for him," Marina said.

"Which Fetchers?" Max asked. "When we don't know who is helping who?"

Marina nodded.

"Shouldn't we report this to The Planet, to the Guilds?" Kaieda asked.

"Who do we trust?" Max asked.

"We can trust Faerae. And Dzuren," Kaieda said. "Pull up the Bluebox, we can message them. They were working on tracing the Venus bounce. They may know things we don't."

"And say what?" Max asked. "Anything we send will be monitored on normal channels."

"They'll send information in some way that's coded, looks innocent," Kaieda said, remembering Faerae's last message. "We could just call the Fetchers and go home. Report it all in person."

"If we are collected by the Retrievers working with Egdar, we might end up dropped on Venus never to be seen again," Marina pointed out. "That would make an easy nothing of us all. You, me, Editha, Freddie, Max…we'd all disappear at once. How handy for my brother. Anony stunted and Egdar's scheme saved in one simple drop."

Well, that's no good.

Kaieda looked at Max, asking, "Why did D'avi send me that recording? What made him do that, as his last act on Earth?"

Marina's phone dinged an incoming text. She looked at it

and then at them. "From Freddie," she said. She read aloud, "IN PARIS. SEEKING SANCTUARY." She looked up. "While you flew overnight to London, he was on a flight to Paris," she said. "He wasted no time coming in this direction."

Kaieda got up and walked to the window, looking across the green landscape. She folded her arms in front of her, trying to hold herself together. *Right when I need to be on Rimalon.* "Contact." *What does that mean? Why didn't Janai say more?*

"Can we check messages again?" she asked Max.

"I'll open the column," he answered, standing up.

"I need to go outside for a while," she said. *Air. Light. That pool. Water.*

"I'll send Jeremy for Freddie once we know when he is coming in," Marina said, texting a reply. "It will be a few hours. Why don't you join Editha, keep her company? We cannot forget her or her loss."

Kaieda nodded. She told Max to let her know if there were new messages from Janai Loa. Then she went downstairs and rummaged through the backpacks to find her swimsuit, one of the few things she'd salvaged on Maui. She put it on, threw a towel around herself, and walked through the ground-level sitting room to the terrace and the pool.

EDITHA STARTLED FROM light sleep when Kaieda said, "Hi," and sat down in the chair beside her.

"Ah, hello…Kayda? I'm sorry, I may be mispronouncing your name."

"Kaieda. Three syllables. Kah-ae-duh. But any pronunciation will do." She looked at the inviting water. "Do you mind if I take a swim?" she asked.

"No, no, of course not," Editha said, waving at the water. "I don't have a suit or I would join you. It looks lovely. Just be careful. She said it's a deepwater pool."

"The best kind," Kaieda said, standing up and letting the towel drop off her.

Editha watched as she walked to the pool's edge and without dipping a toe, dove in headfirst, disappearing beneath the surface. *She's so beautiful. All of them are. What must their world be like? Does my child walk so smoothly? Is he like this? Despite being made by a flawed Earth woman? Is he considered a half-breed? Does he look like me? Like Fenn?* She stared at the water and realized that Kaieda had not surfaced. The water was still.

"Oh no!" she said, standing. *Did she hit her head with that dive?* She went to the edge of the pool and peered down. Everything was dark, thanks to the midnight blue of the pool's underwater surface. Nothing moved below the rippled water.

"Kaieda!" she called at the water. She wasn't a good enough swimmer to dive to the bottom. Nothing happened. "Kaieda! Kaieda!" she shouted.

She was about to turn and run to the house for help when the water in the center of the pool parted and Kaieda swooped into the air. Editha gasped as Kaieda hovered eight or so feet above the water.

Kaieda grinned at her. "Sorry, I didn't mean to scare you."

"How do you…how do you…DO that?" Editha asked.

"We're not supposed to be able to do it here." She lowered a little, hovering a foot or so above the water and directly across from where Editha stood. "It's called lifting. We can do it on The Planet; it has something to do with gravity and the water and tiny gills behind our ears. Our Scientists believe we brought the gills with us when we left. Unlike Earth-bound *Homo sapi-*

ens, we kept them as we evolved. We remain an oceanic people, bound to water. Our chips are supposed to suppress it here. But on this visit, it all works."

"It looks…magical," Editha said. "You're almost flying."

"Not a bad way of describing the sensation." She dropped further down into the water and began treading. "We can breathe underwater for a while. That's why I was under for so long. My gills." She disappeared under the water again. Editha waited. Kaieda surfaced a minute later. "Don't want to scare you this time," she said. "The water is the perfect temperature. Take off your clothes and jump in."

Editha laughed and shook her head. "Not right now and not in broad daylight!"

Kaieda grinned, shook her head, and disappeared beneath the surface. She shot up again in a wet swoosh, hovering two meters above the water. She was high enough to be opposite the back of the first story of the house. She peered into the kitchen and waved at Theone. Editha watched with delight as she dropped slowly back into the water. She swam to the pool's edge and pulled herself onto the rim, then stood and reached for the towel she had dropped. She wrapped herself in it and sat down next to Editha. "Delicious," she said.

"Delicious for you, shocking for me," Editha said. "Fenn never did anything like that!"

They both laughed.

"He could have," Kaieda said. "The Reporters aren't chipped the way we are. Although they probably closed off his gills before he left The Planet." She felt behind her ears. "Max's and mine are still working." She frowned. "I assume closing and cloaking them got skipped in the rush to get us launched."

"I knew every inch of his body, he had no…" Editha stopped. "Wait, he…"

Her mind raced. She'd forgotten about those thin, faint scars behind his ears. Early in their relationship, when he still wore his hair short, she'd seen them, run her fingers over them, asked, "What is this?" He had answered, "A needed repair." Then he had changed the subject by pulling her closer and showering her with kisses and pulling away her clothes. After that, he'd let his hair grow just long enough that the scars weren't visible at all. Editha had thought nothing more about it, assuming it had been some childhood surgery, until now.

Kaieda waited a moment, then said, "I'll bet he loved the water."

"Oh yes—yes, he did," Editha said.

A memory rose, of being at the beach with Fenn and the baby. How he would sweep the baby over the foaming waves and how the baby would squeal with laughter. *Of course. This love of the water, this ability to live in and out of it, is IN them. Gills! They can breathe underwater!*

"It's so strange," Editha said as they stared out over the dark, shimmering pool and beyond to the rolling green meadows behind the house. "You all feel so familiar, yet foreign at the same time. Fenn never seemed like a foreigner."

"It's different with Travelers," Kaieda said. "They prep us extensively, embed the chip, send us on specific missions. The Reporters are here for something different. It's like the short view versus the long one. I'm usually focused on researching particular social practices or a certain window of place and time."

"Fenn did that work too."

"Yes. Fenn taught us how to see, how to observe, how to write about it. I wish I could have met him. I loved the poetry of his writing." She looked away from the garden at Editha. "He was bound not to mention you. But now that I know you exist,

I realize you were there all along. A presence never named. I want to reread it all now."

Editha wiped a tear off her cheek. "Thank you for that. I was writing too. But it's all gone now. Well, most of it."

"Gone?"

Editha nodded. "He destroyed nearly all my journals before we left San Francisco. They were burned, except for a few. I have Fenn's laptop. All his writing is archived there. At least I have his writings if not my own."

"But you kept some of yours?" Kaieda asked.

Editha nodded. "We were in such a rush to leave. I grabbed what I could and"—she hesitated briefly, then said—"hid it from him. Now I'm glad I did."

Kaieda stood. "I'll get a shower and come back," she said. "Max may have some messages for me. It won't take long."

Editha got up as well. "I'll bring one of my notebooks down here," she said.

Editha went to her room to put on a skirt and blouse and a pair of blue sandals she found in the shoe rack. Like everything else, they fit. She found the rucksack and pulled out the journal on top. Then she returned to the poolside. Before long, Kaieda reappeared wearing a blue and white dress for the lunch gathering. It suited her more than the red flowers.

Editha handed her the journal. "It's from the third year of our marriage. We were still living in Ojai. It was such a happy time in our life, but for the one thing…" She stopped herself. *Probably not supposed to talk about it.*

Kaieda accepted the journal and opened it to look at the first few pages. "Gosh," she said. Then she saw the start of one entry and shut the journal. "Very personal!" she said.

"Intimacies," Editha said softly. "I did write about us sometimes."

Kaieda laughed. "I've done some of that too."

"Yes, of course, you're a writer. Do you…have someone on New Atlantis, Kaieda?"

As Kaieda returned the journal to Editha, her hand slipped. In catching the book, leaves fell open and a photograph fluttered out. Kaieda bent to pick it up, as did Editha. They bumped heads. Both laughed as Kaieda picked up the black-and-white photo. On a patterned sofa sat a man, a woman, and a baby that looked a little over a year old. The baby was in the woman's lap, looking gleefully up at her. The couple were both smiling down at the curly-haired child.

"What a beautiful family," Kaieda murmured. *We wanted this, eventually.* She looked closer at the photo. "Wait—that's you," she said.

"Yes." Editha sighed. "And Fenn." She took the picture as they both continued to look at it. "I don't think you're supposed to see this," she said.

Kaieda looked at her, astonished as she realized the photo's content. "You and Fenn had a child!"

Editha nodded. "We had a son," she said.

"What happened to him?" Kaieda asked.

Editha sighed. "I should ask Marina about this," she said. "Or you should."

"Marina knows you had a child?"

"Yes. It appears Marina and Fenn knew everything about each other. Though he never mentioned her."

"We're not…this isn't allowed," Kaieda said, staring at the picture. "What happened to the child?"

"I know only to a point," Editha answered. "From the start of our relationship, Fenn was clear there could be no children. But…once we learned I was pregnant, we decided to go ahead. We couldn't imagine otherwise. After the baby was born, Fenn sort of…lost his mind. At least it seemed that way at times. He was so torn. When the baby was six months old, Fenn started talking about sending him back to New Atlantis. I was shocked. For months we circled the question. Fenn couldn't take me there. I wouldn't consider him leaving and never coming back. Nor could I imagine him leaving me and taking our son with him. What we eventually agreed, and it broke my heart, was that the baby would be taken to New Atlantis to be raised by his cousins. I had to let him go."

Kaieda put her hand over Editha's. "I am so, so sorry," she said. "I can't imagine facing a choice like that. Can I see the picture again?"

Editha handed the photo back to Kaieda. As Kaieda accepted it, Editha noticed the double star tattoo on her hand.

"He's beautiful," Kaieda said, gazing at the baby.

"He had the best laugh," Editha said through her tears. "Your tattoo…" she started.

Kaieda kept looking at the photo. She glanced at her hand and said, "Yes, it's…" She stopped, looking back to the image.

Editha leaned in and gazed at the photo as well. "He was delightful. Funny, endlessly curious. He was always getting himself into mischief of some sort. A rascal."

Kaieda looked at Editha and back at the photo. Then she said, "Oh gods."

"What?" asked Editha. "What's wrong?"

"Wait here," Kaieda said, getting up. "I have to show you something."

"Okay," Editha said as Kaieda rushed back toward the house.

A few minutes later she returned, holding a thick ring several inches in diameter. She placed it on the low table between their lounge chairs. Then she waved her hand twice over it. Out of it, a hologram rose. It was a slightly shifting human figure, a man, perhaps in his early thirties, wearing a metallic military jump suit. He was smiling, looking at the viewer, his head slightly tilted. His wavy brown hair was tousled, his brown eyes sparkled, his face was open and full of life. Everything about him looked effortless.

Kaieda and Editha looked from the image to each other and back again. Editha looked at the photograph again. Then she stared at the hologram.

"He looks like Fenn," she said. "Who is this?"

"He's my…" Kaieda was trying hard not to cry. "He's what you would call my husband," she said, her voice breaking. "Alec."

Editha slowly said, "We named our son… Alexander."

"His mother was Clan Loa. Alec uses his father's clan name, Ta'ava. Normally we go by the mother's clan name. Alec doesn't. He grew up among the Ta'avas. His parents were always open about Alec having been adopted out of the Weller clan. That's our clan for those with unknown or complicated bloodlines." She paused. "The name is so common, the Loas are our largest clan. But…when you said he was curious and a rascal… and then this picture…I've seen pictures of him when he was young, but not this young…"

"This could be him?" Editha asked.

Tears welled in Kaieda's eyes. "I think we have found your son," she said.

CHAPTER 25

THE WOMEN EMBRACED.

"This would make Alec so happy," Kaieda said, releasing Editha. "I don't know if he knows he was born on Earth." She paused, then added, "Probably."

"Is there any way to communicate with him from here?" Editha asked.

"No," Kaieda answered. She smiled and pushed a strand of hair away from Editha's face. "But I can tell you more about him."

"Tell me everything," Editha said, choking back a sob. She looked again at the hologram, Alec standing there with a flirtatious expression on his face. "Is this recent?"

"He made it a few years ago," she said. "As a joke. I haven't opened it in a long time. He's dreamy, isn't he?"

I love you I miss you I miss you I love you

Editha smiled, looking at the image. "He is. All of you are," she said. "He looks so much like Fenn. When we first met."

Kaieda gazed at the image as well. "He's funny, and smart, and"—she sighed—"stubborn. He made this hologram when I was preparing to leave on my third Traveler assignment. I'd complained about our being apart so much. He gave this to me and said, 'Take me along, then.'" She looked at Editha. "We're what's called phero mates. It's like…mated for life."

"We try to do that here," Editha said. "Half the time it doesn't work out."

"For the most part we don't try. We're not very good at monogamy. But for a small percentage of us, it's the only way." She held up her tattoo. "Bonded mates. The tattoo is called a bondmark. Each bondmark is unique to the pair."

Editha smiled mysteriously as she looked closely at the entwined sapphire stars on Kaieda's hand. "Beautiful," she said. "That must have hurt. He has one too?"

Kaieda nodded. "He does. And it did. It's supposed to."

Editha pulled her right foot up onto the lounge chair, revealing her ankle. "Look at this," she said. Below her ankle bone was a tattoo featuring two intersecting green and blue planets.

"Beautiful," Kaieda whispered.

"Fenn insisted. He designed it. He wanted ours in the same place as yours, on our hands. But then he decided our ankles would be better. Less visible, I guess."

"He took you as his bonded mate," Kaieda said.

Max appeared, interrupting the exchange. "Freddie has arrived," he said. "He isn't alone."

"Who's with him?" Kaieda asked.

"Dawn."

"Who's Dawn?" Editha asked.

"We're not sure," Kaieda said, grabbing her towel and heading for the house with Max. Editha followed. They entered the sitting room on the ground level.

"Are they upstairs?" Kaieda asked.

"Top floor," Max answered. "She didn't want him traveling alone."

"Research her," Kaieda said. "Hack whatever's necessary. Find out who she really is."

"What is happening?" Editha asked, sensing the alarm. "Does this have to do with the man who was killed?"

"Possibly," Kaieda said. "Marina may know more."

She and Max continued down the hallway toward their suite.

Editha hurried up the steps to the first floor where she found Marina and Theone in the kitchen.

"We have an expected guest with an unexpected companion," Marina said, seeing Editha. She nodded at the kitchen table, suggesting Editha sit. "You heard about Freddie, the partner to D'avi who was killed?"

Editha nodded.

"He is here. He brought a woman friend."

"Dawn," Editha said, remembering the name Max and Kaieda had used.

"Yes," Marina said. "Tea?"

Editha nodded. "Please."

Marina proceeded to make and serve the tea as they talked. "Max said he and Kaieda met Dawn twice while they were in San Francisco. She's apparently an 'internet influencer,' with fashion. They're trying to find out more." She sat across from Editha. "I have to ask something of you."

"Anything," Editha said.

"We are unsure of Dawn," Marina said. "Will you allow Jeremy to take you to my north London flat until we sort things out? I can send Theone with you."

Editha frowned.

"If I let anything happen to you, Fenn will haunt me from The Deep."

"I don't want to leave," Editha said. "Not after I've just found you, not after what I just learned from Kaieda."

Marina smiled. "I saw the hologram. Your son is a remarkable man."

"You…knew about him?"

Marina nodded. "It is Kaieda's story to tell, since Alec isn't here to tell it himself."

"Kaieda saw the resemblance to Fenn. Have you met him?"

"Alec Ta'ava is well known to many on The Planet. Right now, we need to resolve Freddie's situation and determine who Dawn is and why she is here."

"They can't do that from your planet?" Editha asked, not sure who "they" were.

"It is hard to know who to trust."

Editha's heart sank. All she wanted was to know more of Alexander. Alec.

"I don't want to leave," she said. "Don't make me leave."

Marina was quiet as she poured hot water over filled strainers and into their teacups. "Let that steep for a few minutes," she said.

DOWNSTAIRS, MAX'S HANDS and fingers were flying over the laptop keyboard. Kaieda had changed into a pair of gray jeans and a white tank top, both purchased in Los Angeles. The Bluebox was up. At her slower pace, she was weaving comm threads.

"Lots of messages," she said. "Several from Faerae and Dzuren, one from Mog Weller. Roiboi, of course."

"What from Dzuren?" Max asked.

"Haven't opened them. What of Dawn?"

"Dawn Carlson. Large internet and social media presence

for the last three years. Driving license, banking details, two moves in San Francisco. Before that, a birth certificate, also San Francisco. Nothing of family, graduations, university."

"She springs out of nowhere," Kaieda said.

"Out of the head of Zeus," Max replied, still focused on his research.

Kaieda laughed. "You remind me of a synth I worked with years ago," she said. "He called himself Harlong."

"The Harlon17."

"Yes. He was a great partner."

"If we were human, you would call him my cousin," Max said.

Kaieda stopped her work, looking at him. "You have technical overlaps with Harlong?"

"They folded the best of the Harlon17 into the Maximus5700."

Kaieda went back to unraveling threads. "I knew there was something about you I liked."

Max glanced at her, gave his half-smile, and returned to his research.

"Okay," she said. "From yesterday, Faerae says: SAW INTERSTITIALS LAST NIGHT. DRAMA. ANONY DROP. GOING TO PLANET TODAY. COMM IRREGULARITIES TRACED TO FESTIVAL WAREHOUSE ADJACENT. Sounds like they may have found the drop point for the Venus comms. There's a second one, from late last night. All it says is: CONSPIRACY."

"Understatement," Max said. "Dawn has three traffic tickets from the City of San Francisco and one from the City of Oakland. All unpaid." He set the laptop aside.

"She's one of us, isn't she?" Kaieda said.

"Almost certainly."

Kaieda looked at the next opened threads. "From last night:

RETURN TO RIM ASAP. MY FETCHERS ARE BETTER THAN HIS." She squinted at the words. "What can that mean?"

"He's telling us to send for Fetchers through him, not through the Earth station," Max answered. He got up, took her by the waist, and moved her aside, taking up the column himself. "The next one from Dzuren says: SPOKE TO JLOA. ALEC NEWS."

"That's no different from what Janai sent," Kaieda said.

"Something new has happened," Max replied.

I want to go back. I need to go back.

"Has D'avi's death been reported?"

"Unlikely," Max answered. "Unless Freddie has used their Bluebox. Or unless…"

"Dawn," Kaieda said. "But who would she report it to? Research the Fetcher personnel on Copernican station. Find out who's been posted there over the last five years, any changes."

Max used the Bluebox for that search. Kaieda pondered the messages from Faerae and Dzuren. *We're all coming at this from different directions, but we're all going toward the same things. Roiboi has some kind of off-grid operation. Anony is questioning Earth Policy and in the process threatening whatever Roiboi is doing. It cost Fenn Loa his life. And D'avi his. Faerae said CONSPIRACY. A warning. Maybe that's what D'avi was trying to alert us to, with that silver thread. But he was Roiboi's man. Nothing's adding up. If we can solve the murders, I can go home and find out what is happening with Alec.*

"Is Dawn throwing those knives?" she asked.

"Possible. Or someone we have not yet encountered. Fetcher personnel in Earth orbit have rotated five times over the last five years. One person has served here or elsewhere in the Copernican system throughout. All except one of the transfers and changes look routine. One person left the Earth station three years ago. No record of their continued work with any Guild after that. No record of them on New Atlantis at all in the last three years…"

"Are there any images of that person? A name?"

"Aurora Kaxton."

"Aurora. Dawn."

He nodded, waving at the Bluebox. A 2-D picture materialized, a blond woman with a ponytail.

"That's her," Kaieda said. "Clan Kaxton. Military. Good gods, a rogue Fetcher."

Max's head tilted slightly. "Her service record shows she has extensive training and expertise in hand weaponry."

"Holy Tri," Kaieda said softly. "Why hasn't she killed Freddie?"

"She would know that Freddie is hard to kill. She may be under orders to keep him functioning for some reason."

Neither said anything for several moments.

"If the assignment is to 'tie up loose ends,' she will attempt it with all of you," Max said. "That may be why she has done nothing further so far."

"All of 'you'?"

"I am harder to kill than Freddie."

"Right," Kaieda said. It was easy to forget he was a synthetic. "Stay on the box, let me know what else you find. I'll speak to Marina." She headed for the door. *Synths are nearly indestructible. And very few people know how to turn them off. I certainly don't.*

KAIEDA WALKED INTO the kitchen. Marina and Editha sat with their tea. "We have new information," she said. "Are they still upstairs?"

Marina nodded. "Freddie seems exhausted, if that is possible with his kind."

Editha squirmed slightly. *His kind? What does that mean?*

"Dawn is not what she seems," Kaieda said.

"Summarize," Marina said.

Editha was starting to feel drowsy. "I may go back outside and rest in the sun," she said.

"Don't wander," Marina said. "Theone, will you see M'Lockyer down to the pool?"

Theone nodded. They left. A few minutes later, Editha was alone by the pool. Everything seemed to be floating. She dozed off, wondering, *Was there something in that tea?*

IN THE KITCHEN, the conversation continued.

"Dawn is New Atlantean. Clan Kaxton," Kaieda told Marina.

"Ah. Military."

"Trained in hand weaponry. Science Guild, Retriever sub-guild. Served on Earth orbit and in the Copernican system…"

"There's the Venus relay," Marina observed.

Kaieda nodded. "She went off-record three years ago. Nothing after that with the Science or Military Guilds. And that is when her records on Earth start to appear. Max found enough to confirm it's the same person. There's even a photo."

"Sloppy of her," Marina commented, sipping her tea. She raised the cup to Kaieda. "Would you like some?"

Kaieda shook her head. "We also got messages from Dzuren and Faerae. Faerae used the word 'conspiracy.' Dzuren wants us back on Rimalon."

"Probably a good idea," Marina said. "Dawn will make her move. Keep Max close. He is faster and stronger than any of us, by far. He and Freddie are our protection."

"Do you think Freddie knows Dawn is one of us?"

"Hard to say," Marina answered. "I would guess not. D'avi probably did."

Then so did Freddie.

"Shouldn't we talk with him? Alert him?"

"I will talk with him after lunch," Marina said. "Between now and then, someone needs to be with Editha at all times. I asked her if she would let us relocate her. She declined. We must not allow Dawn private access to her. Editha has been lucky, and she is resourceful, but she's our most vulnerable."

"I can't let anything happen to her," Kaieda agreed. "For Alec. For her."

Marina smiled. "I was watching from the window when you brought the hologram out. She is your family too, Kaieda."

Kaieda stared at her. "You knew about Alec?"

Marina nodded. "Fenn."

Alec kept that big a secret from me? Did HE know?

"I'll sit with her," Kaieda said. "That pool is beautiful," she added. "Deep water for lifting."

"We situated and landscaped it to avoid exposure," Marina said. "Though now, with satellites and drones…" She shrugged.

Kaieda smiled. "See you later."

"Stay vigilant," Marina said as Kaieda departed. "Keep Max close. Lunch at one. By the pool."

KAIEDA SAT IN the lounge chair beside Editha, who was dozing. A butterfly fluttered across the pool. *Max will find me if new messages arrive from Janai Loa or Dzuren.* She considered Dawn, who seemed so young and brash and caught up in herself in San Francisco. *But you're one of us. You hid it well. You're trained by our military. You know the Fetcher protocols. You gave it all up. Going rogue must have been thrilling. The energy here turned you on somehow.* She thought again about her own moment by the Bay two mornings ago, when she saw life sweeping all around her. *It calls us. I haven't read the new Anony messages but they're right, we've lost our way. Our brew of caution and curiosity has turned in on itself. Fenn and Marina saw it. People on The Planet are waking up. But some—gods know who, beyond Roiboi and his minions—are capitalizing on our failures with tactics they shroud and bury in our bureaucracy and our compartmentalization and our assumption of eternal peace for The Planet. We cannot quit Earth, we can't shed our impulse to know and connect with our place of origin. But this planet needs our help. We keep refusing to give it.*

Her eyes fell on the now-shut ring that held Alec's hologram. *And you, you, you, my love. If only I could talk to you. The person I most want to talk with about everything, most of all what it's like to be without you. Do you know your origins? That you're Earth-born? Do you know your parents were bonded? What have you found in the experiment you couldn't resist? What stories will you have for us if*—she shut her eyes tightly—*when you come home? Are you trying to come home? You promised you'd come home.*

She suddenly, desperately, wanted this business on Earth to end. She wanted to return to Rimalon and find out what was happening, what had caused Janai to send the message.

We have a killer in the house. I must stay alive to find out. To see him again. Or let him go forever.

She stared at the dark, inviting water in the pool. Editha continued to doze in the sun. She drifted to sleep.

CHAPTER 26

HALF AN HOUR later, Kaieda sat up. She saw Marina, wearing a long white dress and holding a blue parasol over her head, supervising the laying out of a round table on the terrace beside the pool. Theone placed cutlery and plates and napkins for six precisely, smoothing over the white tablecloth with her hand. A bouquet of stargazer lilies rose in a crystal vase at the center of the table. Theone returned to the house to begin bringing out the food.

Editha was still asleep.

"Looks lovely," Kaieda said.

"We aren't setting out any knives."

Kaieda nodded toward Editha. "Do we tell her about Freddie?"

"There are so many things we could tell her about Freddie. Which do you mean?" Marina asked. "We may want to warn her he looks like Alec."

Their conversation ceased when the French doors to the house opened. Freddie and Dawn emerged, followed by Max and then Theone, who carried a serving bowl of salad. Freddie appeared stricken, his hair uncombed. He wore black jeans, black loafers, a French-tucked black T-shirt, and a black hooded vest. Dawn was better assembled but looked tired. She was empty-handed, wearing her usual blond ponytail and a pair of black tights with a long gray linen sweater. Kaieda went to Freddie and forced herself to hug him.

"I'm so sorry," she said.

Freddie hugged her fiercely and said, "Thank you. It's unreal…" He released her abruptly.

Not Alec's long, luscious hug.

"D'avi thought the world of you, Kaieda," Freddie continued. "I know he didn't act like it. But you were always the one he followed and envied and wanted to be like."

Kaieda looked to Max beyond Freddie's shoulder. Max was watching, impassive.

Kaieda stepped away from Freddie, turning to Dawn.

"You must be exhausted," she said.

Dawn leaned in for a hug, which Kaieda returned. "It's so unfair," she said into Kaieda's ear. "D'avi was so wonderful."

Kaieda let go. What she wanted to do was shove this woman into the pool or better still strangle her for a while. But a confrontation could be deadly.

"Be strong," she said.

Dawn nodded.

"Lunch is served," Marina said, waving everyone to the table. "Max, pour some *vino verde*, we all need it." She looked over at Editha, still dozing in her lounger. "Let her sleep," she said to Kaieda.

Kaieda nodded. She sat next to Max, their backs to the pool. They were across from Freddie and Dawn, who faced the pool. Marina took the seat between Dawn and Max. Theone began serving the first course, a spring pea soup seasoned with fennel and tarragon.

"Oh my God, this is delicious," Dawn said. "I haven't eaten since yesterday morning."

"Theone is a marvelous cook," Marina said. "Freddie, I'm sorry to ask, but did you call anyone, are you making arrangements for D'avi…?"

"I…uh…" He shook his head. "No. I just…left. I couldn't…" He choked.

Dawn put her hand over his. "We'll deal with it once we get back," she said. "They'll release him to you. We'll figure it out."

Max frowned, taking this in. "He has to be sent home," he said.

Freddie looked startled, then said, "Well yes, yes, of course. We'll take him home to his mother…"

"I forget—where's he from?" Dawn asked. "His mother is alive?"

"Has she been notified?" Max asked.

Kaieda knew that D'avi's mother lived near the Capital on New Atlantis. Max had to be fishing to see if Freddie had notified anyone on The Planet about D'avi's murder.

"No, no, I'm going to tell her," Freddie said. "As next of kin, it's all on me. I had to show them our wedding certificate…"

"Wedding certificate?" Kaieda coughed. "You were married?"

"Of course!" Freddie answered. "We got married right after we moved to San Francisco."

Dawn nodded. "I was at the wedding," she said. "So sweet."

Max's head tilted slightly. "You knew them before they moved to San Francisco?" he asked.

"Yes," she said, looking to Freddie. "We met when they lived in…" Her voice trailed off. "Tell them when we met, Freddie."

Freddie put his spoon down and looked off into the distance. He noticed Editha. "Who is that?" he asked.

No one answered. His eyes drifted beyond the pool, toward the meadows rising behind the manor house. "We still had so much more to do," he murmured. He stood up, still staring out. "It just…wasn't possible."

Marina nodded at Kaieda and then toward Editha, who was stirring.

"I'll get her," Kaieda said, leaving her seat.

Max followed.

"Are you awake? Time for lunch," Kaieda said, leaning over Editha. "I need to explain something, about Freddie."

Editha opened her eyes, seeing Kaieda first. Max offered Editha a hand. Editha took it with a smile and rose slowly, then turned and looked at Dawn and Marina. Then she saw Freddie. Her eyes widened in recognition. She gasped, pointed, cried out, and fell against Max, who caught her before she could drop to the ground.

"Oh gods," Marina said, also rising and coming toward them. "Is she all right?"

Max lowered Editha back into the lounger.

Kaieda sat next to her. "Editha…that's not Alec," she said gently, taking Editha's hand. "I know it looks like him but it's not."

"What did I do?" Freddie asked, stepping away from the table.

"You haven't done anything, she's just confused," Marina said. "You do look so much like him."

"Alec who?" Dawn asked.

"My doppelgänger," Freddie said, sliding his hands into his pockets.

"Just wait, we'll get it sorted," Marina said. She eyed Freddie. "Alec isn't the doppelgänger."

Max and Kaieda stayed by Editha. Kaieda kept saying, "It's okay, it's not Alec, we can explain…"

"No, no," Editha kept saying. Finally she caught her breath enough to sit up and twist around to look at Freddie. "That's him!" she said to Max and Kaieda, pointing at Freddie.

"No, Editha, it isn't," Kaieda repeated. "He looks like Alec, I know he does, but that's not him." She tried to help Editha stand. Max also turned to look at everyone at the lunch table.

As Kaieda turned with Editha, she saw Dawn begin to rise. Then Kaieda saw a dark burst of action as Freddie's hands flew out of his pockets at supernatural speed. The sunlight caught a glint of bright metal flying toward them. Then Kaieda was shoved violently toward the pool. Max was pushing her and Editha too. She yanked Editha with her and heard a clatter and a human howl of pain. She and Editha careened into the pool, sinking into the dark water. Editha tried to push to the surface for air. Kaieda dragged her back down and pulled her against her chest. Then she put her mouth over Editha's.

Here is air! Breathe! We talked about the gills! Breathe!

Editha resisted at first, then realized what was happening. She took in a breath from Kaieda. Kaieda pulled them a foot below the surface. The sunlight filtered into the water, providing enough light that their eyes met. She waited, still. Editha nodded.

Good, now you understand I can keep you alive down here. She could see bodies in motion beside the pool. She tightened her grip on Editha. *Do I dare a lift? Can I carry her up? If I lift high enough, I might avoid the danger but…was that knives being thrown? How long can we last down here?* The underwater pressure increased. Kaieda saw a mass of bubbles as another body tumbled into the pool. She pulled Editha tightly against herself. With as much strength as she could gather, she shot up through the water and into the air as high as she could lift. Clinging to Editha, she hovered three meters above the pool, parallel to the tops of the tall cypress trees that surrounded the terrace. She looked down at the scene below.

"What is happening?" Editha asked, holding on to Kaieda tightly, her back turned to the scene below.

Kaieda saw Marina deep in the pool. Dawn was on her back next to the table, struggling to pull herself up, wailing loudly. Her left hand was holding her right arm. Blood was everywhere. Max and Freddie were locked in combat near her, each trying to strangle the other. Freddie's gaze rose up briefly to meet Kaieda's as he saw the two women hovering high over the pool. He held Max off with one hand, ramming his other into his pocket and yanking out another knife.

"No!" she heard Max roar. He threw Freddie to the ground and sank heavily onto his chest. His right hand reached toward Freddie's mouth, as a series of wiry tendrils shot out of his fingers. He rammed the tendrils into Freddie's mouth. For a moment Freddie continued to struggle, then suddenly went limp.

Marina lifted out of the water, stopping short of Kaieda's hover point. Kaieda shifted her position so that Editha, still clinging to her, could see what was happening below. Dawn continued to wail, holding her bleeding arm.

Theone burst from the house onto the terrace, followed by two men in yellow jumpsuits. Fetchers. *Z'eng's Fetchers.* One of them went to Dawn and took her arm to look at the injury. The other went to Max, who was still sitting on Freddie's chest. Max looked up to see Kaieda, with Editha, and Marina, in the air over the pool.

"You can drop," he called to them. "He's turned off."

"What? What does he mean?" Editha asked again as Kaieda lowered them to the water.

"You'll have to swim to the ladder and climb out," Kaieda said, drained.

They dropped back into the water. Editha swam to the side and pulled herself out of the pool. Kaieda followed, and after her, Marina.

"How did you stay under?" Editha asked Marina. "Fenn's gills were closed off…"

Marina smiled. "He had modifications that I declined," she answered.

Freddie lay motionless on the pool deck, his blank eyes staring at the sky.

"Is he dead?" Editha asked, taking a few steps toward him.

"Not exactly," Max answered, getting to his feet. The tendrils from his fingers drew back into his hand and it looked like a hand again.

Editha stared, speechless.

Marina accepted a terry-cloth robe offered by Theone. The Eflos provided others to Editha and Kaieda.

Editha pointed at Freddie, her hand shaking. "That is who attacked Fenn and me. I couldn't see his face that night. But when I saw how he moved just now, wearing all that black… the way his head turned and the shape of him…that's the man who killed Fenn."

"It's not a man," Kaieda said softly. "Not a human man."

Editha looked at her, confounded.

"He's what we call a synthetic," Marina said. "An android. A robot."

"What!" Editha exclaimed. "Those things are real?" Then she remembered the bizarre lines coming out of Max's hand. "He's one too?" she asked, staring at Max.

Kaieda turned to Max. "How is this possible?" She saw Dawn sitting in a chair, one of the Fetchers tending to her arm. Freddie's knife, aimed at Editha, must have nicked Dawn's arm as he threw it. "Is she all right?"

"Her arm will be," Max said. "These are Captain Tso's Fetchers, not the Copernican squad. They'll take Dawn…Aurora… to Rimalon where she will have to explain herself."

"You sent for them," she said to Max.

He nodded. "I suggested Captain Tso look at the Fetcher turnover. He and Commander Z'eng took fast action."

The Gorgon worm hole. Gods sing your gifts and nerve, Dzuren and Henk.

Dawn was close enough to hear him and groaned miserably. "I don't want to go back," she moaned. "Let me stay here, let me disappear here…please, I just want to stay here. I have a life here, it's better here, I'll stop helping Roiboi…"

There it is. The missing link.

"Only Reporters get to stay," Marina said to her. Then she asked the Fetcher next to Max, "How long before you can launch everyone?"

"Creshes are ready, M'Roiboi. We'll have them to the Keeper Colony in thirty-six hours Earth time. Captain Tso is waiting for them. We'll take the Mercury wormhole, spare them the Gorgon." He paused, then added, "Two of our team will stay behind to deal with the relay situation. They're still on the drop ship."

Marina nodded. "High time to shut that relay down. Good luck on Venus." She looked at Freddie, still motionless on the ground. "Are you taking that back with you?" she asked.

"Certainly," the Fetcher answered.

"They have to find out how this happened," Max said. "Why and how and who interfered with his programming. And why he killed D'avi as well as Fenn."

"D'avi was a loose end," Marina said. "But how they programmed Freddie to kill…" She shook her head wearily. "That will be harder to solve."

Editha wanted to scream. She was confused by these strange new men in yellow and Freddie…a robot? Fenn's murderer? A robot that looked so much like her son? *All this talk of wherever whatever Rimalon was and wormholes and who is Dawn and who is Roiboi…?*

"Editha," Marina said. "Things are happening very fast. I am sorry to set yet another challenge before you. However, these men"—she nodded at the Fetchers—"are going to take Max, Kaieda, and Dawn…and Freddie, such as he is…back to New Atlantis. You must make a decision."

"What?" Editha asked, bewildered.

"Either you stay here, or you go with them," Marina said.

"Wait, wait," Kaieda started.

Marina held up her hand, glancing at Kaieda and saying, "It's the only way."

What flooded Editha's mind was *I could meet Alexander!*

"If you go to New Atlantis," Marina continued, "you will be the first person from Earth to set foot there since we emigrated centuries ago." She paused, then corrected herself. "The first full-blooded Earth person. I won't count Alec, given his unusual circumstances. If you go, you will not be permitted to return. You will live the rest of your life on New Atlantis."

"I want to meet my son," Editha said.

Marina looked to Kaieda.

Kaieda stepped forward and took Editha's hand.

Editha saw immediately that whatever she was going to say was not good. "Please don't tell me he's dead," she said, her voice quavering.

Kaieda took a deep breath. "We don't know. He was…is… involved in an experiment. Alec is a Scientist. He's part of a team that's attempting to research the extension of human consciousness, beyond life as we now understand it." She saw

Editha's face go ashen. "I wish I could better explain it," Kaieda said. "He went into a state, something like a coma, for a while after the experiment started and then he…disappeared."

Editha stared at her. "Disappeared?"

Kaieda nodded. "He was just…gone. Vanished. We've had no contact since." She paused, then added, "There's always hope…we may have reason to hope…"

"How long has he been gone?"

"By Earth's accounting, over three years," Kaieda answered.

"Three…years?" Editha murmured.

One of the Fetchers spoke. "Should I move this?" He kicked at Freddie.

"Yes, move him out of here," Marina answered. "Max, they may need your help."

Max nodded. He assisted the two Fetchers as they lifted Freddie and carried him away.

"Good riddance," Marina said as the synthetic corpse was removed. She looked again to Editha. "Your alternative to making a new life on New Atlantis is to stay here," she said. "We can help establish you somewhere of your choosing on Earth."

"I'd want to stay here, or near here, near you…" Editha said. "There's nothing for me anywhere else…" She paused, then said, "And I know too much…"

"We can fix that," Marina said. "We would have to."

"What do you mean?"

"Max can make you forget," Kaieda told her. "He can clear your memory of things."

Editha sat down heavily on one of the chairs near the table. She stared at all of them. "Max is a robot too, isn't he?" she again asked.

"A high-functioning android," Kaieda answered.

"Max must go back to New Atlantis," Marina explained. "If

he is to clear your memory of these events and of us, he needs to do it before he leaves."

Editha took a deep breath. "Either I go to your planet and live there, where my son is missing, and I have no one else…or I stay on Earth, my memory will be wiped of everything since Fenn died, and…I'd live here alone the rest of my life?"

"If you come to New Atlantis, you'd have me," Kaieda said. "I leave for periods of time on assignments but…I'd bring you into our clan, we could make a beautiful home for you, I can introduce you to people…The Planet is a beautiful place."

"Could you take me there, and if he doesn't return you wipe my memory then and send me back?"

"Doubtful," Marina told her. "When it comes to interplanetary policy, our Government is inflexible." She paused, then said, "Either you take this knowledge to our world and live there, or we free you of it and make sure you are established here, as Fenn Lockyer's widow, for the remainder of your days. Only you can decide."

Editha looked again to Kaieda. "You said there is reason to hope?"

"I received a message this morning that there has been some kind of contact," Kaieda told her. "I don't know what it means. If he was confirmed dead, they would have told me. Something has happened. Something." She shook her head.

Marina took Kaieda's arm. "Let's give her a few minutes," she said, leading Kaieda toward the house. Max reemerged. They stood on the upper terrace at the doorway.

"Freddie is folded in a transit box," Max told them. "They want to pull up as soon as possible; they're cloaked on a football pitch that will be full of players when the school day ends." He looked at Marina. "Three creshes," he said. "I assume you will return with us. And Aurora Kaxton."

"What about you?" Kaieda asked.

"I don't need one."

Right, right. They put him in one with me. He didn't need it.

Marina shook her head. "I'll remain here, Max. If that third cresh is filled, it will be her." She nodded back at Editha.

"How did you turn Freddie off?" Kaieda asked.

"The Allan9 has two off switches, neither of them easy to reach," Max said. "You would not want to see me trying to reach the other one."

"Uh-huh," Kaieda said. *Harlong's cousin talking.*

"You'll want to take your Bluebox home, of course," Marina said to them. "We'll deal with the rest, everything in California. Jeremy is good with such things."

"Wait!" they heard Editha cry out as they started into the house.

She came up the short flight of stairs to join them at the French doors. She looked at Max. "I don't know how you change or wipe out memories. I know a lot of people here who would pay you to do that for them. But I want to remember everything." She then turned to Kaieda. "If you will have me, as your…we would say your mother-in-law, I accept." She turned to Marina last. "You have become so dear to me in such a short time. I want to remember you. I want to remember all of you. And I want…"—she took Kaieda's hand—"I want to meet my son. If I can't, I want to see the world where he grew up, the world Fenn came from. I'm getting old. This is a chance to have one last grand adventure in my life."

Marina smiled. "I believe Fenn would agree." She looked to Max. "We can go forward with the Fetchers." She turned again to Editha. "The transport ship is small, Editha. If there is anything you wish to take with you, little though you brought, now is the time to get it in order to make sure there's room."

"My notebooks! Fenn's laptop!" Editha exclaimed. "Is there enough space for those? I don't have any clothes with me, just what I wore on the flight and what was in your closet."

"Change to your dry clothing. They will provide you with new garments after you get to New Atlantis." Marina smiled. "And yes, bring your documents. I know they are dear to you. Meet us in the front foyer on the ground floor. Jeremy will get you to the launch site, it's not far."

"Thank you," Editha said. She hurried for the house.

TEN MINUTES LATER, they were all on the steps at the front door as Jeremy drove up. Marina still wore her terry-cloth robe, Kaieda had changed into a fresh pair of jeans and a T-shirt, and Editha wore the newly laundered jeans and sweater she had worn when she fled San Francisco. The rucksack was on her shoulder.

"This is everything," she said. "Notebooks, Fenn's laptop, and my photo of the three of us."

"That computer will be a relic on New Atlantis," Max said.

"Too bad my brother will not be able to sell it to anyone," Marina said. She hugged Editha. "Be well, my friend. Our paths may cross again one day. I do go back to The Planet. I just don't stay." She then hugged Kaieda. "To you I say, don't give up. And consider the work of Anony. Fenn would say, 'We are trying to continue.' Give it thought, my friend."

Kaieda nodded, hugging Marina back tightly. "Thank you," she whispered.

Max and Marina gave each other a short bow. He then got into the front seat with Jeremy, who raised the glass window between front and back, leaving the back seat to Editha and Kaieda.

"She didn't hug Max," Editha observed as the car began moving.

"No offense is taken," Kaieda said.

A flood of relief washed over her. *We're going home.*

CHAPTER 27

Ten days after return to New Atlantis, midday, NAT-0

"**I** COULD DO IT," Faerae said.

Kaieda is back. Kaieda is on Rimalon. Imperfect situation.

When Kaieda had asked her to join the meeting with Janai Loa, Faerae agreed.

She asked me. Not Editha.

When Janai Loa laid out the plan to both of them, Faerae saw an opportunity. Impulsively, she volunteered. To which Kaieda answered, "Absolutely not."

Faerae slumped in her chair.

I really could do it. I know I could.

"A generous offer, Faerae, but we can't let you try," Janai Loa said. "It's too risky. The team isn't confident enough about the procedure to attempt human intervention. It needs to be a synth."

"Oh gods," Kaieda groaned. "You're going to bring up the Allan9?"

"No," said Janai. "The Robotics team activated it, studied what they could, and then deactivated it. They're still trying to find the coding that enabled him to do what he did on Earth, to Fenn and D'avi. Everyone in the unit is under scrutiny. We think there's a better candidate."

They sat in a small room in the Experimental Wing of the Science Guild. Faerae stared out to the corridor beyond them.

It led to the labs, including the one where Alec's biotube lay. Ten days had passed since Kaieda, Max, Aurora Kaxton, and Editha Lockyer arrived at the Keeper Colony. Ten days since Roiboi, Caspar, and Wofar Tonie were led away. As they departed, Roiboi had pointed at Caspar saying, "It was him."

Maeve Ep had called after him, "Oh Egdar, really. You are the front man. They're going to put you at the edge of The Deep for a long time. But don't worry, Dofi and I will be fine." She'd then looked around at everyone still in the room and said, "It was an arranged marriage."

As he'd disappeared, surrounded by security guards, Roiboi had shouted, "Feck you to the end of pi, Maeve! Feck Anony! Feck you all!"

The last Faerae had heard, Wofar Tonie was free on his own recognizance. Mog Weller had broken the news of the artifact black market. Searches of the homes of numerous Delegates had been launched. Huge citizen protests had arisen, objecting to the kidnapping of The Interstitials. They caused a small riot in the Capital. The Anony movement and their advocacy for change in Earth Policy continued to gain traction.

Faerae found satisfaction in having had a hand in exposing Roiboi. Allou and Luce were back at their posts at the Festival. Sundrae had been hastily promoted to Acting Festival Director by the Guild Chair after Roiboi's arrest. Luce, Dzuren reported, was applying for a library position in the Keeper Colony. Mog Weller had broken more news, reporting Fenn Loa's murder. That caused new shock waves across The Planet. In rare cooperation with the Government, Weller had, so far, withheld word of D'avi's death. Dzuren had convinced her that more information was needed. The identity of the murderer remained undisclosed, to Mog or anyone else beyond those who'd been present at Eswen House, the military inner circle on Rimalon, and the Robotics team that built the Allan9. Until they could ascertain the nefarious link in the programming chain, going public with news of a murderous New Atlantean–built synth was not in the population's—or the Keeper Colony's—best interests.

Once the returnees reached Rimalon, issues had arisen over the two "extra" humans who had arrived with Max and Kaieda. Aurora Kaxton was marked as rogue. She resisted arrest and attempted to stow away on a departing Fetcher ship bound for the Copernican system. The Bubble Guardians and Fetcher team earned their badges recapturing her on the station. Henk Z'eng had summarized it in a drinking session at The Blue Guitar, muttering, "Glad I'm not bonded to her."

Editha Lockyer's arrival had triggered a different drama. Faerae was still appalled by the whole business. First the Team showed up with an Earth woman. Then it turned out that she was the mystery Earth wife of Fenn Loa. Then, from Kaieda, Faerae learned what also remained a guarded secret beyond the Keeper Colony: Fenn Loa's mystery Earth wife had birthed a son with Fenn. That son was ALEC fecking TA'AVA! Which explained to Faerae why, from the moment she returned, Kaieda was focused on only two things: Alec, and Editha Lockyer.

Despite Kaieda's efforts, as well as advance support from Earth Reporter Marina Roiboi, the Guardians at the Bubble had refused to allow Editha access to The Planet shuttle. They directed her to Rimalon to await evaluation of her entry request. Soon after landing, Editha suffered two episodes requiring emergency health intervention. Both were reactions to what, for Editha, was an over-oxygenated atmosphere. The episodes involved chest pains and terrible coughing fits. Faerae had never seen Kaieda as panicked as she was over Editha's condition.

Editha was now adjusting to the Keeper Colony air, which replicated The Planet's atmosphere. Both episodes had been upsetting to everyone involved.

They didn't think of THAT when they brought her here, did they?

The Government review of Editha's entry request had layer upon layer of complications. How to explain a sudden émigré from Earth? Should her relationship with Fenn Loa be made public? If so, how to explain Loa's departure from centuries-old protocol that banned relationships with the Earth cousins? Even if those questions were answered somehow, Faerae wondered, with aggravation, where did it leave the news that Alec Ta'ava had been born on Earth to a New Atlantean and an Earth woman? The circle of people who knew that part of the story was growing. Whispers about it were rampant in the Keeper Colony.

Are they going to wipe all of us? The entire Keeper Colony?

Kaieda refused to go to The Planet until Editha's situation was resolved. She and Editha were housed in tiny side-by-side guest units in the Traveler branch of the residential wing of the Keeper Colony. The Guild Chair required a live meeting with Kaieda to debrief on the disastrous events of Team Seven's short visit to Earth. Faerae had been with her when Kaieda said, "You'll have to come to me."

This had not landed well with the Guild Chair. No meeting had yet occurred.

Dzuren did another inspection at the Festival Warehouse. "You wouldn't believe what's down there, in those hills," he told Faerae on return. "Including that Maui airplane from the beach where Max and Kaieda landed." He added, "Kemmi says hello. We're welcome back any time."

When Editha's health permitted, Faerae spent time with

her and Kaieda. Together the three of them pieced together what had happened on Earth and how it overlapped with events on The Planet and Rimalon. The stories intertwined at last, though not without frustration. Editha asked pointless questions. She constantly wanted to talk about Alec. Faerae found her tedious and annoying. Kaieda was solicitous and patient. The two of them cried about Alec multiple times. If Editha cried, she would start coughing. Then all the attention, to Faerae's frustration, would shift. *Everything was about EDITHA.*

Faerae wanted to comfort Kaieda and inspire her to see the urgency of what was happening with the Earth controversy, see that action was needed. Now. Get her to focus on something bigger than Alec and his fecking Earth mother. After Editha had retired to her room one evening, they at last had a moment for a private conversation. Kaieda had gotten a call that afternoon from Mog Weller. Faerae overheard the exchange. Mog wanted an interview. "A live one! Talk about Anony, Kaieda. You're one of the few who can make a difference right now in getting the Government to reconsider the Earth policies. It could change everything."

Kaieda was upset and noncommittal. "I'll think about it," she had told Mog.

That evening, Faerae had tried to coax her into considering the interview. Kaieda had deflected discussion of any of it, saying, "Right now I have to take care of Editha and sit with Alec and just…hold myself together until we know more."

She wasn't having any further discussion.

An interview could change everything. Faerae came back to that belief again as they sat in Janai Loa's workspace. The People always welcomed word from Kaieda. *How do I get you to do that? Why do you keep holding on? To Editha, and to HIM? Yes, something happened, some part of him reappeared. Remember the last time they tried bringing someone back?*

IT ISN'T GOING TO END WELL.

Faerae had learned the Alec news from Janai Loa the afternoon Roiboi and Caspar were taken away. She'd tried to make small talk as they left the meet room.

"Quite an afternoon," she'd said as they walked together.

"Indeed," replied the beautiful Janai.

"Can I ask…what's going on with Alec?" Faerae ventured.

Janai had weighed the question. "You are close to Kaieda. She deserves the information first, but we haven't had direct contact with her. Yes. Something has happened."

"Is he back?"

"Part of him."

Faerae waited.

"His right thumb materialized in his chamber."

"His thumb?"

Janai nodded. "The thumb and a section of thenar space below it, with part of a tattoo. It looks like part of a star. Something is happening. We're developing a subchamber for…" She paused again. "In case he is able to make more direct contact."

"His *thumb?*" Faerae's mind began racing. *Part of a star tattoo?* She recalled the section of the hours-long bonding ceremony she had not wanted to attend, when Kaieda and Alec removed the gloves from their right hands to reveal their bondmark tattoos. A pair of intertwined, golden-lined, sapphire stars.

"Healthy tissue," Janai continued. "We don't know how, but it is activated, it's his genetic code…we think he may be trying to alert us or tell us something. It behaves as if it is still connected to him. It even moves sometimes."

Faerae had been churning ever since. She'd been present

when Janai met Kaieda on arrival from Earth and broke the news. At Kaieda's insistence, she had led the two of them to Alec's biochamber.

"He's trying to come back," Kaieda had whispered, after reaching down and touching the thumb. When it twitched in seeming response, she'd started crying. Then she had asked Janai, "What can we do? How can we help him? Something of him is here. I can feel it."

"We're working on it," Janai said. Then she dropped what Kaieda later described as "the hope bomb." Alec's thumb was growing. A whisper of calcium, a hint of skeleton, was appearing. The thenar space was widening. More of his double-stars tattoo was appearing. "We think he may be reassembling in the biotube," she had explained to Kaieda. "We think it's organic regrowth. See this?" She'd indicated a thick, transparent, turquoise-lined box nestled at the foot of Alec's biotube. "We call it a c-chamber."

"What is it?" Kaieda had asked, staring at the empty container. Her forefinger was still on Alec's thumb.

"It's a place to house his consciousness," Janai had answered. "If something appears here, we will take it as confirmation. We have a plan to try to talk with him directly. If it works, it will be a major scientific breakthrough. It might open the way to bring him back."

Two days later, a wispy, pale-green cloud had formed in the c-chamber. It stayed. It floated, turned, fluttered, swooped, and danced about in the chamber as Alec's thumb continued to send out its calcium cloud.

Today the full plan was being revealed. Janai explained it was risky, unprecedented. "It involves transferring his consciousness from the c-chamber into another vessel," she explained. "He'll have to make it happen. What we're trying to do is give him a path and somewhere to land."

That was when Faerae offered to be the vessel.

Kaieda sat with Janai's comment that they believed there was a better candidate. Then she said, "Max. You mean Max."

Janai nodded. "Yes. The Maximus5700. We can't damage him, but if it works, he can suppress his programming and let Alec take over. Kaieda, we have no idea, even if it works, how long an exchange would last. Max must agree to it. He's a high-functioning synth with memory, sentience, the capacity to learn and evolve. He has a version of feelings. He's a new kind of being. He's the ideal surrogate for the transfer. He'll know that. But it has to be his choice."

Kaieda nodded.

"There's something else about Max," Janai said. "Another reason he is the right surrogate."

"What?" Kaieda asked.

"You remember we told you that Alec left us samples of his DNA."

"Yeah. I'm still not happy about that."

"We had the samples long before we used them," Janai said. "In the Maximus."

"What!" Kaieda exclaimed.

"The Robotics team has been working for a long time on blending synthetic and biological content," Janai said. "Several previous synth models were laced with human DNA. You worked with one of them."

"The Harlon17," Kaieda said. *Sweet old Harlong.*

"Yes. We used Dzuren's DNA in that one. We learned a lot from it. Very successful experiment. It informed the development of the Maximus5700."

Kaieda smiled. "Max told me that he and the Harlon17 were 'cousins.'"

Janai laughed. "In a sense. When the Max5700 was in development, we decided to work with Alec's DNA. He'd been gone for over two years at that point. They wanted to send the Maximus5700 with you on your next assignment, to test the partnership. The build accelerated when you were proposed for the Earth Traveler Teams. We had to pause the work to devise the Allan9. Replicating Alec's appearance took some time."

"But they didn't put Alec's DNA into the Allan9?"

"No," Janai replied. "It's a facsimile. We used D'avi's DNA. It was part of the deal he worked out with Roiboi. I wasn't given a choice. The Guild Chairs rule."

Kaieda sighed. *No wonder D'avi was so attached to that thing. Alec's good looks and his own DNA. Your parents didn't hug you enough, D'avi.*

Faerae shook her head. "Unbelievable."

Janai continued. "Then came the pressure to finish the Maximus and get him onto the transport with you. We had not a second to spare."

"Max did things in ways that…surprised me," Kaieda said. *The part of him that is Alec. I saw it but didn't recognize where it was coming from.*

"When are you talking with Max?" Faerae asked.

"We want to ask him today," Janai said, "with your blessing, Kaieda. Then do the experiment tomorrow."

Kaieda considered for a moment. "No," she said. "I have to ask him."

"Kaieda, it's too much," Janai said. "It needs to come from us."

"No, it needs to come from me," Kaieda insisted. "I've barely seen him since we returned. I have to ask him."

"You must allow for him to decline," Janai said softly. "Remember his emotions. He and the Allan9 are the most emotionally sophisticated synths in our history. They're going to pave the way for a new era of synthetic life."

"I saw it in Freddie," Kaieda said. "Max keeps his feelings to himself."

Like Alec often did. Does.

"All the more reason to leave him room to say no," Janai said. "Please, let us take it up with him. He'll literally have to close out his own sentient programming and surrender to something else. It's a big ask."

"I really, really could do this," Faerae said.

"No!" Kaieda exclaimed. "Thank you. But no!"

Faerae sighed. "Then I'm not needed here."

"Don't sulk," Kaieda said. "I need you. Just not…for this."

Faerae got up. "Okay, yes, well, I am going back to my station to not sulk and find out the latest on what they've found in the Warehouse and whether Wofar Tonie will be accused of worse than following orders. Let me know what happens."

She walked out of the room and pulled the door shut behind her.

"I love her," Kaieda said, looking after her friend. "But not in all the ways she wants."

"We all want to matter," Janai said.

"She matters. But she wants something I don't have to give. Not to her." Kaieda sighed. "Where is Max?"

"He's in the Colony," Janai answered. "Wait here."

She rose and left the room.

Kaieda waited. *How do I ask this of you? What happens if you say yes? What if it works? You can survive nearly anything. You can DO nearly anything. But would it damage Alec? How will it feel to be with you when it's really Alec, or would it really be…you? What if his consciousness gets trapped inside you? Do we lose you but gain him, in your body? What if this damages his organic regrowth process? We don't know anything! And what if you say no? What then? Do they fire up the Allan9 or build a new one or…what?*

Her mind churned over these questions as well as worrying about how Editha would respond. She decided not to bring Editha into the decision. Impossible to explain. It would do nothing but guarantee more stress when Editha already had to live, stateless, on a moon in an artificial environment orbiting a foreign planet that, if the bureaucracy would just focus, would be her home for the remainder of her life. *If she can fully adjust to the atmosphere. I can't add to all of that. Not until we know more. Not until we reach Alec.*

She was alone in the room for fifteen minutes.

Max arrived.

"Thank you for coming," she said.

He sat down across from her. Looking, as always, perfect. "Director Loa said you had something urgent," he said.

"Yes. But I haven't seen you, how are you? What are you working on? Are you all right here, on Rimalon?"

"Mostly off-loading content from the Earth trip," he answered. "Analyzing details of what worked and what could be improved with the Blueboxes. They're too limited as essential comm tools. Real-time comm exchange needs prioritization. Given everything that happened on Earth, I believe they are on it now."

Kaieda smiled, nodding as he talked. "I agree it needs doing," she said. "It would transform the Traveler program, to be able to have real-time communication with base."

Max nodded back. And waited.

"I have something to ask of you," she said. "But I need you to promise me you'll say no if you want to."

"I can say no."

She then told him more about Alec's absence. Things he probably knew. She wanted him to hear her version. She described the Consciousness Project and its effort to reach into new dimensions of existence, into the unknown. Alec's commitment and disappearance. The long wait. The unexpected arrival and growth of "the thumb." The possibility of connecting what they believed was Alec's consciousness to a surrogate. "If that could happen," she finished, "we could talk directly with him. We could find out what he knows. He might be able to help. We think he wants to come back."

As she talked, she saw his head do its occasional, subtle, processing tilt.

When she finished, Max said, "You want him to come back."

"With all my heart."

"Even though he may be in a dimension that is an improvement over this one."

You understand this instantly and far better than I do.

"We believe he wants to come back," she repeated. "But we can't know for sure if we can't talk with him."

"You want me to import his consciousness so he can communicate through me."

"We all think you are the best candidate," Kaieda said.

"Can I see where he is?"

Kaieda was unprepared for that request but said, "It's down that corridor." She pointed.

Max got up and she followed. They reached the outer door to the lab referred to by the Scientists as the Green Room. Every lab had a corresponding color, depending on the nature of the experiments and projects under way. The Green Room was where *Homo sapiens* life experiments were conducted. The environment inside was temperature controlled and humid.

She lifted her wrist in front of the keypad beside the door.

The lock clicked open. She led Max through the gangway, two meters of transitional space, before entering the room itself. Another lock opened and they passed through. At the far end lay a narrow biotube, two and a half meters long and a meter wide. It sat on a waist-high platform. They approached it. Inside lay a human thumb halfway from top to bottom. At the foot sat the c-chamber. In it floated the foamy green cloud. It began to whirl around as they approached.

Max stared into the tube for a long time. Kaieda said nothing, trying to manage colliding surges of hope and fear. *Please say yes, please say yes,* comingled with: *He's right, Alec could be in a far better place, and this could be so dangerous…we could kill him…*

"He's here," Max finally said, nodding at the biotube.

"How do you know that?" Kaieda exclaimed.

Max made no reply. He continued to stare into the biotube for what seemed an eternity.

"Yes," he said.

Kaieda threw her arms around Max and hugged him. He held her briefly, then patted her shoulder and released her.

"When does this occur?" he asked.

"Tomorrow," Kaieda answered. "Janai can lay out the timing."

"We can go now," he said. "I need to return to the Bluebox project."

"Thank you, Max. Thank you."

He nodded with his half-smile as he opened the door to the gangway.

Her heart pounding, Kaieda hurried to Janai to let her know Max had agreed to the transfer.

That night, she could not sleep. She was too agitated thinking about all that could go wrong. She shared the news with Faerae, who said, "Fine," and "Let me know how it goes." What she told Editha was guarded. "They're doing a big test tomorrow." *Don't raise her expectations.* Then she told herself she needed to take her own advice.

The next morning, Max and Kaieda met at the door to the Green Room. Janai and two of her Scientists were already inside, connecting a pair of long, transparent tubes to the c-chamber holding the green cloud. Max and Kaieda entered and waited.

"You're sure?" Janai asked Max as one of the Scientists gestured for him to come to where he held the thin hoses.

"I'm sure," Max answered, stepping forward. He waited as the hoses were placed, one into each of his ears.

"If he's in there"—the Scientist nodded at the box—"he's going to have to figure it out and make the trip."

"Max, when you sense engagement, you need to shut off your own processing systems immediately," the other Scientist said. "Not your physical systems, just the sections of your hard drive that process memory, personality, emotions, your knowledge. Make full room for him. Set yourself so that when your system reads that he has exited, you'll reactivate."

"Understood."

Then they waited. For several minutes, nothing happened. Max stood motionless beside Alec's chamber. Everyone else kept watching from a few feet away. Janai took Kaieda's hand.

Then Kaieda gasped. The green cloud was slowly inching its way into the tiny hoses, working its way from the c-chamber through the tubes toward Max's ears. As soon as the cloud slid past Max's ears, Max shuddered slightly. His eyes rolled and he took a small step backward. He looked down and his eyes closed. Then he was still.

"He just shut off all but his physical systems," Janai whispered.

Kaieda watched as the green cloud disappeared. The tubes were empty. The Scientist closest to Max reached over and removed the tubes.

Max's eyes opened. He looked down at his hands, wiggling his fingers. He coughed and then said, "Hera become us! A body!" He lifted one foot and then the other. Then he looked around, seeing the Scientists first. "Where are we, is this Rimalon?"

"Yes, sir," one of them said.

"Good, that's...that's perfect," he said. Then his eyes went to Director Loa. "Janai. You can't know what I've—" He stopped as his eyes moved to Kaieda, who stood furthest away.

"Oh," he said, his voice catching. "Kae..." He went to her and pulled her into his arms. "Oh Kae," he whispered into her hair, holding her tightly.

Kaieda half hugged him, frozen and confused. *IS it Alec? It's Max holding on to me? It doesn't sound like Alec but...*

He let go and stepped back. "Sweetheart, it's me. I'm here, I'm...this isn't..." He looked down at himself, and again at his hands. Then he frowned. "It's not my body," he said. "My bondmark is missing, these aren't my..." He looked to Janai.

"Your consciousness has transferred into a synthetic person," Janai told him.

"Yes, yes, that's it! We've done it! Yes. Gods, it feels amazing. The strength." He turned again to Kaieda. "But I don't look like myself."

She shook her head, trying not to cry. She was looking into Max's face. Was this Alec?

He took her by the arms. "Don't be afraid, love. Gods, how I've missed you." His fingers caressed her cheek. "How long have I been gone?"

"Over three years," Janai said.

Max looked pained. "Three years?" He let go of Kaieda's arms but took one of her hands in his.

"Where were you?" Janai asked.

"Hard to explain," Max said. "Another dimension. It's like there isn't any space…except there is. Time is different. It's…" He struggled for words. "It's…curved. Intelligent beings… incredible science…I saw, I talked with the Star People." He shook his head. "Except it isn't talking."

"They still exist?" Kaieda asked with wonder.

"In a way. And I saw uncharted galaxies. The quantum knowledge is…" He shook his head again. "They're so far ahead of us. And I…" He stopped.

Janai Loa spoke again. "Alec, we want to know as much as you can tell us, but we have to get you back with us as fully as possible. In your own body. This transfer is an experiment."

"I'm in a synth," he said, looking again at the tops, then the palms, of his hands.

"You're in the most complex biosynth ever built," Janai said. "But we have your right thumb in the biotube. It's growing into a hand."

"Yes!" he cried. "You cannot know the effort it took."

"You were trying to come home," Kaieda murmured.

"I'm here," he said, nodding toward the chamber. "I just… you can't see me. It's a dimensional, vibrational thing. I never left. I know that doesn't make sense."

He jumped up and down, as if testing the sensation of motion. Then he turned to Kaieda. His hands came again to her arms. "I needed to come back. They wanted to help me, tried to show me how to do it, but I didn't have the skills to recross dimensions…"

Max said he was here. Somehow, he knew. Was it the DNA connection? Who is "they"? The Star People?

"It was enough to start a regeneration process," Janai said. She nodded at the c-chamber. "We have a holding place for your consciousness there, while the physical regeneration continues. Is there anything you can tell us about how to make it work? Are there ways to accelerate the process?"

He looked at the biotube and at the c-chamber. "It's not really regeneration," he said. "But call it what you want. I don't know about acceleration. Time works differently on the…other side; it's not linear. You've done all the right things, the housing and the chamber should work." He looked above and around him. "It's the right environment. Sustain it. You can always bring me back this way," he said, indicating Max's body.

"No!" Kaieda said. "If you're really Alec, I want *you*, not your soul floating around in a synth!"

"We have no idea how long this will hold," Janai said to him. "If you feel any kind of weakening, you have to tell us so we can reinsert the tubes."

"I need some time with her," he said, leaning his head toward Kaieda. Janai nodded. Everyone else filed out of the room into the gangway, then to the outer corridor.

Kaieda stood before him, anxious and confused and hopeful and scared. "I don't know who you are," she said. "I don't know where Max ends and Alec starts."

He took her hand and led her to the bench beside the biotube. They sat. He kept her hand in his, covering it with his other hand. His touch was warm. His voice low, he leaned toward her and said, "Kae, I'm here. It's me."

She looked away. She didn't want to hear Max anymore. "I've missed Alec beyond…words," she said. "I've tried, I've tried to keep going but…he's my heart, he's my…I can't…" She stopped, overcome and unable to hold in the years of grief any longer.

She sobbed, turning back to him and leaning her head against his shoulder. His arm came around her as she cried, holding her close. Recovering, she looked at him and saw tears welling in his eyes. Max's eyes. "Alec is my home," she said, her own tears returning. She whispered it again. "Alec is my home."

His lips brushed her hair. "And you are my home." He cupped her face with his hands as a tear ran down his cheek. "Kae, close your eyes."

She closed her eyes.

"I'm sorry. I'm so sorry. This is so hard. But I'm here. I'm here. I could remind you of the night we met, or the stormy day of our bonding ritual or the nights we spent in the Pelma Hills in the hot spring watching the shooting stars or the fights we had building Arcana. Or the debate about the dog."

Kaieda sniffled and laughed. "No dog," she said softly.

"Dog," he said back, also laughing softly.

She started to open her eyes.

"No, no, keep them closed," he said. "I've been gone a long time. I know it has hurt you. I know you've held on. I can't change any of that..." He sighed. "I can't change how long it may take, to fully come back. But my darling, my beloved, I said I would come home." He lifted her right hand to his lips and kissed her stars tattoo. Then, his hand coming to her cheek, he kissed her lips. "I meant it," he whispered, leaning his forehead into hers.

With the words, and with the kiss, Kaieda's heart turned. She cried again on the shoulder of the person she so loved and so missed. She kept her eyes closed. It wasn't Max's hands holding her close, but Alec's.

"I have so much to tell you. Oh Alec, so much...I went to Earth. I found her. I found your mother."

Max's voice changed slightly. "Kaieda," he said.

She opened her eyes. *Alec is in there.* "You were born on Earth. But you grew up here. She's here, she came back with us."

Max looked astonished. "Here? On New Atlantis?"

Kaieda nodded, wiping her face. "Here, Rimalon." She squinted at him. "Someday you can explain to me when and how you found out and why you never told me about your origin."

"NTK," he said. "My Earth mother is here?"

Kaieda nodded again. "If they do this again, I'll bring her. And don't you dare NTK me."

He laughed. "I want to meet her," he said. "But my father…"

She shook her head. "We'll tell you about Fenn."

A knock on the door interrupted them. Janai entered. "Alec, we are reaching the limit of how long it will work this time." She nodded towards his head.

Kaieda saw tiny flecks of green dancing near his ears.

"Bring me back when you can," he said to Janai. He stood and drew Kaieda into his arms as the assisting Scientists entered. "Stay with me," he whispered to her. "I love you."

"I love you," she whispered back, holding on to him.

The assistants reinserted the tubes into Max's ears. Immediately, the green cloud inched back into the hosing, working its way toward the c-chamber. The transfer finished. The green cloud spun around in its box. The assistants removed the tubes. Max, still holding on to Kaieda, shuddered and then straightened.

"Max?" Kaieda said.

"Kaieda?" he said.

Awkwardly, they let go of each other.

"He's back," said Janai, her eyes on the c-chamber. She looked around at everyone. "Now we work on the regeneration process and consider options."

"Options?" Kaieda asked.

"It may be possible to create a hybrid for him," Janai said. "Until he's fully regenerated. We have the structural blueprint for the Allan9; between that and the programming for Max, we can work quickly."

"Good transition plan," said Max, nodding.

"Thank you, Max," Janai said. "Now we know surrogacy is possible."

Kaieda thanked Janai and the Scientists before following Max into the hallway. They walked together toward the central hub of the Experimental Wing.

Kaieda said, "They told me you have Alec's DNA."

Max nodded. "I do."

"Why didn't you tell me that, when we were on Earth?"

"Would it have made a difference?" he asked.

CHAPTER 28

THREE MORE WEEKS passed. The Government gave conditional approval for Editha's entry to The Planet. Notice of a "special circumstance" was posted on the ticker at midnight the day approval was issued. It went out on a night when VoG was providing comprehensive coverage of Anony support protests in the Capital and three other cities. The announcement noted the arrival on New Atlantis of an Earth-based documentarian who, hosted by Traveler Kaieda Beq-Ta'ava, would be present on New Atlantis for an undisclosed period. The Earther was described as "a research associate of recently deceased Earth Reporter Fenn Loa." Her task on New Atlantis was described as "assisting with interpretation of unpublished records from Loa's vast body of work." Because of everything else that was happening on The Planet, Mog Weller's blowcast noting this mostly unexplained and certainly unprecedented arrival of a woman from Earth gained no traction in the news sphere.

"That won't last," Dzuren muttered to Kaieda after Mog's Editha episode sank without a ripple. "Mog will persist. But it buys some time for the Guild Chairs and Assembly to figure out what to do in the long term with"—he'd shaken his head—"the situation."

Editha's adjustment to the atmosphere improved. Before she left Rimalon, and with her permission, the medical team inserted a chip into Editha's wrist. Along with stabilizing her heart and lungs to better accommodate the New Atlantean atmosphere, they added new knowledge that gave her an easier time understanding The Planet's several dialects. She declined a comprehensive insert of New Atlantean knowledge, telling them, "I'd rather learn it on my own, a little at a time."

Kaieda focused on getting Editha settled at Arcana. They discussed building a second structure on the property so that Editha could have her own place. They walked trails in the forest and meadows, and on the beach. On those walks, Kaieda told stories of the Star People and The Planet's history since their departure. "We have nothing of them except oral history, a few drawings, and the technology they gave us," she said. "It was enough to accelerate what we could do. They left before we could record them. They are like ghosts. Ghosts that left a trail."

"What did they look like?" Editha had asked.

"Like us," Kaieda answered. "But we're not sure that's what they really looked like, among their own kind."

Each night, Editha added to her notebook, expanding on what she had recorded from Fenn's stories and what Marina told her. She promised herself she would do more research at the Atlas once she had permission and learned how to use it.

From Kaieda, she learned more about the bloodlines and hierarchical clan structure, from "the aristos"—the Eps and Roibois—then Loas and S'Iloas, down to the "new clan," the Wellers. The night of that discussion, she'd jotted, "Never underestimate a Weller" in her notebook. The five Guilds, she learned, had subguilds that covered applied and research areas of work and practice. Everyone on New Atlantis had a place in the Guild structure, though at times collisions occurred between Guild agendas, needs, and aspirations. This happened most often between the Science and Philosophers Guilds.

Conflicts had to be sorted out between the Guilds. Without resolution, the issue was sent to the General Assembly. If it still went unresolved, it was passed on to the Triumvirate. As near as Editha could tell, "the Tri" was an opaque combination of the U.S. President and Supreme Court, and the Royal Family.

Eswen mystified Editha. Eswen was clearly revered on The Planet, a reformer who had established much of how things worked and set many of the values New Atlanteans adhered to. "More needed on Eswen," she noted to herself. "Engineer one day, mystic the next. The Mother of Them All."

Kaieda showed Editha 3-D maps of the different regions of New Atlantis and the functions assigned to each region. "Here, Farm Country, nearly all our food production. See the vast lakes beside it? All freshwater, and aquifers. Endless water supply. Nomad, down here, is where the dinosaurs live. And no, we can't go there and see them."

"Why?" Editha had asked, excited at the prospect of seeing real dinosaurs.

"It takes forever to get permits and requires a scientific reason to enter the region," Kaieda answered. "A lot of us aren't a hundred percent sure they're really even there." She pointed at another location, on the other side of the globe before them. "The Desertlands are here. It's not the wasteland you might think. There's a huge engineering station, and the largest military base on The Planet."

"I thought that was on Rimalon," Editha interjected.

"Rimalon is about defense."

They'd spent one evening drinking wine and talking about how Planet culture and technology had evolved over millennia, and the constant intersections with and appropriations from Earthly cultures.

"We're magpies," Kaieda said. "I don't know how else to explain it. We have our own culture, but it's blended with what we have been lifting from Earth cultures for centuries."

"Magpies. Pretty birds," Editha replied. "Do you have them here?"

Kaieda nodded. "Along with so much other flora and fauna from Earth. The Star People encouraged us to bring nearly everything we had and knew. We incorporated it into the plants and animals we found here. You'll love the Marbears here. They're like half-size red-and-buff pandas that eat a wrinkly petaled pink flower called a bobo." She grinned. "Lots more to learn about The Planet."

She also told Editha about the synthetics, and the ethical arguments over them, and about the revival of the Eflosi and their instatement as New Atlantean citizens. Having met an Eflos on Earth, Editha was especially fascinated with the lost, then revived, species. She asked if they could visit an Eflosi settlement.

"I'll have to ask," Kaieda answered. "I've never been to one. Few of us have."

One afternoon, they opened Fenn's laptop. At first, they could not get past the entry screen. Editha did not know Fenn's password. After two days of lamenting and worrying over the situation, Editha had a flash of inspiration and entered a guess. It worked. Now they had access to Fenn's many files and writings that were not in his Bluebox.

Kaieda asked, "What did you enter? What was the password?"

Editha took a sheet of paper and wrote, "Alexander06151987" on it.

"Now I know his birthday," Kaieda smiled, reading it. "His real one."

Kaieda and Editha also toured the Capital and hiked in the

Kemmi Wildlands. With an introduction from Dzuren, Kaieda took Editha to the Kemmi village where they had tea with Kemmi and Mumno. Editha was a great hit with them. She received an invitation to return at any time. They visited the Festival offices, where they learned that Luciena Shoko had transferred to the Keeper Colony Library and Research Center. With special passes provided by Allou Owea, who remained on the Festival staff, they went to museums, art galleries, and performance events.

FAERAE WAS NOT speaking to Kaieda. She'd heard that the experiment to reach Alec through the Maximus was to proceed. *So Kaieda convinced the synth to do it. What is THAT relationship?*

Kaieda had found her at The Blue Guitar an hour after the experiment ended. Faerae was already half drunk. Kaieda rushed to Faerae's booth, shaken and excited.

"We got to him, he got to us," she babbled. "He's still alive, he exists, he…I have to tell Editha! Oh gods, Faerae, he's finding a way back to me. Alec is alive!"

Faerae had stared at her beer. Kaieda took it in. They sat in silence for a long moment. Then Kaieda said, "I thought you would be happy for me. For us."

Faerae took a long swallow of beer. "Terrible way to get drunk," she said.

Kaieda was at a loss. "We've been best friends for almost fifteen years."

"I've been in love with you for almost fifteen years," Faerae replied.

There. Said it.

Kaieda took a breath. "We're doing this *now?*" she asked.

Faerae shrugged.

"I never gave you hope," Kaieda said. "For me, it's Alec. It's always been Alec. It will always be Alec."

"But you did…" Faerae started.

Kaieda looked at her blankly.

Does she remember? She remembers. She remembers. Admit you remember.

They remained silent for a while.

Kaieda repeated, "It will always be Alec."

She got up from the booth and left the bar.

But you did, you did give me hope that one night, that one night, Faerae wanted to scream into her beer and at everyone in the bar and after Kaieda. That one night that changed everything. That one night before they left for their Global Service assignments, when they'd gotten raucous drunk and fell, laughing, into Faerae's bed and kissed and stroked each other everywhere and made what Faerae knew was love and lay in each other's arms the next morning before they went their separate ways for two years. The night that inspired the equation, that one night when everything was not only possible but *happening.* That night that was stronger than what Kaieda had told her two years later when they reunited at a spa. When Kaieda said, "I've met someone." They never spoke of what happened between them before they'd parted. That night was stronger than watching Kaieda and Alec's relationship turn to bonding. Faerae's pain over that lowered the heat; she backed away, kept her distance, concentrated on her military career and made herself into the finest Tracker on Rimalon. But when Alec took on the Consciousness Project and vanished, everything had seemed possible again. She had Kaieda to herself.

That night was stronger to Faerae than anything. Until Alec's thumb and little green cloud appeared.

KAIEDA HAD WALKED away from the bar in misery and sadness, angry with herself and with Faerae. *Yes, I remember that night. I remember the intimate good-bye. I remember the pleasure it gave us both. I treasure those moments. But Fae, it was about letting go, not holding on. I didn't understand it fully until three months later when I looked into Alec Ta'ava's eyes for the first time and everything changed, everything in my heart and body, and whatever my soul is, changed. You can't know the electricity that sparked between us, you can't know how startled and certain we were in that instant and in everything that came after it, the heat, the connection, what it gave us, gives us. GIVES us.*

She'd brushed tears off her face in the Blind Deck. *You can't know what that is. But I tried to tell you. I've tried to show you and keep our friendship alive given…him. You could have respected it, all these years. We both hope. But for different things. It's on you to figure it out. I can barely put one foot in front of the other right now.*

IN THE DAYS after the exchange in the bar, Faerae burrowed into work.

Max visited Kaieda and Editha occasionally. He kept Editha company when Kaieda went to subguild meetings or took extended calls from Rimalon. Janai Loa sent daily updates on Alec's progress. The synthetic and biologic Scientists persisted in the effort to enhance Alec's regeneration, while the Robotics team, assisted by Max, worked from the Allan9 and Maximus5700 schematics to create a new being that looked like Alec. They were attempting, they told Kaieda, to give him realistic housing, blending synthetic and organic compounds until the organic re-creation of his human body completed itself.

The problem with the new hybrid was that, so far, the link with Alec's consciousness could flourish only in the highly controlled environment of the Green Room. The team succeeded with repeat transfers into the hybrid. The connection dissipated unpredictably, forcing his consciousness back into its c-chamber. Meanwhile, his skeletal shape continued to emerge.

"He's got ribs now," Janai told Kaieda one morning.

When Faerae heard that Editha Lockyer's entry to New Atlantis was approved, she spent three nights lost in OP doses. Then she heard Kaieda and Editha were at Arcana.

Never took me there once but takes the Earth woman there as soon as she's approved. Once more Arcana lives up to the name Alec gave it. Secrets. Mysteries. I hate it. I hate him.

After the OP wore off, Faerae spent her off day writing what she now referred to as "the failed equation" over and over on pieces of paper that she then tore up. Then she took the pile to the burn room and set them on fire.

Fecking smoke drifting to nowhere on the moon.

She watched the dark gases vent into the airless atmosphere of Rimalon. *Wish I was that smoke. Wish I could just drift away. Maybe that's the equation. Fprime [s]>37-37 what? Where besides space can I go?*

She fell asleep asking that question and dreamed that Janai Loa invited her to donate her brain to the Consciousness Project. Faerae awoke the next morning with the feeling that would be a relief. Provided her c-chamber was nowhere near Alec Ta'ava's.

The weeks passed. Then she heard Kaieda and Editha were back on Rimalon. Some kind of reunion with Alec was planned.

Rumors about a new synth were circulating. She encountered Dzuren and Janai Loa in The Blue Guitar one night.

Dzuren waved her over to join them and asked, "Have you seen Kaieda? Big day tomorrow."

"If everything holds," Janai added. She waved at someone behind Faerae. A moment later, Luce Shoko stood by their booth.

"Wouldn't know," Faerae answered. She looked at Luce. "Heard you're assigned up here now," she said.

"Research Library!" Luce beamed. "Thanks to him." She nodded at Dzuren. "I love it here."

"Welcome," Faerae said.

"Sit with us, drink with us, lighten up," Dzuren told her. He nodded at the seat beside Janai. "You too, Luce. We have things to celebrate. Both of you should go to the Green Room tomorrow. It would mean a lot to Kaieda."

Faerae frowned. "Why?"

"Witness the experiment," Janai said. "We think it will stick this time. For longer. With a custom surrogate for Alec."

Whatever that means. "I'll think about it," Faerae said.

She didn't stay long. She did not need another of Dzuren's stories about strange encounters on other worlds. She walked the Blind Deck to her quarters, ran for an hour, and fell into bed aching inside and out.

Kaieda was right. Best friends for fifteen years. But I don't know how to be only that. I managed it before Alec left, but it was never only that for me. Even when it was only that.

Yet, deep down, she knew going to the Green Room was necessary.

KAIEDA WAS IN a swirling state of exhaustion, excitement, and uncertainty. When the call came from Janai Loa, saying,

"We believe we can bring Alec up in the new synth for a brief time with you in the Green Room. It's still a hybrid. But it will be his DNA, his structure, his body."

"How much time?" Kaieda asked.

"Minutes, not hours. We don't want a misstep."

Kaieda asked many questions, seeking reassurance that this new "manifestation" would not damage the regeneration under way as his biological body slowly reassembled. The answers she got ran along the lines of "Not that we can tell," and "We don't know for sure but we don't think so," and "You need to balance the risk with the chance to be with him."

She discussed the situation and conditions with Editha. "You must meet each other. Come with me. It will be a short reunion, for now."

Editha agreed to come to Rimalon on the appointed day. She was endlessly fascinated with the New Atlantis moon. "It's like our moon," she told Kaieda. "But your people have made it habitable."

"That was the idea, when the Star People brought us here," Kaieda answered. "As much like Earth as possible, but with resources we didn't have."

Janai Loa greeted them at the entrance to the Experimental Wing Lab. Together, the three women walked to the Green Room.

"Wait here," Janai told them, entering the gangway. The windows were darkened so they could not see inside.

"Will he know who I am?" Editha asked.

"I told him you're here. He wants to meet you," Kaieda answered.

"Oh, you mean when he was…in…"

"When Max was his surrogate," Kaieda finished.

Editha nodded. "But this won't be Max?"

"No," Kaieda said. "This will be Alec. He'll be in what they call a hybrid. If the transfer works again, it will be in a body that is exactly like his."

Editha nodded again, feeling overwhelmed, excited, and nervous. "Do I look okay?"

"You look beautiful," Kaieda answered, smiling as best she could.

Is it really going to be him?

The outer door reopened and Janai said, "Come in now, he's here. But I don't know for how long." She stood to the side as the women entered the outer chamber. "We'll monitor his status," she said to Kaieda.

Kaieda nodded, taking a deep breath and trying to focus on Editha. "Ready?" she asked.

"You go first," Editha said. "He knows you."

Kaieda opened the door. Editha followed. Alec was standing beside a gurney next to his biotube and c-chamber. He wore a silver lab suit. The ear tubes were gone; the Scientists had found a way to do the transfer using nano-quantum entanglement. He saw Kaieda and crossed the room in three steps, sweeping her into his arms. They were HIS arms, she knew: It was Alec. They kissed. Alec lifted her right hand to his lips and kissed her bondmark. Then he showed her his right hand, featuring his identical tattoo. They hugged tightly.

He eased away, looking past Kaieda at Editha. Her eyes met her son's. Alec stared, then asked, "Are you...?"

Before Editha could reply, Kaieda turned and smiled. "Alec, meet Editha Lockyer. Your mother."

He stepped toward Editha, his dark eyes studying her. She stepped toward him, until she was close enough to touch him. Her hand came to his cheek. "You look like your father," she said softly.

He pulled her against him, saying, "I never imagined I would meet you." He looked again into her face, then hugged her again. "Not in this life."

"Can you forgive us?" Editha asked, in tears. "I didn't want to let go, we didn't want to…"

He held her by the arms. "Don't, don't. Everything is as it's supposed to be." He hugged her again. Then he looked into her face.

Kaieda knew he was debating whether to say something more to her; he was wearing his *Shall I tell her this or not?* look. An all-too-familiar expression to Kaieda.

The moment passed. "I am so happy, so grateful, to meet you," he said to Editha. He looked to Kaieda. "What were the chances of any of this?" He looked back at his mother. "We will have more time together. We will. I know it. We have so much to tell each other. And I want to learn about my father." He nodded toward Kaieda. "Watch out for this one for me, will you?"

Editha nodded, grasping his hand. "We'll watch out for each other."

He kissed his mother's forehead. "Thank you," he said. "For this moment. And for my life."

Editha suppressed a sob as she turned to go. She squeezed and kissed his hand. Kaieda pulled the heavy door open for her and saw other faces at the window beyond the gangway. Max stood there, watching them. Faerae was next to him, and on Faerae's other side she could see Luce. She smiled at all of them and pointed at Alec. Even Faerae smiled back.

Editha went through the door, which swung shut.

"Our audience," she told Alec, turning back to him.

He waved at the gathered ones, then took Kaieda back into his arms. "Thank you for bringing her," he whispered.

"She belongs with us now," Kaieda answered, drinking in his presence, his heat, the sound of his voice, his body pressed against hers. She paused, then asked, "What were you going to tell her?"

He grinned. "I can never keep a secret from you, can I?"

"You're actually pretty good at it," she replied. "Earthling."

"We'll make a home for her together, soon," he said.

"However long it takes," she murmured, pressing her head into his shoulder. She saw the faces still at the window beyond the gangway. "I want you to meet someone else," she said. She waved for Max to enter the Green Room.

"Who is this?" Alec asked, eyeing the synth as he stepped in.

"This is my traveling partner, Max. He's the one who disabled the Allan9. And pieced together so much of the mystery." She paused, then said, "He's also the surrogate."

"Oh!" Alec said. He looked Max over slowly. "Handsome," he said. "Brilliant."

Kaieda rolled her eyes. "Max, this is my bonded mate, Alec Ta'ava-Loa."

Max offered his hand. Alec took it, for a firm shake.

"Quite human," Alec observed. He looked at Kaieda. "I'm getting the *Are you kidding me?* face."

"Are you?"

He laughed the laugh she so loved. "Thank you," he said to Max. "For everything you did for her. For us. All of us."

Max nodded, half-smiling back. "It was a collaboration," he said. "You were part of it." His head tilted a few degrees as he processed. Then he said, "I should go. I am glad to meet you, Alec Ta'ava-Loa."

Alec looked at Kaieda and back to Max. "What do you mean, I 'was a part of it'?"

Max opened his mouth to offer an explanation that Kaieda knew would be too long. She held up her hand.

"You're…built into him," she said to Alec. "Your DNA."

"I thought that was the other one!" Alec said. "They told me there was an Allan9…"

"That one replicated your appearance but had none of your biological content," Max started.

"You agreed to let them use your DNA," Kaieda intervened. "They didn't use it on the Allan9. They used it on the Maximus5700. He's…part of you. You'll have to get the Robotics people to explain."

FROM THE OTHER side of the window, Faerae watched as Max and Alec interacted. Alec kept his arm around Kaieda as they talked with the synth.

They fit. How did I never see it before?

ALEC EYED MAX anew. "So, are you my…son? My brother?"

An awkward pause passed as Max returned the look. "Let's go with cousin," he answered.

Alec laughed. "Well done, cousin," he said, giving Max a hug.

Kaieda pulled him away, as Max looked startled. She leaned her head into Alec's shoulder. His arms came around her. "I want you back," she said into his chest. "The real you. All of you."

"It's happening," he whispered. "Have faith."

Luce, at the door with Faerae and Editha, watched Max turn away and head toward the exit door. "That didn't last long," she said.

"They said it would be short this time," Editha said. "But I've met my son. My God, I've met my son!" She wiped her cheeks.

As Max left the room, Faerae saw Alec and Kaieda slip into a tight embrace. Faerae caught her breath, as if seeing them for the first time. The look between them. The certainty. The connection. Faerae swallowed. She didn't feel envy or anger. It was something less familiar. Not hurt. Tears formed in her eyes. *Wonder. This is what wonder looks, feels like. They…belong.* Something inside her released as she wiped her tears away. Her internal knot unraveled. Her sight remained blurry as the outer door opened and Max entered the hallway, joining them. He kept his back to the window, mostly blocking their view.

"Alec is progressing," he said. "They've made something in which he can exist in while that happens." He paused, then added, "Her heart rate changes when she is with him."

Faerae exhaled. A hand rested gently on her forearm. Janai Loa was offering a tissue.

LUCE LOOKED UP at Max. Since coming to the Keeper Colony, she had made a point of meeting as many people as she could, learning names, making herself known. *That's what Allou would do,* she'd told herself. She'd run into Max twice. The second time she introduced herself, he had told her, "I know who you are, Luciena Shoko. The Roiboi refugee. You are called 'Luce.'" They'd met a few times after that at The Blue Guitar, for drinks.

"Do you remember?" she asked him.

"Remember what?"

"When you were…Alec's surrogate?"

"I'm not supposed to," he answered.

Footsteps from down the hallway caused them all to turn.

Dzuren walked toward the group. "What, a meeting of Team Kaieda?" he asked. He peeked into the Green Room window, grinned, then pressed a button on the panel next to the window. A screen lowered, blocking their view. "Looks like Alec is finding his way back. That's good. We need him."

"What will you do next, Max?" Luce asked.

"They will keep me on Rimalon. They've made an accommodation to the rules about synthetics working in the Keeper Colony."

"Excellent," Luce said.

"So," Dzuren asked. "Where do you all belong?"

"Office," Janai said. "A lot of work ahead. We still haven't solved the mystery of Freddie." After a smile at Faerae, she bowed to them all and departed down the hall.

"I'm going back to the Keeper Research Library," Luce said.

Max turned to Editha. "May I escort you as far as the Gateway shuttle?" he asked. "Kaieda may not be free for a while." He looked back toward the Green Room.

"That would be wonderful," Editha answered, smiling at Max. "I think I'll go back to the Capital to do some research in the Atlas today."

He offered her an arm, which she took.

"I'll join you as far as the Blind Deck," Luce said. She thought Max looked wistful.

The three of them set out.

STILL AT THE Green Room's outer door, Dzuren said to Faerae, "Come on. I need to go to The Blue Guitar to find the Twins. They are, and I quote, 'breakfasting.'"

They headed toward the mover platform. Faerae looked beyond the glass at the moonscape and black space beyond. The

Planet was rising. She could see the distant outline of land where it met the shores of the Raja Sea.

She said, "I don't think we should call them that anymore."

He looked over at her. "Who? The Twins?"

"They have names. We should call them their names. Vaylor. Mynar."

They continued walking. Dzuren was quiet for a while. "You're right," he said. "Let's find Mynar and Vaylor. They're being helpful to Henk in sorting out this Copernican Fetcher mess."

Faerae nodded. *Just say it, just ask,* she told herself as they stepped onto the mover. She looked at him and tried to smile, feeling timid. Then she asked, "What can you tell me about pilot training?"

IN THE GREEN Room, Alec and Kaieda were still embraced. A low whirring sound rose.

"No," she whispered. "No, no. No."

"It's time. I can feel it. Fading." He kissed her head. His breath, his warmth, spread across her hair and filled her body. She tightened her grip on him.

He released her. She held on. "We'll be together again before we know it, love," he said. She let go of him slowly. He wiped a tear off her cheek. "Don't cry too much. And don't go far."

She nodded, more tears coming into her eyes. "I'm grounded."

"Stay busy. Stir up some trouble," he whispered. "You know how to do that." He smiled, kissed her lips, and lay down on the gurney next to his biotube. He took her hand. A tremor ran from his fingers up his arm.

"I love you," she said.

His hand started to squeeze hers, then his hybrid body went still. The swirling, pale-green wisps were sweeping back into the c-chamber. In the biotube, his skeleton looked more robust. His arms and hands were complete, intact. She stared at it all, aching.

He is still here. Becoming.

She rested her hand lightly on the c-chamber, then turned away and opened the exit door. She went through the gangway tunnel and walked into the silent, empty hallway. Max had left. So had Editha and the others. Even Faerae was gone.

Good for you, my friend. We'll make things right eventually.

She leaned against the wall.

What now? It depended on the unpredictable pace of Alec's organic renewal. She thought about what Alec had said, and Dzuren, and Marina, and Mog. *They're right. Time to stir up some trouble.* She smiled to herself.

I'll call Mog and give her the interview. We'll talk about Earth, and Fenn, and Anony.

She looked back into the Green Room.

On it, love. Have faith.

ACKNOWLEDGEMENTS

This project was rebirthed in June 2023 at a Creators' Haven artist retreat in Temecula, California. A single chapter of a sci-fi project had been sitting on my laptop for ages. I could neither part with it nor figure out "Where does this go from here?" On that retreat, I came up with a direction for chapter two. That opened the floodgates. I am grateful to my Haven sisters for their encouragement—that week and ever since.

Special and immense gratitude to my friend and fellow writing voyager, Sharon Linnéa. Her insights on and experience in independent and small press publishing were steadying and wise.

I am grateful, too, to several early readers: Richard and Amy Woodbury, Phil Reynolds, Elvi Moore, and Kathy McGuire helped me see the story, characters, and writing with new eyes. Thank you to Sue Green for introducing me to Frank Tetreault, an experienced pilot who gave needed insight into what it takes to "fly the plane," not to mention landing it, when things go wrong. Thank you, Frank.

Eternal thanks to my editor, Carolyn Haley, for her insight, professionalism, and good humor throughout our work together. Thanks, also, to Caleb Jones for the cover art, plus being an exceptional friend in books and in life. Gratitude, too, to Emily Snyder for her superb interior design.

Last, thank you to my family and friends who listened to me talk about this project for close to two years, especially Marsha Purcell, Riley Steiner, Ryan Purcell, Andrea Snyder, Robert Black, Sue Green, Timothy Buckley, and Steve and Jill Smith. I am forever grateful we are in one another's lives.

Bonnie Brooks lives outside Washington, DC, where she works as an arts consultant and writer. She is Associate Professor of Dance Emerita at Columbia College Chicago, having also taught at UCLA. She worked previously as an arts administrator at Dance/USA and the National Endowment for the Arts.